The Kissing Game

**Center Point
Large Print**

**This Large Print Book carries the
Seal of Approval of N.A.V.H.**

The Kissing Game

Kasey Michaels

Center Point Publishing
Thorndike, Maine

To Michele Bidelspach,
who puts up with me.
Thanks, babe!

This Center Point Large Print edition
is published in the year 2003 by arrangement with
Warner Books.

The text of this Large Print edition is unabridged. In other
aspects, this book may vary from the original edition. Printed in
Thailand. Set in 16-point Times New Roman type by
Bill Coskrey and Gary Socquet.

ISBN 1-58547-326-X

Library of Congress Cataloging-in-Publication Data.

Michaels, Kasey.
    The kissing game / Kasey Michaels.--Center Point large print ed.
        p. cm.
    ISBN 1-58547-326-X (lib. bdg. : alk. paper)
    1. Large type books. I. Title.

PS3563.I2725K57 2003
813'.54--dc21

                                                    2003041039

Who lives without folly is not so wise as he thinks.
—FRANÇOIS, DUC DE LA ROCHEFOUCAULD

Chapter One

ALLEGRA NESBITT, only child of the Earl and
Countess of Sunderland, lifted her head and warily
sniffed the breeze with her pert nose, rather like a sprig-
muslin gowned hound attempting to pick up a scent.

She'd been in the gardens for only a few minutes, but
so far nothing seemed wrong here. That was good, for
James, the head gardener. The poor man had yet to fully
recover from the shock of finding that all his pink roses
had, overnight, become yellow roses (three undergar-
deners had pocketed a half crown apiece for staying up
the whole night long transplanting the bushes).

That had been a week ago. Seven full days, an
unusually long time between pranks for Oxie Nesbitt.
He was due; he was overdue, and the entire household
was tiptoeing about on eggshells, waiting. Waiting.

Unless Allegra counted the most ridiculous joke
Oxie had ever played, that being the one that suppos-
edly had them all adjourning to London for the
Season.

She had to admit, he had been playing out that particular baited line for nearly a month now, and showed
no signs of letting it go, finding some other way to
amuse himself at her mama's expense.

The pity of it was that Mama believed him, really
believed him. As if they'd really travel to London.

Ridiculous. What had the Nesbitt family to do with London?

Even more to the point, whatever would London have to do with the Nesbitts?

Allegra walked to one of the side doors leading into the mansion, automatically checking to be sure Oxie hadn't rigged it with a bucket of water that would spill on her as she entered, and stepped inside.

Her parents had been to London, five years ago, when Oxie had first come into the earldom by way of several unexpected deaths and a convoluted chain of inheritance that had left the then dowager countess prostrate on her bed for months.

Oxie Nesbitt, Earl of Sunderland? Why not, the dowager had been known to say almost daily until her death two years previously, just stick a jacket and neckcloth on a pet monkey and turn him loose in Society?

Poor woefully unprepared Society.

Allegra, still unable to succeed in her various and at times ingenious attempts to break out of the nursery, had not accompanied her parents to London on that first, fateful trip, but she had heard about it from Aspasia, her mama's maid.

A fiasco, that's what that sojourn had been, from start to finish.

Mama, always a shy and nervous sort, couldn't remember anyone's name, rank, or any of the social graces she'd attempted to learn from books, because she had married a poor man with no expectations, not an earl.

In fact, she'd yet to fully forgive Oxie Nesbitt for

accepting his title, probably in part due to the horrors she'd experienced in that single trip to London.

Magdalen Nesbitt had curtsied to the bewigged major-domo of one of her hostesses, and in front of half the *ton.* Which had been an infinitesimal faux pas, when put up against the fact that she'd also actually asked the Prince Regent (now *he,* Aspasia told Allegra her mama had said, really looked like a majordomo) if he could kindly point her in the direction of the ladies' retiring room.

Oh, yes. Mama had made quite an impression upon Society. The poor woman still had the occasional night-mare.

But it had taken Oxie himself to bear off the palm. The new earl's frank speech, his boisterous ways, his *pranks,* had been the talk of London for the ten days it had taken Magdalen to convince him that she was dreadfully ill and a rapid return to Sunderland was the only thing that could possibly save her.

They'd left behind them a rash of silly pranks and some angry peers, along with several hilarious anec-dotes about "The Countess of Bumpkin" that would have witnesses to her social blunders dining out on the stories for weeks, and a Grosvenor Square mansion in Holland covers, never to be visited again.

Five years, and the fact that Allegra was now a rapidly aging nineteen, had pushed Magdalen into believing that London had forgotten them, forgiven them, and would welcome her beautiful, eligible daughter with open arms. And, if it hadn't, she'd pretend it had. She would walk over hot coals for her Ally—or, even more daring, down Bond Street.

After all, her darling Allegra was the daughter of an earl. There was a truly stunning dowry. Just a quick pop into the metropolis, where her dearest Ally would dazzle all the gentlemen, take her pick of the best of this year's litter of bachelors, and Magdalen could return to the relative obscurity of Sunderland, little worse for wear.

And Oxie had agreed, with a wink to his daughter, who had scolded him for lifting her mama's hopes when everyone knew that they'd never travel to London again. Ever.

Still, he was pushing this prank too far, even for him.

Magdalen had ordered new wardrobes for everyone, had the traveling coach refurbished, even invited Allegra's dreadful cousin Elizabeth to accompany them to the metropolis so that she could shepherd Allegra into society, leaving her mama safely at home, where she couldn't embarrass herself or anyone else.

Disappointing Elizabeth when Papa finally admitted he'd only been funning them would be the single spot of joy Allegra looked forward to, as her cousin was the silliest, most chuckle-headed, condescending—

Feminine shrieks cut into Allegra's random thoughts, followed by her mama's hysterically pitched, "Oxie! Help, help! Oh, *OX-eee!*"

Allegra picked up her skirts and followed the screams to the large saloon, to see both her mama and Cousin Elizabeth standing on couches, looking about as silly as two women could look without outside assistance (though, considering her mama's fervent invocation of Oxie's name, they probably did have outside assistance).

"I thought he was overdue. If there's one thing to be said for Oxie, he never disappoints," Allegra said as she looked around the room. "Well? What did he do?"

Cousin Elizabeth, her face unnaturally pale beneath her neatly coiled black hair, her equally black eyes narrowed to slits, pointed a finger toward one corner of the room. "There. Right there."

Allegra shook her head, looking where Cousin Elizabeth had pointed. "I don't—oh, I see now. How cute," she said, smiling. She looked at the gaily papered box on the floor, the one whose lid had somehow been transported a good fifteen feet away from its bottom, and then to the corner again. "You thought it was candy, didn't you, Mama?"

Magdalen appeared to be attempting to climb onto the very back of the couch, then reach for and shimmy up the chandelier, which would be a fruitless exercise, as Magdalen was a smidgeon of a person, petite, blond . . . gullible as ever; Oxie's favorite audience. "Of course I thought it was candy, Ally. *OX-eee!*"

"Don't waste your breath, Mama," Allegra said, sighing. "You know he's around here somewhere, watching, but that doesn't mean he's going to come out until he believes his small prank has run its course."

"You're all mad, do you know that? Stupid pranks, calling one's own father by his Christian name. Outrageous!" Cousin Elizabeth declared feelingly as she sat herself down on the back of the couch, folded her small hands in her lap—as if prepared to serve tea from this novel position.

"Yes," Allegra said, walking toward the corner and bending down, "we're all mad. If I were you, cousin, I'd hie myself straight back home, escape this asylum while you still retain your own priggish wits. Ah, here we go. Hello, mousie," she said, lifting the white mouse by its tail, holding it so that she could watch its small, pinkish nose twitch as it inspected her with anxious-looking black eyes. "Poor little precious. Did those noisy ladies frighten you?"

"Oh, for the love of God, child—you're worried about the *mouse?* Just get that disgusting thing out of here. Get it out of here now."

"Yes, Mama," Allegra said, gathering up the two pieces of the box and tucking the mouse back in it, wondering silently how neither her mama nor Cousin Elizabeth had failed to notice the neat pattern of air holes her papa had punched into the lid.

Oxie certainly wouldn't have gotten such a sorry attempt past *her.*

"Cousin Elizabeth? Perhaps you'd like me to put this in your rooms? I believe he'd make a lovely pet for a spinster of two and twenty. Or is that three and twenty?"

"You wouldn't—oh! You're as bad as his lordship, Allegra, I vow it. And, for your information, cousin, I am not quite twenty-one, barely eighteen months older than you. But what about his lordship, cousin? What if he attempts anything like this when we're in London? Well, I should just simply *perish* from the embarrassment."

"You won't have to worry about that, Cousin Elizabeth," Allegra told her, "because we're not going to

London. Mama, haven't you figured that out yet? This is just another of Oxie's small jokes. And a not very funny one, at that, considering that we now have Cousin Elizabeth running tame in our house."

She tipped up the lid of the box, peeked inside. "Among other vermin."

Cousin Elizabeth crawled down from her perch, sitting on the proper couch cushion once more, smoothing her muslin skirts as she balefully glared at Allegra.

"Oh, really? I know just what you're doing, Cousin Allegra. Oh, yes, I know. You're only saying that because you don't want me to accompany you to London. It's just as Mama has said, I'll cast you very much in the shade. How you'll hate that, cousin, mean and spiteful creature that you are, as you seem to positively *dote* on making a cake of yourself whenever possible."

"Yes, that's me, straight down to the ground," Allegra agreed, because what use was there in arguing? "A horribly improper branch on the otherwise prim and proper yet still—dare I say it?—prodigiously ramshackle Nesbitt tree. My father's daughter, my mother's child. Oh, and when we get to London, Cousin Elizabeth—not that we're really going—I should like it very much if you were to address me as *Lady Allegra*. I don't wish to depress your pretensions overmuch, but you have been cast to play the role of charitable gesture on Mama's part in this small farce, you know."

Magdalen watched as Elizabeth ran from the room, one hand pressed to her mouth to stifle her sobs.

"That, my girl, was mean," she told her daughter.

"Not too many years ago *we* were cast as the poor relations, remember?"

"I remember a lot of things, Mama," Allegra said, tucking the box under her arm. "One of them is the single house party we, then playing the part of poor relations as you said, attended here at Sunderland. I remember how Cousin Elizabeth pretended to be my friend, then left me all alone in the middle of the yew maze. It took hours for anyone to find me. I was six, I believe, and still afraid of the dark. Foolish girl, she never thought I'd grow up, or that I'd remember. But I do remember."

"That was naughty of her, but she only mimicked the sentiments of her parents. She's a grown woman now, and you should judge her on her own merits." Magdalen sighed, worked her fingers together in her lap. "And remember this as well, we must be even *larger* than that, Ally. We must also forgive, we must also forget. After all, we are now the Earl of Sunderland."

"No, Oxie is the Earl of Sunderland. That man over there, just coming out from behind the draperies. Hello, Oxie. Enjoy your little joke?"

Oxie Nesbitt hitched up the waist of his breeches, which had begun sagging beneath the considerable weight of his ample belly. He patted at the fluffy white halo of hair that ringed his otherwise bald pate, and sat down beside his wife, lifting her fingers to his lips.

"I hadn't planned on frightening you, pet. Only the gel. But you climbed this couch with the grace of a gazelle, truly you did."

"I should crack your head with the teapot," his wife

said, her heart not really in the threat. "But what is this Ally has been talking about, Oxie? Please say our trip to London is not another of your pranks. I've spent hours and *hours* memorizing the names and titles of all of the Prince Regent's siblings and all of the patronesses at Almack's. Practiced them until my head positively ached. I would just die if we didn't go, truly I would, Oxie."

Allegra put down the box and crossed her arms over her slim waist, stared at her papa. "Tell her," she intoned heavily. "This has gone on long enough. Tell her, Oxie."

His lordship looked at his daughter, looked at his wife, looked at the toes of his boots. "We leave Friday morning at first light," he said, speaking into his faintly soiled cravat.

Then, quickly, he looked up at his daughter. "The trick was on you, Ally, not your mama. I only let you think that so that you wouldn't bolt, run away, before I could get you tied to the seat of the coach."

"Oxie . . . no," Allegra said, shaking her head. "We can't. Don't you remember? Think of who we are. Think of how Mama was so . . . and how *you* . . . and the coffin you propped against Lady Jersey's door? And . . . and the ground pepper in your snuffbox . . . and the silly map you made up, showing a great Stuart treasure buried under the Prince Regent's own Carleton House—people crawling all over his highness's gardens, digging up his posies? And . . . and the—"

"Ancient history, my dear," his lordship interrupted as Allegra searched her brain for more stories told to her by a sniffling Aspasia. "And there were those who jolly well enjoyed my little jokes, not that Lady Jersey was overly amused, I'll grant you that one. As for your mama? Elizabeth will be there to guide her this time, as well as the bear-leader we've hired. What is her name, pet?"

"Mrs. Tomlin," Magdalen told him. "Mrs. Lettice Tomlin, and she's a paid companion, Oxie, and is also acting as our housekeeper. She's a widow, I suppose, or perhaps a spinster. She's to be called Mrs. Tomlin, as a courtesy, as all women of any advanced age in this position would be. But there was no mention of a Mr. Tomlin." She frowned. "Oh, never mind, Ally, we'll just figure it all out as we go on. She came highly recommended."

"Highly recommended?" Allegra rolled her eyes in only partially amused disbelief. "By *whom?* Mama, we don't *know* anybody. None of us has been anywhere but here for the past five years, and before that we were less than nowhere."

Magdalen began fidgeting with the ribbons on her morning gown. "Don't put such a fine point on everything, Ally. I had your papa place an advertisement in one of the London papers, and Mrs. Tomlin replied with the loveliest letter, and references and everything. Why, she's already in residence in Grosvenor Square, making sure everything is ready for our arrival. Oh, Ally, don't make that face. You know how upset I get when you make that face."

"I don't believe this," Allegra said, shaking her head. "We're really going? To marry me off, correct? You're going to drag me to London to get rid of me. Oxie, this is the nastiest trick you have ever played on me."

Magdalen hopped to her feet, put her arms around her daughter. "Oh, darling, don't, please. This is for your own good, truly it is. You are of an age now, nearly as old as your cousin Elizabeth, in fact, and you've just teased her about how she is all but on the shelf, ready to don her caps and raise cats."

"Mice," Allegra said into her mother's bouncing curls. "I thought she could raise mice." Then she shut her eyes, unable to contemplate the disaster that awaited them all in London. "Oh, it will be terrible. Just terrible."

"It will be *wonderful*," her mama corrected, giving her a quick squeeze before putting her at arm's length, smiling at her child. "Your papa has friends, friends from his school days, and they'll all be in London. Surely they'll all have sons. We have a beautiful daughter. We'll have Elizabeth to bear you company, Ms. Tomlin to guide us along the straight and narrow, your papa's money to cushion any falls we might have. Papa has convinced me that we'll be just fine—and I am willing to put my head in the lion's mouth again for you. Although," she ended a little nervously, "your papa says that won't be necessary."

"Your mama's right, Ally," his lordship added, giving Allegra a bracing, nearly staggering clap on the back. "Only thing you'll find around here is men like me, and I wouldn't wish such a sorry match on my dearest baby, or you on the fellows around here, come to think on it. I've already penned letters to my school chums, telling them of our arrival early next week."

"Names, Oxie. Give me names, or I won't believe you. I may not even believe you then. Give them to me now, without giving you time to make them up."

"Names? I'll give you names. Gideon Pakes, he's the Viscount Eaton, no less, soon to be an earl, when his father gets put to bed with a shovel. Sir Guy Berkert, and the last one—what's his name? This would be easier, pet, if you would just stop staring at me that way. Oh, yes, I remember now. Jagger. Walter Jagger. Called him Wally until he bloodied m'nose for me. Wally always was a bit of a spoilsport. Roomed with them at school, you know, along with Elizabeth's papa. Fine chaps."

"Ridiculous," Allegra said, pulling a face. "Friends. Fine chaps. So, why haven't I heard about any of them except for Uncle Frederick until today? Why, you couldn't even remember the last one's name at first, could you? And yet you say they're your friends? Nonsense. Cousin Elizabeth's father, Oxie, has never been your friend. Were *any* of these men your friends? Really?"

"Schoolmates," Oxie corrected. "Long ago and far away."

"Long ago and far away enough that they've forgiven you for tying all their small clothes in knots and hanging them from the lampposts? Long ago and far away enough that they no longer remember the day you put a freshly fed goat in their rooms?"

"It was a family of piglets, and how would you know that, anyway?"

"I know *you,* Oxie," Allegra said, jamming her hands

on her hips. She loved her father, loved the man desperately, but that didn't mean she didn't believe he'd be safer—that the whole world might be safer—if she could keep him in leading strings.

"Now tell me, Oxie. I already know that Uncle Frederick can't afford a Season in London, or otherwise Cousin Elizabeth wouldn't be within a dozen miles of this place, so we'll forget him for the moment. Did any of these three old schoolmates of yours return your letters with missives of their own? Offer you invitations? Acknowledge your letters in any way at all?"

Oxie pushed both hands through his fuzz of white hair. "You know the sad condition of the posts, Ally," he said, not quite looking at her. "Now, please, enough. We leave for London in two days. Accept it, pet, because it's true."

Allegra looked at her mother, who was smiling at her weakly, then to her father, who had this *gleam* in his eye that boded ill for anyone in London who didn't find feathers in their soup or ink in their port amusing occurrences.

She clenched her fists, stuck out her chin. "No. This is going to be an unmitigated disaster. I'm sorry, Mama, but I won't be a part of it."

Oxie took both her hands in his. "Pet, listen to me. I'm the Earl of Sunderland. I have no sons, only you. When I cock up my toes the title goes to—Magdalen, darlin', you've been studying up on all of this for a few weeks. Who does it go to?"

"Your cousin Frederick Nesbitt, Oxie. Elizabeth's father."

Allegra took a half step backward, shocked, for she had that particular failing of loving daughters, that of believing her papa would live forever, and had never investigated the succession.

"Elizabeth's father? That can't be right. Do they know? No, they couldn't, because that couldn't be right. If that were right, Elizabeth would have poisoned your porridge the day she arrived."

"It's true, Ally," her mother told her. "When I was trying to commit names and titles to my memory, I stumbled on the family tree. Your papa is the earl now, but Frederick definitely is next in line."

"Oxie, I'd watch my back, if I were you," Allegra said, only partly in jest. Her cousin's family, well born but poor as church mice since Uncle Frederick's gambling soul had rolled them up years ago, was accepted in Society—but an earldom? Oh, my. What Elizabeth wouldn't do to be Lady Elizabeth and live at Sunderland.

"Ally?" her father prompted as Allegra's mind took her down paths littered with Cousin Elizabeth shooting Oxie with his own dueling pistol, Cousin Elizabeth jumping out from behind one of the suits of armor in the long hall and sticking a knife into Oxie's back, Cousin Elizabeth hiring thugs to beat Oxie, drop him into a sack, and toss him off a cliff . . .

"Hmmm?" she said, shaking herself back to the moment, and to her father.

"I was saying, Ally, that when I shuffle off this mortal coil, you and your mama will be left with the dowager house, some few pennies in an allowance, and to the mercies of Frederick Nesbitt—Frederick, his harridan of a wife, and Cousin Elizabeth, all whose meanness you well remember."

"I won't think about that," Allegra said with that same daughterly determination to see the world only as she wanted it, a view that included both her parents forever in that world with her.

"Sometimes, pet, even you have to listen to me. I'm not always such a noodle, you know. You can see, can't you, why I need you married, and married well? You have to be provided for, and through you, my darlin' wife as well. Everything here is entailed, on loan to whatever earl is in residence. It is time, my pet, for us to be practical."

"And it might also be prudent for you to behave with more charity toward your cousin," Magdalen added.

"I'll try," Allegra said on a sigh. "But it won't be easy."

Chapter Two

*A*RMAND GAUTHIER flicked the reins lightly, his hands soft, his mastery of the ribbons in no doubt to anyone on the loud, congested London street or to the fine pair of blacks in the traces.

Handsome, dashing, Armand Gauthier was also mysterious. No one quite knew where he was from, how he had come into his immense fortune. He never mentioned his parents, as if he had been dropped into England from a cloud not quite three years ago, fully grown.

Or was that cloud purposefully constructed, to hide a

dubious past, a dark and dangerous past?

Had he been an adventurer? A highwayman? The illegitimate heir to some throne? To England's throne?

He had the bearing of a prince, didn't he; had this way of walking into every room as if he owned it, always dressed in his impeccable black and white, always in control of every situation, while finding humor in all areas of the human condition.

Women gushed over him; men felt it to be in their best interests to befriend him.

And Armand Gauthier kept his secrets, mostly by cheerfully confessing to be anything anyone suspected him of being.

An adventurer? Oh, dear, really? Oh, all right, if you insist.

The bastard son of a French prince? Of course, isn't everyone?

The well-recompensed lover of one of England's greatest ladies? Dear, dear, how indiscreet to even mention such a thing. *Wink, wink.*

The *ton* had delighted themselves in trying to ferret out any small piece of information about Armand Gauthier.

His accent—was that American, or French?

His skill with the cards—had he once dealt the cards or rolled the dice to earn his daily bread?

His skill with a sword, with his fists, with a pistol— were these purely gentlemanly pursuits, or did they, too, speak of that supposed dark and dangerous past?

And did it matter? The man appeared to be well bred, was definitely well behaved, as well as sinfully rich and even more sinfully gorgeous.

His eyes were as blue as a summer sky, his hair as black as a winter midnight. Taller than the average, and built along the lines of one of Elgin's famous marbles brought from Greece (but with arms still intact, of course, the observer who made the comparison had been quick to clarify), he cut a fashionable but never gaudy figure as he had moved into Society on the arm of his good friend Simon Roxbury, the Viscount Brockton.

No one questioned Viscount Brockton. No one but a fool would even suggest that Viscount Brockton was trying to foist some lowborn impostor on his friends.

And so Armand Gauthier, his deep pockets, pretty face, and mysterious past, were all welcomed into Society, where he had made himself comfortable for these past three years.

He'd just the previous winter sold his town house on Gerrard Street and purchased the Grosvenor Square mansion that was one of the jewels of the Square when Sir Roger Trembly's luck at the card tables had turned sour and the man needed ready cash in exchange for the fully furnished establishment.

And Armand had not even been in the game.

Now the mansion was his, along with a houseful of servants, fully fitted-out stables, and the remarkable Quincy, the majordomo's majordomo. Deep pockets could buy almost anything, and a pleasing face and manner could at the very least place a sizable deposit on the rest.

With his good friend, Bartholomew Boothe, Armand

had wintered in Sussex and, for a month or more, visited with Viscount Brockton and his bride, before announcing to one and all that he had decided that London needed him, almost as much as he needed London, for he had, at nearly thirty, concluded that perhaps it was time to set up his own nursery. Well, at least *think* about it.

And wouldn't his good friend Bones want to go on the hunt himself? Find himself a wife? Armand broached the question, then had stood back to watch the fun.

Bartholomew, predictably aghast at even the thought of bracketing himself to some simpering debutante, yet alone ever dandling a swaddled babe on his bony knee, had at last agreed to come along for the Season, but he'd made it clear he was only there under protest, and only because he knew Armand still held hopes for another agenda.

Love, Bones had said (quoting his mother, seemingly an expert on all things), had to come unbidden, or it didn't come at all—and even then, it was a good bet that any descent into love would end badly.

Bartholomew's warnings to one side, Armand retained high hopes for a successful Season, even if he failed to find the woman of his dreams—not that he actually expected to find a woman who could fulfill all his dreams. Not that he intended to look very hard.

Still, the chase itself held no small appeal, as well as continuing his private search for at least one more Season before admitting failure, putting a period to his private hopes.

There were times, just recently, when that search

didn't seem quite as important as it once had.

Simon's contentment had stirred a previously unknown hunger deep in Armand's belly. Home, hearth, family. Didn't one always long most for what one has never had, never experienced for one's self?

Perhaps it was time to give up his quest, and do just as he'd said, find himself an acceptable woman and set up his own nursery, his own future, and let the past continue to lie in its obscurity.

And so, this last week of March, he had driven his high-perch phaeton on the last leg into town, with his servants following somewhere behind in the assortment of coaches that were needed to transport all of Armand's massive requirements for the Season from one abode to another.

Armand, who once could carry all he owned in a single square of cloth tied to the end of a not particularly stout stick, smiled now as he momentarily reflected on the vagaries of life. And the luck of the draw.

Bartholomew Boothe sat up beside Armand, his sharp teeth still worrying the skin on the side of his thumb after pronouncing for at least the tenth time that they would come to grief in the crush of traffic, and being proved wrong each time.

Armand had just turned the phaeton out of the worst of the crush of vehicles and into Grosvenor Square when he exclaimed, "Good God, Bones, what's that?"

Bones narrowed his eyelids and looked past Armand, to his left. With remarkable sangfroid, he then sat back, crossed his arms over his thin chest. "It's a fountain, Armand, complete with cherubs and openmouthed fish.

The same fountain that has been in that particular corner of the Square for years and years."

"Yes, but why—who?"

"Oh, you want the particulars? My mistake, I'm sure. Very well. Dredging through my rather remarkable memory, I would hazard that the Earl of Sunderland is in residence, in that pink mansion, just behind the fountain. Boggles the mind, that does."

"Why? The Earl of Sunderland? Really. The name is vaguely familiar."

"Should be. People still talk about him from time to time, although it has been about five years since he's come to town. A terrible failure, his first sojourn to the metropolis. And a memorable one, in case he's hoping everyone forgot. I know m'mother never has. Or me. I can't believe he's back."

"How do you *know* he's back?"

"That's simple enough," Bones said as Armand pulled the horses to a stop in front of his own mansion, gazing at it with pride of ownership. "M'mother's told me tale after tale of how the earl loves mischief, playing pranks. Only Oxie Nesbitt would fill his own fountain with bubbles. At least, he did it the first time he came to London. Seems unlikely it's anyone else but him, don't you think?"

Armand hopped down from the seat as a groom ran to the horses' heads, and looked across the Square at the elaborate structure that, indeed, was still spouting small mountains of frothy bubbles, a virtual rainbow of bubbles that were tumbling out of the stone fountain, onto the cobblestones. They danced in the breeze, glistened as they caught the sunlight; a pretty if ludicrous sight.

"A novel way to announce one's presence. Some people, obviously far less inventive sorts, are content with merely ordering that the knocker be put back on the door," he said, smiling slightly as he shook his head. "Ah, well, Bones, we are here safely, the Earl of Sunderland is to be our neighbor across the Square, and the Season is about to begin. Everything seems to be—well, hello."

Bones, who was standing on the flagway, inspecting himself for road dirt as he surreptitiously rubbed at his bony posterior that would never get along well with a hard bench seat, picked up his head and quizzically looked at his friend. "Hello?"

"Indeed, yes, Bones. Hello." Armand inclined his head slightly, in the direction of the fountain. "I do hope the gods are smiling, and the young lady is in residence here for the Season."

"Young lady? I don't see any—oh, there? What's she doing?"

Armand watched as the small, honey-blond beauty walked fully around the fountain, one hand on her hip, then leaned over, scooped up some of the bubbles, blew them off her hands, watched as they floated away on the breeze. She laughed, shook her head, and all but skipped toward the pink mansion, stealing inside before Armand could do more than feel the first pinprick of attraction.

"Tell me, Bones, would your dearest mama, your own personal bubbling fount of information, know if the Earl of Sunderland has a daughter?"

"If he does, and if that's her, she's probably as dotty as the father. But a pretty enough little thing, I suppose, if you don't mind the bloodline."

Armand hid his quick irritation at his friend's incautious words. "She's the daughter of an earl, Bones. That seems to be a fairly respectable bloodline."

"She's a Nesbitt," Bones explained patiently as the door opened as if Quincy had been standing just behind it, his ears at attention, waiting for nothing more than the sound of his master's boots on the marble steps.

"Yes, so you've said. The Earl of Sunderland. Oxie Nesbitt. Tell me more, please."

"Oxie Nesbitt. Poor and extremely distant relation who unexpectedly backed into the title when the last earl keeled over in the midst of drinking himself stupid, as he did every night of his life. Still fairly young, in the prime of his life, and the man went crashing down."

"Leaving no son, no heir?"

"Correct. We all thought Frederick Nesbitt would come into the title, but this Oxie Nesbitt turned out to be the one, something to do with birth order, m'mother says. Definitely not bred for the title. Rough, crude, and with a talent for mischief, that's what m'mother says, and with a wife who actually asked Prinney to please show her the way to the nearest water closet."

"Really? And nobody thought that was funny? I think that's extremely funny."

"You would of course, Armand. Always said you were a little dotty yourself," Bones said happily enough—he was always happiest when saying something depressing. He followed his friend up the steps,

26

adding, "But remember, sad specimen that he is, Prinney is still our regent, and deserves some respect. That's what m'mother says, when she isn't calling him a fat flawn."

"Good to see you again, sir," Quincy said, bowing his bewigged, powdered head. "I trust you had a comfortable journey."

"Thank you, yes we did, Quincy," Armand said as he handed over his hat and gloves to the bowing major-domo before heading upstairs to the drawing room and the fully loaded drinks table.

"Your mother says quite a lot, Bones," he remarked as he held up a crystal decanter and his friend nodded his acceptance of the offer of wine. Now his interest had been piqued twice, once by the daughter, and again by the father. "I can't imagine why I've never run across this earl. I had thought I knew everyone in London."

"One peek at some honey-colored curls and a shapely ankle, and your mind's gone to mush." Bones took his glass and sat down on one of the couches, crossing one long, skinny shanked leg over the other. "I *told* you. That's because the earl and his countess made such a disaster of their first visit here, so that they went running to ground and have never dared to come back, not even just the earl, on some flying visit to his solicitor or some such thing."

"Not for five long years?"

"At least that long, I'm sure. But if you're right, Armand, and that was the daughter, she looks to be old enough to be popped off. That's probably it. They're here to pop off the daughter. Well, good luck to them, if she's anything like the parents. Society will cut her dead."

Armand put down his own glass, looked at Bones thoughtfully. "We're a mean bunch at the heart of it, aren't we, Bones? Condemning the poor girl before she so much as dips her toe into Society?"

Bones shrugged. "Possibly, but that's the way it has always been, Armand. You should know. If it weren't for Simon—and myself, to some small measure—you would have had a lot more difficulty inserting yourself into the *ton,* being accepted by them all."

"I know that, Bones, and I'm grateful."

"Not that you wouldn't have succeeded on your own, given enough time. But even you must admit having Simon quietly let it be known to the hostesses that he would attend no gathering to which you were not invited? Well, it went a long way, and we all know it."

Armand picked up his half-empty glass, held it up so that the sunlight pouring in through the large front windows made a small rainbow in the wine, the way that same sunlight had colored the bubbles the petite beauty had blown off her hands.

"A patron. Simon acted as my patron, and therefore guaranteed my easy entry into Society. Amazing what one small encounter can do for a person."

"Hardly a small encounter, Armand," Bones said, shifting on his seat. "You two met in that gaming hall, and you took Simon to one side, explained to him that he was being royally fleeced by a sharper, then proceeded to thoroughly trounce the bastard at his own game."

Armand walked over to one of the couches, sat down, crossed his long legs. "I've since taught Simon how to spot a marked deck, among other things."

"Yes, you did. And you paid Simon back in full for any favors last year when you taught him how to fuzz the cards when he went after that rotter, Filton. Oh, have you heard? Filton's in the Fleet, for debt again, of course. I still can't believe he didn't hang for what he tried to do to Callie."

"Yes, Simon told me," Armand said, nodding his head. "And peers rarely hang, Bones, as we both know. But as it sounds as if Filton will be spending the remainder of his sorry life outrunning duns and eventually escaping to the continent with every other penniless gentleman we know, I would like to return our attention to the earl's daughter."

"Oh, must we? I'm uncomfortable with petticoat talk, and well you know it. We could talk about the weather. Yes, let's do that, let's talk about the weather. Do you think it will rain tomorrow?"

"I could become her sponsor, of sorts, couldn't I? Her patron, as it were, as Simon did with me. I have enough consequence."

"I think it might rain." Bones took a deep breath, let it out slowly. "Oh, very well, but only because you're going to insist."

"How well you know me. Now, Bones, talk to me. Tell me if I'm right."

"Of course you're right. You're up to your ears in consequence, which remains a remarkable thing, considering . . . but to sponsor the Nesbitt chit?"

Armand leaned forward, his elbows on his knees. "Yes?"

"Truthfully? I don't know if anyone has that much consequence, not if she's anything like her sire and mama. Because the mama is just as bad, Armand. I remember now, m'mother said she was dubbed the Bumpkin Countess, or something close to that, and the earl played pranks that had half the *ton* ready to hang him from the nearest lamppost. I'm serious, Armand. These two have all the refinement of a pack of party pigs."

"They also have a beautiful daughter," Armand said, closing his eyes, recalling the vision of the pretty little blonde, gaily laughing at the bubbles, appearing both at ease and delighted with the world. "A remarkably beautiful daughter."

"Probably one of the servants, out for a breath of fresh air," Bones said, always more than willing to pour cold water on anyone's hopes.

"No," Armand said, finishing his wine. "She was well dressed, Bones. Small, both in her height and in her slender frame, and with the most adorable point to her chin."

"You saw all of that, from that distance? I don't believe it."

"But you are not interested in petticoats, Bones. I'm not surprised you didn't notice. I, on the other hand, am always interested in feminine beauty. Now, what to do about this? I suppose I would be best served to approach her at one of the balls, one of the parties?"

"Ha! And where would that be, Armand? No invitations will be sent to the Earl of Sunderland, for fear the man will pull one of his pranks and ruin the entire evening. Sally Jersey loathes him, for two, so that rules out Almack's, definitely. The daughter will never be offered a voucher, you can count on that."

"And why does the most rude, crude, and generally improper patroness of Almack's dislike him?"

"He played Merry Mourner, that's why, propping a coffin against her front door, so that when he knocked, then ran, her footman opened the door only to have the lid and a soggy, straw-stuffed suit of clothes fall in on him. Man screamed loud enough to wake Sally from a dead sleep. I'm telling you, Armand, so please listen— the Nesbitts will be on their way out of London again within a fortnight, without so much as a single invitation ever coming their way."

Armand was silent for a few moments, considering all of this as he looked around his lovely new mansion; considering the girl, the unknown earl whose acquaintance he must surely make, the girl again. The girl most definitely.

"Very well. I'll introduce her myself, here, at the party I've just decided I must host in order to show off my latest acquisition," he said at last, unfortunately just as Bones was sipping the last of his wine, so that he had to wait until the man was done coughing and choking before he could add, "What Simon did for me, I shall do for this poor girl. It only seems fair, Bones."

Bones pulled a large white linen square from his pocket and dabbed at his streaming eyes. "I know what you're doing, so don't try to flummox me with all this talk of parties and patrons and pretty little blondes. You're hoping this one may be the one, that this one could be the answer to your questions. A *Nesbitt,* Armand? Oh, I don't think so. It will go badly, Armand. Trust me, it will go badly."

"Yes," Armand said, walking to the window, to look out at the fountain across the Square, smile at the mounding bubbles, "so you always say, Bones, so you always say."

Chapter Three

IT TOOK QUITE A LOT to impress Lady Allegra Nesbitt. She had lived in genteel poverty. She had spent the past five years in the lap of luxury. She had chased frogs out of her bed warmer and had kept her expression blank as the vicar prepared to sit down on his wet-with-glue seat after his Sunday sermon, just two of the hundreds of silly pranks Oxie had put into action over the years.

She'd neatly taken over the running of Sunderland when it became obvious that her dearest, easily overwhelmed mama was not quite up to the job, educated herself beyond expectations for a female by locking herself up in the extensive Sunderland library for at least five hours a day. She'd placated those servants who swore they would not spend another moment in a household run by a man, even an earl, who delighted in putting salt in the sugar bowl, or hanging fish heads in clothespresses.

She'd survived every April Fool's Day, every single

year, and Oxie had been frustrated at not being able to fool his daughter, so frustrated that, this year, he had obviously become desperate.

Allegra waved the rich ivory vellum card in front of her father's face, then gave him a snap of her fingers.

"This is pitiful, Oxie. Shame on you. We've been in town for over a week, completely without invitations to so much as a small breakfast, and now you present me with *this?* A *ball?* Ridiculous. You'd have been better served to try to convince me, as you did Mama, that bits of coal strung on a necklace were, in fact, Newcastle diamonds, and quite treasured. Poor Mama, her neck was black for a week."

Oxie Nesbitt looked from side to side, shushing his daughter. "Please, pet, don't mention that right now. I think your mama has forgotten that it's April Fool's, although it's already gone eleven, and she's not yet showed me her lovely face."

"Nor will she, all day," Allegra told him, tossing the invitation onto a table before seating herself on one of the couches in the drawing room. "If you tried the door, Oxie, you'd see that she's locked herself in her bed-chamber, planning not to emerge until tomorrow. Now, to get back to"—she gestured toward the table—"*this.* Who is this Armand Gauthier? You made him up, didn't you?"

A blur of color swept past Allegra as Cousin Elizabeth swooped out of nowhere to snatch up the invitation. "Armand Gauthier? Oh, my stars—Armand Gauthier! A *ball?* And we're *invited?*"

She closed her eyes, smiled beatifically. "He must

know Papa. Papa promised he would write to his many friends, to tell them I was in town for the Season. Papa's name still carries some weight, you know, even though we've not been in Society since . . ."

"Since *my* papa was proved the Sunderland heir five years ago, and all those nasty creditors began demanding payment for bills your gambling papa had been ringing up with the understanding that *he* was the heir?" Allegra offered helpfully.

"You're a horrid, horrid person, Cousin Allegra, but I don't care, not now that we have *this,*" Elizabeth crowed, then walked toward the windows, still holding the invitation, as if she planned to get a better look at it in the sunlight.

"No more *horrid* than you, cousin. What a silly word—*horrid.* Better, and clearer, to just say that I'm a pain in your—"

"Now, pet," Oxie interrupted quietly. "The line of succession, remember? The dower house, that pitifully small allowance?"

"Oh, piffle," Allegra said, then tipped her head, looked at her father with some intensity. "Are you ill, Oxie? Have you had some ridiculous dream in which you met an untimely end? Why all this sudden worry about what happens to Mama and me once you're gone?"

"I am only being prudent, Ally," the earl told her, sitting himself down on the facing couch. "I knocked on fifty's door three months ago, remember, and the view from the other side makes me realize that I now am looking back on the majority of my life, and forward to whatever few years the good Lord gives me. I'm not entirely insensible you know. I am mortal, we're all mortal."

Then he smiled. "Oh, that's good. I'll have to remember that one, we're all mortal. Catchy, almost poetical, eh?"

"I doubt the bard would have quivered in his boots, had he heard you say it," Allegra told him, looking at her cousin. "Elizabeth? Such an intense inspection. Are we about to see you bite into the vellum, as if you were testing a coin to be certain it's gold?"

Elizabeth, who had been holding the invitation within inches of her eyes, quickly lowered it and glared at Allegra. "I may have been fooled before, but I have learned. I just wanted to be certain this invitation is . . . legitimate."

"Yes," Allegra said, stifling a smile, "those bastard invitations can be the very devil."

"You delight in chasing her, don't you?" Oxie asked as Elizabeth picked up her skirts and raced from the room, aghast at her cousin's earthy language.

"Not as much as I thought I would," Allegra said, sighing as she walked over to retrieve the invitation her cousin had dropped in her agitation. "I think I like her more than I'd expected to—which is depressing in its own way. Leave it to the dratted girl to spoil my fun. Now," she said, sitting down on one of the couches, waving the invitation like a fan in front of her face, "back to this, Oxie, if you please."

The earl spread his hands wide, shook his head. "As God is my witness, pet, I don't know this Armand

Got-yer from the chimney sweep that was here this morning."

Cocking one expressive eyebrow, Allegra stopped fanning herself, inspected the invitation nearly as intensely as had her cousin. "It's real? You don't know him, which means he doesn't know us, and yet here's this invitation. Why?"

"Because I'm the Earl of Sunderland, pet, why else?"

"Really? Nobody else seems to care. We've been watching carriages clog this Square for the past week, coming and going, visiting and partying, and without a single invitation to a single event. Certainly we've seen no invitations from your schoolmates. Not even Uncle Frederick's pleas on behalf of his daughter seem to have sent so much as one invitation our way."

She slapped her palms against her knees—quite an unladylike gesture—and got to her feet. "This bears investigating."

"Investigating? Oh, I like the sound of that, pet. What are you going to do?"

"Do? Why, Oxie, I believe I'm just going to have to take a stroll in the Square, then turn my ankle outside Mr. Gauthier's mansion."

Other fathers would have been shocked, appalled, and put a firm foot down against any such plan. But, then, other fathers weren't Oxie Nesbitt.

"Good, good," he said, nodding. "Carry on, pet, carry on. Oh, but take a maid with you. This isn't Sunderland. We must obey the rules of Society, even though we both know that the person who'd dare to accost you would run away much the worse for the encounter."

Within the quarter hour, Allegra was descending the steps of the pink mansion, setting out to walk the inside edges of Grosvenor Square until she reached Armand Gauthier's door.

With her she brought her favorite chip straw bonnet, a parasol the same sweet pale green color as her gown, a reticule holding a very long, very sharp hatpin—she was daring, not redbrick stupid—and her mama's maid, Aspasia.

Aspasia had been her first choice, as Mrs. Tomlin and Allegra hadn't rubbed well together since their very first meeting.

The hired companion-cum-housekeeper, a straight-spined creature with coal-black eyes and a wardrobe of high-necked, shapeless gowns, wore her morals as close as the tightly coiled black bun on top of her head, and had immediately pounced on Allegra as walking with too long and free a style, with sitting entirely too much at her ease . . . even for making faces at some of the portraits of the near-dozen long-dead Sunderland earls in the hallways.

In short, the woman was a stickler, and a real stick. Cousin Elizabeth adored her, Magdalen nearly worshiped her, and Allegra had—after her third lecture in two days on the inadvisability of crossing one's ankles, even in the privacy of her own home—succumbed to the impulse to make a small visit to the woman's bedchamber.

Mrs. Tomlin hadn't uttered a word of complaint the next morning, after attempting to crawl into her bed and finding that the sheets had been folded halfway, so that she was left with three options: ask for assistance from one of the maids, remake the entire bed herself, or sleep with her knees tucked up under her chin.

Allegra grudgingly gave the woman credit for having some bottom, and not running to the countess with her complaint. At the same time she realized that in Lettice Tomlin she had found a worthy adversary.

Not that she'd even consider taking the woman along on today's little adventure.

Much better the shy, nervous Aspasia, a woman as out of her depth in London as would be a flounder perched on a lamppost. Sweet, gullible, loyal Aspasia, a short, rotund, gray-haired dear with the loyalty of a hound and the brainpower of that aforementioned flounder.

As if to prove Allegra's mental point, the maid, walking two paces behind her, piped up, "Dear my lady, isn't it wondrous that his lordship is going to sup with the Prince Regent tonight? We're all aflutter below-stairs."

Allegra stopped in her tracks, turned to look at the smiling maid. "Aspasia. Think. What day is this?"

Aspasia squeezed her eyes tightly shut, drew her mouth into a pucker as she considered the question. "Monday? Yes, Monday, because we all went to services yesterday. At least a few of us servants did."

Not bothering to explain that her mama had been too nervous to even think about venturing out to a church when no one in London would so much as give her a friendly nod in passing, Allegra smiled and said, "I'm sure you prayed for all of us, Aspasia. Now, to get back to the point. It is Monday, yes, but do you recall the date?"

The maid shook her head sadly. "No, my lady, I surely don't."

"In that case, let's walk as we talk, all right? And I'll tell you the story of the Wise Men of Gotham. This story is very old, dating from around twelve hundred and something, and has to do with a trip King John took to Nottingham."

"My sister, Blasia, lives near Nottingham," Aspasia put in helpfully.

"Ah, wonderful, then the geography is clear in your head. To continue. On his way to Nottingham, on the first day of April to be precise, King John and his entourage were about to pass through the meadow of a small village named Gotham. This, the villagers knew, could not be a good thing for them, because anywhere the king walked became a public road, and this would put paid to their lovely meadow."

"The first day of April?" Aspasia interrupted, a dawning knowledge, and apprehension, scrunching up her pudding features once more.

"The first day of April, Aspasia, yes. The anxious villagers misdirected the king, sent him off in entirely another direction, thus saving their meadow. However, when the king heard about this deception later in the day he was furious."

"As well he should be, made to take the long way round. I know I would be, especially the way my shoes can pinch me," Aspasia commented. "Um, my lady? Did you say the first of April?"

"Aspasia, concentrate, I'm telling a story, one learned

at my dearest papa's knee. The king—the very angry king—sent his officer back to the village, to punish the inhabitants, but they'd been forewarned and were ready for him."

"There's not going to be any supping with the Prince Regent, is there, my lady?" At Allegra's level stare, Aspasia quickly said, "So sorry, my lady. What did the villagers do?"

"You already know, don't you, Aspasia?"

"Yes, my lady, I do. The villagers greeted the king's officer in a real treat, rolling cheeses down the hill so they'd find their own way to the market town. Some were hunkered down at the edge of the pond, trying to drown the fish. They'd put wagons on the barn roofs to give shade. All sorts of nonsense, so that the king's officer went running lickety-split to tell the king about the fools of Gotham, and that punishing them would be useless."

"Exactly," Allegra said as she turned to her left and took dead aim at the Gauthier mansion. "Except that the villagers of Gotham—the Wise men of Gotham—had actually fooled the king. And thus, according to some legends, was born April Fool's Day."

"Pitiful waste of perfectly good cheese, I say," Aspasia remarked. "But no wonder your dear mama didn't so much as blink when I told her about his grace's invitation to break bread with the Prince Regent. She already knew it was all a humbug."

"Poor Oxie. Mama has finally outwitted him this year, I believe. Now, why don't we just walk along and enjoy this wonderful sunshine. Such a lovely day, Aspasia. I vow I could walk this Square the entire afternoon, just to feel the warmth of that sun on my shoulders."

She made a dead set at her target. "Oh, look. What a pretty mansion this is," she said, passing just in front of the building carrying the number contained in the invitation. "Such intricate carving around the doors, and those pillars on either side of it are certainly—whoops!"

She went to one knee, quickly pulled back to her feet by Aspasia, who then encircled her mistress's waist with one strong arm as she did her best to avoid being conked on the head by her ladyship's parasol. "Are you all right, my lady? You took quite a turn there, didn't you?"

Allegra dipped her head, hiding her smile behind the encircling brim of her bonnet. "I . . . I don't know. I may have twisted my—ouch! Oh, yes, yes, I've twisted my ankle on these silly cobbles. Twisted, definitely twisted. Aspasia, I shan't be able to walk all the way back across the Square, not even with your help."

"My stars, what do I do now?" Aspasia asked, just as if Allegra had put the words into her mouth which, in a way, she had.

"I don't know. Perhaps . . . yes, perhaps there is someone at home in this mansion behind us? A footman who could assist you in helping me across the Square?"

Aspasia bit her bottom lip, nervously looked at the mansion, looked at Allegra, looked back at the mansion, as if trying to follow a speeding shuttlecock going back and forth across a net. Allegra counted to five, and then to five once again. The maid's mind worked slowly, sometimes needed a little boost.

"Aspasia? I'm in considerable pain here, dear. I'll tell

you what we'll do. Just you hold on to me as I hop over to the steps, sit down, rest my ankle. Then you can knock at the door, ask for assistance."

Aspasia sucked in her cheeks, looked at the mansion, looked at Allegra, who moaned, deeply, with great feeling.

"I suppose so," the maid said, and Allegra gratefully hobbled to the stone steps and sat down. "What—what do I say?"

Allegra rolled her eyes. You could lead a horse to water, but— "Just tell whoever comes to the door that your mistress, Lady Allegra, daughter of the Earl of Sunderland —you can point to me as you say this, Aspasia—has twisted her ankle badly and needs assistance."

"I can say ankle? Oh, I don't think I can dare say *ankle,* my lady. Not to a footman. It isn't decent."

"Oh, good grief." Allegra dropped her head into her hands, beginning to feel oppressed. "Lower limb, Aspasia. Tell the footman I've injured a lower limb, all right? Can you say that?"

"Yes, my lady," the maid said, taking a deep breath, straightening her shoulders. "Lower limb. I suppose I can say that."

"Praise be," Allegra muttered to herself, and waited for Aspasia to mount the steps. "Lift the knocker, Aspasia," she prompted patiently. "Now bang it against the door, about three times should be sufficient. Soundly, as a knock reflects who we are. Not the timid knock of a servant, Aspasia, nor the imperious knock of a king. But a healthy knock, worthy of the daughter of an earl. Put a bit of shoulder into it."

Aspasia whimpered, closed her eyes, and did as Allegra had instructed.

The door opened almost immediately, and a tall, rather elderly man looked down at Aspasia, his sharp blue eyes skewering her, his powdered wig adding at least two inches to his already considerable height, his ramrod-straight posture advertising that this had once been a military man.

The maid visibly shrank, stepped back two paces. "I . . . I mean, that is, her ladyship . . . can't say where . . . something limb?"

The majordomo gave a snap of his fingers and two liveried footman stepped outside, helped Allegra to her feet, made a chair of their locked arms, and carried her up the stairs and into the foyer, just as if they performed the same duty every day.

Sparing a moment for a quick look-round, Allegra silently complimented Mr. Gauthier for his good taste. The foyer was massive, furnished well, and with a truly majestic set of marble steps rising in a graceful curve to the main floors of the mansion.

She could just barely see the green baize door tucked beneath the stairs, a door that surely led to the kitchens, and a room to either side of the foyer, one with the wide pocket doors firmly closed, the other obviously a small private study where the master of the house met with tradespeople and others not socially fit for the drawing room.

"Mr. Gauthier sends his compliments, my lady, as he happened to be looking out an upstairs window and noticed your distress, then alerted me to that distress," the majordomo said in the tone of one who has little patience with young women who conveniently twist their ankles outside the domiciles of rich, eligible men—a ploy Allegra had already decided wasn't quite as brilliant or original as she had thought when she'd first come up with the idea.

"How kind of Mr. Gauthier," Allegra said, feeling silly as she remained perched on the footmen's arms, wondering if a prudent exit might be in her best interests, but not quite knowing how to make one without looking a perfect fool.

Or, at the least, more of a fool than she looked now, still wearing her bonnet, her parasol remaining open and held over her head because she'd quite forgotten to close it.

"As you cannot wish to be carried up the stairs to the main drawing room much like a sack of meal, I shall beg you to please take your ease in the small study on this floor. James and Clarence will carry you there. James, Clarence, you know the drill. Your maid, my lady, will of course accompany you, to maintain the niceties. Refreshments will be served, and the master will join you, anon. Will you need the services of a physician, my lady?"

"A polite question, under the circumstances. Tell me, what do you think?" she asked the man, because she had learned long ago to recognize fools . . . and those who do not suffer fools gladly.

"Tea and cakes have marvelous restorative powers, my lady, or so I've heard," the man answered without a whit of expression in his eyes. "I should imagine that some rest, possibly some pleasant conversation, will speed the healing sufficiently for you to return to your own domicile."

"My thoughts exactly." Allegra couldn't help herself. She smiled in real pleasure.

She asked the footmen to please put her down, thanking them for their kind assistance, then closed up her parasol, which she then handed over to the major-domo, along with her bonnet. "What's your name, if you please?"

The majordomo drew himself up to his full height, his shoulders thrown back. "Quincy, my lady."

"Well, hello, Quincy. If your master has half the mind and wit you do, I shall indeed pass a pleasant quarter hour here while my injury miraculously repairs itself."

"Then we're agreed, my lady," Quincy said, at last unbending his consequence enough to actually smile at her as he tipped the closed parasol against his shoulder, as if hefting a rifle, ready to march. "Good hunting."

Allegra knew she should at least pretend to be confused, perhaps even be insulted. Instead, she laughed out loud, not even bothering to limp as she turned Aspasia about by her shoulders and nudged the nervous servant into the small study to the right of the foyer.

Chapter Four

*Y*OU CAN'T GO DOWN THERE," Bartholomew Boothe pointed out with all the fervor of a duenna guarding her charge. "It's not proper."

"Proper? And just when, dear Bones, did you decide that I've become in the least proper? I seem to have slept through that transformation," Armand said, checking his appearance in the cheval glass in the dressing room located at the front of the mansion's third floor, carefully adjusting the lay of his snowy white cravat. "I am expected to, as you say, *go down there*. Besides, she's accompanied by her maid, she's a damsel in distress, and I am nothing if not a good host."

"She's a forward, graceless minx who has pretended to turn her ankle in order to get herself into this house and you into her clutches," Bones corrected.

"True, true. I'll admit it, Bones, I'm disappointed in the forward, graceless minx. I had hoped she'd be different from the others, more of an original. Say, be daring enough to faint in front of my curricle as I drove through the park. My admiration for our pretty little blonde has dropped a notch, maybe more."

"Not our pretty little blonde, Armand, but *yours*. And what does this make, Armand? Five twisted ankles since last week?"

"Alas, only four," Armand answered, turning to face his friend. "That being said, I am still quite the popular gentleman since it has been bruited about that I might be considering setting up my nursery, aren't I? I do believe I am quite the eligible *parti*."

"You're vain and disgusting, that's what you are, as well as on an entirely different hunt. These forward young ladies are simply disgusting."

"And you're jealous."

Bones all but choked on his indignation. "Jealous?

Me? Jealous? Don't be ridiculous."

"I offered you Miss Haliburton, remember? As I recall it, you didn't want her."

"Nobody wants her," Bones said, picking up a pair of dice and beginning to throw them, one hand against the other, on a small table beside his chair.

"She's pretty enough, as I know that means a lot to you."

"Oh, and not to you? Remember, I was with you when you all but fell to pieces over the minx downstairs. But Miss Haliburton? The girl has nothing to recommend her. She don't like London, she don't like the country, she don't approve of the waltz, she don't think gentlemen should be allowed to blow a cloud, even after the ladies are retired to the drawing room. I never saw anyone so determined to be unhappy."

"And you would most definitely know about that," Armand said, lifting his glass of wine to his friend, then finishing it off in one swallow. "Very well, if you won't accompany me, I shall be off. Never let it be said I kept a lady waiting."

"And she's definitely the bubble chit?" Bones asked, putting down the dice and following after his friend, obviously deciding that the man could only benefit from his protection. "The same small blonde you've been waxing poetical about since last week? Sunderland's whelp? You're positive? I couldn't quite see beneath the brim of her bonnet."

"The Earl of Sunderland's daughter, one Lady Allegra, if my bribes to the Sunderland servants are to be trusted. Yes, I'm quite sure," Armand said as he headed for the stairs. "As well you know, considering that you've spent the last twenty minutes peering over my shoulder as we watched her slyly make her way to my door."

"Yes, all right, as well I know. I suppose I've been trying to hold out hope that we don't have a Nesbitt in the house. She's here because of that invitation you sent, that has to be the reason. It had to appear like manna from the heavens to that motley group across the Square. She's here to thank you, and then neatly compromise you, bring you to your knees, and from your knees to the altar. Armand, for a supposedly intelligent man, you can be depressingly thick."

"Ah, Bones, but I have you here, to guard me, to protect me from my folly. What could possibly go wrong with my own personal doomsayer at my side, dire predictions at the ready?"

Armand made his way down the stairs, heading for the small study, Bones mumbling something behind him, but still with him.

They both stopped at the doorway, Bones nearly colliding with Armand's back, and looked inside the room.

Lady Allegra was on her feet, those appendages just below her two very sound ankles, inspecting the titles of the few books located on a shelf behind his desk. She was up on tiptoe, as a matter of fact, because she was a definite dab of a female, and the shelf was high.

Her maid, a small, rotund woman, sat on the very front edge of a straight-backed chair in the far corner of the room, her knees visibly knocking, her head dropped forward into her hands. The lament, "Oh, laws, oh, laws," could be heard from time to time, as Aspasia awaited the inevitable.

At Armand's slight warning cough, the maid jumped a good three inches and Lady Allegra lazily turned to glance at him, and then looked to her cowering maid.

"Oh, piffle. Aspasia, you were supposed to stand guard, remember? But, then, intrigue has never been your brightest light, has it, dear?" she said more kindly, then stepped out from behind the desk, looked Armand square in his eyes, addressing her next words to him. "It's to be expected that the truth would out I suppose, as I'd acted in haste anyway, and still haven't formed a suitable new fib."

"I beg your pardon?" Armand said in real confusion, his attention caught by Lady Allegra's greener than green eyes, her honey-gold curls, her faintly husky voice—not to mention her bright, direct manner.

Perhaps he'd been too swift to demote the fair lady to the ranks of an everyday debutante. He found himself backing up, all the way into the foyer, as she rather imperiously waved for him to step to one side.

She joined him there, as the maid's whimpers had grown into rather noisy snifflings.

"How nice of you to pretend not to notice, Mr. Gauthier. I should be limping or, better yet, reclining on that couch in there, my injured ankle—limb, that is—resting on a stool. Ah well, I've already bumbled enough to discard any further presence, haven't I? I suppose the offer of refreshments is withdrawn, and I'm about to see a finger pointed firmly at the door? If I could just retrieve my bonnet, my parasol, and, oh yes," she continued, tipping her head toward the study, "that dear, sweet watering pot in there?"

"Cheeky little thing," Bones said from his position behind Armand, his thin frame nearly hidden, which is probably the way he liked it.

"Go away, Bones," Armand said, not taking his eyes off Allegra, unable to take his eyes off Allegra, from those lively, amused green eyes. "No, wait. I must remember what small manners I have."

He then stepped forward, made a most eloquent bow. "First things first. Please allow me to introduce myself, my lady. I am, as you supposed, Armand Gauthier, and you, if I'm correct, are Lady Allegra, daughter of the Earl of Sunderland. The fellow just now grumbling behind me is one Mr. Bartholomew Boothe. But he's of no matter, as he's about to disappear. Aren't you, Bones?"

"At the moment, no, he's not important, although I am most happy to meet him," Lady Allegra agreed with stunning honesty, her smile wide as she returned Armand's look.

That in itself was an oddity in a metropolis heavily littered with young ladies who either could not or would not meet a man's eyes—at least not without first giggling or simpering, or whatever it was young ladies did, all of it remarkably unappealing.

"I can only commend your sangfroid, my lady." Armand grinned as Bones gave a slight bow before retreating behind his friend once more. "And, now that the introductions are complete and you have the correct target in your sights, would you care to adjourn once more to the relative privacy of my study?"

She spared one last look at Bones, just then hovering at the bottom of the staircase, wringing his hands as if he'd heard that the world would come to an end in five minutes and he wasn't sure if he should try to stop that destruction or be better served to hide himself under a table.

She placed her hand on Armand's sleeve. "I would be delighted, Mr. Gauthier. Shall we?"

Quincy appeared at that moment, carrying a silver tray laden with teapot, cups, and scones, only to be waved away by his master, who felt he'd had enough interruptions for one afternoon.

In fact, he was tempted to not only oust the maid, but to close the door on his majordomo's face, and only the sure knowledge that the man would give his notice immediately stopped him. Bones would forgive him; lecture him, then forgive him. But Quincy would leave him, without a backward glance.

Armand watched as Lady Allegra reentered the room, patted the maid's shoulder, then walked to the couch, sitting down smack in the middle of it. She spread her skirts, letting him know without words that if he wished to seat himself he'd better find another place to rest his rump. She put her hands in her lap, tilted her chin up at him, and smiled, somehow taking on the role of hostess, leaving him the part of opportunistic interloper.

Minx.

"How odd," she said after a moment. "You look . . . almost familiar, as if I've seen you before today. I doubt you've been to Sunderland, but perhaps you've visited

Durham? That's close by. Although I don't fully believe I can see you showing an interest in the architectural marvel that is Durham Cathedral."

"Another not quite novel approach, my lady, one usually employed by clumsy wet-behind-the-ears youths trying to strike up a conversation. Will there be many more?"

She had the grace to lower her gaze. "No. I think I'm done now. Quite done."

"Splendid." He took up his position in front of the small desk, leaning back against its edge, bracing his hands on either side of him. The maid once more dropped her head forward into her hands, effectively removing herself from the situation, much like an ostrich sticking its head into the sand.

"So, my lady," he said, manfully suppressing a wicked grin. "How's the ankle?"

"In much better condition than my pride, now that I've decided that I must be the most recent in a long line of females who have twisted their ankles outside your door," Lady Allegra returned sprightly. "I should have known that any idea that came to mind so readily would be equally apparent to anyone else. Next time, I'll have to throw a brick through your window, with a note wrapped round it. Or has that also been done?"

"Not lately, no," Armand admitted. "What would the note have said?"

Lady Allegra shrugged her slim shoulders.

Gad, but she was gorgeous, her every move graceful, even as she delighted him with the ease she displayed in his presence. No feigned shyness, no simpering. They could be talking man-to-man, except he'd never be able to forget that this unusual young woman was definitely no man.

"Oh, I don't know what the note would say. Perhaps something cryptic, such as *meet me in the park tomorrow.*"

Armand shook his head. "No, that wouldn't do it. Which park? When tomorrow? How would I know where to wait for you, or even who you were?"

She lifted her hands, let them fall into her lap once more. "Details, details. Just like consequences, I barely think of them. How did you know my name?"

He lifted one eyebrow. "We're still being direct?"

She smiled, unleashing yet another round of tingling sensations in Armand's belly, making him glad he had the support of the desk beneath him. "That couldn't have been a question, sir."

"Very well then. I saw you last week, was struck by your beauty, then had one of my servants bribe one of your servants, so that I could learn your name. Lady Allegra. Pretty name, pretty lady."

Allegra shook her head, obviously not believing a word he'd said. "How I wish I could blush, but I've never mastered that particular art. Now Cousin Elizabeth? She could do it, right after she roused from her horrified swoon. But, then, as Cousin Elizabeth would never have dared to beard you in your own den in the first place, I suppose you'll have to take my word on that."

"Ah, yes, Cousin Elizabeth. That would be Miss Elizabeth Nesbitt. I vaguely remember hearing something about her father, Frederick, a man dedicated to losing his last groat at the gaming tables. I have not, however, had the pleasure of meeting your father, the earl, even if his rather unique reputation does precede him."

He watched as her beautiful eyes went cold and hard. "A lapse which you plan to correct with the invitation you sent us to the ball you're hosting next week? Is that your reason for the invitation? My father's reputation?"

Armand pushed himself away from the desk, looked down at Lady Allegra. "Ah, and now I believe we have come to the point of your visit? You came here today to find out the reason behind the invitation."

"My goodness, I can see I would never be able to trick you, Mr. Gauthier," Allegra said, also getting to her feet, so that he had to step back a pace, or else risk succumbing to the desire to kiss her impertinent mouth.

"Have I upset you in some way, Lady Allegra?"

"You admit to not knowing my father, and I can see by the smile in your eyes that you are very aware that yours is the only invitation sitting on the mantel across the Square. Oh, and if you think I could be taken in like a green goose with those silly compliments you've tossed out so glibly, I will tell you that I am not impressed. And, yes, I am upset. Upset that I even bothered coming here today."

The minx had a temper. He opened his mouth, mostly to defend himself, but she cut him off.

"So, now that the gloves are off—yes, sir, I want to know why you forwarded the invitation. Curiosity, perhaps? Or do you expect my father to be in the way of a diverting entertainment? Hope that Oxie pulls one of his silly pranks, perhaps even encourage him to do so, just to enliven the evening?"

He felt his own temper flare. "Well, now I'm stung, my lady. It never occurred to me that the earl would be the evening's entertainment. My reason is much more . . ." He paused, searched for the right words, and found them to be elusive. Shaking his head, he said, "There's no easy way to say this."

Allegra looked at him closely. "Piffle. There was no easy way to say that I pretended to turn my ankle so that I could breach these doors, meet you, and ask you if the invitation we received was genuine. But I did it, sir. Surely you aren't afraid to be as honest with me as I—albeit belatedly—have been with you?"

Armand knew he had three choices if he wished to tell the truth.

He could tell her that he'd seen her last week, at the bubbling fountain, and was struck enough by her amazing beauty that he'd sent the invitation. That would either have her running, screaming, from the house, or picking out her wedding veil.

He could tell her that he needed to meet her papa, investigate yet another possibility in the many possibilities he'd investigated in these past three years. But, then, other than Simon, Callie, and Bones, no one knew about that, which was how he intended to keep the matter.

He could tell her about Simon, about patrons, about his Good Samaritan charitable gesture of hosting a ball in order to help this poor shunned girl and her family enter into Society. This seemed to be the shortest route he could take between having Lady Allegra smile at him . . . and having her slap his face.

Or he could lie, which was always an option. That was his fourth possible scenario, and the one he chose.

Mentally ordering his man of business to pen a few more invitations, he said, "I'm afraid my reason for inviting you and your family to my ball is not in the least earthshaking. My mansion is in Grosvenor Square. Your papa's mansion, my lady, is in Grosvenor Square. And, as it happens, I have issued invitations to every household in Grosvenor Square. It seemed the right, the polite, thing to do, considering that the Square will be clogged with traffic and noise the whole night long. No nefarious reason, no hope of having the earl as the evening's entertainment. Simply an invitation. Is that all right?"

"Oh. I see. Aspasia? We'll be leaving now."

Armand watched as Allegra's expression went even colder, as near to blank as a beautiful, obviously intelligent young woman could manage.

She knew he'd lied; the minx had sensed it, smelled it on him—something. And now she was going to walk away, leave his house, and never come back, not attend the ball. He could sense *that,* smell *that,* feel an opportunity he wanted to explore rapidly slipping away.

Hastily, he offered her his arm, which she refused, and said to her as they walked back into the foyer, "Of course, I wouldn't have thought of a ball at all, and inviting everyone in the Square, if it hadn't been for the fact that I somehow can't get the sight of you blowing bubbles off your hands out of my mind. Do you remember? Last week? The bubbles in the fountain?"

"Now you're just being kind, which I find to be even more insulting than your lies," Lady Allegra said, avoiding his eyes. "Not that I can blame you overmuch, as I've just made a perfect cake of myself. Please forgive me."

"Kind?" Armand chuckled softly. "My lady, I assure you, I am never kind. We could go off upstairs, apply to my friend Bones, who would tell you the same thing. I saw you, and within a heartbeat knew I had to meet you."

"I think we will leave Mr. Boothe undisturbed, thank you," Allegra said curtly, accepting her bonnet and parasol from a stone-faced Quincy. "I'll say I believe you, if it matters that much to you. I understand it all now. You saw me, and wished to make my acquaintance. As walking yourself across the Square and knocking on our door was out of the question, you decided to go to the horrible expense of putting on a ball, inviting the entire Square, just so that you had an excuse to meet me."

She glared at Armand as she tied the bonnet ribbons beneath her pert chin, tucked the parasol under her arm like a field marshal's baton. "My goodness, Mr. Gauthier, are you telling me I look as if I've just fallen to earth in the last rain? Or, as Oxie might say, pull the other one, sport, it's got bells on."

Quincy abruptly coughed into his hand, wheeled about with an almost grateful look on his face as the knocker went once more.

Armand felt the moment, and a frightening amount of

his sanity, slipping away. "No, really," he said, stepping in front of her. "Look—gloves off, all right? There *is* another reason. It's just that I . . . well, it's not something I want bruited about. Yes, that's it. A secret."

Allegra pulled on her gloves, wiggled her fingers into the soft white kid. "A secret? Oh, piffle. And here I was, about to hire a town crier. How depressing. Not," she ended, glaring up at him, "that I have the *faintest* idea what you're saying. Really, sir, you could at least make a small attempt to get your fibs in a row. Even I can do that."

"Sir?"

Armand was caught between wanting to laugh at the absurdity of this conversation and a brief yearning to shake the girl until her teeth rattled. Had he ever encountered a woman like this in all of England? Had there ever been a woman like this anywhere, so open, so frank, so totally uncaring of the impression she made on an eligible gentleman?

"Could you possibly reconsider your obvious decision to never set eyes on me again, and go out driving with me tomorrow afternoon? Say around five? I'll explain everything then."

She looked into his eyes, ran her gaze down his form, then back up again. Dismissed his smartly tailored clothes, his well set up body, his reportedly handsome face, his mansion, his fortune.

"No, I don't think so. And, much as I wanted Cousin Elizabeth to be the first to know, please allow me to offer our regrets as to your invitation, because the Nesbitts will not be in attendance."

"Sir? Really, sir, I think you should—"

"Not now, Quincy," Armand said, returning Allegra's glare. "Look, I know we've gotten off on the wrong foot here, but—"

Her green eyes flashed. "Oh, how *low* of you to refer to my ploy that got me into this house I now wish only to leave."

Armand didn't know if he was on his head or on his heels. "What? Oh, wait. Your ankle? You thought I was—good God, woman, I didn't mean—"

"I say, *sir.*"

"What?" This exclamation came from both Armand and Allegra at the same time as they turned toward the now opened front door.

"Hullo, pet, I'd hoped you were still here. Having a nice coze with the Got-yer man, huh?" the Earl of Sunderland said as he stood just outside, on the steps, a large white *thing* under his arm.

"Oh, laws, here we go again," Aspasia moaned from behind her mistress.

The earl gave Allegra a large grin and a small wave. "Your mama's ordered me locked out. Silliest thing, but if you could see your way clear to toddle back home and let me sneak in behind you, I'd be prodigiously grateful."

Armand blinked as he looked at the fairly squat, definitely round man. "Pardon me, but is that a duck he's got under his arm?" he asked of no one in particular.

"No," Allegra answered from between clenched teeth. "You only think it's a duck. It's a goose, for goodness' sake. Haven't you ever seen a goose before?"

"Yes, but . . . oh, bloody hell, never mind. Please, reconsider. It's just a ride in the park."

Allegra pursed her lips, sort of wiggled them from side to side, as if tasting her possible answers. "May I bring the goose?"

It was a test. Of his resolve. Of his intentions. Of his sanity, definitely of his sanity. "I wouldn't think of taking the air without a goose, my lady. As my friends will all doubtless tell you, I never do."

Finally, she smiled at him again. The same glorious, bright smile that had so rocked him to his heels that first day, again this afternoon. "Shall we ask him what he planned to do with it?" she all but whispered, as if they were friends enjoying some small, private joke. Some small, unexpected intimacy.

"If I hope to sleep tonight, yes," Armand answered just as quietly, guiding her toward the door. "Good afternoon, my lord," he said, one eye on the goose. "So good to meet . . . you both. I'm Armand Gauthier."

"Didn't think you were the lord high mayor," Oxie shot back, reaching into a pocket and pulling out a handful of what looked to be recently deceased worms, then holding out his palm toward his feathered companion.

"Oxie," Lady Allegra warned, "behave."

"And what fun is there in that, pet? Got-yer? Introduce you to Lord Gooseberry here, except telling the wife to come downstairs to meet him only got me tossed on my ear. Women. I warn you, Got-yer, women are wicked, fickle creatures. What they laugh at while you're courting just gets you a foul look—ah! Fowl look! Get it?—after the wedding bell's been rung."

"There's your answer," Allegra said, stepping outside to stand beside her father. "Come on, Oxie, I'll take you and Lord Gooseberry home, all right?"

"Oh, you're a fine one, pet. Teatime soon, you know, and I'm pretty peckish. Got-yer? That was a good thing you did, sending that invitation. Perked her ladyship up no end, I tell you. We'll be here good and early, all spit and polish, and that's a promise."

"But—Oxie, I turned down the invitation," Allegra said, turning her father around and guiding him down the steps, Aspasia trailing along behind.

"Well, turn it back up again, pet, because we're about to cut us a dash in Society. Your mama won't have it any other way, and I'm not sleeping in the dressing room again tonight, not if I can help it."

"Yes, Oxie," Armand heard Allegra say on a sigh before he closed the door, leaned his back against it, and looked at Quincy.

"So?" he asked. "Don't be shy, Quincy, honestly tell me what you think, because my own mind has pretty much turned to mush."

"She addresses her own father as Oxie, sir."

"Yes, I'd noticed that. Rather as if she were the parent, and he the child. Which is entirely possible, considering the goose."

"You didn't know that wasn't a duck, sir?" the major-domo said. "Pardon me, sir, but anyone would know it's a common white goose."

"Quincy, trust me in this, there is nothing common about an earl walking around London with a duck—

goose—tucked under his arm."

"Yes, sir," Quincy said, then asked Armand if he wished a fresh decanter of wine put in the main drawing room, as a nervous, pacing Mr. Boothe had been making serious inroads on the one he'd placed there earlier.

"I suppose two would be overdoing it?"

"Yes, sir, and if I may say so, sir, she's a good one."

Armand, getting his wits back under some control, purposely misunderstood. "The goose?"

"No, sir," Quincy said, his black eyes twinkling. "I was speaking of the filly."

"I knew I liked you, Quincy," Armand said, giving the man a hearty slap on the back as he pushed himself away from the door and headed for the stairs. "Couldn't have done with a man with too much starch in his shirt."

"Yes, I sensed that, sir," Quincy said, watching his new master climb the stairs two at a time, then nodded in some satisfaction and went off to fetch a fresh decanter.

Chapter Five

*A*LLEGRA HAD GIVEN over a solid ten minutes to the idea of packing her bags and heading for Sunderland, her tail neatly tucked between her legs, before realizing that she could run, but she could not hide from the thoughts in her mind.

How could she have behaved so badly? She'd been forward, bold, unladylike, and terribly stupid.

But, then again, she'd never been so stunned, so poleaxed, so nearly made dumb by a pair of startling blue eyes and a smile that turned her stomach to jelly.

A fool. She'd been a fool.

Cousin Elizabeth, in the same situation—not that she would ever have been silly enough to put herself in such a situation—would have simpered or giggled, or both, but she would not have opened her mouth just to repeatedly insert her foot.

What had happened to her? One moment she'd been feeling rather clever, in control of the situation, and the next she'd been turned into a babbling idiot.

All her country frankness had come spilling out, all her "the devil with it" honesty that was what kept her sane when dealing with her parents, the servants, the entire uncomfortable situation she and her family had been thrust into, unprepared, five years ago.

She should have been a boy, that's what her papa had said more than once, especially since he'd become an earl without an heir, come to think about it.

A boy, who could back up his speech with action, who could shrug off the sting of being the poor relation, and not the entirely unsuitable daughter of the entirely unsuitable earl and countess.

Pride. That's what it was. She was overloaded with pride, bogged down by it, made prickly by it, made wary by it. No one would hurt her parents, not while she was alive.

And no one, by damn, would ever hurt her. Because she'd been hurt, didn't like the feeling, and wouldn't allow herself to be hurt ever again, not because of who she was.

Yes, that's what it was. Pride. She was chock-full of it. To her detriment. It was almost as if she went searching for arguments, for slights, for a reason to prove how unsuitable she was to be called Lady Allegra, just because she knew that unsettling high-nosed people was her most shining talent. She'd been doing it all her life, just the way Oxie played his pranks.

She'd been a child who ran, barefoot, through the village, playing with the other village children, free, unfettered; free to think what she wanted, say what she wanted, how she wanted to think and say it. She'd been her own person even as a child, something she'd come to realize now that she was no longer a child, but the Lady Allegra.

That in itself was depressing, and she missed that barefoot child, that happy, carefree child.

No rules—and, thanks to her doting, easygoing parents, no constraints. She'd grown up semi-wild, and then been pushed, unwilling, into a straight and narrow life that now threatened to strangle her.

Even now, at the drop of a hat—or a pair of fascinating blue eyes—the village child in her came rushing out, and the devil with rules and society and all of that claptrap nonsense.

Besides, she told herself, if she tried to conform, after so many years of being given her own head, she would fail, badly.

Sunderland had been relatively safe, but London was nothing more than street after street and square after square of deep potholes waiting for her to tumble into them.

She could never be like Cousin Elizabeth; content to sit and sew, paint watercolors, and wait for some man to decide she had the makings of a tolerable wife and an excellent brood mare.

If she tried, she would fail. Dismally. Probably because her heart wasn't in it, her mind wouldn't allow it, and her spirit craved for more than a home and children and a place in Society. She wanted to *live*. Really live.

Yes, she should have been the son. She could have run wild—more wild than she had—and then bought a commission after her papa came into the earldom and fought in the war, traveled to the continent on a grand tour, spoken her mind, and bloodied the nose of anyone who said a nasty word about her parents.

That's why she had gone to visit Armand Gauthier. To size him up, decide not if the invitation had been genuine, but if the man had plans for using Oxie as his own personal court jester, her mama as gossip fodder for all the high-in-the-instep ladies who couldn't wait for a chance to look down on someone they saw as inferior.

And when he'd lied? When he'd handed her that drivel about inviting the entire Square, then compounded the lie with some silly nonsense about seeing her at the fountain, being struck by her beauty or whatever he'd said—well, that second lie just proved the first lie.

Above anything else, Allegra couldn't abide a liar—unless it was her.

And yet . . . and yet. He had begged her forgiveness, had asked her to go driving with him, had even managed not to burst into snide laughter when Oxie had shown up at his front door, Lord Gooseberry tucked under his arm.

That had redeemed him, slightly.

But she still couldn't forgive him for those wonderful, teasing, laughing, yet totally unreadable blue eyes. Those eyes that had seen more of life than she would ever see. Those eyes that spoke of secrets, that hinted of danger . . . that drew her in even as they revealed only what he wanted her to see.

Who was Armand Gauthier? Allegra had been desperate enough to ask Cousin Elizabeth, who had recognized the man's name on the invitation. Not that the silly girl was much help. Wonderfully wealthy. That had been the sum total of her cousin's knowledge. Uncle Frederick had probably sent her to London with a list of wonderfully wealthy, eligible gentlemen tucked into her reticule and committed to memory.

Oxie had been even less help, as his knowledge of Society extended about as far as the end of his nose, which at the moment was stuck in a book he'd found in the mansion's library, a rather slim volume he'd chuckled over, then hidden beneath his waistcoat when she'd asked about it.

Obviously, there was another prank in the making. That was Oxie. Always off on one of his mad starts. She really should pay attention, she knew, but at the moment, her mind was too full of her own problems.

Strangely, it was Lettice Tomlin who at last came to Allegra's rescue, sitting her down in the main drawing room and telling her that there were things she should know about their neighbor across the Square.

"Your dear mother has brought it to my attention that you have agreed to ride out with Mr. Armand Gauthier this afternoon, my lady," Lettice said, smoothing her black skirts as she sat, with more grace than Allegra had supposed the woman capable of, now that she thought about the thing.

As a matter of fact, there was more than simply grace to Lettice Tomlin. Not more than forty, she still had a finely molded chin, beautifully clear skin, and if her hair was flatly black, it was also thick and, if let out of its bun, probably quite long. Her hands were slim, the fingers narrow, the nails well cut.

Even hidden behind the shapeless gown, Allegra felt certain the woman had a good figure; she certainly had excellent posture.

The right gowns, something more imaginative done with her hair, and possibly an occasional smile, and Lettice Tomlin would be a very handsome woman.

Was there a story about her, one that included a loving husband killed in the war, so that she had been forced to make her own way in the world as a housekeeper-cum-companion? Did she have children? Was she happy?

Did it matter? It should. Everyone's life should matter.

"I said, my lady," Lettice repeated as Allegra's mind chewed on this thought, "that I am aware you are to go driving with Mr. Armand Gauthier this afternoon."

Allegra mentally shook herself, and nodded. "I won't take Lord Gooseberry, though," she said, not realizing she'd made that decision. "I think I owe the man an apology which, of course, I would rather die than give, so he'll just have to be content with the gift of *not* having Lord Gooseberry with us."

Lettice's left eyebrow—remarkably well shaped—lifted a fraction. "I'm sure you know just what you're saying, my lady, but I believe you also should know a little something about Mr. Gauthier before you pursue this relationship with him."

"Relationship?" Allegra sat back against the couch and goggled at the woman. "Whatever makes you think I'm seeking anything even close to a relationship? I just met the man."

"I've also met the man," Lettice said, a ghost of a smile tickling at the corners of her mouth.

"Over the course of the past three years, most all of London has met the man. If he is pursuing you, my lady, which I believe he is, I doubt you will have any choice in the matter of the relationship. What Mr. Gauthier wants, Mr. Gauthier gets. He's a dangerous man."

"Oh, piffle," Allegra said, waving one hand dismissingly. "He's just a man, Ms. Tomlin."

"Very much a man," Lettice pointed out—pointing out the obvious. "He came to London three years ago, unknown, without friends, but not without ambition. He performed a service for the Earl of Roxbury, one I shall not go into here, and in return his lordship sponsored him, took him into the *ton,* introduced him to the small, tight world that is London Society."

"And . . . ?" Allegra urged when Lettice took a moment to extract a lace-edged handkerchief from her pocket, dab at the corners of her mouth.

"And, my lady, Society accepted him, even began to

dote on him. He was soon invited everywhere, and accepted every invitation. And yet, three years later, no one knows a thing about him."

Allegra didn't even bother to dissemble, pretend she wasn't intrigued. "Such as?"

"So many things. Not how he came to be rich, what he did with his life in the years before he came to London. Rumor has it that he was a spy during the war, or that he was a highwayman in France, or a gambler, or that he is an American who had to leave his own country. Some say he is the bastard son of a duke, or perhaps even a royal prince, but I don't believe that. I just know that men who hide their pasts are dangerous men. They always are."

"Why, my goodness, Mrs. Tomlin," Allegra said in amazement. "You're a romantic. I never would have believed it of you."

Twin spots of color stained Lettice's smooth, pale cheeks. "Yes, perhaps I am, or perhaps I have seen more of life, of men, than you have in your few years. I'm not saying Armand Gauthier isn't a good man, even a fair man. But there is something dark behind that smile, something tortured behind those handsome blue eyes. He's hiding something, seeking something. At the bottom of it, nothing else is important to him. I would not wish to be in his way when he finally discovers what he is looking for, because anyone who is will be trampled, quite ruthlessly."

Allegra slowly shook her head, feeling nervous. "Why are you telling me all of this? We're only going for a drive, for goodness' sake. And how do you know about his eyes? Has he been a guest in one of the houses you've worked in over the years?"

Lettice lowered her chin, averted her eyes. "Yes, I suppose that's as good an explanation as any. And he has never been anything but kind to me."

"A kindness you've rewarded by warning me away from the man," Allegra said, standing up as she heard the knocker go on the ground floor. "You have a strange way of showing your appreciation, Ms. Tomlin."

Lettice stood as well, one eye on the doorway. "I've watched you these past ten days, my lady. If I were to pick a woman from all the women in London, I would pick you for Mr. Gauthier. You have the spirit, the fire—dare I say it, the *brass*—to intrigue him. But never to capture him, as he has his own plans, his own goals. Don't set your cap at him, my lady, that's all I am saying to you, for he will break your heart."

The butler appeared in the doorway to announce Armand's arrival, and the man himself entered the room behind him, his curly brimmed beaver in his hand, a smile on his handsome face. That smile remained in place, Allegra noticed, even as his step hesitated, a barely perceptible slowing, as his gaze swept over Lettice Tomlin.

Allegra watched as Lettice's spine stiffened, as the woman's small hands closed into white-knuckled fists. And it occurred to her—if she did not know anything about Armand Gauthier, she knew less than nothing about one Ms. Lettice Tomlin.

Armand stopped a few feet inside the door as Lettice swept across the room, a curiously beautiful black crow, and bowed slightly in her direction as she dropped a quick curtsy in his direction.

"You're looking well, Letty," he said quietly, but not so quietly that Allegra didn't hear him, or Lettice's quick, "And you, Mr. Gauthier," before she was gone and it was just Armand and Allegra, staring at each other.

He did not join her at the arrangement of couches in the center of the room, but just bowed where he was, saying, "The horses and the afternoon await us, my lady."

"And it wouldn't be proper to keep them waiting," Allegra said, gathering up her gloves, bonnet, and parasol that she'd laid on the table. She walked over to him, motioning toward the now-empty landing outside the room. "You and Mrs. Tomlin are acquainted?"

He offered her his arm. "That surprises you?"

"No, of course not," Allegra began, then shook her head. "Yes, that does surprise me. I wouldn't think you moved in the same circles."

"Ah, but there are circles within circles, my lady. Did she warn you away from me? I would think so. I'm convinced that Letty takes her duties very seriously, no matter what they are, and would always be quite protective of the females in her charge. If she believes you are better to avoid me, I should think you might want to listen to her."

Allegra thought over these words as the two of them made their way downstairs, to the foyer, and then out into the watery sunshine that she'd decided was the best London usually had to offer.

It was only after he'd helped her up onto the seat of the finely made curricle and then joined her that she turned to him, and said, "Are *you* now warning me away from you, Mr. Gauthier?"

"I should think you'd want to run like the very devil, yes," he said, flicking the reins so that they moved off, heading out of the Square. "My money may be tainted, even more so than my background. And, as we all know, and I'm convinced Letty told you, a man who does not even own up to his own parents is not a gentleman."

Allegra shrugged at this. "And a woman whose father thinks it the best of good fun to hammer holes into the bottom of his house guests' chamber pots before they retire for the night is not usually looked upon as prime marriage material. What of it?"

Armand had to pay attention to his horses after allowing the reins to go slack for a moment as he howled with laughter. "He didn't really do that, did he?"

Allegra bit back a smile. How she loved shocking him, not that he seemed shocked. He seemed amused, and she liked that even better.

"My uncle Frederick didn't find it in the least funny, sir, running from room to room, trying to hunt up a chamber pot he could use after a night of dedicated drinking. He packed up his family and left the very next morning, vowing never to return. Which, now that I think about the thing, was probably the result Oxie had in mind. We don't care for Uncle Frederick, you understand. Oh, look—there's Oxie now. Oh, dear. I don't think I like this. Whatever is he doing?"

Armand looked to his left as they slowly proceeded along Grosvenor Street, toward the park. "Where? I don't see him."

Allegra was tempted to say that she had been mistaken, that the man she'd seen wasn't Oxie Nesbitt, but both her innate honesty and her fears for whatever the man might be doing got the better of her.

"Over there," she said fatalistically, pointing with the tip of her opened parasol. "See him? He's wearing a smock of some sort, and a leather vest, but I can never mistake that riot of white hair."

Armand edged his team over to the flagway, out of the traffic, and put on the brake. "No, I'm afraid I still don't—oh, wait, yes, there he is. Why is he dressed like that? And who are those other two men?"

Well, here it was, the moment of reckoning, come sooner than she had supposed. Armand Gauthier would either be amused, or run like the devil, as far as he could. Because, if there was a surefire way of measuring men, it was to measure them against her father's penchant for foolishness.

Sighing, Allegra said, "That would be Oxie's manservant, Mersey, the poor oppressed fellow, and I believe the second man is Bateson, one of our new London staff. They're heading up the steps to that house. Do you by chance know who lives there?"

"Yes, I believe I do. Walter Jagger and his son, Rutherford. I don't know the father well, but to use Bones's term, Rutherford is a nasty stick. But, all of that to one side, yes, that's Walter Jagger's town house."

Allegra rolled her eyes. "That makes sense. Fools.

They shouldn't have ignored Oxie's letters. Could you please help me down, so that we can step into the opening of that alleyway? I'd really like to be able to see this without having to worry about any of them seeing me. Do you mind?"

"Not in the least," Armand said, hopping down from the seat, then assisting Allegra to the flagway. "Your father is pulling a prank?"

"I can't imagine another reason for him to be dressed up that way, or knocking on Mr. Jagger's door. Do you suppose the man is home?"

"No, not at this time of day at least. He's either at one of his clubs, or taking the air in the park. Does that matter?"

Allegra closed up her parasol and stepped closer to the wall of the house on the edge of the alleyway. So far, Armand Gauthier was being amused, even helpful. How long would that last?

"Oh, yes, I'm confident it does. I doubt Oxie will want to be seen by the man, although I'm sure he won't remember him. Oxie was much thinner when he was young, with a full head of bright red hair. Now Mersey is letting out his breeches almost monthly, and that wiry halo of white fuzz is far from red."

"I suppose, if I took my time about it, I would understand that," Armand said, removing his curly brimmed beaver as he, too, stood close against the side of the house. "Wait, I think I have it. Your father and Walter Jagger knew each other when both were younger, but don't know each other now? Am I right?"

"Very good," Allegra said, smiling up at him. He

smiled back at her, clearly enjoying himself, and her stomach did that curious *melting* thing once more. Better she should concentrate on the moment at hand, and not her curious, definitely upsetting reaction to this man.

"They . . . er . . . they were schoolmates, eons ago, and Oxie wrote to Mr. Jagger, among others, asking that they help ease my way into Society. Mr. Jagger never replied, which is his own fault, as anyone who knows Oxie even a little bit surely would have explained to him. Uh-oh, someone's opening the door."

They watched as Oxie Nesbitt held out a paper to the bewigged butler, then began waving his arms, talking loudly enough for his voice, if not his exact words, to come to them from across the street.

He motioned to the paper, he indicated Mersey and the other servant with a sweep of one arm . . . and moments later, all three men entered the tall, narrow town house, the door closing behind them.

"They're in. That's Oxie. He can bluster his way anywhere."

"Why do you call your father Oxie? It's not usual, you know."

Allegra shrugged her shoulders. "I'm sure it's not. But he was forever playing pranks on Mama, and Mama was forever calling out his name. *OX-ee.* It's all I ever heard as a child. Said in shock, in surprise, in dismay— whispered, moaned, groaned, shrieked. Oxie, Oxie, *OX-ee.* So I began calling him Oxie, too, and it stuck. He thought it amusing to have this little thing toddling up to him, calling him Oxie, and being nothing but poor country folk, what did it matter, anyway? I'm not going to change now, just because it might shock sensibilities here in town. Why should I?"

"Why should you, indeed. A perfectly respectable explanation. Now what?" Armand asked as Allegra peered around the corner once more, nervously twisting the parasol in her hands.

"Now we just stay here and wait. I have no idea which prank Oxie has chosen, but since Mersey is with him I can fairly well narrow it down to either the tradesman come to perform a service, or the inspector come to inspect."

"Inspect what?"

Allegra shrugged. "Oh, the drains, the chimneys. Whatever. Does it matter? It's what he might take or leave behind that will be of concern to Mr. Jagger. Oh— here we go. Looks like it's the tradesman. I do like this one, much as I shouldn't admit to that, and Mr. Jagger does deserve it. He could have answered Oxie's letter, even if it was to tell him to go to the devil. Oxie could understand that, but he doesn't care to be snubbed. Pranksters rarely do."

"Yes, of course, Jagger should have known that," Armand said rather blankly, then stepped forward, his eyes widening as he looked across the street. "Good God, they're carrying a couch. What are they doing with a couch? That's stealing."

Allegra sighed. "Borrowing, actually. There's a difference. Would you like me to explain?"

"I'd be gratified, yes."

"All right. Oxie pretended to be a tradesperson come

to pick up Mr. Jagger's couch. I don't know the reason, perhaps to fix a wobbly leg, or to re-cover it or dispose of it before the new couch arrived—whatever Oxie thinks the butler will believe. He brought his two workers with him, to carry it, and now, as you see, they're loading it onto the back of that wagon. Tell me, Mr. Gauthier, do you happen to know where either Viscount Eaton or Sir Guy Berkert reside?"

"Berkert? He's somewhere on High Street, I believe, quite near the church."

"And the viscount?"

"Eaton's in Portman Square. I was to a dinner party there last year. Why?"

"Which is closer?"

"High Street, I'd say. Again, why?"

"No reason," Allegra said, keeping her face averted as she led the way back to the curricle as the couch was being loaded into the wagon. "Shall we head for High Street, Mr. Gauthier? We wouldn't wish to miss this. Then we can continue on to the park. I really do want to see the park."

"You know, my lady," Armand said once he was settled beside her on the seat, "if Bones were here, he'd be having an apoplexy."

"Then it's fortunate Mr. Boothe is not here, isn't it, Mr. Gauthier?"

He released the brake, gave a quick flip of the reins. "True, but may I tell him about our small adventure, or am I to be sworn to secrecy?"

Allegra, who had been enjoying watching her father at work, sobered, looked at Armand. Was he having fun at Oxie's expense? Couldn't he simply enjoy the joke? "You think this is silly, don't you?"

"Don't you?"

"No, I don't," Allegra told him, feeling her temper rise. "Oxie is defending his daughter, his wife. He, as the earl, asked a favor of his schoolmates, and they as good as slapped his face for the effort. They deserve whatever they get. If Oxie's methods are a little . . . unique, then that's just the way it is. I'm honored that he cares enough to stand up to the insult to himself, to my mama and me. We'll leave Cousin Elizabeth out of this, as the girl hasn't the wit to know when she's been insulted."

Armand was silent for a few minutes as they headed for High Street. "I think I understand now, my lady, and I offer my apologies," he said as he pulled the curricle into an alleyway across from the town house of Sir Guy Berkert. "Some people put up the knocker, some overflow their fountains with bubbles. Some give the cut direct or even challenge the other man to a duel, and some steal couches. It's perfectly clear now."

"I told you, Oxie is not stealing the couch. He's—oh, you'll see soon enough, here they come. Watch and learn, and remember never to upset Oxie Nesbitt. He may be silly at times, but he is not to be trifled with, not if you wish to hang on to your sanity."

"Or your couch."

"Oh, do shut up," Allegra said, her heart not really in the thing. She was too pleased that Armand Gauthier seemed to be enjoying himself again. It wasn't every man, she knew, who would.

The wagon lumbered down the street, Oxie Nesbitt at the reins. In the back of the wagon, the two servants sat side by side on the couch, Bateson looking pleased with himself, the more refined-looking man, Mersey, appearing for all the world as if he might burst into tears at any given moment.

Oxie jumped down from the wagon seat and approached Sir Guy's door with the two servants, and the couch, bringing up the rear. He knocked, the door opened, and the paper was waved once more, the two servants indicated yet again with a sweep of one arm.

"As tradesmen, they should have gone behind, to the mews, and knocked on the rear door," Armand pointed out. "Both here, and at Jagger's."

"Oh, please," Allegra said, grinning at him. "Oxie's an earl, remember? Besides, just the shock of seeing a tradesman at the front door is usually enough to unnerve the servants into dealing with him quickly, just so that he'll go away again."

And then the three went inside. Allegra silently counted to ten, then watched as the three men emerged again, minus one couch, walked rather quickly to the wagon, and took off down the street.

Oxie was laughing, Bateson was still appearing pleased to be along for the ride. And Mersey was wiping at his bald pate with a huge white handkerchief, looking as if he expected the hangman to come find him at any moment.

"And that's that," Allegra said, motioning for Armand to drive on, take her to the park.

"Oh, I don't think so. I need an explanation, if you

please. How did you know your father was coming here with the couch? And what did he do with it, anyway?"

Allegra sighed. Was it so difficult to understand? "All right, I'll explain. One, the three men—not counting my Uncle Frederick, Cousin Elizabeth's papa—Oxie wrote to are Walter Jagger, Sir Guy, and Viscount Eaton."

"Yes, I've figured out that much on my own, thank you. But can we get back to the couch?"

"Certainly. Oxie and his cohorts, one of them seemingly willing, the other a pawn of Oxie's for so long that he has no choice but to go along with anything the man says, all went to Mr. Jagger's town house, to pick up the couch. They carried orders, signed by Mr. Jagger, I'm sure, probably saying that he wished to dispose of his couch. Are you understanding me so far?"

"Yes, I am, and I'm also beginning to get an inkling of what comes next. Allow me?"

"Be my guest."

"Once they took possession of Jagger's couch, they then knocked on Sir Guy's door, saying they had come to *deliver* the couch Sir Guy ordered."

"Yes, that's always the easiest part," Allegra told him. "Nobody turns down a new couch, now do they?"

"True enough. But to take this a step or two further? Jagger believes he has been robbed, poor man. I can see him now, spitting and sputtering as he comes home to find a gaping hole in his decoration of his drawing room. But, as he and Sir Guy are friends—I'm assuming they are friends—when he visits his friend it will be to see his very own couch sitting in the man's drawing room. With any luck at all, Sir Guy will have sold his own couch, liking this one better. It won't be pretty, at least not at first."

"Exactly. Do you think they'll come to blows? I don't. I think they will look at each other, look at the couch, look at each other again, and then, at one and the same time, cry out *that damned Oxie Nesbitt!* That's what I think they'll do."

Armand pulled into the park, moving toward the line of carriages, curricles, and high-perch phaetons making the circuit. "Don't you expect retribution? No one likes to be made the fool. Aren't you concerned that these two men might decide to come after your father, to bloody his nose, at the very least?"

"No, I don't think so," Allegra said, her heart only skipping a little as she heard Armand's words. "I mean, if they come back at him, he'll only come back at them again, doubled. It would be never-ending. No, Oxie's had his little revenge, at least on two of them. After he's done with the viscount, it will all be over. I hope," she added quietly, looking out over the park, but seeing little—and caring less about the well-dressed ladies and gentlemen of the *ton*—as she wished Oxie could, just for this one time, take a sabbatical from his foolery.

Chapter Six

ARMAND DEFTLY INSERTED THE CURRICLE into the line of traffic as everyone in London who wished to see or be seen clogged the pathways.

He glanced over at Allegra, who wasn't looking quite as pleased as she had earlier, as they hid in the alleyway, watching Oxie Nesbitt perform.

He decided that Allegra was nervous, being out and about, having to face the world that, so far, had been totally ignoring her family.

It couldn't be easy, after all, to know that this world knew her father as a buffoon, and her mother as a country woman of no social competence; the poor relations who were as suitable for the peerage as were mittens for a duck—make that a goose.

"Don't be afraid," Armand said, placing one gloved hand on hers, which were folded in her lap. "They only look like they might bite."

"Pardon me?" Allegra said, looking at him in question. "What might bite? And, secondly, although I should have said it at once, I am never afraid, Gauthier."

Armand smiled, mentally noting the way she'd dropped the "mister" from his name. She was feeling more comfortable with him, comfortable enough to be even more of her frank, wonderfully honest, and earthy self.

Now to decide if that was a bad thing or a good thing, and what he was going to do about it.

He already knew what he *wanted* to do about her, but he had to be patient. Otherwise, Allegra might run very quickly away from him . . . or have her father "borrow" his couch.

As for the rest? Yes, he still wanted to know about *that,* too.

He tipped his hat to the bewigged dowager Duchess of Quorm as her ancient coach lumbered past, then smiled at Allegra. "Allow me, then, to rephrase. Don't be worried, they don't bite."

Allegra frowned for a moment, and then her forehead smoothed once more. "Oh. You think I'm worried about all of these people? Whyever would you think that?"

"Well," Armand said slowly, feeling himself sinking into a quagmire of his own making. "They're very important people."

"Important to whom?"

"They're the *ton*. Society. Influential, titled, the very people whose houses you wish to enter, whose companionship you are seeking during the Season. In short, your success in London depends on these people."

"Piffle."

Armand suppressed a smile. "I beg your pardon?"

"Oh, don't pretend not to understand, Gauthier. You've seen Oxie, and you've seen me. Do you really think there is anything I can do to be *accepted* by these people? Even more to the point, sir, do you honestly believe that I even *want* to impress them?"

"Your mother does," Armand said, not having met the countess, but knowing enough doting mamas to be fairly certain he'd hit the correct chord.

"Yes, well, there is that," Allegra agreed, casting her gaze over the strutting peacocks and beribboned darlings parading themselves about as if hoping for the first prize in some competition. "But I really do hate this. You know that, don't you?"

"I had gotten that impression, yes. Why?"

Allegra turned to him on the seat. "*Why?* How can you ask that? These people care for nothing but the depth of Oxie's pockets, the cut of my gowns, and possibly, just possibly, how gaining our acquaintance might in some way benefit *them*. Not that they haven't already decided that no Nesbitt shall cross their thresholds, dine at their tables, or, most definitely, marry their sons. Which, I might add, I have no intention of doing. Coming to London was my mama's idea, not mine. Definitely not mine."

"Ah," Armand said, tongue in cheek, "the reluctant debutante. That alone, my dear, may serve to make you a sensation. Certainly an original."

"Now you're laughing at me, Gauthier, and I have to tell you I really don't appreciate that. In fact, were I a man, I would punch you squarely in your nose."

"If you were a man, my lady, we would not be having this conversation," Armand pointed out, then tipped his head slightly, to look past the phaeton in front of him, at the open carriage just then coming up the pathway. "But, since you're not, and since we're here, and because you are, I'm sure, a loving daughter who would never wish to disappoint her mama, I think we've just spied out someone who can help you across those thresholds."

Allegra leaned closer to him, trying to see what he saw. "E-gods, Gauthier, who's that?"

The sight was daunting, Armand agreed silently. An overall impression of rouged cheeks, violent violet-striped cloth, a tumble of false curls, and—as usual—an open mouth, emoting a monologue to the oppressed-looking gentleman sitting beside it, advanced on them.

"One of the patronesses of Almack's, hard to port," Armand told Allegra. "Now, be a good girl, don't swear, if you please, and I'll get you a voucher to our holiest of holies for debutantes. I can do that, you know. I'm quite the powerful person. Your mama will be so pleased."

"Oh, dam—dash it," Allegra said, appearing ready to leap down from the seat and race into the safety of the trees. "Don't do this to me, Gauthier. I'm warning you, don't do this."

"Too late," Armand said as the female, still talking nineteen to the dozen, waved at him merrily, and yet imperiously. He was to stop, clog the thick afternoon traffic, and pay homage to Silence. An apt name for a woman who had never experienced a moment of silence in her life.

"My lady, Sir Henry." He tipped his hat, then suppressed a wince as Silence made it obvious by the way she held out her hand to him that she expected him to risk life and limb in order to kiss her gloved fingertips.

"Ah, Armand, ever the gentleman," she said as he felt Allegra's hand fisted into the tail of his coat, pulling him upright on the seat once more. "So good to see you back in town. You know, dearest, how crushed I have been that you rarely have been in attendance at Almack's since your very first Season with us, which is entirely bad of you. You would greatly improve the place."

"A pool of spilled lamp oil and a well-placed flame would greatly improve the place, my lady," Armand said with the smile that allowed him to say what he meant and not be believed as serious.

Silence laughed, brayed like a donkey, causing many heads to turn, see that, yes, it was her again, and then smile painfully as they tried to contain their horses and pretend that they *enjoyed* being held up in line.

"You're a wicked, wicked man, Armand," she said as she narrowed her eyes, looked past him, her gaze drawing down on Allegra. "Pretty. Sits it serious, Armand?" Then she laughed again.

"Serious enough, my lady, that I would be eternally grateful if you were to offer a voucher."

He could see the woman salivating. The hint of gossip, the food of life to Silence, had gained him her full attention. "Certainly, my dear man. And you plan to attend with her?"

"That goes without saying, my lady. I thank you. Now, we mustn't keep everyone piled up behind us when we can much more comfortably have a private coze next Wednesday night. That is the date of your first gathering at Almack's for the Season?"

"Yes, of course." Silence looked at the mass of traffic coming toward her, and then behind her, stacking up like so much cordwood. "Delicious, isn't it? Almost worth being married to the man, to trade on his consequence this way. Not that mine is inconsiderable."

"Most definitely not, my lady. I know grown men who tremble in their boots, just at the sight of you."

From beside him, he heard a quick, choked snigger, and quickly leaned forward, effectively blocking Silence's view of Allegra, whose green eyes had to be dancing a jig at his smooth insult.

"Yes, yes, dribble compliments over me on Wednesday next. Now, quickly, my dear, where am I to have the voucher delivered?"

Armand smiled, tipped his hat once more. "That

would be two vouchers, actually, my lady. One each for Miss Elizabeth Nesbitt and Lady Allegra Nesbitt, in Grosvenor Square. You will, of course, have my undying gratitude, which is so much more pleasant than not having it, isn't it, my lady?"

And then, because he wasn't a stupid man, he gave his horses the office to start up again, leaving Lady Sally Jersey to whirl about on the carriage cushions and toss a few unlovely words at his departing back.

"Dear God. *That* was Lady Jersey?" Allegra said, sneaking a look back at the carriage and the red-faced woman . . . and the widely grinning man sitting next to her. "Oh, she *hates* Oxie," she continued, sitting front once more. "Absolutely loathes him."

"Yes, so I've heard. Something about propping a coffin at her front door in the middle of the night?"

He watched as Allegra's eyelids narrowed. "You *knew* about that?"

"We call her Silence as a sort of joke, as she is anything but, my lady. What Sally Jersey knows, the world knows. So, don't you want to thank me? I even remembered to include your cousin. With any luck, she'll find herself an eligible *parti* quickly and be out from under your feet within the month. I may be wrong, but I've sensed that this would please you."

Allegra looked at him for a long time. "Do you know, Gauthier, I think I like you. You've got a really mean streak in you."

"Yes, so I've been told, even by my friends. Now, shall we discuss the ball?"

"Discuss the reason you invited me to the ball, to be

precise. The *secret?*" Allegra corrected.

"Yes, I did promise to reveal my secret, didn't I? I must have been out of my head, envisioning you walking out of my life forever, along with Oxie and Lord Gooseberry—the latter, by the way, who is *not* invited to the ball. However, a promise is a promise."

She tipped her head to one side, bit on her bottom lip for a moment, then said, "No, I don't think I want to hold you to that promise. I like you right now, Gauthier, and liking you seems to be safer than not liking you. I'd much rather just enjoy the drive. You can tell me who all these people are, and I can picture the ladies curt-sying to Mama, and the gentlemen sneezing the pepper out of their noses after Oxie shares his snuffbox. You know, I was wrong. This could be fun, couldn't it, this going out into Society?"

Armand felt himself becoming drunk on Allegra's smile, on her frankness, her joy at all things ludicrous. "I totally agree," he said, grinning as she lifted her chin, peering at passersby as if they were exhibits at the fair, and twirling her parasol in her happiness.

Allegra said her good-byes to Armand and lightly tripped up the steps, into the Grosvenor Square mansion. She knew she had to go directly to the drawing room, to be interrogated by her mama and, most probably, Cousin Elizabeth, neither of whom had been within five hundred yards of the park or anyone from the *ton*.

And there was plenty to tell them.

She could describe the fine carriages, the mincing,

red-heeled dandies whose shirtpoints were high enough to slice their ears as they turned their heads, hoping someone was watching them.

The massive, rouged ladies decked out in jewels and feathers and six layers of fat.

The silly man dressed all in green, riding in his green carriage, or the man half crowded out of his carriage by the giant poodles that rode with him.

The sight of Lady Jersey's expression when she realized she'd just agreed to send vouchers to the Nesbitt debutantes.

She'd taken only two steps into the room when Cousin Elizabeth was on her feet, advancing toward her. "What happened? Who did you see? Did you see anyone? Oh, you must have seen *everyone*. What were the ladies wearing? Are my gowns suitable, or am I woefully out of fashion? I vow, I'll just *die* if my bonnets won't suit."

Allegra let her run down, then said, "Mr. Gauthier has received the promise of vouchers for Almack's for the two of us. We attend next Wednesday evening."

Which sent Cousin Elizabeth racing out of the room in tears, whimpering something about Cousin Allegra being the meanest, the *horridest* creature in nature.

Allegra watched her go, then went over to the couch, sat down beside her mama, looked at Lettice Tomlin, who was pouring tea from a silver pot. "Well, I give up. There's no pleasing that girl. I was trying to be nice, you know."

"That's two fibs, my lady," Lettice pointed out, handing her a cup. "She must have been very mean to you when you were children."

"Children are often mean," Lady Sunderland said on a sigh. "But not all of them grow up to tell such shocking crammers as you've just done, Allegra. Almack's? Shame on you. That was truly mean."

Allegra looked from Lettice to her mama, and back again. "But it's true, Mr. Gauthier stopped his curricle to talk to Lady Jersey, and asked her to please send vouchers for Cousin Elizabeth and myself."

"Lady Jersey?" Her mama rolled her eyes. "I've lived with your father for more than five and twenty years, Allegra. I think I know a crammer when I hear it. Lady Jersey? She would never do such a thing." She leaned close, as if to confide in her daughter without Mrs. Tomlin hearing her. "The *coffin*, you know."

Allegra nodded, also knowing her mama had a point. "Oh, all right. I wasn't going to tell you, because I think it should have been kept a secret between us, but Mr. Gauthier sort of . . . *tricked* Lady Jersey into agreeing to send the vouchers."

"Probably holding something over her head," Lettice said, nodding sagely. "My lady, I would have to say that we should be expecting vouchers by tomorrow morning. Perhaps I should run upstairs, and tell Miss Elizabeth this wonderful news?"

"No, no, that's all right," Lady Sunderland said, rising, smoothing down her skirts. "Vouchers to Almack's? I . . . I . . . I don't quite know what to say. No, wait, yes, I do. Allegra? Do I have to go? Please say I don't have to go with you."

Lettice stood up, put a protective arm around her ladyship's slim shoulders. "I can act as chaperone for the young ladies, ma'am. It would be my pleasure."

Lady Sunderland let out her pent-up breath on a sigh. "Oh, could you? I'd only make a cake of myself, and this is just too, too important. Oxie—that is, his lordship—so wants Allegra to be a success."

"I believe she already is, my lady," Lettice said, looking over the top of Lady Sunderland's blond head to Allegra, who pulled a face at her.

Once her mama had gone, dabbing a handkerchief at her moist eyes, Allegra turned to Lettice, who was sitting once more, arranging her unbecoming black skirts about her like a queen.

"I think I need to know a little more about Armand Gauthier from you, Mrs. Tomlin, and I definitely need to know veritable *volumes* more about you."

"If we're both to accomplish what we wish to accomplish during this Season, yes, I suppose you do. Where shall we begin?"

Allegra took a sip of tea, looked at Lettice Tomlin over the edge of the rim. "Well, let's see. I told Gauthier that I was no longer interested in hearing his secrets—that is, the supposed secret that had him inviting us to his ball. Now that we've cried friends, it didn't seem right to push at him."

"Friends?" Lettice chuckled low in her throat. "My lady, you and Armand Gauthier can never be *friends*. Women cannot ever have a man as her friend. Definitely not, it's against nature."

"Again the romantic, Mrs. Tomlin?"

"Please, call me Letty."

"As Gauthier did?"

Lettice shook her head. "It's true, what they say. Little pitchers often have big ears. I didn't think he said it quite so loudly."

Allegra pointed up. "It's this domed ceiling, I think. Even a whisper carries to all corners of the room. You'll learn to check out such things, living with Oxie, as you never know what will be useful. For instance, I'm sure he already knows he can never sneak up on either of us in this room. Don't you, Oxie?"

As Lettice looked around the room, the Earl of Sunderland stepped from behind the drapes at the front window, a sheepish grin on his face. "What gave me away, pet?"

"I'd like to say that I heard you breathing, Oxie, but I'm afraid that it was your cologne that gave you away, mixed with the smell of overripe meat. Trying to cover up the smell of wagon? Where did you rent it, a butcher shop?"

The earl came around to the front of the couch, sat down beside his daughter. "You saw me?"

"Saw you, followed you, yes. Tell me, what do you have planned for Viscount Eaton? Gauthier seemed interested, and might even want to help you if you approached him. Poor man, he seems easily amused."

"Got-yer saw me?" He shook his head sadly. "I must be losing my touch. I used to be in and out, no problem. It's that being mortal thing, pet. I'm mortal, and growing more mortal every day. So, you like this Got-yer fellow? I think he's rich. He'd take good care of you and your mama."

"You're like a dog with a bone, aren't you, Oxie?" Allegra said, feeling frustration growing inside her. "This was your idea, yours and Mama's. Not mine. I'm here because you're here, and that's all. I'm not on the hunt for a—"

Allegra shut her lips tightly as an idea struck her. Forcing herself to bat her eyelashes a few times, do her best to look embarrassed, she said, "Oh, all right, Oxie. You've caught me out. I never could fool you, could I? I'm very . . . smitten with Mr. Gauthier."

From her seat on the facing couch, Lettice Tomlin quickly raised her white linen handkerchief to her mouth, to catch the dribbles of tea that escaped her as she choked and coughed.

"That's my girl!" The earl grabbed on to Allegra, enfolding her in a bear hug, rocking her back and forth in his embrace. "I knew it, just looking at him. Well set up, deep in the pocket, and he didn't mind Lord Gooseberry, at least not by more than half. Can't say that for a lot of people, now can you? Now, if we can only get your cousin settled so easily, we can be back at Sunderland before your mama gets any more nervous than she already is. Poor thing, she hasn't set a single foot outside this great hulking place since she stepped down from our coach and raced inside."

He pushed Allegra slightly away from him, holding on to her shoulders. "So, this Got-yer have any friends? Nobody too special, not for Elizabeth, not with the paltry dowry Frederick is giving with her, but surely there's someone?"

Allegra thought about Bartholomew Boothe. Tall, too

thin, nervous, his face pleasing enough, if he could possibly learn to smile. "I'll think about it, Oxie," she said, and was grabbed into yet another crushing hug before his lordship trotted off upstairs to tell his wife the good news.

"You were saying?" she asked smugly, smiling at Lettice.

"I have no idea what I was saying," Lettice told her, sighing. "I'm much too impressed. You're planning to use Armand as a sort of foil, aren't you? Pretending to your poor parents that there's a good chance of a match between the two of you, when you have no intention of doing anything of the kind. That was very quick thinking, my lady."

"Allegra," Allegra said, smiling in real happiness. "Please, call me Allegra."

"How about I just call you a silly, shortsighted, selfish little ninny who deserves to have her ears soundly boxed?"

Allegra's smile disappeared. "What? I thought you said you were impressed."

"I am, with your unmitigated *gall*. You plan to *use* Armand, use his friendship to keep your parents from pushing you at every eligible man who comes within reach. Do you know how—no, I won't say it. I won't tell you that what you're planning is about as safe as climbing into a cage with a hungry bear."

"Because he's *dangerous*. Yes, I remember. But you're wrong, Letty. He's a very nice man who probably did tell me at least most of the truth yesterday. He invited us to his ball because he saw me, was interested in me, and decided that inviting us to his ball was the best way to make my acquaintance. That actually is rather sweet, almost romantic. You should like that."

"And you plan to repay his kindness—his *interest*—by using him as a foil to fool your parents?"

"Oh, don't put your back up, Letty. I plan to tell him. I told you, I think we've cried friends. He even enjoyed watching Oxie today as he pulled one of his pranks. I'm sure he'll help me."

Lettice sat back and crossed her arms, rather smugly. "And I'm sure the sun will come up tomorrow. Of course he'll help you, as long as it helps himself. This will be interesting to watch."

"I don't understand."

"I doubt that you do, Allegra. The world is a funny old place. You leave one life, find another, only to learn that people are just people, and life is just life, just with those people and that life better housed, better dressed. And then, most unexpectedly, you find something you never even knew existed. You find explanations—reasons, if not complete answers."

"Much as it pains me to admit this, Letty, I *still* don't understand."

"I don't expect you to, my dear girl. I could end this, you know, end it today. But I won't. I think both you and Mr. Gauthier should do your own dance, in your own time. And, now, if you'll excuse me, I believe I'll go off upstairs and inspect your wardrobe. You'll want to look innocent and sweet at Almack's. You'll have to practice, won't you?"

For long minutes after Lettice had gone, Allegra sat in

the drawing room, going over and over their strange conversation.

And understanding none of it.

In quite another domicile in Mayfair, someone else understood nothing that was going on. He was in his drawing room (yes, his drawing room; he remembered the drapes), but something was missing.

A very definite *nothing* sat in the middle of the room, behind the low table with the statue of Zeus on it, in the middle of two other tables loaded down with treasures his dear departed wife had adored.

Hating them, he'd still kept them, because what else was there to do with ugly treasures except save them to give to your unloved son the day the idiot ingrate married and got the bloody blazes out of your house.

"Wilkins!" he called out at last as his wine-befuddled senses finally put two and two together and came up with a missing blue on blue brocade couch.

What had his despicable, gambling, wenching sod of a son done now? Paid off a debt with his father's furniture?

"Wilkins! Where the bloody blazes is my couch?"

"Probably hauled away on the shoulders of the pink elephants you see every day about this time," Rutherford Jagger said, strolling into the room as his father turned, staggered slightly, and glared at him.

He stuck out one arm, waving it in the direction of the tables. "My couch! Your mother's couch! It's gone! You sod, how could you do that?"

"Well, sod to sot," Rutherford said, inspecting his fingernails, "I have to tell you that I didn't do a damn thing with it. I thought you did."

Walter Jagger slammed his hands against his chest, nearly knocking himself down in his drunkenness. "Me? You think *I* did this? Why in bloody blazes would I get rid of my own couch? *Wilkins!*"

The butler, having heard his master's voice and deciding that he could safely finish his meat pie before racing off to attend the man, walked into the narrow drawing room, picking at his teeth with a knife. He was a small man, wiry in build, with a sharp, foxy face beneath his slightly askew, faintly dusty wig.

Here was a man with a dedication to doing as little work as possible, who could inspire adoration in slackers all over London.

"Yes, sir? Is there a problem, sir? Have you left your coach somewhere again, and want me to find it, fetch it home?"

Walter Jagger blinked, lurched toward the drinks table. "The cheek of the man," he said, to his son, to the world at large, to anyone who might be listening. "Why in bloody blazes do I keep him?"

"Because he doesn't mind only getting paid when you remember to pay him or he remembers to steal something and palm it off on the streets," Rutherford said, lifting the crystal stopper from a decanter and pouring his father a generous splash of port. "Here you go, drink up. It's nearly eight, and you're still upright. It must be a great trial to you."

"I'd cut you off without so much as a bent penny, if I had one," Walter said, taking the offered glass and heading back toward the couch. The missing couch. Oh, yes, now he remembered. "Wilkins? What the bloody blazes happened to my couch?"

"You sent it out to be re-covered, sir," Wilkins said, rolling his eyes. "You don't remember?"

"Remember? I sent it out? Sent it out where? Rutherford, what's this daft man talking about?"

"Yes, Wilkins, what is this daft man talking about?" Rutherford said, smiling as he shot his cuffs, sparing a moment to admire his new suit of bottle green superfine, the way it contrasted so well with the snowy white of his linen.

He brushed past his father, who was slowly spinning around, deciding where to sit, and went to admire himself in the mirror hung between the two front windows.

Rutherford Jagger was a handsome man, in his own opinion, which was the only opinion that mattered to him. His blond hair done in the windswept style, his rounded chin a Byronic marvel, his gray eyes so remarkably unusual.

It was only his pocketbook, his always-empty pocketbook, that detracted from his perfection. His new suit would be faded and worn and living on a ragman's back before the tailor had been paid, but that was not Rutherford's problem. All he had to do was find himself an heiress and he'd be out of the River Tick, living the good life, and without ever having to see his drunken father again.

Wilkins folded up the small knife and used it to scratch at a spot behind his left ear, a spot that obviously was somehow connected to his brain. "Wait a minute.

I've got it now. You mean you didn't send the couch off to be re-covered?"

"Ah, how I adore watching the workings of a brilliant mind," Rutherford said, smiling at the butler. "My congratulations to you, Wilkins. *No,* my good man, the couch was not sent out to be re-covered. What the couch was, Wilkins, was *stolen.*"

"Oh, God," Walter Jagger moaned.

Rutherford continued, only sparing a moment to smile at his father's distress, "Has the penny dropped yet, Wilkins? Have you figured that out? Figured out that you allowed thieves into this house, then most probably held the door for them *as they carried off our damn couch.*"

Walter Jagger sat down on the edge of the low table, using his ample rump to shift Zeus to the far corner, and dropped his head into his hands.

Wilkins looked to his left and right, as if for possible escape routes, then said quietly, "Oops," and then, quickly, gratefully, "There goes the knocker. Shall I answer it?"

"Now there's a thought to stagger one's mind, the butler asking if he should attend the knocker. Unless it will answer itself, Wilkins, yes," Rutherford said, deciding that he, too, could do well with a glass of port.

A few moments later their guest, without Wilkins leading the way to announce him—as that man had decided a retreat to the small kitchen to be in his best interest—entered the room.

As short and round as Walter Jagger, the man had a rough and red complexion, a bulbous nose that signaled that he, like his friend, was a drinker. His well-made but rather worn clothing proclaimed that he, also like his friend Walter Jagger, had less money in his purse than he believed necessary to the life he led anyway.

He was already speaking: "Strangest thing, Walter. Popped on home from my club and what should be waiting there for me? A couch. Solid enough thing, if a trifle faded. A gift from some admirer, I suppose, and pretty much like yours, now that I think about it."

Then he stopped, stared. "Oh, I say, Walter, old sport, where's your couch?"

If she had been there, Lady Allegra Nesbitt would have been gratified to see Sir Guy Berkert look at Walter Jagger, and Walter Jagger look at Sir Guy Berkert, as the two men, their drink-blurred eyes clearing even as they narrowed, opened their mouths in unison to cry out: "That damned Oxie Nesbitt!"

Chapter Seven

ARMAND LIKED THE FEEL of Allegra's gloved hand gripped around his elbow as they strolled about the Square, taking the air.

They could have strolled to the park, but that would have necessitated a female companion for Allegra, or at least a maid trailing behind her. The fact that Allegra wanted neither told him that this was more than just two people taking the air. Something was *in* the air.

"I appreciate your note, my lady, even though you resisted tossing it through my window, tied around a rock. Quincy would not have been amused."

"Yes," Allegra replied, stopping to pet a particularly oppressed-looking white poodle being walked by an equally oppressed-looking footman. Both wore pink ribbons, and knew well enough to be embarrassed. "Amusing you pales beside upsetting Quincy. He's much too nice a man."

The dog went on its way, and Allegra straightened, looked up into Armand's eyes. She had this way of looking clear inside him; unnerving, and yet exciting.

They were so alike, in so many ways. They didn't belong here, either of them. They might fit, for a while, but they didn't belong. They both had the makings of adventurers in them, perhaps even renegades.

He was tempted to give her a glimpse of who he was. Tempted, yes, but he wasn't that foolish.

"Besides, I couldn't possibly put everything in one short note," she continued. "Or haven't you as yet figured out that I wanted more from you this afternoon than a walk in the Square?"

"I would be disappointed if you didn't," he told her, bowing to a well-dressed lady who went tripping on by, dragging a reluctant toddler—who was pulling a wooden hippo on wheels. The hippo tipped, the child began to wail piteously, and Armand quickly bent to right the toy.

"Oh, thank you, Mr. Gauthier," the small brunette with the harassed expression on her pleasantly pretty face said feelingly. "Georgie here wants to visit his grandmama, and I thought it a lovely enough day to walk to Brook Street, and then his nursemaid—dratted girl—had to run back to gather up George's blanket—

he goes nowhere without it, you understand, and she should have known that—so now here I am, dragging the boy who said he wanted to go where he seems now to not want to go at all."

Then Lady Jane smiled. "And you're not in the least interested in my problems, are you, Mr. Gauthier?"

"Perhaps young Lord George would like to travel to his grandmama's on my shoulders?" He bent down, addressing the small boy. "Would you like that, Lord George?"

Allegra, all set to be impressed by Armand's gallant gesture—or so at least he hoped—instead burst into delighted laughter as the boy reached out, tried to pull off Armand's nose. Pulled hard, nearly bringing Armand to his knees before he could pry those small fingers off of him.

"Oh, *Georgie,*" his mother said on an exasperated sigh as the child giggled. "I'm so sorry, Mr. Gauthier, it's his latest trick, but you bent down too quickly for me to warn you. Did he hurt you?"

"Not at all, my lady," he answered, doing his best not to rub at his stinging nose. Didn't the boy's nursemaid ever think to clip those sharp nails? "So sorry I couldn't have been of service to you."

"Ah, but you were, Mr. Gauthier. You've delayed me long enough for good sense to override my fear that my husband's mother will ring a peal over me for being late. I shouldn't say so, but the woman terrifies me. I'll just wait here until Georgie's nursemaid comes along. *She* can ride Georgie on her shoulders."

Armand laughed, bowed again. "In that case, we'll

wait with you, bear you company. May I have the privilege of introducing you to my companion of the afternoon? Lady Jane Hastings, Countess Chirton, may I present Lady Allegra Nesbitt, daughter of the Earl of Sunderland."

Lady Jane's eyes widened and she leaned forward, grinning. "Nesbitt? Really? Oh, this is above all things wonderful."

"I'm happy to make your acquaintance, my lady." Allegra wavered between a curtsy and a bow, obviously decided on the bow, a slight dipping of her head. Armand silently gave her points for effort.

"Happy, yes, of course. I've been meaning to leave my card, but Georgie here has been down with the sniffles, and this is our first day out. He absolutely *clings* to me when he's ill. I attended a dancing class with Elizabeth Nesbitt, you know. That was *eons* ago, when we were both little more than children ourselves, and I've been an old married woman for almost three years now."

"Cousin Elizabeth, I'm convinced, will be delighted to know that I've met you," Allegra said with a sweet smile. "I can barely wait to tell her."

Armand bit the inside of his cheek, as he already knew that Cousin Elizabeth, who had been twiddling her thumbs in London for the past two weeks, probably would be furious to learn that Allegra had met her old dancing classmate. You just had to know how to listen, to understand what Allegra Nesbitt was *really* saying.

Lady Jane pulled a card from her reticule, a move that—since she had little Lord George's leading strings wrapped around her wrist—lifted the boy a good two inches off the ground.

Armand knew himself to be nasty enough to enjoy the startled look on the boy's face. But it was only fair; his nose hurt like the very devil.

"I say, perhaps you and Elizabeth would be kind enough to drop by tomorrow afternoon, say around three? I'm having a small gathering, nothing too special, to hear a singer my husband has brought over from Italy for me as a birthday present. Such a sweet man, don't you think? I'd ask you, Mr. Gauthier, but I already know the answer, as it would be the same as my husband's—I full well know now where poor little Georgie gets his temper—although you're welcome to attend. Lady Allegra?"

Allegra took the card, noted the address, which Armand knew to be yet another mansion in Grosvenor Square. "We would be delighted, my lady, thank you," she said just as the nursemaid came rushing up, breathless, holding a faintly ratty-looking knitted blue blanket.

"An Italian singer?" she said as she and Armand watched Lady Jane, minus the confining leash of the leading strings, glide away, with the nursemaid—Lord Georgie on her stout shoulders—bringing up the rear. "Tell me, Gauthier, will I like an Italian singer?"

"Probably," Armand told her, offering his arm once more. "Just don't hum along, even if you feel the urge. I don't know why, probably something to do with being an artiste, but they don't like that. And you don't have to believe me. Just ask Bones. He was quite embarrassed when the outraged singer stopped singing, and all that was heard in the suddenly hushed room was Bones's humming. He hasn't been to a recital since."

"Now you're making fun of me, and poor Mr. Boothe as well," Allegra said, "and I barely laughed at all when little Georgie tried to twist off your nose. There's a spot of blood on it, you know."

Armand took out his handkerchief, dabbed at the scratch that he could feel on the side of his nose. "I should have known better than to push my face into his. I probably frightened him."

"Oh, I don't think so. I think Lord Georgie just likes pulling noses. Some of us do. Will . . . will you come along with us tomorrow afternoon? I'm not sure I'm quite up to being out in Society yet on my own. Why, I didn't know whether to curtsy or bow to Lady Jane."

"She's the wife of an earl, you're the unwed daughter of an earl. You curtsy to her."

"Oh, dam—drat. I bowed to her."

He replaced his handkerchief, first surreptitiously taking a peek at it to see that, yes, the little devil had drawn blood. "I know. But I really wouldn't worry about it. She was much too busy with the bloodthirsty little Georgie to notice."

Allegra nodded. "All right, I won't worry about it. I'll just apply to Letty, have her give me a few quick lessons before tomorrow afternoon. You know, I never had to worry about such things at Sunderland."

Armand stopped, which had Allegra stopping as well, looking up at him. "You'll ask Letty? Really?"

"Yes, really. Why shouldn't I? Mama hired her to be our housekeeper and as a companion to Cousin Elizabeth and myself, so that mama didn't have to always be out and about for things like sipping tea and listening to Italian singers. Not nervous as she is, poor thing."

She withdrew her hand from his arm, jammed both her hands on her hips as she turned to face him completely. "And now you're frowning. Why are you frowning?"

"I'm frowning?" Armand said, quickly putting a smile on his face. "So sorry. It's probably more of a squint. The sun, you understand."

"Oh, piffle. You were frowning. Not only that, you had the strangest look in your eyes a moment ago. Tell me, Gauthier. You don't know me well, I grant you, but I'll also grant you that you know me well enough to grant that I'll only pest you until you do. Will you grant me that?"

Armand grinned. "Would you please *grant* me the boon of repeating that last little bit?"

"Gauthier," Allegra gritted out from between clenched teeth. "I've made a fool out of myself, pretending to turn my ankle the other day. I've let you watch Oxie at play. I've seen the way you looked at Letty—heard you call her Letty. Admit it, we've gone beyond dancing about each other. Talk to me."

"You heard that? How?"

"Domed ceiling," she answered matter-of-factly, confusing him even more.

He needed to put her off balance, redirect her mind. "Will you *grant* me the privilege of being my partner as I lead off the ball?"

Her eyes narrowed. "Oh, now that's mean. You

answered my question with a question of your own."

"Yes," Armand agreed. "So? Will you?"

"I suppose that would depend on the dance. Will it be a waltz or a reel?"

"Do you waltz?"

"Do pigs fly?"

"You really have been tucked in the back of beyond, haven't you? Then I suppose it will be a Scottish reel. Does that suit?"

"Agreed," she said, nodding, taking his arm once more as they continued their stroll. "Now, talk to me. Talk to me about Letty."

This was going to be tricky. "I really don't know the woman that well."

"Well enough to address her as Letty," Allegra pointed out.

He liked that Allegra was intelligent, admired her for it, but sometimes it might be easier if she weren't quite so sharp on all suits.

"Letty," he said, then sighed. "I met her last year. She was working . . . working in a house on the fringes of Mayfair."

"Yes? As a companion or housekeeper, I suppose," Allegra prodded as he hesitated.

Armand nodded, happy to grab at that easy explanation. "In charge of the house. Yes, that would be it." Now that he'd begun, he lapsed rather easily into more truth, carefully shaded. "There was some trouble with a rather inebriated gentleman guest one evening when I was visiting for some gathering or another, and I happened to be nearby. Wonderful man that I am, I came to her assistance."

"Someone backed her into a corner? One of these great pillars of Society who look down on Oxie and Mama? Oh, that's dreadful. Poor thing."

"She left that house soon after that, vowing to better herself, and I can see now that she has. So," he ended, remembering his earlier misgivings. "Letty is to accompany you to Lady Jane's? Dare I ask—to Almack's as well?"

"Unless Mama changes her mind, which I highly doubt, yes. But you see a problem in that? Oh, wait. Are you afraid she'll see the man who tried to hurt her?"

"No," he said quickly, too quickly. "I really don't. I doubt the man, deep in his cups, even remembers the incident. I'm confident she'll be fine, now that I've overcome my first misgivings. Letty's a wonderful woman. I admire her . . . grit. Now, wasn't there something you wanted to say to me, before Lord Georgie's interruption?"

"One I should probably be grateful for, as it delayed what I need to say," Allegra told him as he steered her toward a small bench near the center of the Square.

She sat down, waited for him to be seated beside her, then turned to look at him.

It felt intimate, sitting here with her, the shade cast by her parasol shading them both, putting them in their own small world. If they were in a country garden, rather than in the middle of this busy Square, what would he do? A stolen kiss? Yes. For starters.

No wonder mamas were so careful with their daughters.

"Do you like me, Gauthier? I think you do. I think we get along famously, actually. So tell me, do you like me?"

"I beg—I beg your pardon, my lady?"

Allegra rolled her eyes. "Oh, don't go all stiff and formal on me, Gauthier. You heard me."

Armand prudently scooted himself a little bit to the left on the iron bench, because he really wanted to scoot himself a little bit to the right, then grab Allegra into his arms and kiss her senseless.

He hadn't spoken to a woman this open and honest since he'd left . . . no, he wouldn't think about that, of how free and easy his life had been then, unbound by the social constrictions of London. That had been a different life, lived in a very different place, and he'd made a conscious decision to remove those memories from his life as he searched for a different past, a different future.

But a better past? A better future?

Suddenly he wasn't sure. He hadn't been sure for all of these three years, now that he thought about it. Had it taken this cheeky, open, totally disarming girl to make him see that his time here in England could be limited?

Allegra slapped her fisted hands against her knees. "Oh, piffle. Now I've gone and done it, haven't I? I've left you speechless, insulted you. The blunt-speaking country miss of no manners and less sense, showing herself not to be a lady. Dress her up, take her to London, and she's still Ally Nesbitt, with dirt on her face and at least one skinned knee, probably come by as she rolled on the ground, doing a very good job of beating up Harry Pigeon—he was the local knacker's youngest—for pulling her hair. I'm sorry, Gauthier."

Armand smiled, rather envying the knacker's son. "Harry Pigeon? How old were you?"

"Twelve, I think," Allegra said, sighing. "Before Cousin William cocked up his toes and Oxie got saddled with the earldom, that's for certain. After that, Mama grabbed me, dragged me along to Sunderland, and begged me to make a lady out of myself. Obviously, it didn't work."

"I had a bit of a rough and tumble youth, myself," Armand said, taking one of her hands in his, teasing her into releasing her fist. "But it's easier for a man, isn't it, my lady? We can swagger and swear, even bloody noses, and be forgiven."

"You can cross your legs, too," Allegra said, pointing at his legs, neatly crossed at the thigh. "Do you know how I long to do that again? Cross my legs, maybe even kick my foot in the air a few times. It would be heaven. But Letty says I can't, not if I want to be a lady. Knees together at all times, both feet flat on the floor. I hate it."

"Listen to what Letty has to say about knees and feet and where to keep them, my lady. She knows." He hid a rueful smile, continuing: "It seems we keep going in circles. From you wanting to tell me something, to Letty, back to you, back to Letty. Are you really so reluctant to talk to me? You did send the note, remember?"

Allegra tugged her hand away from his, sighed. "All right, as I hate being missish. Gauthier," she said, lifting her chin, "I told Oxie you're courting me."

There were a few birds in the Square, chattering and singing. Across the way, two young boys in short pants were rolling a hoop. A closed coach rumbled by, stopped at a mansion on one corner of the Square. A child laughed.

Armand heard, saw, none of it.

"Excuse me?"

"Oh, don't look so shocked," Allegra said, obviously feeling braver now that she'd said what she'd said.

She'd said that? She'd really said that?

"I mean it, Gauthier. And it's your fault anyway, because you gave me the idea. Or am I wrong, and you didn't hint that you're hosting a ball just as a means to meet me? That you saw me at the fountain and were entranced, or enraptured, or some drivel like that."

How he was enjoying himself! "Drivel? I spout drivel? Good God, I didn't know. Drivel, you say?"

"Drivel," Allegra repeated evenly, and it was obvious she believed what she'd said—and believed nothing he'd said. "But it gave me the idea, when Oxie started in again the other day about me making the acquaintance of a rich, eligible gentleman, marrying him so that Mama and I would be taken care of when he dies."

"Oxie—that is, the earl is dying?"

"Not soon, unless I kill him," Allegra said without rancor, crossing her legs as she leaned toward Armand. "Look. I'm here because Oxie is trying to pop me off— Lord, how I hate the way that sounds. That's no huge secret. It's why everyone is here in London, at least all the debutantes, and at least half the unmarried gentlemen. I'm also here under protest—mine."

Armand nodded his understanding. "All right. I'm following you so far. You've crossed your legs, by the way. And you're kicking the air."

She looked down at herself, uncrossed her legs. "Oh, piffle."

"Piffle. I hear you say it, my lady, and somehow I think what you're really saying is *Oh, bloody hell.* Why is that?"

"Because that's what I'd rather say, I suppose," she told him, getting to her feet, readjusting her parasol over her head. "Do you have any idea how I long to throw this silly thing away, and let the sun warm my face? But then I'd get freckles again, and if you haven't spent every night for two weeks sleeping with crushed straw-berries and cream slathered all over your face, drying and itching, Gauthier, well, then you haven't known hell."

He held out his arm, began walking her back to the Sunderland mansion, because if they stayed together much longer tongues would begin to wag.

Which didn't bother him quite as much as it probably should.

"All right, I'll finish this, since I see you're steering me home so that you can run home yourself, pack your bags, and grab the first ship leaving port, headed for places unknown."

"I'm steering you home, as you say, my lady, because I have promised Bones I'd meet him at his club. He worries like a hen with one chick if I'm late." If she could be bold, he could lie, if not with complete impunity.

He certainly couldn't tell her the truth, or she'd find a way to use the strict social rules to her own advantage. He was in enough trouble as it was.

"Oh. I'm sorry, Gauthier. Prickly, aren't I? I should really try not to be so thin-skinned. I don't think London brings out the best in me."

"That, my lady, is yet to be seen. So far, London does not know you. But I am delighted that you've decided that I should be the one by your side when the city is introduced to you."

"By my side? Surely not constantly, Gauthier. Once a week," she said, nodding. "That should be enough to keep Oxie happy. And it's not as if we'll be going any-where, except for your ball. Yours is still the only invi-tation on our mantel."

"Don't forget your voucher for Almack's. And now the invitation from Lady Jane," Armand reminded her. "Who knows what comes next. You may need to have the mantel braced with heavy nails, to hold up the weight of your invitations by next week."

"Oh, I hope not," she said, and Armand could tell that she was deadly serious.

It angered him.

"What is it, my lady? Do you feel inferior to the people here in London, or superior? Enlighten me, please, because I swear I don't know which it is."

Allegra stopped just at the bottom of the steps to the mansion, gave out a deep sigh.

"I don't know, Gauthier. The people here are probably no better or worse than those living around Sunderland, those in the village where I grew up. You can find mean and spiteful people wherever you go, coming from every station in life. Mostly, it's Mama and Oxie I'm worried about. They have such foolish *hopes* for me, and they're all wrapped up in this trip to London."

"Then perhaps," he heard himself say as his finer nature grabbed his unwary tongue before his self-serving self could lock that finer nature behind a stout door, "we should not hurt your parents more by allowing them to believe that you and I—"

"I know, I know," Allegra interrupted with a wave of her hand. "I've thought about that. I had thought only of a light flirtation, enough to keep Mama happy and Oxie from constantly reminding me that he's mortal. But it would be building them up, just to let them down, wouldn't it? Yet I don't know what else to do. I will *not* marry just because Oxie has taken it into his head that he's mortal."

"He isn't?" Armand couldn't help himself. This time he smiled.

"Of course he is, Gauthier. Don't be silly. But to try to *sell* me in exchange for creature comforts this way? It's so unlike him. If I marry, it will be in my own time, not just because he and Mama wish it. Why, if he'd listened to such nonsense himself, even as the poor relation he'd have been married off to some vicar's daughter, very prim and proper and genteelly impoverished, instead of Mama, who is wonderful, but not at all socially accept-able. Mama is a miller's daughter, you understand. But they were in love, so I think it all very grand of both of them. Why would Oxie suddenly wish less for me? It makes no sense."

Armand folded his arms across his chest. No, it didn't make sense. But, suddenly, something else did.

"Maybe this has less to do with popping you off, as you call it, and more to do with Oxie. Maybe he's playing a prank on you? Keeping you stirred up—as I'm sure he knows you are—just so he could come to London once more? He does seem to be enjoying himself."

Allegra was silent for a few moments, obviously chewing on this new thought. "He has rather worn out every one of his pranks at Sunderland. It's sad to watch him begin to repeat himself, and to hear people saying, *Oh, that's just Oxie Nesbitt pretending to be a ghost again, pay no attention—although those clanking chains are new, aren't they, and add a rather nice touch?*"

Armand bit on his knuckle, to squash a laugh.

She looked at Armand. "Is that it? Could it be? Oxie's just looking for a new audience, and knew mama had vowed never to return to London? Popping me off is the only reason she's here, that we're all here."

Those green eyes flashed, then narrowed. "How could he raise Mama's hopes this way, and upset me in the bargain? Oh, if this is true. If this is true, and it begins to sound reasonable to me, I'm going to have to turn the tables on him. You know that, don't you?"

Armand took a step backward, performed an elegant bow. "In that case I, my lady, am of course *entirely* at your service."

She tapped one foot against the cobbles. Tapped a finger against her wonderfully belligerent chin, in tune with the tapping foot.

"All right," she said at last, taking the finger from her chin and pointing it at Armand. "Nothing really changes. We are going to pretend—*pretend*—that yes, we are courting, that you are courting me. Seriously courting, not just the light flirtation I'd considered earlier."

"That, I suppose, would include meeting every day, and not just once a week? Just so I have this clear in my head, you understand."

"Whatever you think is best, yes. And we'll argue, I'll run, weeping, to my room, and then we'll be together again, we'll argue again, as if I must be trying very hard to be the willing daughter, finding myself a husband, but so unhappy as I am forced to choose any husband who will have me. Remember, London isn't welcoming me, is it? You're probably the only suitor I'll see."

"If you open my ball with me, if we see each other every day, if I make it known that I am courting you, then yes, everyone else will stay away. I say that with all modesty, but no one will wish to interfere if they believe I've set my sights on you."

She looked at him curiously. "I knew you had depths. How wonderful to have people tippy-toeing around you, Gauthier. My compliments."

"My thanks," he said, bowing to hide his smile. "Now, back to your father, if you please?"

"Yes, Oxie. He'll feel so guilty, wresting me from my happy home, wondering if I'm really in love, or just trying to make him happy. Oh, he'll be so at sixes and sevens, riddled with guilt. And *then,* just when Oxie realizes that he's about to accomplish what he had no interest in accomplishing, we'll have a falling out."

"You'll be throwing me over, I imagine. Will I need to go into a sad decline, or will getting myself entirely and publicly drunk be enough?"

"Oh, stop worrying about yourself. I'll let you be the one to cry off, if it's so important to you," Allegra said with a dismissive wave of her hand.

"God, I could adore you," Armand said, but she wasn't listening. She was pacing now, the parasol bobbing over her head.

"I'll have to let Mama in on the plan straight off, so that she's prepared, but Oxie will be so upset with himself to think that he brought me here for his own purposes, just to have his little pet's heart broken. Then— *then*—I'll tell him it was all a hum, and we can go home. Mama really wants us to go home. I think she realized this trip was a mistake before the coaches had even left Sunderland. Even better, Gauthier, I'll wager that this will be the very *last* time Oxie tries to trick either Mama or me. I love him, I truly do, but his pranking can grow tiresome."

"Yes, about that," Armand said, stepping in front of her to stop her pacing, gain her attention. "What do I get out of all of this? So far, it would appear that I'm to be the laughingstock, the poor jilted beau, or the cad who has dumped you. I like you, my lady, but—"

"Allegra," she interrupted. "If we're seriously courting, Gauthier, you should call me Allegra, shouldn't you? I give you permission. I can do that, can't I? Please, call me Allegra. No. Ally. That's even better."

"I'm flattered, truly, *Ally,* but the question remains—where is the benefit to *me?* Or aren't you aware of the definition of the word *bargain?* I believe it means there will be benefits on both sides. Doing a good deed is some reward, but I don't think it's enough. I'm sorry to be so shallow, but there it is."

She took a deep breath, raising her slim shoulders, then let it out slowly. "You're right. I'm being selfish. Very well. I've already told Oxie that you enjoyed chasing Jagger's couch to High Street. How much would you enjoy being in on his next prank? Remember, Viscount Eaton is still to be punished. I know Oxie, and I know he won't rest until he's played a prank on his lordship as well."

She lowered her chin, muttered, "Among others, that is. The silly man probably came to London prepared with a list. Oh, why didn't I see this sooner? It's all so *obvious* to me now."

"I could be a part of the next prank?" Armand rubbed at his forehead, wondering if he was really asleep in his own bed, and all of this afternoon was one long, confusing dream. "Oxie would allow that?"

"I think so, yes. He's already told me Bateson was more eager than accomplished, and I doubt Mersey is up to handling much more, at least not on his own. So, yes, it could be arranged. After all, you're my beau."

Her grin was as close to evil as he'd ever seen, and then she winked at him, sealing him into the role of co-conspirator.

He'd never been winked at by the daughter of an earl.

"Ally, I believe we have a bargain."

"Good. But you'll need a little practice, before you go out with Oxie."

"Practice," Armand repeated. "Now where in the world do I apply for that?"

"To me, of course, Gauthier. I am my father's child. Even if I don't play pranks anymore myself, I was his helper until Mama put her foot down and made him leave me at home. I think it was right after we'd put a cow on the squire's roof. I don't know who was most shocked, the Squire Handley, or the cow. Will you be able to meet me here tomorrow?"

Gauthier had to take a deep breath, to rid his mind of the picture of a younger Allegra braced behind a reluctant cow, helping to boost it up a plank laid against the edge of the squire's roof. His sides already hurt, from trying to control his mirth. God. Bones would be in nervous hysterics when he told him . . . no, he wouldn't tell him. This was between Allegra and himself. He wanted to keep it that way. Intimately that way.

As she was waiting for him to answer, he said, "Tomorrow? You're going to hear Lady Jane's Italian singer tomorrow, remember?"

"Oh, piffle," she said, and he grinned. He so enjoyed hearing her say, "Oh, piffle."

"I think I have the solution. I have been invited, in a way, so I could escort you and your cousin tomorrow, leaving Letty free to indulge in her own devices."

He saw the quick flash of intelligence that so very often sparkled in Allegra's green eyes.

"Circles, you said, Gauthier, and now we're traveling

in them again, back to Letty. Don't you want her to go with us tomorrow? Why?"

Why indeed? If Letty had applied for the position of both housekeeper and companion, who was he to question the woman's judgment?

He stepped back, bowed. "I shall be here promptly at a quarter of the hour tomorrow afternoon, to escort all three of you ladies to Lady Jane's. We'll walk, unless it rains. Afterward, we'll deposit the two ladies back here, and go off to practice pranking. Is that all right?"

Allegra nodded. "It's perfect. Oh, this is going to be such *fun*."

Yes, Armand agreed silently. *Fun.*

Chapter Eight

$\mathcal{P}$RYING A WEEPING FEMALE off one's shoulder is not as easy as one might think. Allegra learned this as she stood, nearly staggering under the weight, as her taller, heavier Cousin Elizabeth clung to her, caught between tears and laughter.

"Cousin . . . back off, if you please," she said, trying to sidestep the two of them toward the couch, and finally succeeding in pushing Elizabeth out of her arms. "Good God, Lizzie. It's just an Italian singer."

Her cousin collapsed onto the couch, wiping at her eyes with her handkerchief, then noisily blowing her nose. "No, no, cousin. You don't *understand.* This is *it.* This is the beginning. Tomorrow, the music recital, and the next day the world. The ball, Almack's. Dearest, *dearest* Lady Jane. All my dreams, my hopes, coming true at last."

"Yes, aren't you the lucky one," Allegra said dryly, rolling her eyes at Lettice Tomlin, who was, as she seemed always to be, pouring tea for them all.

"Oh, I am, I *am.* I know that. And, much as it astounds me, I owe it all to *you!*" Elizabeth declared, looking rather surprised.

Allegra pressed her hands against her breast. "*Me?* Oh, I don't think so. Face it, Lizzie. If it were up to me, you'd be knitting slippers or socks or whatever in your father's run-down estate in Hampshire. It was Mama who thought to drag you along to London."

Elizabeth tipped her head to one side, considered this. "Yes, but you're the one Mr. Gauthier saw, and you're the one who dared to visit him, and you're the one who met Lady Jane and made sure I was included in her invitation. You may try to be awful, cousin, and you can be. But in your heart, you're good. You're really, really *good.*"

Allegra opened her mouth to point out that Gauthier had tricked the two vouchers out of Lady Jersey, and that it had been Gauthier who had introduced her to Lady Jane.

"Well, not precisely *good,* cousin," Allegra found herself saying. "You're happy, then? You'll understand why I ask, as you are crying, you know." She wet her lips, made a small face. "You cry a lot, don't you?"

"A-hem, a-hem."

Allegra turned to Lettice. "You have something to say, Letty?"

"No more than you should, my lady," Lettice said,

handing over a teacup. "Just that I think it lovely that you and your cousin are rubbing along together this way. Your mama will be so pleased."

"But she won't attend with us tomorrow, will she?" Allegra said, understanding that Lettice had, very nicely, just told her to shut up. She sat down beside her cousin— then quickly stood up again as Elizabeth attempted to take her hand. "I'm sure she'd be welcome."

"The countess is happiest in her own house," Lettice pointed out, stirring her tea. "At the moment, she's tucked up on the chaise in her room with a soft knit blanket over her legs, reading one of Miss Austen's books and having herself a good laugh as well as a good cry. Why upset her with thoughts of going out into Society, meeting up with those who intimidate her? She's already horribly fretful over the thought of attending Mr. Gauthier's ball."

"She won't go," Allegra said, sitting down once more, this time beside Lettice. "She'll cry off at the last moment, with the headache or something, but she won't go. Oxie will, for our sins."

That seemed to bring Elizabeth out of her happy, rather benevolent haze. "Oh, *must* he? Wouldn't he rather stay home with Aunt Magdalen?"

"Perhaps he'll be good," Allegra said into what was soon a tense silence. "And, then again, perhaps not," she added, shrugging. "Dearest cousin, would you care for more tea?"

"Oh, I would, yes, thank you." Elizabeth leaned forward, her hands clasped together in her lap. "And you can tell me all about Lady Jane. Is she still so pretty? Is she fat, now that she's had a baby? It's a boy, isn't it? I believe I read about the birth in Papa's newspaper about two years ago. She'd hate it, if she got fat, because her mama's fat, and I can remember her telling me she'd rather *die* than have to have her maid all but stepping on her back to lace up one of those horrid corsets. We giggled about it, I remember. I don't know that I want to get fat. Oh, and does she still talk so fast, nineteen to the dozen? Honestly, that sweet girl could *talk!*"

Allegra exchanged glances with Lettice, happy to see that the woman—even if she would a-hem, a-hem again if Allegra said anything even slightly mean—had at least seen the humor in Elizabeth's words, and that fact that, after spending the past weeks nearly silent as a clam, the girl had turned into a veritable chatterbox. Amazing.

"Lady Jane is quite lovely," Allegra said with all honesty. "But, yes, she does talk nineteen to the dozen. Charmingly."

Then she threw her cousin another bone, actually feeling in charity with the girl. "It took her only a heartbeat to recognize the name Nesbitt, and inquire about you, Elizabeth. It would seem she has fond memories of the dancing class you attended together."

"Oh. That," Elizabeth said, blushing furiously. "That . . . that was a long time ago. We were preparing for the day we'd make our debuts here in London."

She sighed, dabbed at her watering eyes. "The waltz wasn't even yet in vogue, you know, considered far too risqué and forward for gentle ladies. Now, of course, everyone waltzes. Except me. I have no idea how the dance is performed."

She tried to smile, not quite succeeding. "Our dancing master was so funny. What was his name? Oh, yes, Mr. Odo Pinabel. Jane and I—all the girls—called him Mr. Odious, behind his back. What a silly man. Ah, it was wonderful, and so, so long ago."

About five years, Allegra thought, feeling unexpectedly guilty as she looked at her cousin's pretty, but extremely sad face.

Why hadn't she seen it before now? If she had been upset at being ruthlessly yanked out of her simple life and into that of being the earl's daughter, well, wasn't the same to be said about Elizabeth being stripped of the life she'd led since birth, her expectations, her dreams?

Suddenly Allegra felt very bad. She'd been thinking only of herself, and only of how Elizabeth had been as a child—as her mother's child, as Uncle Frederick's child.

But now Elizabeth was a grown woman, and if silly, she was not mean. She'd tried, early on, to be mean, but she couldn't seem to sustain any real nastiness. In fact, if she were any easier to be upset, yes, even hurt, Allegra knew she'd have been honor-bound to punish anyone who dared to hurt her.

She was, after all, blood.

Allegra slowly put down her teacup, looked at Lettice, who nodded, seeming to be able to understand what she was thinking.

"You know what, Elizabeth?" she said as brightly as possible. "Mr. Gauthier has asked me to lead off his ball with him, and I nearly had to decline, as he'd planned a waltz. We're to do a Scottish reel, which any child can do, but perhaps it would be nice if I could learn the steps to the waltz. We both could, couldn't we? What was your dancing master's name, Elizabeth? Or didn't you have those lessons here in London?"

Elizabeth pressed one hand to her mouth for a few moments, trying to control her tears, then said, "Yes, yes, here in London. Mr. Pinabel, Mr. Odo Pinabel. Oh, but the ball is on Saturday. Still, I'm sure he'd come, straightaway, if Uncle Oxie paid him well enough. You'd do that? You'd really do that for me?"

"And for me, Elizabeth," Allegra pointed out reasonably. "I'm not entirely unselfish."

"But you do protest too much. Oh, *cousin,* you're just too, too, *good!*"

"Oh, piffle. If I'm so good, Letty," Allegra asked in genuine confusion as she watched her cousin all but race from the room, overcome by tears, "why is it the dratted girl bursts into tears every time I talk to her?"

Armand sat at his ease, enjoying the spectacle of Bartholomew Boothe in full, near-apoplectic fury.

Bones paced the carpet in Armand's study, periodically stopping, turning to face Armand, opening his mouth to say something or pointing at him, then blowing out an exasperated breath and going back to his pacing.

Bones stopped again. "You . . ." he began, waving a finger at Armand. "You . . . I don't believe it!"

"It was a couch, Bones, and I had nothing to do with it."

Bones threw up his hands. "The couch? This isn't about the couch. You're going to . . . you said that—well, you can't. You just can't."

"Court her? I can't court her?" Armand uncrossed his long legs and got up, headed for the drinks table. "Whyever not?"

"Why not?" Bones's eyes nearly bulged out of their sockets, and his face had turned a rather unbecoming red. "Because . . . because—well, damn, Armand, as if you don't know why. How could Simon desert me like this? He should be here. He'd know what to say."

Armand poured two glasses of wine, handed one to Bones as that man reached the end of the carpet, was about to make his turn. "Simon, my friend, would only tell you what I'm telling you. Simon would tell you, Bones, that I do what I do."

"That's all well and good, I suppose, when doing what you do has to do with why you came here, came to England in the first place. But this? Walking about London on that girl's leash, pretending to be courting her? That's not a prank, Armand. Propping coffins against doors is a prank. This is . . . this is lunacy."

Bones gestured with both arms as he said *lunacy,* and half his wine sloshed out of the glass, onto his shirt cuff. "See? See this?" he said, holding out his dripping arm. "You did this, and we're already late for Lord Hereford's. How am I supposed to go all the way back to m'mother's and change? We'll be late, and I don't like to be late. I *hate* being late."

"Bones, calm down. Sit down. No, don't. Just stand there, and strip down. I'll have Quincy order a footman to fetch a clean shirt from my valet, and you'll be good as before. Unless you're planning to fall into a swoon, or foam at the mouth. Neither appeals, by the way."

Bones looked at his damp cuff, then at Armand. "Oh, I didn't want to go anyway. Hereford's a boor, always going on about his salmon fishing. Don't even like salmon. Who eats pink fish? Not me, I tell you. M'mother says it's unhealthy. But I will take that shirt. I feel soggy."

Ten minutes later Bones was wearing a dry shirt and a new neckcloth as well, the cuffs of the shirt only slightly too long, and sitting in one of the leather chairs in front of the small fire in the fireplace, rubbing a snifter of brandy between his hands.

"Feeling more the thing, Bones?" Armand asked from the facing chair. "You know, I didn't mean to upset you."

"You never do," Bones answered. "Nobody ever does. But you all do it. Courting the Nesbitt chit. There goes your hard-won consequence, Armand, dumped right into the Thames, tied down with a rock."

"I think you're wrong, Bones."

He looked up, just with his eyes, keeping his chin still very close to his bony chest. "Oh, really? Well, I spoke with m'mother about the Nesbitt chit the other day, and m'mother says—"

"Bones," Armand interrupted, "I don't want to be mean-spirited, really I don't. But you passed thirty on your last birthday. Do you still really care so much what your mother says? Isn't it time you decided what *you* think, what *you'll* say?"

Armand watched as Bones blinked a time or two, then sat back, his arms hard against the leather arms of the chair, his feet solidly on the floor—as if a strong wind had just entered the study, pushing him backward, holding him immovable.

"Bones? Are you all right?"

Bones let go of the arms of the chair, sighed deeply. "By God, lightning didn't strike, did it? No clap of thunder, no white-hot bolt burning you to a crisp where you sit. I wonder what would happen if I tried it?"

Armand rubbed a finger beneath his nose, hiding his smile. "Why don't you give it a try?"

"All right." Bones stood up, walked to the center of the room. He stood very still. Cleared his throat a time or two. Said, "I think it all sounds like the greatest of good fun, Armand, I think you should do it. Play this prank with the Nesbitt chit. She sounds like a very interesting young lady."

And then he ducked down, his knees bent, his gaze directed at the ceiling. After a moment, he raised himself up again, smiled at Armand. "Nothing. Nothing happened. You know, Armand, if m'father had known that, he might have had a happier life."

"And probably a longer one," Armand said quietly. "Now come here and sit down, and tell me what *you* think. Do you believe what you just said, or am I heading for all sorts of trouble?"

Bones sat down, picked up his snifter once more, and looked straight at Armand. "You really want to know what I really think—just me, and nothing to do with m'mother? All right. You're a dead man, my friend, but you don't know it yet. Does that answer your question?"

"Fairly well, yes," Armand said, draining his own snifter. "Why?"

"You still really want to know what I think? Even after I said you're a dead man?"

"As my personal doomsayer for these past three years, albeit secondhand from your esteemed mother, Bones, yes, I really want to know what you think."

"All right," Bones said, settling himself against the soft leather. "One. Simon is no longer here, so even though you are popular, you've lost his consequence. And I don't have any, Lord knows. Anyway, those who might have suffered you, not really liking you, believing you to be some lowborn gambler or whatever Simon foisted on them, could see this Nesbitt connection as a reason to begin to back away from you, undoing the work of three years. That's just number one."

"Gracious, what a fickle world we inhabit here in Mayfair. But you overestimate, Bones, how much the approval of the *ton* means to me."

"Which brings us to two. You may not care about how you're perceived by this fickle society here in Mayfair, but you're still hunting, Armand. Do you really want the field to get smaller?"

Now it was Armand's time to stand, begin to pace the carpet. "I've about given that up, Bones," he said, avoiding his friend's eyes. "The Captain was wrong. He had to have been wrong."

"And the handkerchief? The jacket?"

"Mean nothing, less than nothing. Bones," he said, turning to look at his friend, "I've been in nearly every great house in England, and there's nothing that even remotely comes close to fitting any possibility the Captain concocted, anything I'd thought, even hoped. No, it's time to stop. In fact, it might be time for me to leave England."

"But you're English!"

"Am I? We don't know that, not for sure. And even if I am, a handkerchief and a coat don't make me the long-lost son of one of the finest families in England. That's a boy's dream, not a man's."

Bones rubbed the snifter between his hands, watching the liquid swirl inside the glass. "I'd miss you."

Armand smiled. "I'd miss you, too, Bones," he said. "But, before I go, why not have a little fun at Society's expense? Playing pranks with Oxie Nesbitt, and running a rig on Society with little Allegra? Well, I might go, Bones, but I wouldn't soon be forgotten."

At last, Bones smiled as well. "You've got a wild streak in you, don't you, Armand? I think I would have liked to have been you, at least for one day. You'd never have allowed yourself to be put so firmly under your mother's thumb."

"Since I never knew the lady, no, I suppose not." Armand sighed. "Ah, Bones. Have you ever noticed? No one's happy with their own lot, everyone else's looks better to them. I thought England would solve my problems. And I've enjoyed myself, enjoyed"—he spread his arms to indicate his study, his entire mansion—"all of this. But, do you know, Bones—there are times I'd give half of it to walk barefoot on a warm beach, when I'd give anything to be that boy who didn't even own a pair of boots."

Bones put down his empty snifter. "Is that it, Armand? Are you hoping that running all over Mayfair with Oxie Nesbitt, playing pranks and raising a rumpus, courting his daughter—that it will all serve to sully your name, make it easier for you to leave?"

"Possibly. I'd have to think on that, won't I? And I don't know what I have to go back to, Bones. The Captain is gone, most everyone I knew is gone. Betrayed and forced to leave. There's no one there for me anymore."

"Do you know where they went?"

Armand nodded. "Last I've heard, he was plying his trade from Campeche."

"Campeche? Never heard of it."

"Some call it Galveston Island, but that probably means just as little to you. I don't know the place myself. No, I won't go there. The Captain would turn his back on me, send me packing. He made that very clear when he ordered me here, to England."

"He cared for you."

"In his way," Armand said, eyeing the bottom of his empty snifter. "Come on, Bones," he said, picking up his friend's jacket, holding it out to him. "Enough of this maudlin business. Let's go celebrate my last evening as a free man, for tomorrow I surrender to Lady Allegra."

Bones slipped his arms into the jacket, then turned to Armand. "But you both know you're only funning, right? Only trying to trick the earl on her part, and tweak Society's nose on yours? Nothing's actually going to come from any of this nonsense?"

"Absolutely," Armand said, then frowned at Bones's back as he followed that man down the stairs, out into the night. "Absolutely. I think."

Allegra stood in front of the mirror in her bedchamber, openly admiring herself.

Bless her mama for her thick honey-blond hair, her green eyes that seemed to please Armand Gauthier. Bless her mama for her small but well-formed body.

Bless Oxie for his sense of fun, his love of life, and for passing that gift on to her. Bless him allowing her, indeed, encouraging her, to spread her wings, dare to be her own person.

She leaned closer to the mirror. "Because you're having fun, aren't you, you shameless creature," she told her smiling reflection. "Against everything you thought when they dragged you to this city, screaming and kicking, you're having *so* much fun."

Allegra stepped back, smoothed down the skirt of her palest yellow muslin gown, drawing her fingers along the lace-edged bodice, slowly skimming them over the skin that bodice bared to her eyes. Would bare to Armand Gauthier's eyes.

Did he know she was interested, even against her better judgment? Could he tell?

Had he yet considered the possibility that the daughter of a master pranker had set out to trick him into falling in love with her?

Not that she had.

"I'd never do anything like that," she told her reflection as she pushed at her soft upsweep of curls, lightly slapped at her cheeks to bring more color into her face. "Never."

Her reflection seemed to look at her with raised eyebrows, a look of speculation.

"Well, I wouldn't!" Allegra said with some feeling, turning away from the mirror. "I didn't even think about it until late last night, when I remembered how handsome he is. How he seems to enjoy himself in my company. How I feel when he smiles at me."

She picked up her reticule, the dreaded parasol. "Oh, piffle. I'm smitten. I'm actually smitten with the man. How depressing. But it's not too late to call the whole thing off. I'll just—"

Allegra turned around, glared at the door. "Who is it?"

The door opened, and Lettice Tomlin walked in, looking the same as she always did. Black hair, black gown, dead-white face devoid of expression. "Miss Elizabeth is having some problem with her toilette, my lady. I thought you should know we may be delayed."

Allegra looked to the mantel clock. It was nearly half past the hour of two. "The devil we will. Tell her we'll go without her."

"You've already forgotten?"

Allegra looked at Lettice's frowning face. "What? What have I forgotten?"

"You're now in sympathy with your cousin, and the two of you have cried friends." Lettice sighed. "And please don't tell me you didn't mean it, because I am not such a looby. You looked at Miss Elizabeth in a whole new way yesterday as she bared her feelings to you. In fact, you pitied her."

Allegra pulled a face, realizing she didn't much enjoy having her finer nature, if that's what it was, pointed out to her. "Maybe."

"So you'll wait for her? Your mama is with her, helping one of the maids with her hair. I'm sure she'll be ready on time. This is very important to Miss Elizabeth, her initial entry into Society."

Allegra nodded her head. "She probably goes to bed every night, dreaming about making her curtsy to Society. While I've been taking to my bed every night these past five years, wishing myself out of Sunderland and back with my childhood friends."

"Even now?" Letty asked her. "I may be wrong, but you seem more contented now to stay in London, to even become a part of Society."

Allegra averted her eyes, plucked at the ribbons on her gown, the one she hoped would impress Gauthier all hollow. "It isn't entirely tedious."

"No, my lady, that's true enough," Lettice said, heading toward the door. "Mr. Gauthier is many things, but I doubt he is ever tedious. I'll go check on Miss Elizabeth, see if I can hurry her along."

"That wasn't what I—oh, why am I even bothering?" Allegra said as the door closed behind Lettice. "That woman sees entirely too much for my own good."

Chapter Nine

LONDON HAD BEEN BLESSED with five straight days of pleasant April weather, with very little rain. Armand was pleased by that happy circumstance as he walked across the Square, heading for the Sunderland mansion.

He liked seeing Allegra in the sunlight. It was in the sunlight that he'd first seen her, and she seemed to positively bloom on sunny days. Not like a lily, elegant and cool, but like a dandelion, all warm and joyful. Touchable.

And she liked the sun, had told him so as she complained about having to use a parasol.

He rather liked that ever-present parasol. He could close his eyes, and picture Allegra carefully picking her way across a hot, sandy beach, her skirts drawn up slightly so that he could see her bare feet, her parasol held above her head as she looked like an acrobat crossing a high wire.

He wondered if she could swim. So many people couldn't, even most of the sailors he'd known, which he'd never understood. But the Captain had explained that being able to swim when tossed into the ocean a thousand miles from shore was more of a torture than just sinking into the water, giving up the spirit.

Armand disagreed. Where there was life, there was hope. With his own history, how could he ever believe otherwise?

He should have bought an estate on some cliff overlooking the ocean. Maybe then he wouldn't be so restless. But the purchase of his home, not more than twenty miles from Simon's estate, had seemed reasonable.

At the time. Before the itch that had begun last year had settled into him like a nettle stuck under his hose.

Become a permanent part of him.

For two years the hunt had been enough. The wondering, the hoping, the thought that the Captain had been right, had been enough.

But Mayfair was small, the *ton* just as limited, and he'd exhausted his options without any success. So, for the past year, he'd traveled all over England, even into Scotland and Wales, with a similar lack of success.

In truth, he didn't know why he was still here, except that the mansion in Grosvenor Square had been as close to a gift dropping into his hands as anything else in his life, and he couldn't ignore it.

No. That wasn't it. His friendship with Simon kept him here; with Simon, with Bones. He hadn't come to England for companionship, but for answers.

Was it so terrible that he had not gotten what he came for, if the exchange was Simon, was Callie, was Bones—was the thought that maybe, just maybe, he was on the verge of building himself an entirely new life?

So he'd given himself one more Season, had even entertained the idea of finding himself a suitable wife, settling down on his estates, becoming the sort of man he admired, like Simon. Simon was so obviously happy, so obviously in love with his Callie. Content.

And perhaps he'd been right to stay. Lord knew he was attracted to Allegra—to Ally. He believed he actually could see the two of them together.

But not here. Not on this damp, foggy, often cold island.

He didn't want to leave this woman, not yet. But he

knew he could not stay. Another world was calling him.

What was he so worried about, anyway? Theirs was just a flirtation, a game. He was enjoying himself, would continue to enjoy himself. This was no time to think about anything more permanent—like making an obviously adoring daughter choose between her parents and a man like him.

And yet . . . and yet.

He could see Allegra lying in the middle of a rope hammock, swinging her bare legs, holding her arms open as he dove toward her, nearly sending the two of them spinning off onto the ground.

He could see her poised on an outcrop of huge rocks, braving the ocean's spray, her skirts and hair blowing, the breeze carrying her delighted laughter to him.

He could see her standing with her hands pressed against the rails of a wide veranda, watching for him as he rode to her through the avenue of live oaks hanging with Spanish moss. Home from his journey, home to her.

And he could see her on that beach. Over and over· again, he could see her on that beach.

"Sir? Excuse me, sir?"

Armand blinked, realizing that he must have climbed the steps to the pink mansion, lifted the knocker to announce his presence.

He didn't even remember passing the fountain.

"Yes, good afternoon," he said quickly, stepping inside the foyer. "Armand Gauthier, to see Lady Allegra."

The butler blessed him with the rather abrupt nod that

told him he was known and expected, then ushered him toward the stairs.

"No need, no need," Allegra called out, leaning over the banister that curled around the first floor of the mansion. "Here we come." Then she turned her head, called out, "Now or never, Elizabeth. I mean it."

Armand, who had been enjoying the view, dipped his head slightly, smiled.

The girl was totally without pretense. It was not in Allegra, he knew, to keep him waiting when she was as anxious as he to be on their way, just because ladies were supposed to keep gentlemen waiting.

When he looked up again, it was to see Allegra bounding down the stairs, one hand held out about an inch above the banister, a wide grin on her face.

"I've had to poke her with a stick a time or two, but Cousin Elizabeth will be down shortly, I promise. I vow, how can a woman begin dressing at ten, and still not be ready at two?"

She held out her hand—ah, something new she'd learned, probably at Letty's knee—and he bowed over it, daring to touch his lips to her skin for just a breath of a second. "Then it must have taken you days, my lady, for you are magnificent. My compliments."

"Oh, Gauthier, what humbug," she said, withdrawing her hand, then she smiled up at him, obviously pleased with his compliment. "Besides, I thought you were going to call me Ally."

"You race headlong into any situation, don't you?" he asked her, longing to reach out, run the tip of his finger down her cheek. "We can't be too obvious, or your father will smell a rat."

She nodded. "True, true. And I think I did say something about arguing with you, didn't I?" She stepped back, cleared her throat, then said loudly, "I don't care if you think we'll be late and want to leave without her, Gauthier, I'm telling you—we wait for my cousin. How can you be so unreasonable? One more nasty remark, and you can just take yourself off without either of us."

The pocket doors to the downstairs study opened and Oxie Nesbitt stepped into the foyer. "Pet? Who you yelling at that way? Oh, Got-yer. You again. Seeing a lot of you, ain't we?"

Armand looked to Allegra, who was grinning the grin of a cat with canary feathers sticking out from the corners of its mouth. One moment he was her suitor, and the next he was little more than an obnoxious pest.

Wonderful.

"Good afternoon, my lord," he said, bowing to the earl. "I've come to escort your daughter and her cousin to Countess Chirton's to hear an Italian singer."

"Why would they want to do that?" Oxie asked, frowning at his daughter. "You don't even talk Italian, do you, pet? Bet Elizabeth don't, either. Oh, well, maybe you'll like the tune, and can hum along."

Allegra looked at Armand, and they smiled at each other. "Oh, I don't think so, Oxie. What's that you're carrying? Isn't that the same book I saw you reading the other day?"

The earl tried to slip the slim volume beneath his coat, but Armand caught a quick glimpse of the title: *Smith's Amusements: Tricks, Ploys, and Sundries Mischief.*

"Nothing much," Oxie told his daughter. "Just a little something about field drainage. Got to know such nonsense, being an earl and all."

"Uh-huh," Allegra said, and Armand felt sure that Oxie would want to put the book under lock and key if he hoped to keep his daughter from finding it. Digging a hole in the floor of the cellar, then dropping the book in, covering it up again, and placing a hulking piece of furniture over it might not be sufficient.

"Oxie?" Allegra said, stepping closer to Armand. "Gauthier has something to ask you."

All right, Armand corrected, holding back a wince. How about we dig a hole in the cellar floor, drop *Allegra* into it, cover it up, et cetera, et cetera.

"What? Something to say?"

"Yes, and so do I," she continued. "I'll go first. Oxie, Gauthier has volunteered to help you hoax the viscount. You are going to prank him, aren't you?"

"Who? Me?"

The man looked as innocent as he sounded, which was not at all.

"Yes, Oxie. *You.* You're going to prank him. Gauthier wants to go along, help you."

"At which time, I would like to speak to you about another matter, yes," Armand broke in, not liking the way Allegra had taken charge of everything, even though she was saying precisely what he wished to say.

How odd. He wondered if he had a contrary streak never before acknowledged until Allegra had come bounding into his life, turning that life upside down. He had always been such an easygoing man.

"You're not going to ask him now? I thought we'd agreed—no," Allegra said shortly, cutting herself off. "Never mind, I'll just go upstairs, grab Elizabeth by the hair, and get this afternoon over with, all right?"

"Nettle-y little thing sometimes, you know," Oxie said as Allegra all but flounced back up the stairs. "I steer clear of her then, at least until she's fed. Food works wonders with her, I've learned. I could have had six sons who ate less than that little scrap. Next time you'll know. Feed her, boy. Otherwise, she might bite your head straight off."

"Yes, my lord, very interesting. I'll remember that," Armand said, and then said no more, because he was in danger of saying too much.

"So," Oxie went on, patting his own ample stomach. "You two getting along? As well as my Ally gets along with anyone."

"I . . . um . . . we seem to enjoy each other's company, my lord, yes, at least for the most part."

"Thought so," Oxie said smugly. "People don't think I see all that I see, but I do. You seem nice enough, Gotyer, so I'll say yes, you can see her, court her. And you don't have to come along with me on my visit to the viscount tomorrow, if you don't want, just to get me alone, ask my permission. Don't want a man with his heart not in the trick. I have enough trouble with that dieaway Mersey."

"On the contrary, my lord," Armand said as earnestly as possible. "I would very much enjoy myself, I'm sure. And, as for my acquaintance with your daughter, I'm—"

"You're going to break your heart, that's what you're going to do," Oxie interrupted sadly. "My little pet would rather eat dirt than spend the rest of her life dressed to the nines and traipsing about London town, rubbing elbows with people she knows to be as false as a harlot's promise of affection."

He leaned toward Armand. "Not that I'd know about that last bit. It's just a saying, Got-yer, that's all. I'm as true as a husband can be. But you take my meaning, don't you? Because I like you, Got-yer."

"Thank you, sir," Armand said, bowing. He didn't incline his head too far, however, because this conversation was making him dizzy, and he didn't want to topple over, make a complete cake of himself.

"Don't thank me. I thank you, son. You've got those two girls going out and about, just as m'wife wants, and I do thank you for that. Hadn't hoped for it, either, with no one answering my letters. Just don't see more in my little girl than what I'm telling you. This town life ain't for her. Don't know why I didn't see it before. Maybe I did. But her mama wants this, poor dear. Poor dear's going to be just as disappointed as any young buck who starts chasing that little girl's heels."

"You're telling me to go away, my lord? Warning me away from your daughter?"

"No. No, no, no. That wouldn't work. She'd just go after you, to find out why you'd left." He stepped even closer, so that Armand had to bend down, to listen to the man's whisper.

"Here's the thing, Got-yer. M'daughter ain't hanging out for a husband, never wanted to come here in the first place. Fought us all the way, both her mama and me. But now she's here, and she's obedient, in her own way, and I'm beginning to worry that she might—well, that she might think I brought her here to marry her off."

Armand digested this. Allegra may have been right. "And you didn't?"

"No-o-o," Oxie said, shaking his head. "That's how I got her *mama* here. Pay attention, Got-yer."

"Maybe if I could take notes?" Armand said, trying not to laugh.

"No need for that, either. Look, it's simple. Plain as glass. I wanted to come to London, see some of my old friends—ha! Didn't know I didn't have any, but that's all right, too, because it made it easier for me to pick my vic—er, targets."

"You wanted to come to London to play pranks?" Armand asked helpfully, eager to tell Allegra that they'd been right, completely and absolutely correct.

"Sort of run my course at Sunderland, Got-yer," Oxie said, sighing. "You can only put so many cows on a roof, boy, let me tell you. Sad fact, but true. It was time for some town tricks, ones without cows, for one. So, to get where I wanted to go, I told m'wife I wanted to marry Allegra off, which thrilled her all hollow, and told Allegra I *needed* to marry her off, because otherwise, when I cock up my toes, she and her mama would be left at the mercies of her uncle Frederick. Wouldn't wish that on anybody."

He looked up at Armand, frowning. "You getting any of this, Got-yer?"

"I believe so, yes. What I don't understand, my lord,

is why you're telling me."

"Because you're all arsy-varsy over my little girl, that's why. Stands to reason. Nobody else would dare come within ten feet of a Nesbitt, and nobody else has, come to think of it. Besides, you've been good to us, which I already thanked you for, if you've been paying attention."

"Yes, I believe I do remember that part, my lord," Armand told him, pinching the bridge of his nose between his fingers.

"And now you want to help me with my pranks. I tell you, Got-yer, you've won my heart. But you won't win my little girl's, and you need to know that, so that you won't be hurt. I play pranks, yes, but I'm not a nasty man."

"Would you mind, my lord, if I at least tried to win your daughter's heart? Now that I've been warned."

"Knowing she's only in your company to please me— or to scare me into taking her home?"

Armand smiled. "How strange. I seem to have a slightly higher opinion of myself, my lord. I believe Lady Allegra *likes* me."

Oxie scratched at the fluffy puffs of white hair above his left ear. "Well, you ain't repulsive, I'll give you that. But, no, I don't see it. She may pretend to enjoy herself, to make her mama happy, to try to tease me into thinking she's sacrificing herself for me, but that's all. When the Season is over, the three of us will head back to Sunderland. Maybe sooner, as her mama really doesn't enjoy being here."

He patted his jacket, and the book hidden beneath it.

"But not quite yet. Well, I'll be off. Things to do, Got-yer, things to do."

"Yes, my lord," Armand said, bowing as the man headed back into his study.

He stood there, thinking over the events of the past two days.

He had agreed to pretend to court Allegra, at her request and for his own private enjoyment, all in order to frighten her mischievous father into believing she was going to sacrifice herself for him. Which would prove to her father that he should not prank her any-more—or her mother, either, Armand felt sure.

As living with Oxie Nesbitt and his pranks, much as he was amused by the man in small doses, would soon send Armand screaming into the night, he certainly understood Allegra's reasons for what she hoped to accomplish.

He also now knew that Allegra had been right, that her father was not really concerned with marrying her off, but only having a new audience for his pranks.

But, ah! Should he tell her that she'd been right? Should he tell her that her father was very much onto her trick, so that there would no longer be any reason for her to continue this sham courtship?

After all, if the two of them just sat down, told each other the truth about their feelings, then the father would be free to play his pranks and then go home, and Allegra wouldn't have to run her own rig meant to frighten her father into never playing a prank on her again.

Which would mean she'd dismiss Armand from his

promise to pretend to court her, wouldn't it?

He smiled, and it was a smile as evil as Allegra's had been when she'd laid out her plan to him yesterday.

Tell her?

Hardly.

Although, rather than trying to keep all of this intrigue straight in his head, it might be easier to just toss Allegra over his shoulder and drive hell-bent for Gretna Green.

That thought, that had flown into his head unbidden, quite effectively wiped the smile from Armand's face.

Allegra sat in the last row of horribly uncomfortable chairs arranged in Lady Chirton's drawing room, using her kid gloves to fan herself.

Too many people, too many strong scents—not all of them perfume.

Too many songs that all sounded the same and went on forever and ever. Lemonade that was not only warm, but watered.

And an idiot sitting in the chair beside her.

"Tell me again," Elizabeth whispered into Allegra's ear. "Bartholomew Boothe? It's a wonderful name. So why is he called Bones?"

Allegra looked across the room, to where Boothe stood beside Armand, the two of them looking very different—one looking oppressed, the other quietly amused.

The oppressed one—Bones—looked uncomfortable, both in mind and body, fidgeting, wincing when the higher notes rang out, shaking the crystal chandelier.

"He looks," Allegra whispered back at Elizabeth, "as

if he was once a much shorter man, but somebody stretched him, then forgot to feed him for six months. He's a tall, thin sack of bones, Lizzie. Even his face is long and bony. Nobody was going to call him *Chubby*."

"Oh," Elizabeth said, fiddling with the strings of her reticule. "Well, I think that's just mean. He seemed very nice when Mr. Gauthier introduced us. And it was very kind of him to come here today, just to help bear us company. Too bad there were no more chairs."

A perfumed, turbaned woman who sat in the next row turned around, glared at Allegra. *"Shhh!"*

"So sorry," Allegra whispered, and the woman turned around again.

Allegra waited a few moments, then leaned closer to her cousin. "I'm sure he is extremely nice, Lizzie," she whispered. "Nice enough to have agreed to come here today, and to walk you and Mrs. Tomlin back across the Square once this caterwauling is completed. But I don't think that means you should immediately write home to Uncle Frederick, have him post the banns."

The turbaned head swiveled on a thick neck. "I said, *shhhh!*"

Allegra fought the urge to stick out her tongue, and only smiled, shrugged her shoulders. "So, *so* sorry."

She then peeked at her cousin, and immediately regretted her words. Elizabeth's eyes were bright, and she was blinking to hold back tears.

"Don't you start," Allegra all but hissed at Elizabeth as the singer hit a note only a few unfortunate people and any dogs in the vicinity could hear, and everyone stood, clapped. "I mean it, Lizzie. I'll pinch you."

Elizabeth nodded, still blinking furiously, and politely clapped along with everyone else. "Wasn't that wonderful? Wasn't he talented?"

"Talented? Wonderful? The singer? Elizabeth, I had no idea you had a tin ear," Allegra said with a laugh, standing on tiptoe, hoping to see Armand and Bones heading in her direction, ready to rescue her, get her out of this room, this house, this nonsense.

And, like magic, Armand appeared, being the sort of man who seemed to move effortlessly through crowds of silk and satin and overfed flesh without problem.

"Since we arrived too late for much more than grabbing you two ladies the first seats we could find," he said, "now is the time for us to approach our hostess and offer our thanks for a truly enjoyable, uplifting experience. You've never heard the like, you'll hear the man's sweet voice in your ears for days and days, and so forth."

"Oh, piffle," Allegra said, mostly because Armand seemed to smile when she did. He smiled now. "Except that part about hearing the man's voice. I think that sound will follow me to my grave."

"Or," Armand offered, "we can say that you needed to return home at once, my lady, as you've got the headache, leaving Mr. Boothe here to make your apologies, and then escort Miss Elizabeth and Mrs. Tomlin?"

Elizabeth grabbed Allegra's arm with both hands, panic in her eyes. "You'd leave me? With just Mr. Boothe? Just the two of us?"

"And Mrs. Tomlin," Armand pointed out. "This will give you time to see Lady Chirton, renew your acquaintance. Oh, and to meet Mrs. Boothe."

If Elizabeth had looked panicked before, she was now as pale as the proverbial ghost, in real danger of swooning. "His wife?"

"His mother, Miss Elizabeth," Armand said, looking around the room. "Ah, there she is. The rather imposing-looking lady in the yellow turban who is, apparently and predictably, reading poor Bones yet another lecture. I believe she was sitting in front of you, as a matter of fact."

"Oh, marvelous," Allegra said flatly. "She turned around to shush us. Well, to shush me. Twice. I don't think she even looked at Elizabeth. Let's go meet her, cousin. This ought to be interesting."

"No!" Elizabeth blurted out. "No, Allegra, that's all right, you don't have to go. Really, you don't. Mr. Gauthier? If you could please take me over to Mr. Boothe and his mother? And then you and my cousin can be on your way."

She turned to frown at Allegra. "Where are you going, anyway? You shouldn't be out and about without a proper chaperone, you know. Oh, what am I saying?" she said, making a face. "That's precisely *why* you're doing it, isn't it?"

"I adore how well you've come to understand me, Elizabeth," Allegra said, pulling on her gloves. "But we won't leave the Square, I promise. Now, be a good little debutante, and smile prettily at Mr. Boothe while being gracious to his mama. I've every confidence you'll have them both dangling from your shoe strings before the afternoon is over."

"You do?" Elizabeth asked, flushing. "Oh, you're probably just saying that. But there's just some *something* about that man. He looks so . . . so *oppressed*."

"Yes, I've thought that same thing myself," Allegra agreed, winking at Gauthier.

Armand coughed into his fist, then quickly offered Elizabeth his arm, ready to escort her across the room, perform the introductions, first telling Allegra to stay where she was and he'd be right back to get her.

Allegra nodded, then felt a presence behind her, turned to see that Lettice had made her way from the row of chairs set up for companions and chaperones, and was now watching Elizabeth's progress.

"That's Matilda Boothe," she said quietly. "The woman could lead troops into battle, except she wouldn't need troops. One bellow from that mouth of hers, and Attila's soldiers would have run screaming for their mamas."

"You've met her, Letty?"

"Heard about her," Lettice said, craning her neck, the better to see what would happen next. "Stickler. High in the instep. Leads that son of hers around by a ring through his nose, just as she did the father—except when she wasn't looking. Oh, the things I could tell you about that man."

"Tell me," Allegra said, her eyes twinkling. Did Letty have any idea how different she sounded at the moment? How far she seemed from the black crow of respectability she presented to her mama?

"I think not," Lettice said, smiling. "But I am willing to wager that she would rather eat that silly turban than say a single civil word to a Nesbitt. Watch. When Mr. Gauthier does the introductions, we should be able to know the moment he says your cousin's name."

Allegra, rethinking her decision to set Elizabeth off on her own, took two quick steps in her cousin's direction, ready to rescue her.

"You don't want to do that, my lady," Lettice said, taking hold of her elbow, the chaperone once more. "Mr. Gauthier will handle everything, I'm sure."

"I don't *want* Gauthier to handle it, Letty," Allegra gritted out from between clenched teeth. "I sent Elizabeth over there, into the lion's mouth, and it's up to me to make it right."

"Yes, but I believe you may have forgotten your sword in your other reticule," Lettice said, her tone dripping sarcasm. "Look. Mrs. Boothe's complexion has just gone as red as those drapes over there. Ah, there goes her head, chin pointing toward the ceiling, the better to look down her nose on your cousin."

"Poor Lizzie. I'm going over there."

"No, no, don't do that. Mr. Gauthier will—well, I'll be damned for a tinker."

Allegra first turned to goggle at Lettice, unable to believe what she'd just heard the woman say, and then looked back to the quartet standing under the chandelier, a small island in the middle of a room suddenly gone silent. Watchful. Definitely eager to listen.

Which was fairly easy, as Mr. Boothe's voice was a quite clear and carrying baritone.

". . . what I just said, Mother, and repeat now, is that I will be escorting Miss Nesbitt to Armand's ball on Saturday evening, and would you care to accompany us, or would you prefer to sit at home, tending to your knitting?"

"My God," Allegra said quietly. "I hadn't thought that man would say boo to a goose."

Neither, apparently, had anyone else in the room, as everyone took a step forward, some of them whispering to each other, some of them smiling, rolling their eyes, and one of them—Allegra couldn't tell who it was—actually applauding, with real fervor and appreciation, as no one had done when the singer had taken his final bows.

"Come along, if you please," Armand said quietly, appearing beside her once more, Bones and Elizabeth tagging along right behind him, peeking back over their shoulders. "I think that turban is all that's holding her brains in place. Her head could explode at any moment, and I'd rather not watch."

They were all outside before, as the saying goes, the cat could lick her ear, at which time Armand gave Bones a congratulatory clap on the back that sent the man reeling toward the gutter.

Bones gathered himself together, tugged on the lapels of his coat, and goggled at Armand. "I said that? I heard that . . . but did I *say* that?"

"You said it, Bones, and beautifully. I'm proud of you."

Bones gave his lapels another tug, did something with his face that Allegra was pretty sure was his attempt at a smile. "Sometimes I amaze myself, Armand, I vow it. I said that? I stood up to her?"

And then his features crumbled into a frown—where they seemed to be more comfortable.

"Oh, good God, I *said* that. I'll go home tonight, Armand, to see my belongings stacked on the doorstep. What have I done?"

"Stood up for yourself, and most especially for Miss Elizabeth," Armand told him. "Let your mother know you wouldn't allow her to say anything cutting to Miss Elizabeth. Striking out for your own independence. All of that. And you're welcome to stay with me until you find somewhere else to lay your independent head. More than time to cut the leading strings, Bones."

Allegra, surprised at herself to realize she had protectively taken Elizabeth's hand in her own, stepped forward. "Thank you, Mr. Boothe. I thank you, and my cousin thanks you. Sir Galahad could not have defended the Nesbitt name any better with sword and shield. Elizabeth. Thank Mr. Boothe. Elizabeth?"

She turned to look at her cousin, then winced. The girl had such a silly, besotted look on her face that it was . . . well, it was embarrassing, that's what it was.

So she looked at Bartholomew Boothe. He looked, if that was possible, even sillier than Elizabeth, as the two ninnies stood there, just staring at each other.

"All right, Elizabeth, never mind. You can thank him later. When you locate your tongue, as well as your wits. Gauthier? Do you think we can continue with our plans now? Leave these two in Mrs. Tomlin's protection, and move on? Before my stomach turns entirely."

Chapter Ten

ARMAND LOOKED AT ALLEGRA, seeing that the flush of anger, and probably of bemusement, was still riding high on her cheeks as they walked toward entirely the opposite side of the Square than Bones and his ladies. Heart-whole herself, she had been dumbfounded by her cousin's lovesick behavior . . . rather as he had been watching Bones.

"Since I seem to be leading here, I probably should ask. Where are we going?"

"I haven't the faintest idea," she answered dully. "You know, Gauthier, I've lived my life in the country, and haven't seen a lot, so perhaps this means little to you. But I have to tell you honestly, I never saw anything like that in my life."

"Bones and your cousin? I believe they call that love at first sight, being pierced by Cupid's arrow. Nearly disgusting, isn't it?"

"Nearly? Oh, I'd say completely. Elizabeth was gaping at him like a positive looby, and I really believe Mr. Boothe had begun to *drool*."

She tipped her head up at him. "How does that happen? This love at first sight silliness? Do you think it's like an illness? Dear God, I hope it's not *catching*."

"I don't think you have to worry about that, Ally," he said, dropping into the easy familiarity she'd allowed him at their last meeting. "You seem to have remained free of any such affliction, in my presence at least."

"Well, I should hope so. And if I thought I'd have to

put in a turn acting like the village idiot to convince Oxie that he'd forced me into breaking my heart over you, Gauthier, I'd rather give up the whole idea. I can find other ways to punish him."

"Almost daily, I'd imagine, if you put your mind to it," Armand said, and meant it. "But to concentrate, just for a moment, on something you said, Ally. You think that people in love remind you of the village idiot?"

"Don't you? Or was I alone back there, and you didn't see what I saw? If that's really love. It might just be that the two of them had something go *sproing* inside their brain boxes when that singer hit one of his high notes. Oh, and before we move on to any other subjects, Gauthier, let me tell you that it will take some time for me to forgive you for Lady Chirton's invitation. I've heard more tuneful squawking in a barnyard."

"Signore Bellucci is all the rage," Armand teased. "Lady Chirton has scored a real coup, getting him here from the continent where, I understand, he has been royally feted. In fact, I imagine she is now the envy of half the ladies in Society."

"Society." Allegra all but spat the word. "Did you see those women, Gauthier? Powdered to look as if they're three days dead, then rouged. Feathers and turbans and silk and satins, all of it covering up bodies that remind me of the butcher and blacksmith in our village. Except the butcher and the blacksmith smelled better, and were probably two stone lighter than any of them."

"I'd say you weren't impressed. The ladies, I'm convinced, will be quite crushed."

"Under the wheels of a carriage, with any luck at all.

They spend their days getting ready for their nights, and only use their minds to think up ways to insult those they think beneath them. There's not a brain among them, I swear, Gauthier, not if they allow themselves to believe that singer we had to suffer through could carry a tune in a bucket. And these people have the gall to look down on my mother, on Oxie? How *dare* they!"

Armand would have answered Allegra, if he'd known what to say. Because she was right. Society could be mean, petty, and see only what they wanted to see in the mirror when they looked at themselves.

But that wasn't all of Society.

So he said that. "What you saw today, Ally, wasn't all of Society. There are some fine ladies and gentlemen. Poets, scholars, brave soldiers. I am proud to have many of them as my friends. Don't judge all of Society on your parents' experience, on one afternoon, on one unhappy old woman."

"Mrs. Boothe." Allegra sighed. "Letty said she leads Bones—Mr. Boothe—around with a ring through his nose. Is that true? Is that why he was so overset? Because he'd spoken up to his mother?"

"Call him Bones, Ally. He'd like that, especially now, if he thought you'd put in a good word for him with your cousin," Armand answered, smiling. "And, yes, it's true. Or it was. I must admit I'm amazed that Bones would finally stand up to her. I may have said some-thing to him, but I think it was your cousin who finally gave him the backbone to say what had to be said. Truly, I'm amazed."

"Not as amazed as Bones himself. He looked ready to

faint, once he'd realized what he'd done."

They moved out of the Square, stepped onto the flagway on Brook Street.

Allegra stopped, looked around. "Well, we won't flog that subject any longer, because it only upsets me. There seems to be enough people here for what I've got planned. Time for you to practice."

"Here?" Armand said, looking around the fairly wide street in the heart of Mayfair. He recognized nearly everyone on the flagways, populated mostly by gentlemen taking the air. "We're going to pull the prank here?"

"No, Gauthier, *you're* going to play the prank here. I'm going to watch. I'd do it myself, to show you how, except that no one listens to females." She looked up at him. "You did say you wanted to do this."

"I did? My memory is rather jumbled these last few days. Will I have to carry any pieces of furniture?"

"No," Allegra said, grinning as she reached into her reticule. "This is just a simple prank, just to get your toes wet, as it were, before you go off with Oxie. He taught it to me when I was no more than five. You can do this, Gauthier. I have everything you need right here."

He watched as she pulled out a length of heavy string, handed it to him.

"I'll just move back here, into the alleyway, if you don't mind, out of the way, and watch. You, Gauthier, pick a gentleman of your choosing, approach him, and tell him that you're on a mission, something, from the royal whatever, and you've been charged with taking measurements along this street."

"Measurements? Of what?"

"No, no, no, Gauthier. Never too many details. People begin to smell a hum if there are too many details. You must just be firm, and authoritative, and act as if you know exactly what you're doing."

"Fine, good," Armand said, nodding. Then he grinned at her. "What am I doing?"

She rolled her eyes at him. "What you're doing, Gauthier, is just what I said. You're taking measurements for the royal something-or-other. I'm not going to do everything for you. Surely you can make some of this up on your own? You will ask the gentleman you've chosen if he will do you the immense favor of assisting you in your charge by holding one end of the string for you."

Armand looked at the gentlemen passing by the alleyway. He saw an earl, two viscounts, and a royal duke and his entourage.

"You want me to ask one of these gentlemen?"

"As Oxie would be the first to tell you, you're in London, and London is chock-full of wonderful targets. What fun would it be, Gauthier, to prank a chimney sweep? I'm sure that's why Oxie's here, to match his wits against all these toplofty peers who think they're smarter, better, than anyone else. It's more of a challenge. And more of a triumph, I'd imagine."

"Good point, good point," he said, nodding his agreement.

"Thank you. Now, if I might continue?"

"I wouldn't stop you for the earth, my dear," Armand said, truly enjoying himself.

"Piffle. Now, you position the gentleman precisely where you want him—I'd make something of a business about that, if I were you—and hand him one end of the string. Then, once that is finished, you repeat what you've just done with another gentleman, preferably one some distance from the first gentleman. It's a long string."

"Hopefully not long enough for me to hang myself with this prank. And then?"

"And then, Mister Faint of Heart, you come back here, and I'll tell you what happens after that. Now, go on. I guarantee that you'll enjoy yourself."

Armand looked at the coiled length of string, looked at the gentlemen on the strut in their high collars, curly brimmed beaver hats, wasp-waisted jackets, impeccable hose. He knew these men, liked most of them, tolerated the rest of them, wished none of them ill will.

And, if he wanted to stay in Society, he would do nothing to upset any of them.

"And you'll stay here?"

"Right here. I promise."

Armand nodded, began to walk away, stopped, turned to her once more. "And you'll behave? I'm playing this prank on two other people, correct? You're not really playing a prank on me?"

"Why, Gauthier, you don't trust me?"

"It pains me to say this, but not with my back turned, no."

"Oh, would you just *go,*" Allegra said, shaking her head.

Armand smiled. He felt good. He felt, he knew immediately, better than he had in more than a year, perhaps more than he had since coming to this damp island, trying to insert himself into a life it was entirely possible he did not really enjoy.

"Wish me luck," he said, taking aim at one gentleman in particular, and once more setting off on his mission.

"Gauthier! Heard you was back in town. Pity Roxbury couldn't pry himself loose from that new wife of his. M'wife told me you're hosting a ball. What? This Saturday, isn't it? Yes, that has to be it. She's all aflutter, Gauthier, which is the same as to say this ball of yours is going to cost me a small fortune in ribbons and gewgaws. I say, what's that in your hand?"

Armand looked at his hand. "String, my lord?"

"Yes, yes, not blind, you know," the Earl of Buckhaven said. "What's it for?"

"Oh, nothing," Armand said, rather protectively cradling the string with both hands, having decided on his strategy. "A small service I'm doing for . . . well, I was sworn to secrecy, as a matter of fact. Bringing in a crew of workmen would be too obvious, so I've been— well, as I said, sir, I'm doing a small service."

"Secrecy, eh?" His lordship leaned closer, so that Armand could smell the gin that was always a part of the man's toilette. "I like the sound of that. Now come, give over. What are you doing?"

"I can't say, not directly, but—" Armand looked to his left, to his right, then gave a crooked, "come closer" sort of hand gesture to the earl. "You know how it is, my lord. The man is always planning some new folly. Look at Carleton House. Look at that nonsense in Brighton.

Look at that enduring shambles at the bottom of Portland Place, definitely look there, my lord. Ripping down, building up."

"Prinney?" the earl said, both eyebrows climbing his forehead. "You're talking about Prinney, aren't you? More building? He's going to be ripping down Brook Street next? Good God, man, why? Hasn't he dug up enough debt for everyone? What does he plan? Another crescent? A new square? A man could make a small fortune, Gauthier, if he knew just what, where, to put his blunt. Always said these were tumbledown buildings, ready for nothing but hacking to pieces so something better could be built."

"Is that so, my lord," Armand said, pressing the looped-up string from one palm to the other, as if he were flattening a cake for the oven—neatly calling attention to the string once more.

"Measuring, Gauthier? That's what you're doing, ain't it?"

"I didn't say that, my lord. In fact, I would have to say, if anyone should ever ask, that we never had this conversation. Now, if you'll excuse me."

He turned away, actually took two steps, before wheeling about, striking a pose as he looked at the earl. "I say, my lord, would it be too much to hope that you might—no, I won't ask."

"Ask, ask," the earl urged helpfully. "Not one to shirk assisting the Crown, not me. And God knows I can keep a secret."

"Well . . . in that case, my lord. Do you see that man over there? Because I fear I need the help of two assistants. Shame I didn't think of it sooner."

The earl squinted, looked across the street. "Lovelace? You've told him? Good God, man, his tongue's hinged at both ends. Tell him, and it will be all over Mayfair before supper tonight."

"Not yet, my lord, no, I haven't told him. Do you have another suggestion?"

"Stap me, man, of course I do. Can see Prinney picked the wrong man for this intrigue. Lucky thing you found me. Look, over there, see that beggar? How he's allowed on this street is beyond me, but he's good enough. Perfect. We'll use him."

Ah. His lordship now believed himself a part of the conspiracy. How helpful.

"Very good, my lord. I think that can be arranged. Now, are you sure you wish to do this?"

"Absolutely," the earl said, holding out his hand.

Sheep. The world was full of sheep.

"Here you go then, my lord," Armand said, handing the earl one end of the string. Then, just because he couldn't resist, he solemnly added, "And may I say, sir, a grateful monarch thanks you."

"Yes, yes, just don't tell him, that's all. Don't tell *anybody*. I know I won't."

Armand smiled. "Yes, my lord, I have every confidence that you won't."

He then stepped out onto the roadway that was mostly free of carriages and the like at this time of the afternoon, unrolling the string behind him, allowing it to lie on the ground as he mounted the opposite flagway, approached the beggar.

The man held out his hand. "A penny, kind sir?"

"Oh, I think that could be arranged," Armand said, fishing in the small pocket in his waistcoat, pulling out a few coins. "But I ask something in return. A personal service for me, if you don't mind."

"'Ere naow, Oi ain't one 'o dem man milliners, yer knows. Oi gots m'pride. Take yerself to the Garden, iffen it be a pretty boy yer after."

"Not that sort of service, my good man," Armand assured him. "I'm in need of someone to hold this end of string for, oh, ten minutes. Nothing more."

He held out the coins in one hand, the string in the other, and turned to look at the earl, who was nodding in some satisfaction. Oh, what an obedient man he was, taking direction from the earl, who seemed to now believe this entire exercise to be his own idea.

If he were to listen closely, Armand swore he'd probably be able to hear the earl *baaa*. He could never be Oxie Nesbitt, but he was beginning to understand the thrill the fellow got from hoaxing his fellow man. Rather like bluffing at cards, but quite a different ante.

"But not here," Armand told the beggar, knowing he had to do something at least reasonably official-looking. He looked up at the building directly in front of him, then cupped his hands around his eyes, peered down the street. Took hold of the beggar by the shoulders, carefully positioned him three feet to his left, looked down the street once more, adjusted the beggar's stance once more, then smiled, as if declaring himself satisfied.

"Jist 'old dis 'ere bit o'string?" the beggar said as Armand handed him the end.

"For ten minutes, yes," Armand said as he pulled the string tight, so that it was now stretched across the street, at least three feet above the cobbles. The thought crossed his mind that he could have tied small, colorful streamers to it in places, just for the effect of the thing.

"An' dat dere flash cove 'olds ta t'other end? Coo, imagine dat." The beggar gave the earl a jolly wave.

The earl, bless him, waved back.

"How perceptive of you, yes," Armand said, giving the beggar's position one last adjustment. "Good man."

With a jaunty salute to the earl as he passed him on his way back to the alleyway, Armand rejoined Allegra. "Well, that was more fun than I'd expected. Now what?"

"How long before another carriage or whatever makes its way down the street?" she asked him.

He shrugged. "At this hour? Everyone is either strolling on foot, or parked in a club somewhere. I'd say at least ten minutes. That's how long the beggar promised to hold the string, by the way."

"Yes, I saw that. It's rather cheating, hiring a dupe. But, as this is your first time, I suppose it's all right. Do you see that man behind us, at the far end of the alley? The one carrying a tray?"

Armand, who had been watching the earl as that man importantly held the string taut, connecting himself to the beggar, glanced down the alley. "A meat pie seller on Robert Street. What of him? Is he a part of the prank? I thought you were going to tell me what happens next. So far, I just have two men holding a string."

"Yes, that's exactly what you have, Gauthier. And

that's enough, don't you think? As for us, I'd say what we could do next is for you to nip off down the alley, at which time you can buy me a meat pie, as I got no refreshments at Lady Chirton's. Then we can stand here safely out of sight in this alleyway, and watch what happens next."

Armand looked at the earl once more, saw the man earnestly explaining to two other gentlemen precisely what he was doing standing at attention on the flagway, holding one end of a length of string. So much for secrecy.

His shoulders began to shake. "You know what he's doing, Ally? He's telling the whole world that he's doing a private service for the Prince Regent."

"Oh, very good. The Prince Regent, himself? I knew you'd think of a tolerable story." She cocked her head to one side, blinked at him. "Gauthier? The meat pie? Or have you forgotten?"

"Your father was right. You do get prickly when you need to be fed. Oh, all right, I'll be back directly," he said, all but running down the alley to purchase one of the greasy pies. He was back within moments, and peered out from the safety of the alley, to see what had transpired in his absence.

"How did—?"

"How did the beggar lose his end of the string? That is what you're asking, isn't it?"

"That, and how the end of the string got to be in Sir Arthur Greeley's hand, yes. Last time I looked, he was standing with the earl."

"Your Sir Arthur paid him to let go, naturally," Allegra

said, unwrapping the pie and taking a healthy bite. "Um, delicious."

Gauthier waited, impatiently, while she chewed, then swallowed, before continuing: "The beggar held out for a bit before he agreed. I believe the man will be living fairly high on the hog until he drinks all his new fortune away."

Just then, a dray wagon loaded to the gills with casks came lumbering down the street.

"Good God, man, *no!* This is a disaster!" he heard Buckhaven bellow as he pushed his companion—a very well-dressed man Armand couldn't immediately place—into the street, smack in front of the slow-moving wagon. "Stop him, Reggie. Stop him!"

"'Ey! Wot's yer doin'?" the driver of the wagon called out, reining in his huge horses, pushing the wooden brake forward, then quickly, and angrily, hopping down off his seat. He was the size of a mountain, and he was pushing up his sleeves, showing off forearms as big as Armand's thighs. "Yer gets outta m'way."

"Don't let him pass, Reggie, whatever the cost," the earl warned, his eye still on the string, careful not to move so much as an inch, obviously for fear of throwing off Armand's measurements.

Sir Arthur joined the chorus: "I'm not moving from this spot, I swear it. Reggie!"

Reggie looked at the hulking driver, looked at the string. Then he turned to the earl. "Freddie? Here's a puzzler for you, if you don't mind. What the devil are we measuring?"

The earl opened his mouth to speak, looked around—

obviously trying to locate Armand, who was pressed against the bricks beside Allegra. "Where's Gauthier? He was here a minute ago," he said, confusion in his voice. "Stap me, man, I don't know. I *don't know!*"

"Freddie, you *ass!*" Sir Arthur said, throwing down his end of the string.

The earl held his end, now hanging loose, for a few moments, then dropped it as if it had turned red-hot.

The man named Reginald Underwood—Armand recognized him now, one of Society's hangers-on, but not a stupid man—smiled at the wagon driver, tipped his curly brimmed beaver, and quickly walked out of the street.

It was all Armand could take. He grabbed Allegra's hand—the last of her meat pie went flying—and pulled her toward Robert Street. They ran, hand in hand, laughing like mischievous children.

They finally stopped near the end of the shaded alley, and Armand pulled her with him as he leaned back against the cool bricks, laughing so hard he thought he just might hurt himself.

His arms around Allegra, their bodies pressed close together, half holding each other up, he said, "Did—did you see the *look* on the earl's face?"

"As if he'd stuck his thumb in his Christmas pie, and pulled out a hulking great elephant?" Allegra said, laughing along with him.

"God knows how long they would have stood there, if that wagon hadn't come along. Probably until pigeons began perching on their heads. All their consequence, Ally, their titles, their fine clothes—and just *standing* there, holding two ends of the same silly piece of string, feeling important and smug."

"And all without the faintest notion *why*," Allegra added, holding on to his upper arms for balance. "Oh, Gauthier, my sides hurt. You know those men will hate you now. They won't *say* anything to anybody, or else look complete fools, but they'll never speak to you again."

"I know, and I'm crushed, really. So crushed, I think I may just have to start wearing a bow made of string on my lapel when I go out in the evening. Everyone will ask about it, and I'll just have to say that the Earl of Buckhaven swore me to secrecy."

They laughed again. But, slowly, that laughter died away, as they both realized that they were somehow standing chest to chest, neatly locked into an embrace.

"This," Armand said quietly, bracing his hands against her slim shoulders, "is not a good thing."

Unbelievably, he saw a spark of pure mischief flash in Allegra's green eyes. "You mean being here, Gauthier, in the alleyway?"

"You know what I mean."

"Oh, you mean standing here, like this?"

"Ally . . ."

Her grin lit the entire dim alley. "Why, Gauthier. I don't believe this. You're afraid of me."

He resisted the urge to blurt: "I am not!" Instead, he decided to call her bluff, answer what had to be her challenge to him.

"I could kiss you, you know," he said, his grip tightening on her shoulders, so that he could feel the heat of her body, just as he could feel her softness, pressed against his chest.

"You wouldn't dare," she answered cheekily. "You're a gentleman."

"You think so?" he drawled, pushing one leg slightly forward, insinuating it between hers. "You know, Ally, you aren't the first to make that mistake."

And then, as her eyes widened, he slanted his mouth against hers.

When he stepped back a few moments later, he wasn't quite sure if he felt her trembling under his hands, or if it was he who trembled.

"Well," she said quietly, after lightly licking her lips—and weakening his knees with the innocent yet alluring gesture, "that was interesting, wasn't it? Could . . . could we try that again?"

"That, Ally, would not be a good idea."

"Oh, piffle," she said so vehemently that he blinked. "If you're no gentleman, Gauthier, I'm no lady. I'm just a country girl, with the normal country girl's curiosity. Society's rules are for Society's ladies, not me."

"You're the daughter of an earl," he pointed out, realizing that he was in no hurry to push her away, break this intimate contact.

"I'm Oxie's daughter," she said. "You could hang a thousand titles around his neck, and he'd still be Oxie, and I'd still be his daughter. And I'm proud of it, and him. Oh, drat it, Gauthier—come here."

He felt her hands reaching behind his neck, grabbing at him, pulling him toward her.

He wasn't an idiot. He allowed himself to be pulled.

He dropped his hands from her shoulders, entwined them around her waist, half lifted her to her toes so that he could crush her against him.

Her mouth was warm, moist, and he sensed the hint of a smile curving her lips.

Minx. She thought she had shocked him, had tied him all in knots.

Maybe it was time he took control of this particular situation.

He eased his mouth from hers for a moment, then captured her again, this time insinuating his tongue between her lips, probing at the soft, wet warmth of her.

He heard her sharp, hissing intake of breath, felt her stiffen beneath his hands. But she didn't struggle to be free of him.

Bless the girl, she also didn't have the faintest idea what to do with her own tongue. She might protest that she was no lady, just a simple country miss, but she was about as experienced in lovemaking as a newborn babe.

So he showed her what to do. By his example, by running the tip of his tongue along her teeth, by skimming his tongue over the roof of her mouth, by gently sucking at her, until instinct overrode lack of experience, and she allowed him access to her tongue—challenged it to a duel with her own.

She was a quick learner.

And his knees got weaker.

"Coo! Don't see dat everyday."

Armand stiffened at the meat pie seller's words, and he reined in his desire, and his brain—which had left the alleyway long since—pushing Allegra away from him slightly, then cradling her head against his chest, shielding her face from view.

"If you ever want to see anything else again, my good man, I'd suggest you find yourself another corner," he said to the meat pie seller, who was gone before Armand had finished his threat.

He felt Allegra's shoulders shaking and knew without being told that she wasn't crying, weeping in embarrassment. She was laughing.

"Stop that," he told her, grabbing on to her shoulders and moving her sideways, so that he could escort her onto Robert Street. He couldn't chance Brook Street again, not because of the duped gentlemen, who were probably long gone, but because he knew Allegra's lips would be red, and puffy, and everyone would know he'd just kissed her senseless in the alley.

"Oh, Gauthier, don't be mean," she said, playfully pushing her hip against his before stepping away, positioning herself in front of him, tipping up her head to look at him in the dimness. Nearly dancing, like a delighted wood sprite.

God. He'd been right. She looked thoroughly kissed. And eminently kissable. Stronger men than he would have chanced life and limb to kiss her again.

"You know," he said, forcing himself to come to his senses, "I think I've just been used."

"Used?" She shook her head. "In what way?"

"I don't know yet," he answered honestly. "I'm already helping you with your prank against your father, so it can't be that. Perhaps you're just curious, like a cat, and these last few minutes have been in the way of an experiment."

She bent her head, avoiding his eyes. "And if it was an experiment?"

Armand took a breath, let it out slowly. "Then I don't think I like it," he said honestly. "Contrary to what you've learned at your father's knee, my lady, all of life is not a joke. People can be hurt."

At that, her head jerked upward. Her cheeks had gone pale, her eyes wide. "A joke? Is that what you—? You think I'd—? Oh, you big *dope!* I thought we were friends."

"Friends? What sort of friends?"

She lifted her shoulders, shook her head. "I don't know. But don't you want to find out?"

"Yes," he admitted honestly, "I do. But there are constraints, rules. It's not proper for us to—oh, bloody hell, Ally. You know damn well that I can't be kissing you, holding you, without also marrying you. Maybe somewhere other than here, in Mayfair, where the rules aren't so stringent but—no, it's just not fair to you."

"To me? Fair to *me?* Why is it that men can do what they want, but women must sit in a corner with their watercolors? This is just a body, Gauthier," she said, spreading her arms to indicate her slim frame. "Why shouldn't I find out why I have it?"

"Because," Armand said with a shake of his own head, "that would make you a harlot. Oh, and since you're an earl's daughter, it makes me a debaucher into the bargain. Not that I'm not interested."

"Oh, piffle. You're just a coward. I'm deeply disappointed in you, Gauthier," she said, then turned on her heels and walked ahead of him to the corner.

Feeling the fool—which he was rather becoming used to feeling—he chased after her, this shapely little scrap with the honey-gold hair and the determined mind. "Ally—wait. You can't go marching through London alone. Ah, you've stopped. Thank God you've got some sense."

"I was merely getting my bearings, Gauthier. I turn left now, correct?"

"Turning you over my knee sounds more reasonable, but yes, we turn left. Now, take my arm, and try not to do anything else outrageous until I get you home again, at which time I think I'm going to crawl back to my own house and lie down in a dark room with a cool rag on my forehead."

She laughed. Looked up at him. Turned his knees to water yet again. "It was nice, wasn't it? Go on, admit it. You want to do it again. Oh, I really do like you, Gauthier, I really do. You're . . . you're an education."

"Wonderful," he muttered as they walked along. "Have you deliberately set out to be ruined?"

"Ruined," she repeated in disgust. "Nobody calls a gentleman ruined, if he keeps a thousand women. And it's not as if I intend to marry, ever—not to any high-nosed stickler of Society who'd soon want nothing more than to hide me away in the country, where I wouldn't embarrass him. But does that mean I should forgo every pleasure? I just wanted to know what I might be missing, that's all. And I do like you, so I thought you wouldn't mind."

"Well, I do mind," Armand told her. "Are you really serious?"

"I don't know. I only thought of this back there, in the alleyway, and I do have this terrible habit of speaking my mind before I really know my mind. But, yes, I think so."

"And if I were to refuse? Would you go after the next man you met?"

She stopped dead on the flagway, glared at him. "How could you even *think* that! I picked *you.*"

"I'm . . . flattered," Armand said, knowing he was getting in too deep. "As a matter of fact, I—"

"Armand? *Armand!* You sly old sea horse! Thought it was you, boyo. And who was it said you was dead?"

Armand froze in his tracks, slowly turned around to see his past bounding toward him from across the street. The older Irishman's face was split in a huge grin beneath his mop of graying red hair, and his ill-fitting suit could do little to disguise either his broad shoulders or his bowed legs. *All the better to climb the mast, don't you know.* That's what Colin always said, with a wink of one Irish green eye.

"Conor," he said, clasping the man's hand strongly in his. "What are you doing in London?"

"You know how it is, boyo. Sail long enough, and you'll be making every port. Have to make a penny now and again, and with the Captain off on one of his starts, I set out on m'own. But it's not the same, boyo, not the same. What ship are you with? I'm here on the *Orleans.*"

"I'm not—please, let me introduce you to Lady

Allegra Nesbitt, daughter of the Earl of Sunderland. Lady Allegra, an old acquaintance of mine, Conor O'Neill."

He watched as Allegra held out her hand to Conor, smiled at him as the seaman took her hand, gave it a mighty shake, and then frowned as Conor looked at him.

Armand sent up a quick, silent prayer that the man would keep his mouth shut.

So much for prayers.

"An earl's daughter? And would you be looking at those clothes, now? Armand, you sly one, you sure landed on your feet, didn't you, boyo? And here we all were, sure they'd hang you soon as look at you."

Chapter Eleven

*A*LLEGRA BRUSHED PAST the bowing servant holding open the door for her and headed directly for the stairs, lifting her skirts a good three inches above her ankles and taking those stairs two at a time.

Behind her, unknown to her, the appreciative young footman silently thanked his lucky stars for his clear eyesight.

She barely hesitated as she came to the wide first-floor landing, quickly turning to her left and making a dead set for the drawing room. She pushed back the pocket doors and burst into the room, already calling out, "Letty? We have to talk—now!"

But it was only her cousin Elizabeth who rose from her seat on one of the couches, and headed toward her, hands fluttering. "Allegra, dear cousin. I've been waiting for you. I have such *news!*"

Allegra looked around the otherwise empty room. "Not now, Elizabeth. Where's Letty?"

"Letty? Oh, you mean Ms. Tomlin?" Elizabeth shrugged. "Somewhere in Bond Street, with Aunt Magdalen, I should imagine. Your mama actually asked to be taken to the shops this afternoon. Something about reading something in some book, then deciding that women of her age are obliged to wear turbans into Society. I so hope she doesn't mean like Mrs. Boothe."

"Mama? In a turban?" Allegra, momentarily diverted, sniffed in amusement. "She wouldn't dare. And if she thinks to stick a feather in it, I'll just have to have Oxie lock her in her rooms until she reconsiders, comes to her senses. Now, when will they be back? When did they leave? Elizabeth? Hello. You aren't answering me."

Elizabeth tipped her head to one side, looking at her cousin. "You look . . . you look different. Flushed. And there's something about your lips. Oh, dear. Did you get stung by a bee? I did that once, you know, right on my lip, and I had to stay hidden away in my room for two days, until it went down again. Should I send one of the servants out for some dirt? You spit in it, turn it into mud, and then pat it on the puffiness, to help draw out the stinger. I'll just go now and—"

Allegra raised a hand to her mouth, scrubbed at her lips for a second. "I wasn't stung. There's nothing wrong with my lips."

"No? But there is something, Allegra. You're almost . . . dewy."

"I just ran up the stairs, Elizabeth," Allegra told her firmly. "I'm sweating."

"Ladies don't sweat. They don't even perspire. They become dewy. Mama told me so," her cousin said, then shook her head, obviously discarding the subject for the one she preferred. "Mr. Boothe walked me back to the mansion, Allegra."

"I believe that had been the plan, yes," Allegra said, going over to the drinks table, just to open the silver bucket and scoop some ice into a glass, add a splash of lemonade from a crystal carafe. Bless Oxie for his single affectation as a wealthy earl, that of always having precious ice at the ready. The man actually had it carted in from the countryside, packed in straw.

"I know, I know, that's what you'd planned, but he was so very *nice* about it. We didn't come directly back here, but strolled the Square for a good quarter hour. Mrs. Tomlin came back on her own, as Mr. Boothe assured me that would be proper, as we weren't going to leave the Square. Although I didn't see you and Mr. Gauthier the whole time."

"It's a big Square. Almost huge," Allegra said, talking around the soothing ice chips on her tongue.

Her *tongue.* Oh, God! Why hadn't anyone ever told her tongues could do that? Then again, who would tell her? Her mama? And who could she ask? Again—her mama?"

Oh, where was Letty! The woman had slipped earlier today, said "damned for a tinker." Black crow gowns or not, this woman, Allegra felt certain, knew about tongues. *She* hadn't been sleeping in the country for the past nearly nineteen years, then never getting dressed without checking to make sure Oxie hadn't filled her half-boots with porridge, Allegra just knew it. Letty Tomlin had *lived*.

Allegra thought about going to her room, pacing until Letty returned, but knew she had to be polite, inquire about Elizabeth's day. Besides, she was interested. Good gracious, who wouldn't be?

"So, cousin, if it wouldn't be telling tales, what did you and Mr. Boothe talk about as you walked?"

Elizabeth, who had returned to the couch, sat looking at the twined hands in her lap. "Oh, we didn't *talk*. Not really. We . . . we just *walked*."

She looked up at her cousin. "He's so sweet. And quite handsome, don't you think?"

Allegra involuntarily swallowed a rather large chip of ice, her eyes immediately watering as she coughed, hoped she wouldn't choke. "Hand—handsome? Oh. Oh, yes, of course. The man is as close to a Greek god as I've seen outside of picture books."

"You really think so?" Elizabeth's face was flushed with color.

Be good, a voice whispered in Allegra's head. *It's you who has had a horrible day, not Elizabeth. And, after all, one woman's walking scarecrow could very well be another woman's golden Adonis.*

"Handsome yes. So tall . . . and . . . and so . . . so tall," Allegra confirmed. She turned her back for a moment, in the pretense of pouring herself more lemonade, and crossed her eyes.

"And so brave," Elizabeth went on, oblivious to

178

Allegra's attempt to keep from laughing out loud. "The way he stood up to his mama, telling her she could just stay away from Mr. Gauthier's ball if she didn't like the idea that he was going to escort me there."

She leaned back against the cushions, sighed deeply. "Defending me because I'm a Nesbitt, here with your parents, and ignored by so many. But not by Mr. Boothe. Oh, no. He defies convention, ignores Uncle Oxie's horrid reputation, and tells his mama that he's escorting me to the ball. He's like a knight in shining armor."

"How brave of him. Tell me, Elizabeth, do you happen to know what we'll be served for dinner tonight?"

"Dinner? Oh, no. I'm sorry, I don't. Why do you ask, Allegra?"

"Because I won't be eating it," Allegra said, rolling her eyes. "For some reason, since entering this room, my appetite is well and truly gone."

"Yours, too?" Elizabeth sort of wriggled about on the seat of the couch. "I vow, the butler brought me tea and cakes earlier, and I couldn't touch so much as a *bite*. I'm much too happy to eat. Oh! I forgot, Allegra. I want to tell you my other news. Aunt Magdalen and Mrs. Tomlin were gone when I returned home, but they left a note. Mr. Odo Pinabel will be here at ten tomorrow morning for our waltz lesson. Isn't that famous!"

Allegra pressed her hands to either side of her head and paced the length of the carpet. If she answered her cousin, maybe the bird-witted creature would shut up, and then maybe Allegra's head wouldn't throb so badly.

"Wonderful, Elizabeth. As a matter of fact, I can't think of anything more wonderful."

Oblivious, as usual, Elizabeth sat and preened. "I shall waltz with Mr. Boothe. His hand in mine, mine in his as I hold up my skirt—there are these little *loops* attached to skirts now, I'll have to be sure I have one on my ball gown—and we go whirling, whirling, *whirling* around the floor. His other hand so lightly touching my back. It is all *so* intimate."

Allegra thought of her stolen moments in the alleyway. "Cousin, you wouldn't recognize *intimate* if it came up and nipped you on your—oh, never mind. When did they leave, do you think?" she asked, nearly running to one of the windows overlooking the Square. "Shouldn't they be back by now? I really have to talk to Letty."

"I'm sure there's something wrong, cousin. You're acting very strangely. I know you said you were fine, but I really think you're upset."

Still looking out the window, Allegra smiled. Upset? She looked upset?

She'd allowed Armand Gauthier to kiss her. She'd kissed him. She'd all but begged him to do more than kiss her. That was bad. That was very bad. But then there'd been Conor O'Neill. And *that* had been very much worse.

Upset? Yes, she was upset. But that's the least that she was. There probably had not yet been a word invented that described how she really felt.

Still, she hadn't known her cousin to be a master of the understatement. What possibly could have given her away? Perhaps she'd begun to foam at the mouth. Even Elizabeth couldn't help but notice *that.*

She really had to calm down, regain control over herself. It wasn't like her to let anyone know how she felt about anything.

Allegra slowly turned around, grabbing back at the windowsill with a white-knuckled grip, and faced her cousin. Smiled. "Wrong? No. I already told you, Elizabeth. Nothing's wrong. Nothing at all, really. What could be wrong?"

Elizabeth spread her hands. "Well, you were with Mr. Gauthier. Perhaps he upset you in some way?"

"No," Allegra said under her breath, "that shoe is fairly well on the other foot, at least for the most of it." Then she walked back over to the couches, sat down across the table from her cousin.

She felt about to burst.

She couldn't talk to her mama about Gauthier because her mama wouldn't understand. She couldn't talk to Letty, because that woman wasn't here. But Elizabeth was here. Elizabeth was nearly of an age with her. Elizabeth was even in love, or so she thought. Perhaps she could talk to Elizabeth, her cousin and new friend.

"We did argue, yes."

"Oh, no!" Elizabeth leaned forward, her expression all concern. Uncomfortably close to horrified.

Allegra found herself wanting to hug her cousin, who really was being sweet. She had badly misjudged the girl, because Elizabeth cared. Lord bless the girl, she really *cared.*

"Allegra! Does that mean we won't be going to the

ball? Oh, how *could* you! I'll just *die* if we aren't going to the ball!"

It was only after she'd slammed the door to her bedchamber that Allegra realized that *she* had been the one to run crying from the drawing room this time.

She never cried. And she most certainly never bolted from a room, sobbing into her hands, like some ninny. What was happening to her?

All she had done was to come to town, meet Armand Gauthier, and her entire world had turned upside down.

Conor O'Neill slouched on one brocade couch, his booted feet propped on the low table, a water tumbler three-quarters full of wine in one hand.

"I'm telling you, boyo, I keep waiting for some starched shirt to come charging in here, telling us to get our mangy selves out to the gutter where we belong," he told Armand, who sat on the facing couch, feeling overdressed, overfed, overfinanced, and somehow disloyal as he longed to ask Conor to remove his scruffy boots before the table was scratched.

"You don't have to worry about that, Conor," he told his old friend. "This is all mine. Really."

Conor dropped his head back on the couch, looked up at the chandelier hanging overhead. "It's like you died and went to heaven, boyo. All yours? I don't think the Captain lives this well. Hells bells, I know it. Bet you even have those water closet things in here, don't you now? Beats pissing off a deck all hollow, don't it?"

Armand smiled. "I imagine some would say we could use the balconies overlooking the Square, but I think

Society might frown on us. Now tell me, Conor, how is the Captain? When did you last see him?"

"Two years? Who counts, boyo?" Conor put his feet down, sat forward, and began pulling at his badly tied neckcloth. "Took this here mess of clothes as part of my bounty years ago. They fit then, don't now that I'm eating better, feeling worse. But I wore 'em anyways, seeing as how I was walking about town, seeing what I could see. Never thought I'd see you though, boyo. Not after the Captain turned you off."

"He didn't turn me off, Conor," Armand corrected. "Not that it was a mutual agreement for me to go my own way. You know the Captain. When he has an idea, it's good as done. He told me I had a duty to go to England, so I've come to England."

"And landed yourself in one deep gravy boat, boyo," Conor said, gulping down more wine. "So you found 'em, did you?"

"No, I didn't," Armand said, shaking his head. "As a matter of fact, I've about given up on that one. It was more the Captain's idea than my own, anyway. I've actually been giving some thought to going home."

"Home, is it? And where, I'm asking, would that be, boyo? Tossed out of Orleans, tossed out of Barataria, tossed out of Santo Domingo, out of everywhere. One minute we're patriots, and the next we're filthy pirates and no one wants to know us. It's good you left, boyo. There's nothing back there you'd want to see, not anymore. The *bos* is working for the Mexicans now, sad to say."

"It's that bad?"

"Worse than that. Most of the mates are scattered, and the rest are dead. Excepting those who went with the Captain, and none of them were happy about that. It's just that there was nowhere else to go. I heard that even Beluche and Dominique Youx have gone their own way now, if you can believe that, leaving the *bos* to surround himself with the scum of the earth. And then there's Old Rummy. He got himself hitched to some widow woman in Orleans. Says she worked some of that voodoo on him, but I know better. The man saw himself a soft cushion for his old bones, and took it."

Conor had referred to the Captain as the *bos*.

How long had it been since he'd heard that?

How long had it been since he'd last seen the *bos* relaxing in his hammock beneath shady trees on the edge of a bayou, strumming his mandolin?

How long since he'd stood beside the *bos* on a rolling deck, felt the salt spray on his face, heard that blood-stirring cry coming from high in the masts: "Merchant to starboard, riding low in the water!" Then the flag would be run up, and the chase would be on.

Those days were over, those days that had been his life for as long as he could remember, since before the age where he could remember. Yet, he had no great wish to return to that particular part of his life. After Orleans, the Captain had seen that, and tossed him out, wresting a promise from him that he'd come here to England, to London.

"I miss New Orleans," Armand said, not realizing he'd spoken out loud. "I've thought . . . a house like this? Why here? Why not upriver, along the bayous out-

184

side of Orleans?"

"Boyo?"

"Hmm?" Armand said, shaking himself back to the moment. "I'm sorry, Conor. Did you ask me something?"

"And that I did. Twice, as a matter of fact," Conor said, grinning at him. "But mayhap you don't want to be telling me about the lady. A real looker, boyo. Daughter to an earl? Never saw the likes of that one in Barataria, don't you know. First lass I've seen in years has all her own teeth."

Armand didn't know why, but Conor's words struck him as hilarious. He threw back his head and laughed, a full-throated sound that did a lot to ease the tension he'd felt tightening inside his chest for months.

Allegra listened for footsteps, then yanked open her bedchamber door and grabbed Lettice Tomlin by the elbow, dragged her inside the room and shut the door, leaned against it.

"My lady?" Lettice said, unruffled. "Is it possible you wish to speak with me?"

"Where have you been?"

"Oh, let's see, where was I?" Lettice said, walking over to the elaborate vanity and sitting down with her back to Allegra. She touched at her hair, leaned forward to inspect the hairline, actually. Not that Allegra took much notice of the action.

"Ah, yes, I remember now. I've had a busy day, all in all. Italian singers, rebellious sons, giggling idiots, and all topped off by a visit to Bond Street, at which time your mother, dear lady that she is, had a near apoplexy at hearing very ordinary prices for kid gloves here in our not always fair metropolis."

She swiveled on the bench seat of the vanity and smiled at Allegra. "I told her I'd heard that some shop-keepers price by the finger, and she delighted everyone in the shop by stating, quite loudly as a matter of fact, that her Aunt Beulah, who lost one arm to the elbow in an accident involving an angry brown spaniel and a kitchen fireplace turning wheel—I didn't ask for details—would have approved. Oh, yes, a quite lovely day."

"That's Mama. Quiet as a church mouse, except when she should be." Allegra, momentarily diverted by both the story and Lettice's calm delivery of it, nearly smiled. But then she became serious once more. She trotted over to the high tester bed and launched herself onto it, sitting cross-legged in the middle of the satin coverlet.

"What is a sea horse?" she asked, leaning forward, her elbows on her knees.

"Sea horse?" Lettice frowned.

"Yes. I think it must be some sort of fish, but if someone called a *person* a sea horse?"

"Where on earth did you hear—never mind. I don't think I want to know. Really, I don't."

Allegra worried the side of her thumb with her teeth for a moment, ignoring Lettice's protest. "So if someone—say, a sailor—were to see you and call you a sea horse, and then say that he'd thought coming to England would have gotten that sea horse hanged, it would probably be because something that sea horse did had upset someone here in England? I'm fairly sure I have this right, Letty, but I want to hear you say it, too."

"Hanged? Good God, girl, what did you hear?" Lettice said, getting up from the vanity bench and walking over to the bed. "Tell me everything."

"I don't know if I should," Allegra said. Then, deciding she'd at least shown some reluctance, she took a deep breath and told her story about the meeting between the Irishman and Armand Gauthier.

"Gauthier introduced us—the man's name is Conor O'Neill, and he seems a nice enough person—but then he whisked me away so quickly, nearly running me back here, that I didn't have a chance to do more than ask Gauthier a dozen questions. None of which he answered, dreadful man that he is."

"I see," Lettice said as she began to pace, talking more to herself than to Allegra. "What a clever man. He tells the truth so, naturally, no one believes him."

"Letty?"

"Hmm? Oh, excuse me, my lady. I was just mumbling to myself." She stopped pacing and looked at Allegra piercingly, as if trying to decide what to say, if anything.

Allegra could barely sit still. "Well, try mumbling a little louder, if you please."

Lettice tipped her head to one side as she continued to look at Allegra. "So, you have no idea what happened today? No inkling? No thoughts at all?"

Allegra bowed her head. "I have a few," she said quietly, then looked at Lettice again. "I wouldn't let anyone hurt him, if that's what you're asking. Really, Letty, I wouldn't. But I have to know. I really do."

"Because you're curious?"

"No! That is, yes, I'm curious. I won't fib and say that I'm not, because I wouldn't believe anyone else if they told me such a hum. But could he be in danger? That's what worries me, Letty. Mr. O'Neill didn't say much, but what he did say makes me think that Gauthier could be in trouble if anyone were to find out whatever it is nobody knows."

She winced at that last statement. "Oh, you know what I mean."

Lettice sighed, then boosted herself up onto the mattress, looked at Allegra. "No one knows much about Armand Gauthier, my lady."

"Allegra. Remember? I really wish you'd call me Allegra. Especially after I've heard you say *damned for a tinker* at Lady Chirton's. As a matter of fact, I think we could become fast friends."

"You certainly are doing your best to prove yourself *fast* . . . Allegra. All right, I'll tell you what I know, mostly because I have a feeling I'll know no peace until I do, and because if you go around Mayfair asking stupid questions you could possibly get the man killed."

"Then it's really bad?" Allegra asked, her stomach fisting into a knot.

"That I don't know," Lettice told her. "I doubt it's good. Mr. Gauthier appeared in London, seemingly out of nowhere, about three years ago. He was befriended by the Earl of Roxbury and introduced to Society. With his pleasant manner, his good looks—and his fat wallet, naturally—he was accepted, if never understood."

Allegra nodded, drinking in all of this information.

"So he's not really English? We're sure of that now? I didn't think he was. His voice is so soft sometimes, almost a drawl. And"—she felt herself blushing—"almost warm."

Lettice rolled her eyes. "Save me from romantic females."

"I am *not* romantic, Letty. You are, remember? And Elizabeth. No, I take that back. You are nothing near Elizabeth. That would be an insult to you. Now, tell me more."

"There isn't much more to tell. Mr. Gauthier cut a wide swath through Society, making friends with both the high and the low, being pleasant, amenable, and apparently forthcoming about his past. He has admitted to being a gamester, a secret royal, a nabob who made his fortune in India, a highwayman, a pirate. Whatever anyone suggested, he agreed to be. Soon, everyone stopped inquiring."

Allegra latched on to the last one. "A pirate? He said he was a pirate?"

"Among everything else, yes," Lettice said quietly. "Where best to hide, but in plain sight?"

"Because Mr. O'Neill called him a sea horse? Because Mr. O'Neill is a seaman, and knows Gauthier?"

She fell back against the mattress, staring up at the canopy over her head. "Good God, Letty. I'd thought it, but to *say* it? A pirate."

"We can't know that for certain, Allegra," Lettice pointed out, and Allegra lifted her head, glared at her. "Oh, all right. It does seem possible, doesn't it?"

"He can't know that I know," Allegra said, staring up at the canopy once more. "Nobody can know that I know. I just wish I knew why he was here, why he came to England in the first place."

"He's on a hunt," Lettice said, walking back to the vanity table, leaning forward once more, pressing her fingers at her hairline. "From the ballrooms to the brothels, he's been on a hunt from the first."

Allegra pushed herself up onto her elbows. "How do you know that? As a matter of fact, how do you know Gauthier so well? He told me he'd done you a . . . a service, in some house where you were employed. Is that true?"

Lettice's fingers stayed in their action of pulling back her hair, peering into the mirror. "He said that?"

"He did. He said something about some boor trying to hurt you—he probably meant kiss you, didn't he?"

Lettice stood up straight, turned to Allegra. "Is that so difficult to believe, Allegra? That some man would want to . . . kiss me?"

"Oh, no, of course not! But you'll have to admit, Letty, that it's passing strange that I should know so few people in London, and those people know each other."

"We are a small society, Allegra. Now you have to promise me that you won't pest Mr. Gauthier about his past, even about this Mr. O'Neill, who is probably at this very moment having himself a hot bath and a warmed brandy, thinking he's died and gone to heaven."

Allegra pressed her hands against her ears, shook her head. "It won't be easy, Letty. I've got a million questions buzzing around inside my head. A pirate? Really?

And not English? American, then, don't you think? Wouldn't that mean that he preyed on English ships? Isn't that why we'd want to hang him? How am I ever going to *not* ask him those million questions? Because this is exciting, Letty, you have to own it. I knew there was something different about Gauthier, something that has *drawn* me to him from the first. I'm not a lady, Letty, and he's no gentleman."

"I believe that Mr. Gauthier has made himself very much the gentleman, Allegra," Lettice said sternly. "But that is on the outside. I doubt that, even after three years in Society, it goes too deep, all the way through him. Scratch that gentleman, Allegra, and you'll still find a dangerous man. I'd remember that, were I you."

"Oh, piffle," Allegra said, even as she felt a nervous fluttering in her breast. A pirate. She actually had kissed an actual pirate. She had dared that pirate to kiss her again, more than kiss her.

No wonder he had entered into their prank this afternoon with such enthusiasm. After years of walking the straight and narrow, even a silly prank must have been a great release to him—a man who had sailed the seven seas, perhaps with a cutlass between his teeth, plundering, raiding, taking his fortune where he found it.

It was the stuff of heroes, or at least Allegra saw it as such.

Even more the stuff of heroes was the notion that Gauthier had come to England on some sort of quest.

Was he looking for the English captain who had slain his father in an unfair fight on some blood-slick deck? Was he on the hunt for booty—it was called booty, wasn't it?—lost to him when one of the English ships slipped away from him? Had he come in search of a beautiful woman he'd seen on that deck, then lost his heart to her as only heroes can?

No. Not that last part. Definitely not that last part. She didn't like that idea at all.

"Do you think Bones—Mr. Boothe—knows all of the truth?" Allegra asked, another thought hitting her. If you couldn't go in through the door, sometimes you could slip in an open window. Oxie had taught her that.

"He might," Lettice agreed. "But he won't tell you, or that silly little widgeon down the hall, in case you were thinking of including your cousin in any plot to ferret out Mr. Gauthier's secrets."

Allegra grinned. "I am so transparent to you, aren't I, Letty? Such a pity that I know so little about *you*. Will you tell me one day? I should like to think I'd learn at least one small secret while I'm stuck here for the—*shhh!* What's that?"

Lettice shook her head, answered quietly, "I didn't hear anything. What did you hear?"

Putting a finger to her lips, signaling Lettice to complete silence, Allegra tiptoed to the door, flung it open . . . and Oxie Nesbitt, who'd had his ear pressed to the wood, tumbled into the room.

From his knees, he looked up at his daughter. "Oh, hello, pet. I was just . . . just passing by."

"Really, Oxie? And you heard nothing?"

"Nothing. Not a peep," he said, walking on his knees until he was near enough the open door to give it a few good knocks with his knuckles. "Thick as a plank, this door. The trick is to listen at the keyhole, but you don't talk loud enough, pet. Too many years of knowing me, too many times I taught you too much."

He got to his feet, brushed off his knees. "Well, I must be off. Your mama bought a few gewgaws she wants to show me. Good thing, too, her getting out and about, and all of that. See you at dinner?"

"At dinner," Allegra agreed, then let the door slam behind her father as she turned to Lettice. "The fat's in the fire now, Letty."

"You think he did hear?"

"I can't be sure, not yet," Allegra said, frowning. "But I have a feeling we'll know soon enough. I'm going to have to stay stuck to Gauthier like sticking plaster now, you know. Just so I can warn him if I smell one of Oxie's pranks in the making."

"He'd prank him? Why?"

"Why? Because he's Oxie, that's why."

"But what could he do?"

Allegra shrugged. "I don't know. Show up at Gauthier's ball with a parrot on his shoulder and a black eye patch? I doubt he could figure out a way to have a peg leg, but he'd do something. Oxie always feels honor-bound to do *something*."

Chapter Twelve

CONOR O'NEILL peeked around Armand's shoulder, peered through the window overlooking the Square. "You've been watching that poor girl like a gator lying in the swamps, boyo, getting ready to bite.

How long are you going to wait before you go out there? It'll be coming along to dark before soon. Not like you to hang back, as I recall the thing. Why, I remember that time in Santo Domingo when——"

"Stubble it, Conor, if you please," Armand said, letting go of the sheer drape and stepping back from the window.

"Oh, no, no," Bones protested from his seat on one of the couches. Bones was only a little less than three-parts drunk, partially inebriated on love, the rest of his currently mellow state the result of his effort to forget that his mother had thrown him out of the house. "Go ahead, Conor. Tell us. Really, I want to hear. And don't forget the details. I can't tell you how long I've waited to hear stories about our friend's dark and dangerous past. Amorous exploits would be nice, too. I have so few of my own."

"Bones," Armand warned, heading for the drinks table to pour himself a glass of wine. "Forgive me, but I find I'm not in the mood for a recital of my past indiscretions."

"Ah, an indiscretion into the bargain. How wonderful," Bones said, turning on his seat, to look at Conor. "We'll talk later," he said with a small conspiratorial smile and an exaggerated wiggle of his eyebrows (which also served to wiggle his rather large, protuberant ears, poor fellow).

Armand walked back over to the window.

How long would she stay out there? What did she hope to accomplish by staying out there, walking around the fountain, pretending to take the air—which had to be turning damp now, as fog had begun to creep into the Square. Fog, and dark.

Was she dressed warmly enough?

And why would he care, even think about such a thing?

An hour. She'd been out there for nearly an hour. That was a long time to pretend an overweening interest in a fountain.

If he called for his carriage, would she come running across the Square, to stop him before he could drive off?

No.

She *knew*. Oh, yes, she *knew*. She knew he saw her, knew he wouldn't drive away, leave her standing there.

How did she know that?

She knew that because, if she wanted to see him, he naturally had to want to see her, too, so she'd make it easy for him. That was how the girl's mind worked.

What bothered him is that, barely knowing her, he'd already figured out how her mind worked. And appreciated it. She was as devious as the *bos* himself, bless her, and as determined to have things go her own way.

"Enough is enough. I'm going out there," he said to no one in particular, putting down his glass.

Bones unfolded his length from the couch. "I'll just go along with you, if you don't mind. Maybe she'll invite us into the mansion, and I can see Miss Elizabeth?"

"You want her, Bones, you go get her on your own—and not right now," Armand said, heading for the hallway. "Conor, why don't you and Bones head down to the inn where you've stowed your bag, and bring it back here. Give Bones a tour of the wharves. Just don't lose him."

"I want to see Miss Elizabeth, Armand. I've seen the wharves," Bones protested.

"Not where Conor will be taking you," Armand said, hesitating at the doorway.

"You know, it occurs to me that my new mansion is getting a bit crowded. You, Bones, and now you, Conor."

"Yes?" Conor asked. "So what of it? Is it changing your mind you are, boyo? Do you want us to leave?"

"No," Armand answered, smiling. "I like it. I don't think I was meant to rattle around in all these rooms by myself, either here or on my estate."

"Estate, is it? Hoo! Didn't know about that. Guess you couldn't invite the *bos* and the others, though, even if I have a feeling he'll be looking for another place to tie up his hammock pretty soon. Aren't that many gallows in all of England, I'll wager."

"Gallows?" Bones grabbed on to Conor's sleeve. "There's things you never told me, aren't there, Armand? But hanging? We can't do that. Not after all these years. Can we?"

"No being sure," Conor said, draping an arm over Bones's shoulders. "One thing you can never trust, boyo, and that's the word of a honorable man with his own ambitions. The *bos* said that, boyo, remember?"

"I remember," Armand said. "A promise is a promise as long as it is politically advantageous. After that, it's nothing but a worthless promise written on an equally worthless piece of paper."

"And no use crying over, right, boyo?" He looked over at Bones, winked. "Let's head for the docks and my gear, while I tell you a tale or two of just what we were about back all those years ago. We'll lift a few pints, and I'll tell you about the *bos*."

Armand turned back toward the stairs, meeting a waiting Quincy in the downstairs foyer. The man held out his hat and gloves to him, obviously having anticipated his needs.

"Saw her, did you?" Armand asked, patting his hat against his head, taking his gloves.

"I thought she might come knocking on the door, sir, but then I realized that her ladyship would never play the same card twice. An interesting young lady, sir."

"A pain in my—very good, Quincy. Both the gentlemen will be going out for a while, but will be residing here for an indefinite period, so we'll need two chambers, and some provision for Mr. Boothe's valet. Mr. O'Neill probably will want to care for himself."

"Yes. Someone should, sir," Quincy said. "Will Mr. O'Neill be attending the ball, sir?"

"The—damn, I didn't even think about that." He rubbed at his forehead, believing this slight headache behind his eyes might become a permanent part of his life. "What do you think, Quincy?"

"Me, sir? I don't think Mr. O'Neill would be quite comfortable in such company."

"No more than such company would be comfortable with him," Armand said, sighing. "And the sad truth is, Quincy, I'd rather spend the night talking with Conor than with half the people I've invited to this ridiculousness. What does that say about me?"

"That you are a man learning who he is? Sir."

Armand looked at his majordomo, then a slow smile curved his mouth. "And the lady, Socrates? What wisdom do you have about her?"

"Enjoy her, sir," Quincy said, bowing. "She seems a most enjoyable lady."

One more circuit around the fountain, and Allegra felt sure she'd be dizzy enough to go staggering off across the Square and get run down by one of the carriages that seemed to be appearing more and more frequently as the sky darkened, and the fog gathered.

Lettice had given her one hour, no longer, to try to lure Gauthier to her, warn him about Oxie. That hour was very nearly gone, and still the man hadn't appeared.

What was taking him so long?

He had to know that she'd seen him. Standing smack in front of a window, lit from behind by the chandelier that was also visible when she peeked across the Square. Pulling back the drapes like some nosey old tabby watching the street. Moving away, coming back, checking to see if, yes, she was still out here, waiting and pacing and wishing she'd worn a heavier pelisse.

How could she *not* have seen him?

He should be ashamed of himself.

She gave in to the growing wish to rest herself for a moment, and gingerly sat herself down on the outer rim of the round fountain.

Ah, that was better. She could wiggle her toes inside her thin-soled slippers that were such faint protection against the cobbles. Rest her legs. Reconsider what she was doing out here, sneaking out here in the hope Gauthier would see her, come to her. Explain to her.

Because warning him about Oxie was one thing. Knowing exactly what secrets Gauthier held was another and, frankly, more interesting.

And he'd seen her. But had he come out here, talked to her, explained to her? No, he hadn't. Yet still she waited, like some brainless ninny, some *needy* female.

How pathetic.

Allegra slapped her palms against her thighs and stood up, having decided that pathetic was something she had no intention of being, at least not where Armand Gauthier was concerned.

"Retreating so soon, Ally?"

She stopped, her spine stiffening. She refused to turn around, irrationally angry that he'd been able to sneak up behind her in the descending gloom. "Arriving so late, Gauthier?" she returned sprightly.

Armand moved to stand in front of her. "I wasn't sure it was me you were waiting for. You could have—how do I phrase this politely? You could have decided to broaden your experience with entirely another gentleman?"

Her head snapped up and she glared at him. "What *are* you talking about, Gauthier?"

His smile infuriated her, because it was openly teasing, and because of her reaction to it, the way all her bones seemed to soften just at the sight of it.

"Well, I'm crushed, certainly," he said, holding out his arm to her. "Are you telling me you've already forgotten our kisses of this afternoon, and your none too subtle hints that you would consider further amorous advances in the form of an educational experience?"

"I didn't say that, Gauthier. I never said that. Educational? Piffle."

"You came damned close to it, Ally," he said as he seemed to walk aimlessly . . . yet still in the direction of the narrow carriage drive to the left of her father's mansion.

"Well, I lied. I do that a lot, Gauthier, so don't be too impressed with yourself. I have no intention of taking a lover. I don't want one, I don't need one."

He tipped his head so that he could whisper his next words in her ear. "How would you know?"

How she hated him when he was right. She didn't know. But, after his kisses of this afternoon, she had begun to realize there were experiences in life that she had been lacking, experiences she doubted she'd ever find once she and her parents retreated once more to the safety and near nunlike seclusion of Sunderland.

Because Armand Gauthier, damn him, wouldn't be at Sunderland with her.

"Ally? Aren't you going to say anything?" he asked as he stopped for a moment, looked about as if for witnesses to whatever it was he planned to do next.

"Not yet, no. I'm still devising painful ways to murder you. Where are we going?"

With one last look around the Square, he had grabbed her hand and was half pulling her toward the narrow carriageway. She had to lift her skirts with her free hand, moving with him, her smile wide, her heart pounding in anticipation.

She'd thought she could goad him into doing some-thing wild, something reckless.

Bless the man, he didn't disappoint her.

Into the shadows between the Sunderland mansion and the building close beside they went . . . then stopped . . . turned to each other.

"You knew I couldn't resist your temptation, didn't you?" he asked, sliding his hands beneath her pelisse, linking them around her waist.

"Actually, I came out here for quite another—oh, what does it matter? Don't just stand there, grinning like a loon. Kiss me, Gauthier."

My, but he was an obedient man in some things.

Allegra felt herself being brought close and hard against Gauthier's chest, their lower bodies touching as well, their bellies, their thighs.

She put her hands on his shoulders, looked up at him to see that his smile had fled, taking hers with it.

She had no second thoughts, although she felt certain that Gauthier was giving her a moment, giving her the time to change her mind, even slap his face in order to protect her own honor.

Foolish man.

So she tugged on his shoulders, silently telling him she was ready, and he obliged her by dipping his head, capturing her mouth with his own.

This time, she was prepared for him. She didn't keep her lips firmly pressed together, but allowed them to soften in a small smile, open against his gentle assault.

They kissed, and they kissed, and they kissed, and

then she felt his hands moving up from her waist, skimming over her midriff, capturing her breasts in his hands . . . and the bottom fell out of her once safe world.

She gasped into his mouth, stood on tiptoe so as to give him greater access to her tingling, singing body.

He turned both their bodies in a circle, then stepped back so that he leaned against the stone wall.

She felt his hips grind closer to hers as he buried his mouth against the side of her neck, as his hands worked their magic with her body.

"Well," he said, his breathing rough as he pushed her away, "that's enough of that."

Allegra slowly opened her eyes, tried to focus. With some effort, she got her mouth to move, forced a few words past her throbbing lips. "Yes . . . I suppose so."

She pressed her palms against his chest, felt the rapid, unsteady rise and fall of it.

"That's not going to happen again," Armand told her, his tone making his words sound depressingly like an order to himself rather than a promise to her.

She felt stung enough to say, "Well, there's a pity, Gauthier. And just when you were getting good at it."

He picked her up at the waist, carried her to the center of the narrow lane, put her down again. "I've heard of imps sent here straight from hell to torment poor mortal men, but until I met you, Ally, I didn't believe it."

Allegra regained some of her humor, because even if he'd spurned her—e-gads, *spurned* her? what a ridiculous word!—she most certainly had enjoyed herself.

In fact, she'd only begun to worry that she wasn't prepared for whatever came next when he'd stopped, so now she had time to think about this half hunger, half fear; reflect, and decide if she wanted to pursue whatever it was that did come next.

She already thought she probably would.

"I'm not the only imp sent here straight from hell to torment you, Gauthier," she said, working to pull her pelisse about her once more, as it seemed to have slipped halfway around her neck. "Or, should I say, straight from Sunderland. There's also Oxie."

"Your father?" Armand patted at his pockets, pulled out a slim cheroot, stuck it, unlit, between his teeth. "Why? Is he hiding in the shadows, ready to pop out, announce that I've compromised his daughter and demand an immediate marriage?"

Allegra rolled her eyes. "Don't be so silly. As if I'd do anything so commonplace as to attempt a compromise. Or so arrogant, either, Gauthier. What makes you think I even want you?"

He cocked one eyebrow. "If you're about to offer me payment for services rendered, Ally, I have to tell you that I don't want it."

"Services rendered?" All right, now she was angry again. The man had her so confused, she didn't know if she was on her head or on her heels. "How dare you, Gauthier? Was it me who grabbed you, pulled you in here? I think not. Why not just admit it? We enjoy each other. We do enjoy each other, don't we?"

"Who are you?" He leaned forward slightly, his eyelids narrowed. "You're nineteen or so, correct? Not a woman of the world? Just a little country miss with no experience?"

Allegra bristled. "That's not my fault."

"Your *fault?*" Armand threw back his head, laughed out loud. "If ever I saw an innocent so dead set on ruining herself . . ."

"Oh, stubble it," Allegra said, turning to leave the narrow carriageway, and leave the obnoxious Armand Gauthier to his own devices.

But she couldn't do it. She couldn't do it because if Oxie had overheard her, and whatever happened next could be partially her fault. The man needed to be warned. Even Letty had agreed.

She took a deep breath that lifted her shoulders, then blew it out angrily, turned back to him to see him looking at the cold end of his cheroot, glaring at it so hotly she was surprised it hadn't burst into flame.

"Look," she said, walking back to face him, "there's something you need to know."

"Oh?" he said, one corner of his mouth lifting into a smile. "Then you know where I left my usual good sense? Wonderful. I've begun to miss it."

"Oh, piffle, Gauthier. We kissed, that's all."

The other side of his mouth lifted, his white teeth appeared as his smile widened. "Only a kiss, Ally? You *were* here a few moments ago, weren't you?"

"Don't do that, don't be snide," she warned him, lowering her lashes because looking at him reminded her of how it had felt to have his hands on her. "And I don't see why a little curiosity has to be made into such a huge problem. I like you, Gauthier, it's as simple as that. I thought we were friends."

"Friends." He shook his head. "We're damn close to

becoming lovers, Ally, or hadn't you thought of that? Not that I can blame you, as I'm having trouble believing it myself. But you make it damn hard sometimes for me to remember that you're the daughter of an earl."

"Yes," Allegra said on a sigh, "it's a trial to me, too."

He laughed again, and she looked up at him, felt herself smiling, relaxing, once more. She really did like this man. Perhaps more than she should. Not that she'd tell him that. Because, if she told him that, he'd probably start treating her the way everyone thought she should be treated, and that would not only be stiff and boring, it would ruin any chance she had to get to know him better.

And she so wanted to get to know him better. And then there was Oxie . . .

"I didn't come out here to kiss you, you know," she said as he replaced the cold cheroot between his teeth. "I came out here, Gauthier, lured you over here to be truthful about the thing, to apologize for something . . . and to warn you that you could be in danger."

"Warn me that I'm in danger?" His smile vanished. "You know, Ally, if any other woman had said those words to me, I'd take them with a shrug of my shoulders and a polite *oh, my*. However, with you? Should I be ducking for cover? Perhaps changing my name and announcing a repairing lease on the continent?"

"I don't know," Allegra answered honestly, trying not to wince. And then, because there was no sense in putting it off, she said what she had to say. "It all depends on whether or not we English still hang sea horses."

The ensuing silence was so chilled that she shivered, before Armand threw down his cheroot, glared at her.

"So much for believing Conor's remarks scooted straight over the top of your head. I knew I'd only been deluding myself to put my hopes in that one."

Allegra pressed suddenly trembling hands to her cheeks. "So it's true? You really are a pirate? Were a pirate?" Yet another shiver ran through her. "Good God, Gauthier—you're a *pirate.*"

"We much preferred to call ourselves merchants of happily discovered commodities. And we never took from our own. So, no, I would say I was not a pirate. Not in so many words. Perhaps an unlicensed privateer?"

She shook her head. "I've been reading a few things I found in our library this afternoon, Gauthier. The only difference between a pirate and a privateer is in *who* gives you the right to prey on another nation's ships."

A small tic began to work on one side of his jaw. "We never asked permission. And those who bought our goods never asked too many questions, either."

"I see. But you never took from your own, as you said. Your own would be America, correct? But you preyed on English ships, didn't you? Spanish ships?"

"Preyed is such a *nasty* word, Ally," he drawled, that slight smile appearing once more.

"Did you sail out of Boston? Privateers sailed out of Boston, didn't they?"

"There were many ports," he answered, searching his pockets for yet another cheroot. "But that's all in the past, Ally, years in the past. Nobody cares anymore."

"Oh, I doubt that, Gauthier. I mean, even if no one would actually hang you, I doubt they'd want you sitting at the dinner table with them. Why, you could have killed some of their friends, even their family. And don't tell me you never killed anyone, because I am not a child, and this is not a fairy tale."

His expression hardened. "If you're not a child, Ally, I suggest you stop sounding like one. Now, as I am not going to stand here and try to defend myself against what I'm sure you're convinced are very logical arguments—why have you warned me? Who did you tell about me? Have you perhaps sent a notice to the papers? I really should know."

She'd been put firmly in her place, and it hurt, feeling the coolness he radiated, the near disdain. So, in her usual reaction, her back went up. "What makes you think I told anyone anything?"

His laugh was short, sharp. "So that I won't be too insulting, let's just say I'm making a guess. Now, who did you tell? Letty? That would be an obvious choice."

"I . . . I may have mentioned something to her," Allegra said, wishing herself out of this narrow lane, safe and snug in her rooms, even back at Sunderland. "Oh, all right, *yes,* I told her. I had to, Gauthier, so that she could help me to understand. After all, Mr. O'Neill said you'd be hanged."

"If they hanged fools, yes," he said quietly. "All right. Letty's no problem. Who else?"

"Why isn't Letty a problem?"

"Don't, Ally. Hasn't your curiosity already done damage to any hopes I might have to continue here in society? Now, who else did you tell?"

Allegra muttered into the collar of her pelisse.

"I didn't quite hear that."

She muttered again.

"Oh, all right. I heard that," he said, walking a few feet away from her, then turning around, looking at her accusingly. "You told your *father?* Of all the simple, cork brained, idiotic—"

"He was listening outside my door when I was telling Letty," Allegra interrupted, chasing after him, stopping not a foot in front of him, tipping back her head to glare up at him. "How was I to know that, Gauthier? Besides, I don't know what he heard, even if he heard anything at all. And if I knew how *ungrateful* you'd be, I wouldn't have stood around out here for an hour, freezing my toes off as the fog rolled in, just to warn you."

"All right, all right," Armand said, beginning to pace. "So he may know, he may not. And what does it matter? He goes nowhere, sees no one."

"He wanders about the city, but on his own, yes. We've still not had any other invitations but yours."

He whirled on his heels, facing her again. "The ball. He'll be at the ball."

Allegra nodded her agreement. "I don't think there's any avoiding that, yes. But tomorrow he pulls his prank on Viscount Eaton—you're still going to help him, so he won't be able to create any more mischief then. Saturday is the ball, which Mama has her heart quite set on. If Oxie has no more pranks planned, I believe I will be able to find some way to get us all out of town and back to Sunderland by the following Saturday. Elizabeth would have an apoplexy if we left before she could attend Almack's."

"How would you get everyone out of town? By saying I've broken your tender, *innocent* heart? On top of everything else, I get to play the cad. No, wait. Perhaps we'd agreed that I could play the brokenhearted and spurned admirer?"

She shook her head. "I really don't remember, and it doesn't matter how we might have worked it out. It was never a good plan. I've quite given it up."

"I have to tell you, Ally, I'm crushed," Armand said, and she heard a bit of humor creeping back into his voice. "And I don't even know whose heart has been broken. You know what? We should have drawn for it. Is it too late for me to fetch a pack of cards?"

"I wish you'd take this all more seriously, Gauthier. We've progressed beyond playing a prank on Oxie to teach him a lesson. If he overheard me speaking to Letty, he'll feel honor-bound to use the information to prank you in some way, tease you with what he knows, what he thinks he knows. He has no choice, it's in his nature."

"And you're afraid he'll do that in a . . . in some public way?"

"He could. I've thought about confronting him, asking what he knows, but that would only make him more anxious to ferret out any of your secrets he doesn't already think he knows. Do you understand that?"

"It vaguely frightens me to acknowledge it but, yes, I did understand that. What I don't understand is how you've decided that I care if anyone knows about my past. Those days are behind me, as is the late war. If I can forgive England for burning down Washington, I think England can be generous enough to forgive me for commandeering a few ships, for bearing arms against the Crown. It wasn't treason, Ally. As you've already figured out somewhere in that rather frightening brain of yours, yes, I'm an American."

"Which you've hidden from everyone, to hear Letty tell it," Allegra pursued.

"I didn't know Letty liked to gossip."

"It wasn't gossip, Gauthier, and if it was, it was yours. A highwayman? A bastard prince? A nabob? Why, you even agreed to being a pirate. If there is a mystery hanging about your shoulders, you helped to put it there."

"Which doesn't mean I've hidden my past, but just that I'm guilty of enjoying myself, granted, sometimes at the expense of those who should know enough to mind their own business."

"No, I don't believe that, not for a minute. Not after what Letty said."

"A veritable fountain of information, our Letty. What did she say?"

"That you came to England for a reason. Hunting something, Letty says. If everyone knew who you really were, what you had been, you wouldn't have been able to enter Society so easily, would you? Hunt for whatever you're hunting for? You kept your past a secret, Gauthier, so don't tell me it doesn't matter."

He scratched at the side of his head, just above his left

ear. "How long have I known you, Ally? A week? Five years? Two minutes? How have you found out so much about me, when no one in Society has done so in three long years? Really, I'd like to know."

"I don't know," Allegra answered truthfully. "Perhaps it's just that, living with Oxie, I've had to be more *aware* of everything. Besides, I met Mr. O'Neill. That was an accident. I didn't *plan* it, Gauthier, for pity's sake. I know you're upset, but surely you realize that much."

She turned away from him, took a few steps, turned back as another thought hit her. "Wait a moment."

"Uh oh," he said, returning the cheroot to his pocket. "Here we go. I was wondering how long it would take for that devious brain box of yours to come to what you'll obviously see as a logical conclusion."

"You're not upset. Not really. You're angry, but that's to be expected. But not the way I thought you'd be. You're not worried about what Oxie might say, what might happen. You don't care."

She advanced on him, poking a finger into his chest. "That's it, isn't it? I've found out—by mistake—about your past, and *you don't care.* Why? Have you given up whatever search you came here to perform? That's it, isn't it? That's the only reason you wouldn't care if Society turns its back on you, isn't it? Either you've found out what you wanted to know, or you simply don't care to know it anymore. Which is it?"

She stepped back, looked into his eyes. "And another thing. Are you leaving London, Gauthier? Because I think you should tell me if you are."

"Why? Would you miss me?"

She lifted her chin. "This conversation, Gauthier, is over. Please present yourself at ten tomorrow morning, prepared to help Oxie with his prank. And for God's sake, man, *don't* turn your back on him."

Then she lifted her skirts, and ran out of the carriage lane and up the steps to the mansion.

Chapter Thirteen

THE CLOCK ON THE MANTEL struck the hour of two as the fire in the fireplace slowly died and the candles began to gutter in their holders.

Armand sat slouched on one of the couches, his dark hair faintly mussed, his jacket gone, his neck cloth hanging loose, his long legs spread out in front of him.

A wineglass dangled from his fingertips.

Facing him on the other couch, Conor O'Neill struck much the same wine relaxed pose. Except that his bootless feet rested on the tabletop, a small courtesy he'd granted Armand, who now had a less than wonderful view of the holes in his friend's hose.

Beside the sailor, tucked up on the far corner of the couch, Bartholomew Boothe had gathered his long, bony body into a near-fetal position.

Armand, without lifting his chin from his chest, said, "I know why I'm drinking, Conor, and I'm fairly certain I know why Bones here is drinking, but I'll be damned if I know why you are."

"And since when have I needed a reason, boyo?" The older man scratched at his belly, burped. "We Irish are a melancholy lot, don't you know."

"Maybe I'm Irish, Conor," Armand said, taking a sip of wine. "I'd never thought of that one."

"The *bos* said you was English, boyo, and he ought to know."

"Why? He was still a child himself when I appeared. He could have been wrong."

"The *bos* was never a child, boyo. He was running smugglers from Barataria Bay from the time he could crawl, or so the story goes. Sailing his ships, taking his prizes, playing in society, dancing with the fine ladies. Ah, boyo, it's almost worth it all, just to have such wondrous stories told about you while you're still around to hear them. Nobody'd tell stories about me, one more sodden, broken-down Irishman."

From his corner of the couch, Bones whimpered softly. "Whole town is probably wagging their tongues about me. Ungrateful whelp. M'mother nursing a viper at her bosom. Rude, thankless son."

He lifted his head from the arm of the couch and looked at Armand. "You know her, Armand. I'm about to become a legend in the family. The unappreciative, turned-off son."

Armand raised his eyebrows. "Bones, you're past thirty years old. How long before the whole town would be talking because you *didn't* leave your mother?"

Conor chuckled low in his throat. "But they wouldn't be calling him a pretty boy, don't you know. Not anyone with two eyes in his head. Sorry, boyo, but facts is facts." He winked at Armand. "Never before met a man with so many elbows."

"Ah, but Miss Elizabeth seems to find him handsome," Armand said, happy to be thinking of something other than how his own life had been turned upside down and inside out since meeting Allegra. And he thought he was still holding up fairly well. If he looked as downtrodden as Bones did at this moment, sounded like the melancholy Bones, he'd probably have to kill himself.

Bones slowly unbent his lanky frame and sat up. "She's the most beautiful woman I've ever seen," he said with the solid conviction of the libation-impaired. "A goddess."

"A Nesbitt," Armand added facetiously.

Bones groaned and sank back into his former self-protective position. "M'mother said our children could be born with horns. She said she'd never speak to me again. She said my uncle George married beneath him and died a sorry, broken man. She said—"

"I'm sure she did, Bones," Armand said, going over to the drinks table to refill his glass. "My only wonder is that you *listened*."

Bones stretched out his long body once more. "Always have, Armand. Don't know why."

Conor looked into the bottom of his empty glass. "Never knew m'mother. M'father neither. Never thought of that as lucky, until now."

Armand sighed. They were becoming maudlin.

"Bones, I'm meeting with the Earl of Sunderland tomorrow morning, at ten. I'm sure he wouldn't mind if you accompanied me as far as the mansion. Who knows, Miss Elizabeth might even be an early riser, and you could catch a glimpse of her."

"Really?" Bones leaned over the back of the couch, to smile at Armand. "Could I do that? It wouldn't be too presumptuous of me?"

"I don't think so. They seem to have a rather . . . different idea of what's proper over there."

Bones nodded, then said, "But why are you calling on the earl? God, man, are you asking for her hand? Oh, wait. Do you think that's the only way to keep her from telling everybody about that pirating stuff?"

"Best damn pirates and smugglers ever born," Conor said, toasting his former occupation. "And the best damn soldiers Old Hickory ever did see. Pardoned and all. Heroes. Right, boyo?"

Armand winced inwardly at Conor's words. The man spoke at the drop of a single glass of spirits, never thinking of the consequences. He'd thought about taking him along in the morning, for his meeting with the earl, and was glad he hadn't yet mentioned it to the man. With any luck, Conor would still be snoring at ten tomorrow.

"What's an old hickory got to say about anything?" Bones asked, carefully getting to his feet, pulling down his waistcoat. "You didn't tell me that story, Conor. Americans make ships from hickory? I didn't know that."

"Don't worry your head about it, Bones," Armand said, taking his friend's elbow and guiding him toward the hallway. "You'll want to get some rest before meeting with Miss Elizabeth tomorrow morning."

Walking the exaggeratedly careful walk of the foxed,

Bones said, "Good thought, Armand. Must be at my best. Might even think of something to say this time. Tongue stuck to the roof of my mouth today, you know. She may never want to see me again, think I'm a dullard."

He tugged Armand around, headed back toward the couch. "Maybe I need another drink. I can still think a little."

"No, you don't," Armand told him firmly, redirecting him toward the hallway once more.

This time Bones made it as far as the doorway, then took hold of Armand's shoulders, gazed blearily into his eyes. "How does it happen, Armand? How does one day change everything you ever thought, everything you've ever wanted? Yesterday, all I wanted was for the days to pass so we could go to that mill outside Wimbledon, and now I wouldn't leave London if you were to tell me Gentleman Jackson himself was going to step into the ring again."

He blinked, slowly, twice. "How does that happen, Armand?"

"Damned if I know, Bones," Armand answered honestly. "But it does happen."

Sleep was impossible.

At last Allegra decided she needed to go back downstairs, pick up the book on pirates and privateers she'd found in the mansion's extensive library, and bring it back upstairs to bed with her.

Armand hadn't said he'd been a privateer, at least not one with a letter of marque, or whatever it was he should have had in order to go sailing all over the ocean, capturing merchant ships from other countries.

He'd said they hadn't asked "permission."

That made him a pirate. Lawless. Reckless.

Was the man insane? Why had he ever come to England? If anyone here were to find out about his past?

Was whatever he'd sought been so important? And if it was, why wasn't it important anymore?

Allegra walked down the hallway, watching the hem of her night rail as she kicked at it with every step she took, her mind nearly aching with questions.

Then she stopped, looked at the sliver of light beneath Lettice Tomlin's door.

It had gone out two minutes ago. Very late for the housekeeper-cum-companion to be awake inside the bedchamber stuck between those of her cousin and herself.

Lettice, Allegra remembered vaguely from their first day at the mansion, had set herself up in a room behind the kitchens, but Magdalen had put a quick end to that, saying the woman should be upstairs, available, and within easy reach if she were needed by either of the debutantes.

Lettice, Allegra also remembered, had protested the move.

Obviously, the woman enjoyed her privacy. In her same position, Allegra also would have liked to be as far from the family she served as possible.

Still, with Allegra wide awake, and her head still so full of unanswered questions, she could only consider it a happy by-product of her mother's good intentions that

Lettice was here . . . and so very available.

She knocked, lightly, not wanting to wake Elizabeth, then waited a moment before trying the knob. Ah, the door was unlocked.

"Letty? Are you there?" she called out quietly as she stepped inside the room, closed the door behind her. Blinking so that her eyes would become accustomed to the rather faint light, she had a moment's hesitation, thinking that perhaps all she'd seen was the light from a dying fire, and the woman was fast asleep.

Then a smell tickled at her nose. A fairly unpleasant smell.

"Letty?"

Allegra advanced farther into the room. There was the bed, not yet turned down. There was the fire, still burning low in the hearth.

But no Lettice Tomlin.

Her eyes now fully adjusted to the dimness, Allegra saw the half open door leading to the small dressing room.

"Letty?" she called out again, moving toward the dressing room. "Letty. I'm sorry to disturb you, but I really can't sleep and—good God!"

Lettice Tomlin, who had been sitting at her dressing table in her night rail, a towel draped over her shoulders, half turned toward Allegra while at the same time lifting that towel to cover her head.

"Go away."

Allegra shook her head. "I don't think so, Letty. What on earth is that on your head—and your eyebrows, too? It looks as if you've dumped a pot of tar on yourself.

And why does it *smell* so badly?"

Lettice didn't answer her.

"Oh, well, if you think keeping your mouth shut is going to have me feeling all embarrassed and contrite that I broke into your privacy, Letty, I suppose you have at least one more thing coming," Allegra said flatly, folding her arms across her midriff. "Now come on, give over. What are you doing?"

"You should have been spanked more as a child," Lettice said, unwrapping the towel, which was now spotted black all over.

"I was never spanked."

"Yes, and it shows," Lettice said, using one end of the towel to wipe the black mess from her eyebrows. "So, since I need to stick my head in a bucket right now, I suppose I'll tell you. I'm adding color to my hair."

Allegra blinked. "But your hair already looks as if you've rubbed it all over with lampblack. You mean you have it look like that *on purpose?*"

"Allegra . . ." Lettice said in a rather threatening manner, so that Allegra backed up as Lettice stomped past her, on her way to the water pitcher and basin on the other side of the small dressing room.

It was almost painful, watching Lettice dump water over her head, lather her hair with a huge bar of brown soap not once, not twice, but three times, before the water at last ran clear.

There was a price for beauty, Allegra knew, and many women gladly paid it.

She'd never thought there was a price to be paid for homely—or anyone who would go so far to pay it.

At last, Lettice took the clean dry length of toweling Allegra handed her, and wrapped it, turbanlike, around her dripping tresses.

"I suppose you want an explanation?"

"Who? Me? Would I be that crass, after invading your privacy, seeing something I clearly was not supposed to see?" Allegra grinned. "Oh, yes. Definitely."

Lettice pulled her dressing gown more closely around her slim body and headed for the bedroom, carrying her brush with her. She stopped in front of the fireplace and unceremoniously plopped herself down, unwrapped the towel, and began working at brushing through her hair. "Vile stuff," she said, "and it plays hell with knots."

"I imagine so. And you forgot to mention the smell," Allegra said, sitting down on the carpet as well, crossing her legs and leaning her elbows on her knees. "None of which explains why you, or anybody, would deliberately do such a thing to herself."

"I'm vain," Lettice said, not looking at Allegra. "My hair is graying, and I like it better with the gray carefully hidden."

Allegra tipped her head to one side as she thought about this. "No, that's not it. You're a pretty woman, Letty. I've noticed that, you understand. But those horrible black gowns? That even more horrible black hair? If you were vain, those black gowns would have been the first thing to go. Mama offered to buy you some new ones, remember?"

Lettice brushed at her hair, wincing as she hit knot after knot. "If I had any sense, I'd cut it all off." She gave another angry tug, said, "Oh, what made me think this would work?" Then she threw the brush across the room and dropped her head into her hands.

"Letty?" Allegra moved closer, put a hand on the woman's knee. "You're crying? Please, I didn't mean to make you cry."

"I'm not crying," Lettice said, grabbing at the damp towel and wiping her eyes. "I never cry. Crying gets you nowhere."

"Yes, I've often thought that myself," Allegra agreed, searching her mind for some way to calm this woman she'd begun to look on as a friend. "But throwing a brush is sometimes fun, isn't it? I can go get it, so you can throw it again if you want?"

"I should have known this wouldn't work out so easily, that I'd eventually be found out." Lettice threw down the towel, looked at Allegra. "Maybe I'm lucky it was you, Allegra."

"Oh, yes, definitely. Let's see. Elizabeth would swoon dead away, and Mama would—you know, Letty, I have no idea what Mama would do. With Oxie about, she's rather gotten used to surprises, shocks."

"This is more than a shock, I'm afraid. I never should have done this. It was hopeful but stupid. Stupid, stupid, stupid!"

Allegra sighed. "I can't agree or disagree, Letty, because I have no idea what you're talking about. Even so, I want to help you. First, I promise I'll tell no one you've been pouring tar or whatever all over your head. I can't promise more than that, because I have absolutely no idea what it is you did that's so stupid, stupid, stupid."

"Excuse me," Lettice said, getting to her feet. "As long as I've got nothing more to hide, I may as well make myself comfortable."

Allegra watched as the older woman opened the drawer to the small table beside her bed and pulled out a cheroot. Lettice placed the thing between her teeth, then bent down, lit the end on one of the candles on top of the table.

She drew in deeply on the cheroot, closed her eyes, and blew out a thin stream of blue smoke. "Oh, that's much better."

"May I try?" Allegra asked as Lettice returned to sit down on the hearth rug once more.

"No, you may not. I've done enough damage here."

Allegra propped her chin in her hands once more. "That sounds as if you're considering leaving, Letty. You know, of course, that I can't allow that. You're the only person in my whole life who understands me. Except for Gauthier, of course, but he's so angry with me, and I'm so angry with him, that I don't think we can list him, do you?"

Lettice's smile started out slowly, but grew. "I do enjoy you, Allegra. You remind me a lot of myself, when I was younger, of course, and thought being head-strong was the same as being independent. You're very fortunate. Being what you are, and who you are, makes it easier for you to be daring without having to pay the consequences. My life, on the other hand, has been overloaded with consequences."

She inhaled on the cheroot again, blew out another stream of blue smoke. "All right, Allegra. Let me tell you a story."

"A true one?"

"I'm past lying. This was my last chance."

"Nothing's changed, Letty," Allegra assured her. "You know you can stay with us as long as you want. Besides," she added, grinning, "I finally found out from Mama that yours was the only answer to Oxie's advertisement for a companion and housekeeper. The Nesbitt fame, or infamy, seems to have spread from the top of Society and filtered down through all the layers there are here in London. Trust me, your place with us is assured."

"That advertisement seemed like a gift from the gods," Lettice said, holding up the cheroot, staring at its lit end. "Oh, very well then—from the beginning?"

"Please," Allegra said, going over to retrieve the hairbrush, then settling herself behind Lettice, brushing the woman's hair. "And don't leave out a single solitary thing. Especially how you and Gauthier know each other. I never quite believed either of you on that one, you know."

Lettice was silent for a few moments, as if gathering her thoughts, and then began: "My name, my real name, is Lettice Toms. I grew up in Lower Beeding. Pretty little village where my father served as assistant vicar. I hated it, I hated the life there, and longed to come to London. When I was fourteen, my mother died, leaving me to my father's sermons, and more rules than you'd ever imagine. So I left, sure I could be an actress—something."

"An actress? Really? Oh, how wonderful!"

Lettice turned her head, smiled at Allegra, and the smile was sad. "You're so young. I remember being that young. But, at fourteen, my youth was gone."

Allegra began to feel uncomfortable. This was not going to be a nice story. "I'm sorry, Letty. Please, tell your story."

"Much of it isn't for your ears. I was met when I climbed down off the stage, all my worldly belongings in one small bag I carried with me. A very nice woman, who told me she'd help me get lodgings at a reasonable rate, and even employment—as a milliner in her shop. I was going to make lovely hats for the ladies of Society, right up until the moment I trod the boards at Covent Garden."

Allegra's hands stilled in the act of working out a tangle in the damp hair. "She lied to you?"

"Afterwards . . ." Lettice said, leaving out something that Allegra was fairly certain she already knew, "well, I couldn't go home, could I? So I traveled from house to house, and became quite popular with the gentlemen. There were a few, more than a few, who wanted to set me up in my own establishment, but I always refused. I worked, and I saved, I sold the jewelry I was given, and finally was able to buy my own . . . establishment."

Allegra thought her eyes might pop straight out of her head. "You owned a house of—no!"

Lettice took the brush from Allegra's hand as she turned to her, smiling. "Being the daughter of an assistant vicar had its benefits, Allegra. I was reasonably well educated, knew my manners. I gathered my own flock, you could say. But I was never happy."

Allegra nodded, sure she knew what was missing in Letty's life, as it was now what she wanted out of life. "You wanted a husband, children."

Lettice laughed. "Dear God, child, no. I wanted to trod the boards. Although, as I told myself, I was an actress in my own way, and a very good one. Then I met Armand Gauthier."

Allegra shook her head to clear it of thoughts of Lettice as a madam, running a bawdy house—dear God, a *bawdy house.* "You met Gauthier at your . . . at your house?"

"Oh, don't be so shocked, Allegra. Men are men. They visited for the company, the cards, the drinks, and, yes, for my ladies. Mr. Gauthier, I believe, was there for the cards, and to meet as many people as he could. From the beginning, I knew that he was on some sort of hunt. He tried to hide it, but his questions were a little too pointed for me not to notice that he had a more than casual interest in learning names and faces."

Allegra nodded her head. "I think he's finished with all of that. Either he has given up, or he thinks he's found what he's been after. Oh, I'm sorry. I didn't mean to interrupt."

"There's little more to tell, really. Mr. Gauthier visited about twice a week, and we had some lovely talks. That's all he ever asked of me, Allegra. To talk."

Allegra felt her face growing warm. "I believe you. Besides, what does it matter to me?"

"Lie to yourself, my dear, but don't think you can lie to me, or to your heart. Now, before you protest again, let me finish this. We have to be up and about early tomorrow for your waltz lesson."

"Oh, piffle. That particular exercise couldn't matter less to me. I won't be going to that silly ball."

"And you've told your mother this?"

Allegra dropped her chin against her chest. "Oh, all right. I may go. But I won't waltz with Gauthier. I'd rather die."

Lettice laughed, and tossed the cheroot into the fire. "How very dramatic, Allegra, and what a gigantic crammer. You'd crawl across hot coals to have just one dance with Mr. Gauthier."

"I really hate that you know me that well," Allegra said, getting to her feet. "Besides, we were talking about how you and Gauthier know each other, remember?"

"I remember. One night, nearly a year ago, one of my . . . customers decided that beating me with his boot would be the height of good fun."

"Oh, Letty." Allegra felt tears stinging her eyes.

"Mr. Gauthier was still in the house, playing cards downstairs, and he heard my . . . my protests, and came to the rescue. Once I'd . . . once I'd healed, I decided to sell the house, find some other way to live. Something I could be proud of, you know? Mr. Gauthier was a big help there."

"How?"

Lettice smiled. "He purchased the house from me, at a very good price."

Allegra gasped. "Gauthier owns a bawdy house? A brothel?"

"Only for as long as it took him to either find other work for my ladies or convince them that they, too, had a chance for new lives. Then he sold the house." She smiled. "To a milliner. A real one."

"And you, Letty? What did you do?"

Lettice shrugged. "I went back to Lower Beeding. My father was dead, but I wanted life in that village so badly. Everything I'd thrown away a quarter of a century earlier, I now wanted. It wasn't to be, of course. I was recognized, the gossip started, and I was forced to sell up again, leave again. That's when I remembered something else Mr. Gauthier had said to me."

Allegra continued to pace, amazed by everything she heard. "What had he said to you?"

"He'd said, among other things, that I could be whoever I wished to be. All I had to do was *be* that person, and everyone would believe what their eyes told them."

"Yes, that sounds like him, sounds like what he's done, himself."

Lettice sighed. "I decided that I wanted to see Society, not the way I'd seen it, but the way Society sees it. One way to do that, the only way to do that, was to be whoever I wished to be."

"You *wished* to be a housekeeper and companion?"

"Running one house is much the same as running another. I was ready for a boring life, or so I thought. There would be problems, I knew, but I could surmount them. My red hair was much too recognizable, so I made it black. I packed away all my wardrobe and replaced them with the dowdy gowns you seem to disapprove of so vehemently."

"You look like a crow in them, Letty."

"Yes, I know. A woman no one notices. That was the

point of the exercise. And then," she said, "the gods smiled. I saw the earl's advertisement. What better way to avoid the possibility of being recognized than to live in the household of a man who had not been in Society in five years? Not that he'd been in Society before that, or had ever . . . visited my establishment."

"You knew about us?"

Lettice nodded. "In my former occupation, Allegra, I heard almost everything. Coming to work for the earl would be perfect. A small dip into Society, for I knew the invitations would not be coming fast and thick. A few months of practice, using your family shamelessly, I agree, but learning, gaining experience, so that my next position could be better, and the next better than that. Except . . ."

"Except?" Allegra prodded.

Lettice spread her hands. "Except, I *hate* this. Oh, I very much like your mother, even your cousin Elizabeth, your father—even if he did do something strange with my bedsheets that first week."

"Um," Allegra said, feeling her cheeks flushing again, "that wasn't Oxie. That was me. Sorry."

"Really? Like father, like daughter? I should have known."

"I shouldn't have done it," Allegra admitted. "I sometimes do stupid things."

"So do I," Lettice said, beginning to braid her damp hair. "One of them, alas, was thinking I could like this life any more than I liked life back in my village. I wouldn't have lasted two days, Allegra, if you and your family weren't so . . . so . . ."

"Unusual?" Allegra said helpfully.

"Unusual, yes," Lettice agreed. "Thank you. And then Mr. Gauthier came on the scene, and you began poking at his past, and, well, I admit to an interest of my own. I would not like to see the man hurt in any way."

"No," Allegra admitted, leaning against the side of Lettice's bed. "Neither would I. So—what do we do now?"

Chapter Fourteen

ARMAND HAD EXPERIENCED less trouble dragging seawater-wet cargo over a soft sandy beach than he did in getting Bartholomew Boothe to walk across the Square as the clock neared the hour of ten.

"Maybe this isn't such a good idea," Bones said for at least the hundredth time. "Maybe I should just leave my card. M'mother is at home to visitors on Tuesdays, but this isn't Tuesday. Do you think most ladies are at home on Tuesdays? Otherwise, I should just leave my card, turn down the corner, that sort of thing. Polite. Well mannered. God, my head hurts. I woke this morning thinking two dogs died in my mouth. I really shouldn't go, you know. I don't think this is such a good idea."

"All done now, Bones?" Armand asked as they approached the steps to the pink mansion. "One last bleat, perhaps? Or maybe you intend to make a break for it before anyone answers our knock? Remember, I've heard it's difficult to run with one's tail tucked between one's legs."

"Oh, go ahead, mock me," Bones said with a sharp

nod of his head—followed by a quick moan. "I thought you was my friend."

"I am your friend, Bones. Otherwise, I would have dunked your head in that fountain and been done with it. But don't worry, I couldn't drown you. You can complain and worry more without taking breath than any man I know."

"But we aren't invited. At least, I'm not invited. You're invited. How did you get invited again, Armand? My mind's a little muzzy on that one."

"I'm doing the earl a small service," Armand said as he lifted the knocker. "Which means, in case you're wondering, that I shall be leaving here in a few minutes, if the earl is ready and waiting for me. You, on the other hand, will either be granted an audience with Miss Elizabeth, or still be standing out here on the steps, muttering to yourself about an opportunity lost. It's your choice."

"You're a hard man, Armand, and cold. I thought you'd have more pity."

"Well, I don't. Ah, here we go."

Armand informed the butler of his mission and gave him both his and Bones's names as they stepped into the foyer. "His lordship is expecting me."

"Yes, sir, Mr. Gauthier, sir," the butler answered, bowing. "I'm to bring you upstairs the moment you arrive, sir. Will Mr. Bartholomew be joining you, sir?"

"No."

"Yes."

"Oh, all right, *yes*. Damn you, Armand."

Armand chuckled under his breath as he and Bones

followed the butler up the stairs, having disposed of their hats and gloves on the large table set in the middle of the black and white tile floor of the foyer. "Buck up, Bones. It's only a female. Besides, I think she's smitten."

"Smitten? Smitten?" Bones took the stairs two at a time, catching up with Armand. "Really? You wouldn't just say that, Armand, would you? That would be cruel."

"Cold, hard, and now cruel. Bones, I don't know why you put up with me."

"Neither do I," Bones said, shaking his head. "I've a penchant for fast companions, that's what m'mother said."

Armand halted just at the top of the stairs, motioned for the butler to wait a moment before announcing them, then turned to his friend. "Bones, if I hear your mother's words coming out of your head one more time, I may have to push you down these stairs. There, was that cold, hard, and cruel enough for you?"

Bones looked at him for long moments. "You've got other things on your mind, don't you, Armand? It's the girl, isn't it? Lady Allegra. She's got you bound up in knots. I could enjoy watching you, if I weren't shaking in my own boots. What a sorry mess we are, both of us."

Armand didn't try to contradict his friend. Not when Bones was right. He was tied up in knots. Not all of them were of Allegra's making, but she now figured in all of them. The way thoughts of holding her, making love to her, thrilling her as she had so innocently thrilled him had haunted his dreams for the few moments he'd actually found sleep last night.

As for the rest of it? He didn't know whether to hope, or to curse coincidence.

"We're ready," Armand said to the butler, then looked quizzically at Bones as the butler moved off down the hallway, taking them past the open door to the main drawing room. "Hear that, Bones?"

"Do I hear music?" Bones said, tagging along behind Armand. "Yes, I do. Is that a waltz?"

Ah, the girl was practicing for the ball. Armand hid a smile as the butler stopped in front of a set of double doors, then pushed them open, the sounds of a waltz being played on a pianoforte growing louder as the doors opened.

"Yes, Bones, I believe it is. Don't bother," he then said quickly as the butler drew in breath, ready to announce their presence.

The butler, a man who looked about as happy to be a part of the Nesbitt household as a man chained to a wall in preparation of heading for the chopping block, bowed quickly, and just as quickly disappeared.

"We shouldn't go in unannounced," Bones said from behind Armand, standing so close that Armand could smell the peppermint on his friend's breath.

"We aren't going in yet, Bones. We're . . . observing."

"No, you're eavesdropping," Allegra said from behind Bones, who grabbed on to Armand's shoulders as he jumped half out of his boots.

Armand turned slowly, to see Allegra standing there, grinning at him as if they'd never argued—or kissed. "Lady Allegra," he said, bowing to her, "I'm afraid you've caught us. My apologies."

"Accepted," Allegra said as she walked past him, motioning for both men to follow. She stepped just inside the door of the large ballroom, then stood with her back to the wall.

"Mama and Oxie are learning the waltz for your ball," she told them, inclining her head toward the center of the room, where her parents were turning and swaying, and Lady Sunderland was intermittently exclaiming, "Ouch! Oh, Oxie, be careful!"

A rather thin man dressed all in black, and looking as if a small, furry animal had nested on his head, danced along beside them, his hands held out to an imaginary partner as he counted off: "One-two-*twree,* one-two-*twree.* And dip, and turn, and one-two-*twree.* Yeths, m'lord, my lady, yeths! Shimply dee-vine! And one-two-*twree!*"

"Twree?" Armand said quietly, imitating the man's affected lisp. "Who is that? And why do I think I remember him?"

Allegra grinned at him. "That, Gauthier, is Mr. Odo Pinabel, the premier dancing master in all of London."

"Callie learned from him, Armand, remember? Simon's mother engaged him."

"Everyone engages him, according to Mrs. Tomlin," Allegra said. "How do you like that thing perched on his head? Do you think it's dead yet?"

"If not, it would probably be a mercy to kill it," Armand said, turning to Bones. "Bones? Did you see that thing on his—Bones? Oh, for the love of—come on, sit down. And for God's sake, man, *breathe.*"

"What's wrong?" Allegra asked as Armand guided Bones to one of the straight-back chairs lining the ballroom.

"It's your cousin. I didn't see her at the pianoforte. Obviously, Bones has. Come on, Bones, in and out, in and out. Breathe, Bones."

Allegra sat down beside Bones and took one of his hands in both of hers. "My goodness, Mr. Bartholomew, you're as much of a looby as my cousin, aren't you? I think that's wonderful. Gauthier? Don't you think this is wonderful?"

"I think I may be ill," Armand said, but he smiled. "Bones. You have to pull yourself together before she sees you. Not that you aren't handsome and dashing, and all of that, but your face is as white as a sheet."

"I . . . I'll be fine, fine," Bones said, taking a large handkerchief from his pocket and dabbing at his damp forehead. "I just had a small turn there, nothing more."

"Should I ring for some water?" Allegra asked, then looked to the middle of the room as the playing stopped. "Oh, never mind, they're done now. Gauthier? Are you still agreeable to assisting Oxie?"

"I'm looking forward to it," Armand said as his lordship, having spied them, quickly kissed his wife's hand, then approached. "My lord," Armand said, bowing.

"Yes, yes, that's me all right. Ally? Did you see us? Weren't we splendid? How thoughtful of you to suggest that your mama and I learn the waltz. She's all a-flutter, you know. Well, Got-yer? Time we were off."

"Yes, my lord," Armand said as Bones, who had manfully struggled to his feet, tugged at the hem of his coat.

"First, my lord, may I have the pleasure of introducing to you my friend, Mr. Bartholomew Boothe?"

"Of course, of course," Oxie said, patting at his ample stomach. "You could use half of me stuck to you, couldn't you, Boothe?" he asked, then laughed. "Maybe more than half. Is he going with us, Got-yer? Don't need him."

"No, you don't," Allegra put in smoothly, "but we do. Mr. Boothe? Mr. Pinabel is a very competent teacher, but the man seems to dine on onions, even at this hour of the morning. Dancing with him is rather a trial. So, if it would be possible, sir, do you think you could partner my cousin and I as we learn the steps? My mother will play for us. Mr. Bartholomew?"

"I . . . but . . . I suppose so."

"So gracious, Mr. Boothe," Allegra said, winking at Armand. "Please, come with me and let these gentlemen go about their business."

She led Bartholomew away, the man's knees only slightly wobbly, looking back over her shoulder to say, "We'll expect you both back in one hour. Oxie? Be good."

"She thinks she's the parent and I'm the child," Oxie said as he headed for the doorway, Armand bringing up the rear. "Probably right, too. So, Got-yer. We'll just see where Mersey is, because he has everything we need."

"What we need for what, my lord?" Armand asked as they went down the stairs to the foyer. "I'm afraid I still don't know what service I'm to provide."

"Oh, don't you go worrying about that, Got-yer. I'll explain everything on the way to the viscount's house in

Portman Square. Never did like Eaton, you know. Worst of the bunch, if you ask me. But that was all right, Got-yer. They could snub me. But to snub my girls? I begged nicely, Got-yer, I really did."

"Yes, my lord," Armand said as a footman ran ahead to open the door of the closed carriage that had appeared in front of the mansion. "So this is more of a revenge than just a prank?"

Oxie settled himself against the squabs, the entire carriage rocking under his weight, and grinned at Armand. "No, this is a prank. I'm not a mean man, Got-yer. Not a mean bone in my body. I only play pranks."

He picked up his cane and banged it against the roof of the carriage, and as he fell back against the squabs when the carriage moved forward, said, "I'm only playing this one to even things out, and because Eaton has to be expecting it. None of them will be expecting what comes next."

"What comes next?" Armand repeated, looking at the man, wondering if he should press him for details, then warn Allegra. Her father was probably having even more fun here in London than she'd anticipated, and warning her might be good for everyone.

"Never mind, Got-yer, never you mind. Just something I read in a book. Now, let's talk about how you're going to prank Eaton, all right?"

"I thought I was to be your assistant," Armand said, with just a hint of trepidation.

"No. No, no, no. I'm just along to watch and enjoy. Eaton'll be looking for me now that I've already had my fun with Jagger and Berkert. But he won't be expecting you, Got-yer. You understand now? That's the beauty of it. It's above everything wonderful that I can do this, Got-yer, being an earl and all. Only fun in the thing."

Armand looked at the man, careful to keep his voice calm, only politely interested. Here was his chance to learn more of what he now desperately needed to know, for his own comfort. "You don't enjoy being an earl, my lord?"

"God, no," Oxie told him, shuddering. "Wasn't born to it, you know."

"I had heard something like that, yes."

"Ha! Bet you heard more than that, Got-yer. The last earl lost his only son at sea more years ago than I can count, so everyone knew somebody else in the family would fall into the title someday."

Armand had heard this, yes, but only after writing to Simon in the country, and reading the reply that had arrived only yesterday, explaining everything, had his interest deepened, his suspicions mounted. "The son died at sea? He was in the Royal Navy?"

Oxie shook his head. "No, nothing like that. The two of 'em, Harry and his bride, sailed out to one of those islands to check on holdings there. Let's see, what was it? Sugar plantation? Something like that. There's one letter tucked away somewhere at Sunderland, saying they were about to start home to England after about a year out there, but they never arrived. Never heard from again. Pity. Damned pity."

"And the son had no children, no heir?" He already knew the answer from Simon, but had to hear it from Oxie.

"Nope. Just the son and his bride. Took the earl another twenty-five years to drink himself to death. Never the same after he'd lost Harry."

"So you became the earl—what, five years ago? It came as a shock, you say?"

"Nobody was more surprised when I got stuck with the title, except maybe my cousin, Frederick. Who would have thought that a cousin of a cousin who'd married a village barmaid—Maisie, m'mother, God love and rest her—could have put out the next earl, I ask you."

He leaned closer to Armand. "Third wife, you know, and none of the others had whelped even once. Frederick's sure m'father was cuckolded, but in the end he couldn't prove it, so here I am. M'poor wife, she's as much a fish out of water as me, rattling around on that huge estate. We knew how to be the poor relations, you understand. The servants boss her, because they can, and I play my pranks, just to keep from being bored to flinders."

"And your daughter?"

"Ah, Allegra. She has the makings, but she refuses to do more than keep her mama happy, you know? I'd give it all up in a heartbeat, if it weren't for the money. Towering heaps of it, Got-yer." He grinned at Armand. "I'm not stupid, you understand."

Allegra haunted the windows overlooking the Square, waiting for the return of her father's carriage.

She'd spent an enjoyable hour, watching Elizabeth and Bones waltzing together, even though she'd somehow been condemned to dancing with Mr. Pinabel and his onions.

Still, it was worth the sacrifice to see two such tongue-tied and obviously lovestruck people make total idiots of themselves.

She'd never be like that. Mooning over someone, staring into his eyes as if she'd never seen eyes before, blushing and stammering and generally acting as if she'd misplaced her brains.

Still, Elizabeth seemed happy enough, and so did Bones. Happy enough, and finally comfortable enough with each other, to announce that they were, with Lettice along as companion, heading for the park on foot, to take the air.

Lettice had seemed happy enough to go along, her black gown rustling as she walked, her blacker than black hair so in contrast to her whiter than white skin.

Allegra had watched from the window as the trio set off, trying to imagine Lettice with red hair against that same white skin. Perhaps a green gown, to match her eyes.

She'd be stunning. Not quite as old as Allegra's mother, Lettice had a slim frame, good posture, and a chin line that had only just begun to show some hint of softness.

Imagine her at nineteen, at five and twenty. She must have had half of London in love with her, desiring her.

And now she hid behind that hair, those gowns, and longed for another life. Not life in her village, not life as a housekeeper or companion able to at least be out watching Society, if not really a part of it. Where would she go next? Was it wonderful, or frightening, to have a whole world of possibilities in front of you?

"Ah, they're back," Allegra said to the empty drawing room, and ran toward the hallway, grabbing up her hat, pelisse, gloves, and parasol as she went.

The front door was just opening, her father stepping inside, as Allegra went racing past him, down the steps to where Armand was waiting.

"You knew I'd be here, waiting for you?" she asked, tying the strings of her bonnet.

"I'd hoped," he said, his eyes bright, full of mischief.

"You're looking pleased with yourself," she said as she unfurled her parasol and began to walk.

He followed along. "You noticed? What gave me away? This grin I can't seem to wipe off my face?"

"That would be it, yes," she said, looking up at him. Oh, how his smile affected her! "Oxie didn't tell me what he was going to do. What was it? Did he learn that the viscount would be away from home and somehow bribe the servants so that he could sneak in the poor man's curricle in pieces, put it back together, and set the horses in their traces—all in the man's drawing room? He hasn't done that one since the squire was visiting his sister. No, he couldn't have done that. It would have taken too much time."

"He's actually done that?"

"Oh, yes," Allegra said, twirling her parasol between her fingers. "Except it was a wagon, complete with hay. The squire is my father's favorite target, poor man. So? Are you going to tell me?"

"Not until you tell me why we're speaking again. I

thought you never intended to see me again."

"Is that a complaint, Gauthier?" Allegra asked, avoiding his eyes.

"Merely an observation. And stop looking so meek and mild, Ally, or I'm going to have to kiss you."

"Here? In the middle of the Square? Oh, I don't think so, Gauthier. You seem to have a penchant for pulling me into alleyways."

"I'm not even going to explain that to you, because I'm in no mood for another argument." He touched her elbow, directing her toward the fountain, then indicating that she should perch herself on the edge of it while he stood there—obviously still so full of energy that the last thing he wanted to do would be to sit down.

"Oh, very well. I won't say I'm not anxious to hear everything. What happened? Which of Oxie's pranks was it? You went to the viscount's house?"

Armand put his hands out in front of him, both to stop her questions and in an effort to put a sort of *frame* around what he would say next.

"All right," he said, then took a deep breath, grinned. "God, it was funny."

"Yes, yes," she urged. "Funny. You begin to frighten me, Gauthier. You aren't going to start pranking in earnest, like Oxie, are you?"

"No, I've had my fun," he told her. "Your father explained everything to me on our way to Portman Square while Mersey, poor fellow, whimpered in the opposite corner of the carriage."

"Poor Mersey."

"Yes, poor Mersey. Anyway," he continued, obviously eager to tell his story, "we arrived in Portman Square, and Mersey got out, retrieved everything he needed from the boot, and set off. I was to give him ten minutes to get himself in position, then follow."

"Where did Mersey go?"

"Another marvel. Your father did some investigating, as he called it, and found that the town house attached to the viscount's is empty save for a skeleton staff. Not only did he find that out, but he somehow got himself a tour, that house being laid out exactly the same as Eaton's next door. Oxie's a man for details, I've decided. Anyway, a few coins to one of the footmen, and Mersey was expected, granted access, and climbed to the roof."

"Ah, the roof," Allegra said, wiggling against the stone fountain. "I think I know what you'll say next."

"Perhaps, but let me tell you anyway. I waited those ten minutes, then went to Eaton's door, banging on it with the side of my fist. I brushed past his man who said the viscount was still in bed—which Oxie had also anticipated—raced up the stairs, straight into Eaton's bedchamber, which overlooks the mews behind the house. The man sleeps in the nude," he added, making a face.

Allegra pressed her fingers to her mouth. "Oh, dear. That was unfortunate for you, I imagine."

Armand gave a wave of his hands. "But that doesn't matter. I just barreled into the room, yelling that I needed to get up to the roof immediately, as there was a man up there, threatening to jump off."

"Ah, yes. The man on the roof."

"Don't interrupt. I grabbed Eaton's dressing gown, flung it at him, as much for my sake as his, then dragged him to the window overlooking the mews. He was still half asleep, but when the body went past the window—"

"He woke up very nicely?"

"He *screamed*. I was supposed to be the one who grew faint, giving Mersey time to get down off the roof, but when Eaton looked out of the window, saw all that blood? I had to slap his face a few times just to get him to pay attention to me."

"At which point, while Mersey and Oxie were gathering up the cloth they'd put down, and rolled up the straw dummy and the spilled cow's blood in it, took it away, you told the viscount that you needed him to see to the body while you went and fetched the Watch."

"Exactly. I had to half drag him down to the door, then left him to go out to the mews, to look for the body that wasn't there."

"Meanwhile, you ran to the front of the town house, grabbed Mersey, and ran him back to Eaton, telling him that you'd been so lucky as to find a member of the Watch right there in the Square."

"You're taking most of the fun out of this, you know," Armand said, frowning.

Then he brightened. "Mersey may not be a jolly volunteer, but he can put his heart into it once he's given no other choice. I left him there, threatening to take Eaton to the Watch house to explain what he did with the body, because I was much too close to laughing, and spoiling the joke. Ally? Have you ever seen a man in breeches and dressing gown, trying to explain that a body was there, he'd seen it, but now it was gone?"

"Mersey warned him he'd be back later, with his superior, to question the viscount some more?"

"That was the plan, yes. Do you think Eaton will spend more than five minutes packing, before he heads to his country estate?"

Allegra stood up, brushed down her skirts. "I shouldn't imagine he would, if it weren't for the other prank, the one Oxie played on Walter Jagger and Sir Guy. As it is, I would guess it took only a few minutes before the viscount was cursing Oxie—and you—quite soundly. Another bridge burned, Gauthier. Why are you doing this?"

At last, he sobered. "I'm really not sure, Allegra. But I think it has something to do with how very civilized I've been these past three years. I think I've decided I don't want or even need to be civilized anymore. Thanks to you and your father."

Allegra's heart slammed hard against her breast. "Or because you've either found what you came to London to look for, or you don't care to find it anymore? Because you're leaving? Going back to America? Back to—you know, what you used to do?"

"A wise man never tries to walk the same path twice, Allegra," he told her, guiding her back toward the mansion. "It's time to move on, not repeat the past. To be truthful, this wasn't even my dream."

"What wasn't your dream? Coming to London? You know, Gauthier, I make a fine showing of pretending I know what's going on, but I don't. What was *your* dream?"

His smile was slow, and warm. "I'm learning that now, Allegra. The ball's tomorrow night. Will you have time to walk out with me again tomorrow? Say at eleven?"

"Yes, I think I will." She bit her bottom lip, looked at him from the second step, so that she was almost at eye level with him. "I caught out Letty last night, rubbing color into her hair. We . . . we had a long talk. You're a good man, Gauthier. You were very kind to her."

"I wonder," Armand said, his smile fading. "Sometimes, with the best intentions, we think to make changes when, perhaps, change is not what's needed. At least, not on the outside. Until tomorrow, here, in the Square?"

Allegra nodded. "Until tomorrow."

Then she turned, ran up the last few steps, and raced inside the mansion, not stopping until she was safely in her room, where she could think more about the puzzle that was Armand Gauthier.

Armand slowly walked back to his house on the opposite side of the Square, barely noticing that he had to dodge carriages and laughing children chasing hoops or dogs, even walking past Lady Harper and her maid without so much as tipping his hat.

He was lost in a world he didn't quite recognize, but that at the same time felt vaguely familiar.

A world of laughter, of silliness, even a hint of danger.

Being truthful with himself, he knew a part of him still longed to know about his past, even if that now meant learning things he might be better off not knowing . . . for Allegra's sake.

But what he knew most of all was that he was rapidly falling in love with Allegra Nesbitt.

"And a good afternoon to you, Quincy," he said as he entered his own mansion, handed over his hat and gloves. "Fine day, isn't it?"

"Somewhere, sir," Quincy answered solemnly, handing him a folded sheet of paper with a broken wax seal on it. "This arrived while you were gone, and as Mr. Boothe was also away from home, I took the liberty of opening it, worried that it might be some emergency."

Armand took the folded letter, held it in front of him. "And was it?"

"That isn't for me to say, sir. It was brought here not an hour ago by a young lad who had been given a penny to make the delivery."

"Really?" Armand looked at the letter again, at the sealing wax that had no discernible crest pressed into it, and then at Quincy once more. "I'm not going to like this?"

"I doubt it, sir," Quincy said, bowing. "Again, my apologies for opening the note, but it was not specifically addressed to anyone in this household. And begging your pardon again, sir, may I just say that I've truly enjoyed being in your employ, and have nothing but respect and admiration for you, sir. You're what my late major would have called a fine right-un."

"Good God, man, am I dead? No, never mind. Quincy, thank you," Armand said, and he headed up the stairs, tapping the piece of folded paper against his thigh until he'd entered the empty drawing room. Tossing the paper onto the drinks table, he fortified himself with a glass of wine before opening the missive.

There was no salutation, no signature. Just the message; short, and potentially damning.

We are all mortal. Don't worry, your secret is safe with me.

Chapter Fifteen

WALTER JAGGER'S SMALL DRAWING ROOM, a good meeting place because there was no curious wife in the household and their club was not private enough for serious conversation, became clogged with angry and definitely nervous male bodies late that same afternoon.

The conversation ran the gamut, becoming more frank as the amount of spirits imbibed increased.

"It's Nesbitt," Sir Guy Berkert declared, dropping himself into the blue on blue striped couch that had so lately and briefly resided in his own drawing room. "It has to be Nesbitt. Again, I say, ignore the letters."

"Yes," Jagger agreed hopefully. "We should just ignore them. He just wants to watch us chasing our own tails."

"That's easy enough for you to say, Walter," Viscount Eaton grumbled. "But the man could spread rumors, lies, or even follow up on these first letters with demands for payment of some sort. He's gone too far this time, turned mean. I refuse to have my pockets bled. But, and this is paramount, I cannot and will not allow my name to be unjustly sullied, Walter. M'father's turned ninety last month and is hanging on to life by a thread. I could be the earl any day now—everything I've always hoped for, soon to be mine. I have too much to lose if Nesbitt tries to destroy my good name. You may not understand that, as you've not nearly the consequence I've got."

The viscount looked around the faintly shabby room, wrinkled up his nose. "Or as much to lose."

"Everything is everything, Gideon," Jagger pointed out, "whether it's all that you've got, or all that I've got. All I've got is my good name and a son to pass that name to when I die. Trying to bleed me would be like trying to suck blood from a turnip. But you're right, I can't risk it."

"Your son? Hell, man, you don't even *like* Rutherford," Sir Guy said, sparing a moment from slurping up free liquid libations. "Call him the devil's spawn, you do. Heard you, just last week."

"True enough, but it's the . . . the *principle* of the thing. Yes, that's what it is, the *principle* of the thing. Guy, surely you can see that. That and the fact that I do *like* being in Society, you ass."

The viscount laughed. "Walter was attempting to sound noble, saying all that about Rutherford. Leave him his pride, Guy."

"Oh, that. Pride. I understand that, I suppose." Sir Guy looked at his empty glass, then headed for the drinks table, where he had already stopped several times, making serious inroads on Walter Jagger's supply of faintly inferior port. "It's not fair, that's what it's not. He already pranked Walter and me. Why include us in this? It's your turn, Gideon. We were done."

"He wouldn't *dare* try anything with me," the viscount declared, knowing he'd take to his grave the tale of himself in breeches and dressing gown, desperately trying to explain the absence of a body that had so recently flown off his roof. After all, he was a viscount, a man of consequence. Or had he already said that?

The viscount put down his wineglass, deciding that he'd drunk enough. He had to choose his words carefully in order to reveal what must be revealed, keep hidden what must stay hidden in order to preserve his standing as the leader of this small group, remain the one who would not stupidly fall victim to one of Oxie Nesbitt's pranks.

"Yes," he said now, "you were done, Oxie having pranked you both, and he knew better than to come after me. That's why I can't be sure it's just Nesbitt this time," he explained to his two cronies, watching for their reaction.

Neither of them even so much as perked up their ears. He had surrounded himself with idiots.

"I said, it may not be just Nesbitt this time," he repeated, ever hopeful.

"Really? Who would you have it be, then, Gideon?" Jagger asked, sounding even more oppressed than he had earlier. "Wish you hadn't said that. And then you went and said it again. I'd much rather it was Nesbitt, to tell you the truth. Nobody pays attention to him."

"Our secrets are safe with him, that's what the notes said," Sir Guy grumbled. "How would he know our secrets, or be able to tell them to someone else?"

"Your secrets, Guy. I have none," the viscount declared.

"Well, isn't that jolly good for you," Jagger said, a bite in his tone. "Or perhaps you just think you've kept yours better hidden. Otherwise, what was all that about your damned consequence? You can say you're worried Oxie would make up lies, or that you don't have a secret, Gideon, but you do. Don't you?"

"Very well, Walter, if it makes you happy, yes, I have a secret. Now what? Do I get to watch you gloat?"

Jagger spread his arms, calling for order, as he was, after all, the host. "I think we can agree that no man who has lived a good deal of his life is free of anything that could cause, um, embarrassment, if it were to become common knowledge. Even you, Gideon."

"And I still say it's Nesbitt," Sir Guy declared, tossing back his drink. "At the bottom of it, I suppose I don't trust the man with *my* secret. Do either of you trust him with yours?"

"No," Jagger said, looking at the viscount.

"No," the viscount said quietly, feeling encouraged. "No, I don't."

Jagger collapsed onto a chair. "We should have done something about the daughter, that's what we should have done. Answered his letter, agreed to be of assistance. Or for Freddie's girl, at the very least. Freddie was a good'un, for a Nesbitt. Why didn't we do that?"

"Because helping Freddie's chit would also be

helping Oxie," the viscount reminded him. "I would sooner man the winch to help hoist Prinney's tonnage onto his horse than assist Oxie Nesbitt in anything, except perhaps into his grave."

"Thirty years, Gideon," Sir Guy reminded his friend. "Surely we could forgive pranks thirty years in the past. Schoolboy pranks. We should have forgotten them."

"What? Writing to my father in my name, saying I'd decided to convert, become a Catholic priest?" The viscount shuddered. "I was plucked from school so fast I didn't know my head from my heels, and subjected to a blistering lecture that I can still remember in my nightmares. Lost two quarters' allowance, too, just for having a *friend* who could write anything so terrible. Forgive him? I don't think so. The man's pernicious."

Walter Jagger cocked his head toward Sir Guy. "Remember what he did to us, Guy? Sending us off to that brothel, or so he called it, as a treat for your birthday he said, just to find out all those fancy painted ladies had cocks? Luckily for me, it didn't take me as long to figure it all out as it did you."

He chuckled low in his throat. "You were running, Guy, and screaming, and hanging on to your breeches while your chubby white arse was hanging out for all to—"

"Shut up," Sir Guy growled. "Just shut up. God, I hate that man. Pernicious? Is that what you called him, Gideon? He is that, boy and man. The whole family is probably pernicious, seed, breed, and generation."

"And we can't chance that he's merely pranking us. He actually may know something. The sneaking bastard."

"Really, Gideon? Then you're definitely saying you *do* have a secret terrible enough that you wouldn't want it bandied about London?"

"As you said, doesn't everyone? I think we've already agreed. For the love of God, try to keep up, Guy. But, as I also already said, I'm afraid it could be much worse than that."

"How?"

"As I said—twice now, this will be the third time— Oxie may not be alone in this letter business. He may have brought someone else into his confidence."

"Oh, yes, you did say that, didn't you? I think I don't want to think about that, but I'm not drunk enough yet, I suppose. Oh, very well. Who?"

Ah, finally. The viscount looked at both men, counted to three, to build their interest, and their apprehension. After all, he needed these men. And wasn't that, among everything else he had to bear, a bleeding pity?

Taking a deep breath, he said what he had to say.

"Armand Gauthier. He's been hanging around the Nesbitt chit's shoe strings, and I have it on good authority that he and Oxie are thick as thieves. Never liked Gauthier. Something too smooth about him, and he's always entirely too interested in everyone for my comfort. Or haven't you noticed? Man asks more questions than a doting father interviewing a prospective suitor."

"Armand Gauthier? The bastard prince? Brockton's friend? Oh, that can't be good. Not if Oxie's talking to him. Are you sure, Gideon?"

"I'm sure. And he's not a bastard prince. He's nothing

that we can know for sure, although we've all heard the rumors that include everything, including the possibility of a dark and nefarious past. He gets his money somewhere, my friends. Could *he* be a blackmailer? Could he have been asking his questions and then bleeding half of London dry these past three years while smiling in everybody's faces—laughing in everybody's faces, stabbing them all in the back? We can't know, can we? What we *can* know for certain is that he and Oxie Nesbitt have been seen together around town. They're as close as inkleweavers."

"But—how do you know that? Thick as thieves? Close as inkleweavers? Have you seen them for yourself? Is that it? Have you seen Gauthier with him, spoken to Gauthier? What do you know for certain, Gideon? We can't go off half-cocked, not on something this important, now can we?"

The viscount angrily glared at his friends. As if he'd tell them about Gauthier racing into his bedchamber, making a complete idiot of him. "Do you really want to waste time questioning me? I'm telling you, if Oxie Nesbitt knows anything, Armand Gauthier knows it now as well. And probably the wife, and the daughter. All of them. Pernicious Nesbitts."

Jagger sighed. "So what do we do?"

Gideon Pakes, Viscount Eaton, a man with much to lose, said, "Shut them up. We have to find some way to scare Oxie back to the country, where he belongs. Failing that, we may have to shut them up, the whole pernicious family. *Permanently.*"

"Maybe . . ." Sir Guy offered hopefully, "maybe my

secret isn't all that terrible?"

"I know your wife, Guy, remember?" the viscount said quietly. "Do you really want her to know?"

"God." Sir Guy buried his head in his hands.

"Everyone would turn their backs to me," Jagger said, then moaned. "Everyone."

"So we're agreed? Gentlemen? First we try to scare him off. And if that doesn't work . . . ?"

In the silence that followed, Rutherford Jagger tiptoed away from the doorway where he'd been eavesdropping, a smile on his face. "So," he whispered under his breath, "dearest papa has a secret. Even more important, and potentially profitable, the pompous viscount has a secret. I should know that secret. It's time I made the acquaintance of one Oxie Nesbitt, before one of those three drunken sots puts a bullet in the man's knee while aiming for his brain . . ."

Saturday dawned foggy and rainy . . . and whining.

Allegra sat at the table in the morning room, poking at her plate of eggs and ham, trying to block out Elizabeth's near wails about the damp in the air, the way her hair "just will not behave in weather so foul. I shall be a mess, a veritable *mess!*"

Allegra stabbed her fork into a piece of ham, held it in front of her, and gave a moment's thought to shoving the pink meat into Elizabeth's craw in order to shut her up. "So your hair curls," she said. "I fail to see the problem. Or am I wrong, and what it really does is turn bright blue and begin emoting Latin verse?"

Across the table, Lettice Tomlin coughed into her

linen serviette.

"Oh, you just don't understand, cousin," Elizabeth protested hotly. "I look such a *child* when my hair curls. I can already feel myself getting all . . . all *wooly*. And I wanted to look so *elegant* for the ball tonight. What will Mr. Boothe say when he sees me?"

"Poor, poor Cousin Elizabeth," Allegra said, looking at her cousin's mass of black hair, that looked just fine to her. Her own problems should be so infinitesimal. "I can just hear Mr. Boothe when he sees you. Let's see, Elizabeth, how does that go? Oh, yes. 'Baa, baa, black sheep, have you any wool?' "

Elizabeth stiffened her spine. "That is not *at all* funny."

"Isn't it?" Allegra looked at Lettice, who refused to meet her eyes. "I like it. And you could answer, 'Yes, sir, yes, sir, three bags full. One for my master, and one for my dame, and one for the little boy who lives down the lane.' Lord knows the two of you should be happy you'd found *something* to say to each other, instead of just making cow's eyes at each other. Or is that sheep's eyes?"

"Well, she's been nicely and predictably routed," Lettice said, picking up her teacup as Elizabeth ran from the morning room. "Am I to believe you wished to speak privately with me? Or are you just being mean this morning?"

"I was not being mean," Allegra said, putting down her fork. "Oh, all right, perhaps I was. But did you hear her? Five minutes, I swear, of nothing but how she has a spot on her chin as huge as a mountain, and how she's sure her gown will be woefully out of style, and how she only has her mother's pearls and how they'll pale next to everyone else's jewels. And then the hair? It was just too much. I did her a kindness by shutting her up before she could remember she's also a Nesbitt, and nobody wants her at the ball anyway."

Lettice tipped her head to one side, contemplated her charge. "And what about you? Your gown is pressed and ready, not that you seem to care. Don't you want to talk about how you'd like your hair styled for the evening? And what jewels will you wear?"

Allegra shrugged. "I don't know. Some pearls I suppose? Don't debutantes wear pearls? Or garnets? It's not important."

Cupping her chin in her hands as she rested her elbows on the table, Lettice said, "Really. And just what *is* important?"

"All right," Allegra said, propping her own elbows on the table. "Tell me this. I was supposed to meet Gauthier this morning at eleven, in the Square. How do I do that, now that it's raining? We can't be private here, and I know we can't go to his mansion. What do I do? How can we be private?"

Lettice sat back, looked at Allegra through slitted eyelids. "Private? Why private?"

"We have to talk, that's why."

"Talk? Is that all?"

"Well, of course it—why? What are you thinking?"

"I'm thinking, Allegra, that I know you better than you know you. Talk? About what?"

Allegra looked toward the door to the hallway. "You

know. The *sea horse*."

"You're still not satisfied with his answers?"

Picking up her fork, Allegra began pushing the remnants of her breakfast around her plate. "Not entirely, no. He still hasn't told me why he came to England in the first place."

"Has he offered?"

"Yes. No. Oh, blast it, Letty, he hints. *Hints*. The man is driving me insane. And last night Oxie told me, quite innocently, that he and Gauthier were talking about the last earl, and the earl's son, the one who died at sea so long ago. I know you said Gauthier asks questions of everyone, but why was he asking questions of Oxie? What about us could possibly interest him?"

"Perhaps Mr. Gauthier was just making conversation?"

"No."

"Perhaps he is, like you, just nosy?"

"You don't believe that any more than I do, Letty. I don't like questions, I like answers."

Lettice got up, crossed over to the doorway, slid the pair of doors shut, then returned to the table. "Has he touched you?"

Allegra knew she could lie. To her mother, even to her father. And they'd both believe her. Lying to Letty, however, was about as productive as begging Oxie to stop spreading glue on doorknobs.

"Well?"

"He . . . he may have kissed me."

"And you want more," Lettice said, her tone fatalistic. "I remember those days. Ah, love."

257

Allegra looked up, straight into Lettice's sad green eyes. "You've been in love, Letty? I thought—"

"You thought I was a ruined girl who grew up a ruined woman, yes. But that doesn't mean there weren't times when I had hopes, when I believed, if only for an instant, that one of my . . . gentlemen would offer more than a cozy nest where he could visit me after leaving his wife."

"Oh, Letty, I'm so sorry," Allegra said, reaching a hand across the table, to take the woman's fingers in hers, squeeze them comfortingly. "But I don't love Gauthier. Really."

Lettice smiled. "Yes, my dear idiot, you do. You can tell yourself whatever you want, that you're in town against your will and might as well have an adventure— anything you want—but I know better, so don't try to tell me differently. He intrigues you, he teases you, he maddens you. And you love him."

Allegra took back her hand, stood up from her chair, and began to pace. "Love? I feel something, I'll admit that, Letty. But love?" She turned to look at her friend. "How would I know?"

"Are you worried about him?"

"Yes."

"Do you want to know everything about him, everything that happened to him before he met you, so that you can know him even better?"

"That's just because I'm nosy. You said so yourself."

"Really? When you see him, do you recognize his walk even before you can see his face? Does your heart flutter when he smiles? Are his kisses enough, or is there so much more you want him to give, want to give him in return?"

Allegra felt her cheeks growing hot. "I can't answer those questions."

"You just did, my dear, you just did. God, I was a fool to think I could be anything but what I am. It's about time you knew who *you* were, Allegra. Anything else just wastes precious time. Come with me."

Allegra followed Lettice as she opened the sliding pocket doors, heading for the servant stairs that led up to the bedrooms.

Once in Lettice's room, the older woman opened the drawer in the table beside her bed.

"You're going to have another cheroot?" Allegra asked, confused.

"No, I'm giving you this," Lettice said, holding out a large key on a brass ring. "Here, take it."

"What . . . what is it?"

"I have a small house, in Half Moon Street. It's empty, in Holland covers, and there's only one servant, Ruthann, who was with me . . . before. She's very discreet. If you're serious, Allegra, I'll send a note over to Mr. Gauthier's mansion, telling him to bring a closed coach around to the mews, and you can give him the key to my house. I'll also send a note to Ruthann, telling her to expect you. I repeat, she's very discreet. You and Mr. Gauthier can . . . be private there."

"To talk," Allegra said, closing her fingers around the key, feeling it bite into her palm. "Only to talk."

"Please, Allegra. If I'm going to go to hell for this, don't lie to me, too. At the very least, humor me into believing I'm playing Cupid, and with nothing but happy endings in sight. In short, my dear, I'm going to trust you. Moreover, I'm putting my trust in Armand. If he agrees to accompany you to Half Moon Street, I'll know his intentions are honorable."

Armand looked up from his morning newspaper, cocking one eyebrow at Quincy. "Another note? How ominous."

Bones put down his fork, looked across the table. "A note? A billet-doux? Armand, you sly dog, you."

"Sly all right," Conor O'Neill said, pausing in the act of slopping up a half-dozen eggs. "Didn't know the boyo could read," he added, winking at Bones.

Armand waited until the majordomo had turned and left the room, looking after him, sure the man had read the unsealed note, and not quite sure if the man approved or disapproved. "If you two will excuse me a moment as I read this?" he asked, opening the single page.

He read the few lines, looked toward the doorway, knowing now that Quincy most definitely did *not* approve. Nobody of any sense would. And yet, for him, the note sealed his fate—or Fate was pushing him toward an ending he had just lately acknowledged that he must face, sooner or later.

He had preferred later, when he was more sure. More sure of himself and his information, more sure of his conclusions, more sure of Allegra's heart . . . but he should also have known Allegra would not grant him a minute more than she could manage.

He folded the note neatly, tucked it into his pocket. "And now, if you two will excuse me even further? It would seem I have a pressing engagement."

"A woman," Conor said, nodding. "You go on, boyo. Bones and me, we'll stay here and eat your breakfast up for you. It's the least we can do."

"No, it's not. And he can't go. Armand, have you forgotten you're hosting a ball here tonight? Quincy is a marvel, but he can't do everything. Any moment now there will be deliveries of flowers, and the musicians will be lugging in their instruments, and someone will have to tell the staff where the chairs go, and where the orchestra goes, and where the flowers go. And the food? What about the food?"

Armand smiled. "But, Bones, you're the expert in such matters. I'd assumed you'd be in charge."

"Me? Oh. Well. It's not that m'mother didn't raise me to know all of this, now is it?" Then he frowned. "But why should I do it? It's your ball."

"Miss Elizabeth will be here, I believe?" Armand pointed out, knowing that would get his friend's attention. "I plan to tell her how masterfully you prepared the entire event. She'll be so impressed, won't she, Conor?"

"Impresses me all hollow," Conor agreed. "Only partying I ever planned was me, a bottle, and a soft spot to fall when I got too drunk to stand. Come on, Bones, I'll help."

"But you just said you know nothing about balls, parties. How can you help?"

"I know a lot about bottles, that's how. Nobody'll pass off any second rate spirits on Armand here, not with me around to taste it all. Ain't that right, Armand? Same goes for the food. I know my food, that I do."

"Then it's settled," Armand said, smiling. "Thank you, gentlemen. I'll be back . . . when I get back."

He headed for the foyer, to see Quincy standing there, holding out his gloves, hat, and a cloak to protect him from the mizzle outside.

"My coach is, I assume, already waiting for me?"

"It is, sir. I pride myself on anticipating every possible occurrence. Sir."

"Even when you've read my private note, and are assuming that I am off now to debauch a fair lady?"

"You wouldn't do that, sir. It remains my expectation that there will be the announcement of a betrothal this evening."

"Your hopes run higher than mine, Quincy. I'm wondering if I'll *live* until this evening."

Quincy frowned. "There's a problem, sir?"

"Yes, there most certainly is. There's one hell of a problem, and I'd be the worst sort of bastard if I didn't tell the lady *before* even entertaining the thought of doing anything else, even proposing marriage," Armand said, tapping his hat down on his head, and heading for the coach.

Chapter Sixteen

ALLEGRA FELL ONTO THE SEAT of the coach, slightly breathless after her mad dash through the downpour from the kitchens, where she had caused more than one maid to stare, openmouthed, as she had stood there with a heavy black veil over her head, draped down over her shoulders.

The veil, which belonged to Lettice, had been Allegra's idea. After all, if a person is going to indulge in an intrigue, that person should at least show she's willing to enter into the spirit of the moment. Go incognito, that sort of thing.

She pushed up the veil now, blowing as it was, sodden with rain, it stuck to the tip of her nose, and looked across the coach at Armand. She grinned at him.

"Hello there, Gauthier. Isn't this fun?"

His smile did something very strange to her stomach. "So, you're enjoying yourself? How wonderful for you."

Her smile faded. "What's the matter? Don't tell me you're going to be a spoilsport, and after all the trouble Letty went to, poor thing."

"Yes, Letty. She did go to a lot of trouble, didn't she? One wonders why."

More nervous than she cared to admit, Allegra busied herself folding the black veil, smoothing down her damp hair that definitely did not have a tendency to curl in this sort of weather, drat it anyway. "Oh, that's easy. Letty is a hopeless romantic."

"Really?" Armand raised one eyebrow as he took the veil from her lap, slid it through his fingers. "Or would that be *hopeful* romantic?"

"I wouldn't know," Allegra said, fidgeting on the velvet squabs. "How far is it to Half Moon Street?"

"Far enough for me to ask a few questions, you to answer them, and me to decide if this coach goes to Half

Moon Street or back to Grosvenor Square."

"Oh." Allegra twisted her hands in her lap. "You're going to be proper, aren't you?"

"Having been all but propositioned, via a third party, no less? Yes, I am. I must be a fool."

At that, Allegra's head flew up and she glared at him. "Propositioned? Oh, that's just ridiculous, Gauthier. What do you think is going to happen? That we're going to Half Moon Street, and the moment we're through the door I'm going to . . . going to *jump* on you?"

Damn him and his crooked smile! "Now there's an intriguing prospect. Maybe I should just consider myself fortunate and be done with it. *Jump* on me, you say? Why, Lady Allegra, the mind does boggle."

"Oh, shut up, Gauthier," she warned tightly, plucking at her skirts, which were also damp. She should have forgone the veil and worn her hooded cloak. But she'd gone for the dramatic, the nearly silly, and now she was sitting here, half drowned, with her sprigged muslin gown all but plastered to her body.

And she was sure Gauthier had noticed, damn him.

She crossed her arms over her midriff, realized that this only pulled the material of her bodice more closely against her. Not that she could cross her arms across her bosom, because then Gauthier would probably laugh so hard at her that he'd fall off the seat in his hilarity and she'd have to kill him.

"Would you care to borrow my cloak?" he asked as she repositioned her hands in her lap, then rethought even that, and gave up pretense, grabbing on to either shoulder as if shivering from the cold and damp—

which was a good trick if she could pull it off, as she'd never felt so *overheated* in her life.

She nodded, unable to trust her voice, or her temper, then grabbed the cloak as he handed it to her, quickly slipped it over her shoulders. "Thank you. I'm cold."

"Yes, I'd noticed," Gauthier said with a level look at her now-covered bosom, and Allegra felt hot blood rushing into her cheeks. "So? Are you going to tell me why we're heading for Half Moon Street?"

Allegra rolled her eyes. "Because it's raining, silly."

"Oh, I see. It's raining. Meaning, if I'm following you correctly, that we could not meet in the Square?"

She narrowed her eyes. "Are you deliberately trying to make me mad at you?"

"In truth, I think I am. But that's because I don't want to dwell too closely on why you thought it so necessary to speak with me this morning, considering the fact that you'll be in attendance at the ball tonight. You *will* be in attendance, won't you?"

"Do I have a choice? I don't think so, not unless I want Elizabeth wailing loud enough to bring the roof down on all our heads. And why are you afraid of *why* I wanted to speak with you this morning?"

"I don't think I used the word *afraid*. Although it might fit."

"Stop that," Allegra said, pressing her hands to her ears. "Just stop going in circles, Gauthier, and acting as if this is all one big, silly debacle of my making. And, for God's sake, stop hinting that I'm out to seduce you."

"Well, now I'm crushed. I've always wanted to be seduced."

Allegra slowly pulled her tense fingers into fists as she glared at him, as a low groan escaped her lips. "That's it. Bang on the roof, or whatever it is you do to get your coachman's attention, and have him drive back to Grosvenor Square."

"Oh, I don't think so. Now, I'll promise not to interrupt again, and you can tell me why we're going—*may* be going—to Half Moon Street."

"Well, it's not to jump on you, that's for certain," Allegra bit out. "Oh, all right, make faces, Gauthier, but I will ignore them. I needed to talk to you privately about who you are, and what you've been looking for that you're not looking for now, if you're leaving and if you'd tell me if you were, and—"

"In other words," he interrupted, and she was grateful for that interruption, "you want to know everything about me. How like a woman."

"Piffle," she countered. "Most women only want to know the depth of your pocketbook and if you're invited to the best parties."

"Too true," he agreed. "It's only a few who worry about whether the man in question is in danger of getting his neck stretched."

"Oh. That. Yes, all right, I'm worried about that. Especially since Oxie might know more than he should, which he almost always does, and then decides to play some sort of prank on you, which is nearly a certainty."

"He already has."

Allegra's head shot up. "What? He already has? Oh, God, what has he done?"

"I'm only guessing that it's your father. Perhaps you

can be more certain?"

She watched as Armand reached inside his waistcoat and came out with a single sheet of paper, then passed it to her. Still looking at him, she reluctantly unfolded the paper, and then just as reluctantly looked down at it, read the two damning lines.

"We're all mortal? Oh, Lord, yes, that's Oxie. He was very struck by the thought when he first said the words, while we were still at home at Sunderland. He said he'd have to remember them. I should have known then that this was the same as him saying he'd feel honor-bound to find a way to *use* them someday. But the rest is rather sinister, isn't it, or at least could be, if you didn't know the note was from Oxie. Thank goodness he sent it to you, and not to anyone who wouldn't be quite so understanding. Because he doesn't mean any harm, Gauthier. You know that, don't you?"

"That's the one thing I do know, Allegra," Armand said as the coach turned a corner, began to slow. "What I'm not as sure of is if I'm the only one who received such a note. Or have you forgotten Jagger, Sir Guy, and the dear, near naked viscount? Do you think one prank was enough for him where they are concerned?"

Allegra refolded the paper, handed it back to him, hating that her fingers were shaking. "He did prank all three of them so, yes, he could be done."

"Except that he was avidly reading a book the other day—*before* he eavesdropped at your door—and seemed very pleased with himself. You saw the book, didn't you? Saw the title?"

"Not the title, no, not that I haven't tried. He hid it too

well, drat him, although I will find it sooner or later. I always find him out, sooner or later. But you saw it? What was it?"

"Ah, I've committed the title to memory. It's *Smith's Amusements: Tricks, Ploys, and Sundries Mischief*. Just the sort of title to appeal to his lordship, don't you think?"

"Oh, dear."

"Yes, I thought much the same myself."

"So there *could* be others who got the same note."

"Again, I thought so myself. Ah, we're here. You may continue borrowing my cloak. That way we'll both arrive damp, rather like a matched set of idiots."

"Uh-huh," Allegra said, not really hearing him, but just waiting for him to exit the coach so that she could follow him.

The rain was coming down so hard now that she didn't dare lift her head to inspect the exterior of the small house, but only ran quickly up the few steps, and past the door being held open by a gray-haired woman dressed in lavender satin, and wearing enough face paint to make Allegra blink in surprise and faint shock.

"Well, hello there, ducks," she said, winking at Armand. "Letty said it was you."

"And a good morning to you, Ruthann. You're looking well."

Ruthann patted at the slipping topknot on her head. "I do my best. You're only past your prime when you think so, that's what I say. Not that I mind a warm bed without anybody else's cold feet in it, if you get my meaning," she added, giving him yet another wink. "Well, come on, come on. The fire's lit upstairs in Letty's room, just as she asked. Rest of the place is cold and covered in sheets like I'm living with ghosts, I say. But Letty will come to her senses soon enough, and come home."

Allegra froze to the floor of the small foyer, looking at Armand. "Letty . . . Letty's *bedchamber?*"

"Oh, she speaks. That's good, Mr. Gauthier. For a minute there, I thought she was just pretty."

"Of course I speak," Allegra said, stung. "Why wouldn't I speak? Hello, Ruthann, Letty told me you've been with her for years and years. I'm—"

"A lady without a name, miss, a lady I've never seen, not even now. As a matter of fact, I'm talking to myself right now," Ruthann broke in quickly. "Isn't that right, Mr. Gauthier. Now, go on up, and I'll be hauling up some tea and cakes in a minute. There's already wine up there. I remember just what you like, Mr. Gauthier. I even turned down the bed for you."

"Turned down the—no! That's not why we're here. We're here to—oh, piffle," Allegra said as Ruthann and her lavender satin gown disappeared through a doorway under the narrow flight of stairs.

"Come on, nameless lady who isn't here," Armand said, touching her elbow as he directed her toward the stairs. "Or has the joy gone out of the intrigue?"

Allegra shook off his hand, grabbed at her skirts, and stomped up the stairs, muttering, "The world is full of narrow minds, that's what it is. Narrow minds and lascivious minds, and I don't know which is worse. Why can't two people be alone, that's what I wonder, be able to *talk* to each other without a dozen other people standing about, listening? It's stupid, that's what it is. S-t-u-p—*stupid*."

She stopped in the narrow hallway, looked to her left and right in disgust. "Where now?"

"I haven't the faintest i-d-e-a," Armand said from behind her. "But I'd say Letty's room is probably the one with the open door, wouldn't you?"

"Oh, don't try to be funny, Gauthier. I can't believe this," Allegra said, setting off once more. "Could we go to a pub? No. Could we ask to be alone in either of our houses? No. Anyone would think that there's no way a man and a woman can be left alone for two minutes without either the man or the woman *lunging* at the other one like some barnyard—"

Allegra's eyes went wide as she looked at Armand's face, which suddenly was right in front of and very close to hers. Close enough that his mouth was on hers, as a matter of fact, as he held on to her shoulders and turned her, backed her into Letty's bedchamber.

She heard him kick the door closed behind them, and was forced to grab on to his arms as he turned her yet again, pushed her up against that shut door as his assault on her mouth continued.

Well, perhaps not an assault. Not when she considered that she was kissing him back for all she was worth.

"What . . . what was that for?" she asked, more than slightly breathless, when he finally released her.

"We won't be disturbed. Ruthann would never open a closed door, or even knock on one for that matter. And, to answer the question you did ask, I was shutting you up before you could dig a hole with your tongue that neither of us would ever be able to climb out of," Armand told her as he moved away, heading toward a small table holding a silver tray, a decanter, and two wineglasses. "Did it work?"

Allegra touched her lips with three fingers. "Yes, I suppose it did," she said, trying hard to ignore the notion that her knees had gone numb.

"Then that's all right, isn't it?"

"All right? I don't know. But I'm sorry, Gauthier. It's just that London is so full of silly *rules*. I mean, I'm already ruined, as far as Society is concerned, just by being here. But you? Oh, you're just fine, now aren't you? You'd get pats on the back, winks from your cronies. A few *huzzahs,* a few glasses lifted in toasts, a few *well done*'s thrown in for good measure. It's not only not fair, it's sickening, that's what it is. Mostly," she ended as her defiance began to bog down beneath her apprehension at the sight of Letty's bed, "it's not fair."

He handed her a glass, then indicated that she should seat herself in one of the two scarlet and white striped chairs in front of the fireplace. "London rules also include some compensation for the female, Ally. I would be considered a rotter by some, and never allowed near another innocent debutante. Your father could demand that I marry you, or he could call me out, shoot me down."

"Oxie doesn't even know which end of a pistol to point," Allegra said, dropping into one of the chairs. She looked around the small room. "Everything is so *little,* isn't it? The rooms, I mean. I like it, it's very cozy. And colorful. Definitely colorful."

"Red usually is," Armand agreed, settling himself in the facing chair. "It's rather Letty's signature, I believe. Red hair, red drapes, red rugs, red—well, you name it. Scarlet, really, and not exactly red, now is it? She said it was the color of her profession, and what her clientele expected, but I think it's because she was so pleased that she's a redhead who actually is flattered by the color. Seeing her in black is *startling*."

"She hates it," Allegra said, looking around the room, wishing it wasn't so small, or the bed so large. "She'd have left us already, except she rather likes me, I think, and wants to make sure you don't come to any harm because of befriending us."

"And because she has every faith in you discovering all my secrets," Armand added. "Remember, I know the woman."

Allegra nervously dipped a finger into her wine, then ran that finger around the rim of the glass. "She is interested. After all, you know all her secrets, don't you?" She dipped her finger again, then licked the wine off with the tip of her tongue.

"That would be arrogant of me," he answered as she looked up at him to see that he was watching her intensely. "As a matter of fact, I *was* arrogant. Believing I knew what was best for Letty, what would make her happy. Perhaps, instead of urging her to follow an old dream, I should have just helped her engage some strong men to guard against any further incidents. Clearly, her return to her childhood home didn't work out the way she'd hoped."

"No, it didn't. Just as believing she'd be happy to live a quiet life here in town, able to move in Society as a companion, see inside the houses she'd never otherwise see, has not proven any better. I think she misses . . . this."

Armand crossed one leg over the other, also looking around the room. "No, not just this. The *freedom*. I think she misses the freedom of being in charge of herself, and able to do what she wants, when she wants, with whom she wants. After being her own woman for so long, she chafes at Society's boundaries."

"Like me," Allegra said, shifting on the chair, drawing one leg up beneath her. She cocked her head to one side, looked closely at Armand. "Like you?"

His smile all but dazzled her. "And how, may I ask, have we moved away from Letty, and gotten to me?"

"Because that's why I'm here," Allegra answered honestly. "Why are you here?"

He surprised her by abruptly rising from the chair and heading back to the drinks table. His back was turned to her, but she could feel a new tension in the room that had nothing to do with the wine or the turned down bed that had so dominated her thoughts a few moments ago.

She put down her wineglass, made to stand up. "Gauthier?"

He returned to the chair in front of the fire, without his wineglass. He sat down, his hands on the arms of the chair, gripping the fabric, and looked at her for long moments . . . long, hard moments.

"This isn't going to be easy," he said at last. "It wasn't going to be easy before, but now it's doubly difficult.

I'm not ready to say what I'm going to say, but I have to agree with you, Ally. We needed to be alone, somewhere we couldn't be disturbed. Somewhere that you couldn't run away from me before I can make you understand."

Allegra swallowed hard as she pushed herself back against the soft cushion of the chair, twisted her fingers together in her lap. "You're scaring me, Gauthier."

His smile all but broke her heart. "I imagine I am. And here you thought I'd only hoped to get you alone so I could kiss you senseless. More than kiss you senseless."

"Oh . . . oh, no, no, I didn't think that. Really. I just thought we could talk, get to know each other better. I certainly had no thoughts of the two of us . . . the two of us . . . *doing* anything . . . that is, not that we *couldn't,* but . . . because I did rather hint that I might . . . and you seemed agreeable and . . . well, we *have* already . . . oh, piffle," she said, rolling her eyes. "Who am I lying to here, Gauthier? You, or me?"

Armand threw back his head and laughed, that laughter melting most of the tension out of the air.

"I could adore you," Armand said as he sobered, then quickly shook his head, as if to at least mentally erase the words he'd just said. "And now, Ally, I want you to be very quiet while I tell you a story. Can you do that?"

"Be quiet? Honestly?" Allegra bit her bottom lip, thought about the question. "No. I doubt that I can. But I'll try, all right? Are you going to tell me why you came to England?"

"I'm going to tell you any number of things, and yes, they're all connected to why I came to England."

Allegra bent up her other leg onto the seat of the chair, tucked both of them beneath her skirts, made herself comfortable, as if ready to listen to a bedtime story told by her mother. "I'm ready."

Armand smiled. "God help me, she thinks she's ready," he said, almost to himself, then stood up, retrieved his wineglass.

"All right, Ally, here we go. I don't know where I was born, who I am, who my parents were. I do know where they died, and how, but that's all I know."

Allegra, who had been bravely smiling as she waited for Armand to speak, lost that smile as her heart gave a quick, painful squeeze. The man had definitely begun his story with a *bang*. "Oh, Gauthier. I didn't know."

"I didn't expect you to. I do expect you to believe me, because what I'm going to tell you is too fantastic for it to be a lie."

Allegra opened her mouth to speak, then quickly shut it again and just nodded.

"You're charming when you're attempting to be obedient, although not very convincing," he said as he walked over to stand behind the high-back chair.

"I was found, about thirty years ago, in the bottom of a long boat, the sort that is carried aboard trading ships and the like."

"No one knew your age? You were just a baby, weren't you?"

"Ally, we'll be done with this today, or next Tuesday. Which would you prefer?"

"Sorry," she half-whispered into her chest. "Go on."

"Thank you. The long boat was adrift, around fifty

miles from shore, I'm told. There was a name painted on the side of the boat, but it has been lost to memory—or nobody wanted to admit that they knew it in the first place. That possibility definitely exists, as the long boat may have been put off because the main ship was sinking in a storm . . . or because the ship had gone down after being attacked by pirates."

"Yes, I understand," Allegra said, nodding. "Go on."

Armand took a sip of wine. "Inside the boat, besides myself, were a man and a woman, both dead. It appeared that they had probably died due to lack of water or food, and they'd been nearly cooked by the sun. It's supposed that I was their son, because the man's jacket had been made into a makeshift canopy to protect me, and although I was much the worse for wear, I had obviously been taken care of, given any water or food they'd had to give."

Allegra felt her bottom lip begin to quiver, and looked away from Armand's face, because the pain she saw there all but broke her heart.

"My parents, I'm convinced they were my parents, were left where they were, and I was lifted out, wrapped in my father's jacket, taken onboard the sloop that had sent the seamen to inspect the long boat."

Armand paused, took a deep breath. "Then the sailors used a boat hook to poke holes in the longboat, sending the two bodies to the bottom."

"Oh, Gauthier, no."

His smile was wan. "There was little choice, Ally. They'd been dead for at least two days—in the heat, in the sun. Not even pirates try to strip valuables from such terrible corpses."

"So . . . so all you had was your father's jacket? Do you still have it?"

"I do. The jacket, and a ladies' handkerchief with initials embroidered on it. It had been employed to cover my bare bottom, or so I was told."

Armand pushed himself away from the back of the chair and walked around, sat down, leaning front as he placed his elbows on his knees. "I was taken to Santo Domingo, where I was put in the care of a succession of women I can't remember, and, a few years later, in the company of one boy, who I most certainly do remember, will never forget. I think he was only about five years old when I came onto the scene, and he was already a figure to be reckoned with—and I truly do mean that. Born to glory, that's one way of putting it."

Allegra didn't want to interrupt, but Armand seemed to be getting lost in thought, in his memories. "A boy took care of you?"

"Hmmm, yes. Not at first, of course. But once I was able to walk, to talk, to toddle around after him, worshiping him. He liked that."

"We all like that," Allegra said. "So you became friends?"

"Yes," Armand said quietly, still far away from her, "friends."

Then he shook his head, as if to clear it. "My childhood, such as it was, passed, and each time my friend and his brother moved on, I moved on with them, finally to a place called Barataria Bay."

"Barataria? I know that name. Oh, wait, isn't that the

name of the land sought by Cervantes's *Don Quixote* when he went on his quest?"

"Yes, it is. You've read Cervantes?"

"There's not a whacking great lot to do at Sunderland, Gauthier. I think I've read every book in the library there. Now, this Barataria. It's in America?"

"In America, in a land very newly become a part of America. Near the city of New Orleans. The Captain made it his base of operations. The Captain and his brother, young in years but old in experience, set up an empire. Our own small empire."

"The Captain being the boy, once he was grown? What operations?" Allegra's eyes widened. "My God, Gauthier, you were raised by *pirates?*"

He smiled. "There are worse fates."

"Yes," Allegra said in some disgust. "You could have been raised by wolves."

Again, Armand smiled. "I lied to you, you know, earlier. We did have letters of marque, issued through Cartagena. That's a Spanish republic."

"You sailed for Spain? Oh, Gauthier, that's not good. That can't be good at all."

"Tuesday, Ally, remember?"

"I'm sorry. Continue, please."

"There's so much more, but I can tell you about Barataria another time, about my life there. Suffice it to say for now that the Captain saw that I was educated alongside him, through him—the Captain is a very educated man. A gentleman."

"A gentleman pirate?"

Armand smiled. "Yes, as a matter of fact. Many called

him that. But let's travel forward a few years, so I can get this done, out of the way."

He rubbed his hand across his forehead, as if sorting out what he felt he needed to say.

"We were . . . our own community in Barataria, on the island of Grande-Terre, to be more exact about the thing. Over one thousand men, and their families. We coexisted with New Orleans, sometimes happily, sometimes not so happily, especially after a new governor was appointed." His lip curled slightly. "William Charles Cole Claiborne. W.C.C. himself."

Armand shook his head. "To be fair, the man had been handed a thankless job. We're an independent sort in New Orleans, and Claiborne had to attempt to rally us all around the idea that we were now Americans—civilized Americans, which we most certainly were not. He and the Captain, to put it succinctly, didn't get along. In fact, Claiborne put a price on the Captain's head, which the Captain responded to by putting a higher price on Claiborne's."

"I think I would have liked your Captain, Gauthier."

"And he would have liked you, Ally. Anyway, the years passed. When the war came, and New Orleans became a British target, the Captain and his thousand men—well, who knew where those loyalties might lie."

Allegra's eyes widened. "You fought for the British? Oh, Gauthier, that would make everything so much easier."

"Yes," he said, smiling. "It would have, wouldn't it? But that's not what happened. We were . . . approached by the British, but the Captain chose instead to offer our services to the Americans."

"Oh."

"Yes, that was Claiborne's reaction to the Captain's proposal." Armand stood up again, began to pace. "In exchange for pardons for the Captain, his brother, for all of us, we'd fight the British for him, prove ourselves to be loyal Americans, once and for all. Barataria was crucial, Ally, and Claiborne knew it. So we sat back, waited for Claiborne to come to us, agree to our offer."

Armand loosened his neckcloth slightly as he stopped, turned, looked at Allegra.

"We were joyful when the *Carolina* and about a half-dozen gunboats appeared offshore early one morning. Our people saw the American flag, and many ran to the beach, cheered, while the Captain and I stood on the veranda of his grand house, watching. The Captain was nearly preening. And then the gunships opened fire."

Allegra half hopped out of her chair. "The *idiot!* Why would he attack you?"

"Why, indeed. The Captain stood on the veranda, his house tumbling down around him under the heavy cannon fire, asking much the same question. The watch tower was shattered, the bell hung there to warn against attack falling to the ground. Soldiers landed on the beach, began torching the men's huts, houses. I had a devil of a time pulling the Captain away, making him realize we had to leave, we had to run into the swamps, or else be captured.

"'Never,' the Captain kept saying as we ran, as we hid, 'never have I attacked an American ship.' He was dumbfounded, and he was pretty much destroyed. His ships confiscated, all his goods taken, many of his men arrested."

"I can't believe this, Gauthier, but I think I pity the man. He offered his help, and this was the thanks he got? What did you do next? Is that when you came to England?"

"No, not quite yet," Armand corrected, leaning against one of the tall posts of Letty's canopied bed. "The Captain didn't give up that easily. We weren't completely ruined. We'd always had arms and stores hidden, in case they were ever needed. So he offered his men, his cannon, everything he had to Old Hickory— General Andrew Jackson, who had arrived in New Orleans, again in exchange for pardons for himself and all the rest of us. Jackson turned us down."

Allegra sighed. "You Americans. Are you all idiots?"

"Jackson only knew the Captain was a pirate, a smuggler. So the Captain paid him a small visit one night. They met, they talked, and we joined Jackson's small army. One thousand of our men, seasoned fighters, and all of our stores of ammunition."

"Jackson had to have been grateful for that?"

"He was. He was also impressed with our men, how well they fought. We sent the British running for their lives, Ally. The pity of it, the bleeding pity of it, was that the war had been over by the time of the battle, but none of us knew it. The British lost two thousand men who never should have been in the field in the first place. Brave soldiers, who had stood against Napoleon, mowed down in their scarlet coats as they tried to bring organized war against a band of clever pirates fighting from the bayous, the swamps. They never had a chance. We were luckier, and lost only forty men."

There was so much more Allegra wanted to know. She wanted to know about Barataria, and the years Armand had spent there. She longed to know more about the Captain, about the battle. If she had a lifetime to listen, she probably would not get her fill. But she also knew this story wasn't as important as what would follow, the reason Gauthier had come to England.

"We were heroes, for a while," Armand said softly, his eyes closed as he spoke. "But then the rumors began, rumors that the Captain had attacked an American ship years earlier, after swearing that he never had. The truth of it was that one of his ships did disobey orders and attack an American trader, years earlier, and the man in charge had been hanged for it—by the Captain himself. Still, we were blamed, and New Orleans became . . . uncomfortable."

"And that's when you came to England?"

He pushed himself away from the bedpost. "That's when the Captain threw me out, yes. Many of the men disbanded, went their own way. We never rebuilt Grande-Terre, there was no point. The Captain said he would never leave New Orleans, but handed me my father's coat, my mother's handkerchief, and said it was time I found out who I am. When I disagreed, he knocked me over the head, and I awoke aboard ship, heading for England."

"He loved you," Allegra said, blinking back tears. "You know that, don't you?"

"I know he thought he'd done what he believed to be

best for me. About the same way I interfered in Letty's life. You'd think I would have learned, wouldn't you?"

Allegra unbent her legs and stood up, walked over to Armand. "You've been here for nearly three years, Gauthier. Looking for your family. What have you found? Because you have found something, haven't you?"

He looked at her for long moments, then ran the tip of one finger down her cheek. "I'll go down, see if Ruthann still has that tea. My throat's dry from all of this, and the last thing I want is more wine."

Chapter Seventeen

ARMAND CARRIED THE SILVER TRAY up the stairs, taking his time as he went, not because he might spill the tea, but because no matter how difficult telling his story had been, what had to come next would be even worse.

He had her sympathy now, and had counted on that, shameless as he knew himself to be, dragging up anything that would make him seem less than the bastard he knew himself to be.

The door stood ajar, and he nudged it with his hip, then entered the room. "Ally?" he said, looking toward the fireplace.

"Over here," she answered, and he turned, having to hold tightly to the tray in order not to drop it in the shock of seeing her sitting cross-legged in the middle of the bed. "Just put the tray down here," she said, patting the mattress. "My feet don't touch the floor in that chair, and I was getting uncomfortable."

"I'm supposed to believe that?"

"You could try," she said, grinning at him. "Now come on, put that down, and join me. I want to hear the rest of your story."

Armand's heart sank. Ally was so transparent. She wanted what she wanted, and she wasn't going to be coy or simpering about it, either.

Little did she know she could soon be tossing the teapot at his head.

"All right," Armand teased as he put down the tray, sat himself on the edge of the mattress. "Just be gentle."

"Oh, stop smiling, Gauthier. You're not as amusing as you think you are."

"Yes, ma'am," he said, then stood up for a moment, slipped out of his jacket and waistcoat, undid his neckcloth. "I see you've rid yourself of your shoes."

"Letty's bedspread," she pointed out. "I didn't want to ruin it."

"Then I'll remove my boots. For the same reason."

"Yes, for the same reason."

Armand turned away, looking for a boot jack, sure that Letty would have one nailed to the floor somewhere, for the benefit of her gentleman callers. And there it was, over in the far corner.

Now in his hose, he returned to the bed, sat on the edge of the mattress once more. "The rest of what I'm going to tell you, Ally, what I *need* to tell you, may have you hating me. I thought you should know that."

He watched as she spooned sugar into her cup, avoiding his eyes. "I could never hate you."

"Yes, well, we'll see. Now, where was I?"

"You were on your way to England."

He nodded. "All right. Now I've arrived, armed with my share of our bounty—ill-gotten fortune, some might say—my father's coat, and one embroidered handkerchief. Miracles may have been wrought with less, but I didn't have an easy time of it, until I chanced to meet Simon Roxbury—Viscount Brockton. He eased my way into Society and, eventually, I took him into my confidence."

"So he began helping you?"

"He and Bones, yes. Even Letty, a few others who didn't know precisely what I was about, but who seemed to enjoy being helpful in exchange for saying they'd befriended Simon's new friend. But I had no luck. None."

"But you have had some luck now, haven't you, Gauthier?"

"Yes, I have. Whether it's good or bad luck, however, remains to be seen. Ally," he said, reaching out to take both her hands in his, "I've scoured England, Scotland, Wales, hunting for a name to fit the initials, a story that came at least close to mine, and I found nothing. Nothing."

"Until . . . ?" Allegra urged, squeezing his hands.

Armand knew he could delay no longer. "Until I looked across Grosvenor Square, and saw a fountain full of bubbles and, for the very first time, heard the name Nesbitt."

He watched as Allegra looked at him blankly. Then she blinked. Her spine stiffened as she sat in the middle of the mattress. She pulled her hands free of his. "Tell me," she said quietly. "For God's sake, Gauthier, *tell me.*"

Armand pinched the bridge of his nose between thumb and forefinger for a moment, then looked at Allegra again, worried over her newly pale complexion.

"Yes, let's do this quickly. I hadn't heard the name Nesbitt because your father hadn't been to London in five years. Which didn't matter, because the initials didn't fit. The handkerchief carries the initials S.T.C."

Allegra made a face, repeated the initials. "You're right. There's nothing familiar about those initials."

"But then I spoke with Oxie, and learned that the late earl had a son, who had traveled close enough to the southern coasts of America to whet my interest."

"Oxie told me you two had spoken about the earl's son. That would be Harry, yes. He and his wife. But that was"—her eyes widened—"that was more than thirty years ago. Oh, my God, Gauthier!"

"It gets worse," he said, anxious to have his story done. "Even before talking to Oxie, I had written to Simon, asked for his help, as I had, at last, another avenue to check. One last hope, before I gave it all up, stopped searching. Good man, Simon, and very thorough. I received a note from him yesterday, hand-delivered by one of his grooms. Harry, the earl's son, married one Sarah Charlene Tate. I realized I must have had the initials wrong, that the T in the center was larger than the other two letters, and had to indicate Sarah's last name."

He lowered his head, knowing he could be damning himself in Allegra's eyes. "My mother's maiden name."

She said nothing. She didn't bolt from the bed, or scream at him that he was lying. She did nothing.

"Ally?"

She blinked at him. "You're the earl. Oxie isn't the earl, Uncle Frederick isn't the earl. *You're* the earl. You're Harry's son. It has to be true, Gauthier. It just has to be true."

Relief struck at Armand so hard he nearly staggered as he rose from the mattress, took up a position on the floor, looked at Allegra. "I can't prove that, Ally. Nobody can prove that. Ask anyone. There was never any word that Harry ever sired a son."

She scrambled to the end of the bed, hopped down, then grabbed at the tea tray and placed it on the floor before taking hold of Armand's arms. "There are letters, at Sunderland. I'm sure there are, because Harry and his wife—your mother—were away for more than two years. Surely there must be something in one of those letters?"

Armand shrugged. "Oxie mentioned one letter, but that's all. The one Harry wrote to say he and his wife were sailing home. Not every letter sent to England makes it there, so who knows if Harry ever wrote to his parents about a child."

He watched as Allegra bit on the side of her thumb, obviously thinking nineteen to the dozen.

"All right. We'll go to Sunderland. We'll find that letter. We'll find all the letters. Then we'll take the jacket, and the handkerchief, and we'll fix this." She looked up at him, tears in her eyes. "We *have* to fix this, Gauthier. Surely you can see that?"

God, how he loved this woman.

"Ally, think. Any claim I might have would be damned difficult to prove. Your uncle could lodge a legal protest. And remember this—if I'm the earl, you and your family are totally out of the picture." He smiled wanly. "Unless your father decides to shoot me. Isn't that amazing? Oxie could be my *heir*."

"Oxie could be the happiest man in the world, and my mother the happiest woman, if you'd give them a small allowance and a house somewhere, and let them go back to being who they want to be, because they never wanted to be the earl and his countess."

"And you?"

She stepped back, tipped her head to one side. "What about me?"

"We could be related to each other, Ally."

"Oh, piffle. Oxie's barely related to the old earl—your grandfather. And Uncle Frederick even less so. Besides, what does that—oh."

"Yes," Armand said softly, moving forward, slowly edging her back toward the bed. He laid his hands on her waist. "Oh."

She covered his hands with her own. "You know, I really didn't come here for this."

He raised one eyebrow as he smiled down at her.

"No. Really. I didn't. I didn't come here to learn that Oxie's not an earl, and you are, certainly. But I don't mind, I really don't. Isn't that odd? It's . . . it's almost a relief."

"You're amazing," he said, edging her back a little more, so that she was blocked against the side of the bed.

"Yes, I am, aren't I?" She took in a deep, shuddering breath. "Am I? Am I really?"

"Amazing," he whispered, bending to speak the word into her hair. "And I want you so badly I'd gladly give up anything I own or hope to have, if we could make this afternoon last a lifetime."

"Oh . . . Gauthier," she breathed as he covered her mouth with his own.

He could be making the biggest mistake in his life. Armand knew that. Allegra could be making the biggest mistake of hers. He doubted she realized that.

And that's the last rational thought he had for quite some time, because Allegra opened her mouth beneath his and he was lost from that moment.

Somehow, they were on the bed, lying beside each other, locked in each other's arms.

Somehow, her gown was undone, and his hand covered one bared breast as Allegra sighed into his mouth.

Somehow, her hands found his chest . . . and the nervous bumbling of her fingers as she slipped open his buttons nearly unmanned him.

Are you sure, are you sure?

No, he hadn't said the words out loud. He should have, but he didn't. He'd opened his mouth to say the words, but what came out instead was, "God, Ally, how I want you."

Her response was so very much like her that even in the heat of his passion and the niggling of his guilt, he had to chuckle: "Oh, shut up, Gauthier, and kiss me again."

So he kissed her.

He kissed her mouth, her hair, the tip of her nose. Her closed eyes.

And then he moved lower, captured her nipple in his mouth as her sharp intake of breath sent yet another thrill singing through his body.

Slowly. Gently, he told himself, as Allegra slid her hands around his neck, drew him closer. He could feel her back arching as he drew the tip of his tongue over her taut nipple, as he melded his lips around her, suckled her.

Her gown was gone. Vaguely, he thought he could remember having some help from Allegra in that department, and he knew it was she who had kicked herself free of the hampering skirts and underpinnings.

He had to see her. She clung to him, not quite the wanton he knew she wanted to appear, burying her head against his chest as he levered himself up, looked down at her body.

So slim, yet curved. So creamy white.

He touched a hand to the flare of her hip, skimmed his fingers down her thigh, then back up again, to press his palm flat against her belly.

He could feel her melting, even as he knew himself to be hard, taut, and growing more aroused by the moment.

Sitting up abruptly, he rid himself of his shirt as Allegra slipped her legs beneath the coverlet, then disposed of the rest of his clothing and joined her.

She lay very still for a moment, and he raised his head, looked at her.

"We're done?" she asked in a small voice.

His smile grew as he looked into her eyes, as his hand trailed down her body, heading for the juncture of her thighs. "Done? Oh, darling, we haven't even started."

She gasped as his fingers found her, opened her, began stroking her.

A virgin. He knew she was a virgin, and needed careful attention.

He didn't think she knew. Or cared.

Her body began to move, pushing against his questing fingers. Her right hand began a quest of its own, finding him, capturing him, driving him nearly out of his mind with her inexperienced, tentative touch.

This was all so wrong, and yet so right, so natural. The foregone conclusion to what had begun the day he'd seen her alongside the fountain, blowing bubbles off her hands.

He kissed her breasts, her belly, and she released him, lying back against the pillows, allowing him to do what he wanted, yet not just allowing it, but encouraging his every move, his every caress.

Slowly, he led her to the precipice. Listening to her breathing as it quickened, feeling her muscles tightening, sensing her complete surrender when she raised her legs, bent her knees, fell open to him.

"Oh . . ." he heard her say, her voice full of wonder as he led her toward the edge. "I didn't . . . I never . . . *Oh* . . ."

Armand held her as she convulsed around him, as her body gave her the very first lesson in why she was born, why she had been formed as she was.

And then she was moving. Swiftly, like a cat, she

turned into him, grabbing on to his shoulders, pulled him toward her. "More," she said, her eyes still closed, her cheeks wet with tears. "You, Gauthier. I want *you*. I must, because I'm *aching* for you."

Armand knew he'd have to be three days dead not to respond to her plea, and even then he might have managed it.

His mouth melded to hers, he rolled her onto her back, eased one knee between her legs.

She wouldn't allow him to be gentle. He should have known that.

After only a small resistance, he was inside her, held tightly within her, nearly his full weight pinning her to the bed.

Her arms went around his shoulders as he lay there, trying not to explode, but only moving slowly, drawing out, moving in, holding himself in check . . . until her legs went up, locked around his hips.

Together, they rode the wild waves that threatened to engulf them. Together, they entered a world he'd thought he'd known, and that she'd never experienced.

When she came, when he followed, that world stood still . . . and Armand knew that after a lifetime of travel, he was home.

Anywhere Allegra was . . . that was his home, and she was his family. All he'd ever wanted, all he'd ever need.

"You're awfully quiet," Armand said as they rode back through the puddled streets to Grosvenor Square, sitting beside each other on the squabs, their hands entwined.

Allegra leaned over, kissed his cheek. "I'm thinking up questions. I think I've got about a dozen, so far. There will probably be more."

"So I've been warned?"

"Absolutely," she said, snuggling against him. "I want to know all about Barataria, your life there. What it's like living in America, free to do anything you want."

"Within reason," he pointed out, lifting her hand to his mouth, kissing it. "There are a few rules."

"Shhh, don't spoil it. I want to think you can go where you want, do what you want, and nobody tells you it isn't proper, or what's expected of you, or will reflect badly on your title. Piffle!"

Armand leaned closer. "I've had this dream, in my mind, of you walking along a warm, sandy beach— barefoot."

She turned to grin at him. "You see, you see? I couldn't do that now. I could, when I was a child, before Oxie became the earl. Now I can do it again."

Her smile, she knew, now veered on the coquettish. "Of course, I'd have to find that warm, sandy beach, now wouldn't I?"

Armand gently flicked a finger at the tip of her nose. "I'll propose in my own good time, thank you."

Allegra's smile faded, and she looked away from him. "I wasn't supposing anything like that, Gauthier. Besides, you're the earl, and will have to stay here, in England."

He caught hold of her chin, turned her face to his. "I *may* be the earl, and I go where I want."

"Oh, really? And where do you want to go, Gauthier?"

"At this moment? Back to Half Moon Street," he said, kissing her cheek. "So you're right, I can't always do exactly what I want. Ah, the coach is slowing. We're here."

Allegra felt an absolutely irrational impulse to burst into tears. She had to leave him? Even for an instant? An instant was too long. The hours between now and the ball tonight would be an eternity.

"I'll miss you," she said, then winced, knowing how silly she sounded.

But he seemed to understand. "I'll miss you, too, Ally. We'll have to do something about that, won't we?"

She bit her lips between her teeth and nodded, then said, "Don't make me do it all, Gauthier. I think I've chased you quite enough."

He laughed as the coach drew to a halt. They lingered over one last kiss, and then Allegra sighed, opened the door. "Until tonight? Not that I'm doing the pursuing, you understand."

"Until tonight, and I think I'll be able, just possibly, to restrain myself from—how did you say it?—jumping on your body the moment I see you. But just barely."

Laughing, and yet still inexplicably close to tears, Allegra hopped down from the coach and ran for the door to the kitchen.

She gave a moment's thought to heading toward her bedchamber via the servants' stairs, then decided she should at least poke her head into the drawing room, to see how her parents were doing, and if Elizabeth was sitting there, all powdered and primped and curled, waiting for the clock to strike eight.

Allegra entered the drawing room and stopped, seeing her father standing over one of the couches, waving his unfolded handkerchief like a fan.

"Oxie? What are you up to?"

He glanced in her direction, then returned to his fanning. "Oh, hullo, pet. Could you perhaps help me a little here? Your mama's gone and done a faint."

Allegra rolled her eyes as she walked over to the couch. "What was it this time, Oxie? Not another mouse, I hope. Honestly, if you aren't going to have any more sense than to keep pranking Mama we're going to have to send you to bed without your supper."

"Allegra?"

Allegra bent over the back of the couch, took her mother's raised hand in her own. "Yes, Mama, it's Allegra. Shall I kill him for you?"

"Oh! Oh, no!" Magdalen wailed, bursting into tears.

"What?" Allegra asked her father. "What did I say?"

"Well, pet, you said you could kill me," Oxie Nesbitt reminded her with a grimace.

"Ordinarily, that wouldn't be so bad, I suppose, and no more than you've ever said. But, you see, I was out in the mews just a while ago, blowing a cloud—you know how your mama hates when I do that indoors— and this . . . well, this *knife* sort of appeared, and sort of stuck itself in the door behind me."

Allegra grabbed on to the back of the couch with her free hand, her knees having gone weak, so that she momentarily feared that she might fall down.

"Oxie? Someone . . . someone tried to kill you?"

He shrugged. "Oh, I don't think so, pet. I'm sure it was an accident."

"Oxie, nobody throws a knife at somebody by *accident*." Allegra took a deep breath, tried to get herself back under control.

"Mama, you stay here and rest. Oxie, come with me!"

"Oh, again, I don't think so, pet. I should stay here, lend my comfort and support to your—"

"Oxie—*now!*"

Allegra closed the morning-room doors behind her and leaned against them, glaring at her father. "Who else, Oxie? Besides Gauthier, who else? Sir Guy? Jagger? The viscount? *All* of them?"

Oxie walked over to the table, pulled out a chair, eased his bulk into it. "I don't know what you're talking about, pet," he said, fingering the lace edge of the table-cloth. "Haven't a clue."

"Oh, really," Allegra said, hanging on to her temper by a rapidly unraveling thread. "Perhaps, then, I can refresh your memory? How's this, Oxie? *We're all mortal. Your secret is safe with me.*"

Oxie made a face. "Got-yer. Wasn't safe with him, was it? What did he do, come running to show you? I thought I liked the man."

"You should like him, Oxie, because he came to me, rather than calling you out and blowing a hole straight through you. This isn't a joke, Oxie, a prank. This is *dangerous.*"

"Dangerous?" Oxie snorted. "Don't be silly."

Allegra walked over to the table, placed her palms on

it, and leaned down, to speak directly into her father's ear. "A *knife,* Oxie. That's not dangerous? Now come on, talk to me. Give me the names."

He continued to prod at the lace, poking one sausage-thick finger through a small hole and enlarging it. "Just . . . just the ones you mentioned, pet," he said at last, then looked up at her. "But I don't know any secrets."

"I know," Allegra said, then had to ask, "not even about Gauthier?"

"Oh. Him. I did hear something, but I'm not sure what it was. Something about sea horses? But it's of no matter. Everybody has secrets, and that's the beauty of the joke."

Allegra sighed in relief and stumbled to a chair. "Oxie, do you know what you've done?"

"Nothing terrible, pet," he said defensively. "In the book, it said that you just send notes to everyone, and then watch them as they go around, looking at everyone they see, trying to figure out who sent them the note. I thought it would be . . . well, rather jolly."

Allegra pushed back her chair and stood up. "Rather jolly. Oxie, you're hopeless. And you're staying home tonight, do you understand? You and mama both. Neither of you is leaving this house until I can make things right with those three men, before one of them actually does kill you. And you know what—there'd be many who wouldn't blame them."

"And Got-yer," Oxie added, obviously trying to be helpful. "Don't forget about him."

Allegra closed her eyes, all her new knowledge skittering across the front of her mind, all her new hopes, her bright dreams. "Oh, don't worry about Gauthier, Oxie. Trust me, we won't soon forget him."

"Did I invite him?" Armand asked Quincy out of the corner of his mouth as Rutherford Jagger left the short receiving line—composed, as it was, of only Armand and Bones—and headed off into the ballroom, one of the last stragglers to arrive.

"You did not, sir," Quincy said, handing his employer a glass of wine. "Shall I have him removed?"

"No," Armand said, accepting the glass. "You invited the rest of Mayfair. What difference does one more man make? But tell me. What about his father? Walter Jagger?"

"He was on the list, yes."

"And Sir Guy Berkert? I should remember, but meeting and greeting two hundred people can blur most any mind. How about Viscount Eaton?"

Quincy rolled his eyes upward, as if checking through a list tacked inside his forehead. "I believe so, sir, both of them. I employed lists I found drawn up by the wife of my former employer and then left here when they departed for the countryside."

"And did your former employer travel in the best circles?" Armand asked, grinning. He probably should have paid more attention to this ball, but he'd had other things on his mind. Allegra on his mind.

"Yes, sir, he did, although he also had a penchant for inviting certain gentlemen he thought easy marks at the card table."

"Which explains Walter Jagger, doesn't it, if not the

son? Thank you, Quincy."

Suddenly Bones grabbed on to Armand's arm, just above the elbow, and squeezed it convulsively.

"If I were to turn my eyes to the left, Bones," Armand said quietly, "would I see Miss Elizabeth Nesbitt?"

Bones nodded, said something that sounded faintly like *"Gaaak."*

"Buck up, Bones, you can do this," Armand said encouragingly, then turned to see Allegra, Miss Elizabeth, and Letty Toms walking toward them. At last!

Allegra looked beautiful, bed-able if not biddable.

Miss Elizabeth looked innocent and demure and as if she might be having trouble remembering how to breathe.

And Letty Toms—no one would call her Lettice Tomlin tonight—her bright red hair done up on top of her head and laced through with pearls, clad in a low-necked gown of deepest scarlet, had already caused one passing servant to walk smack into a post.

"Ladies," Armand said, bowing over Allegra's gloved hand, squeezing it even as he pressed a kiss against the soft kid. "You're late, woman. I was about to come get you."

Allegra grinned at him. "We had to wash Letty's hair at least half a dozen times. Be happy we're here at all, Gauthier. Now please say hello to Elizabeth before she faints."

"I want you here, with me. We'll send them off on their own. If anyone else shows up, they can damn well find their own way to the ballroom."

"My thoughts exactly," Allegra said, moving so that

she stood beside him.

"You're being obedient. Why does that frighten me, do you suppose?" Then he bowed to the other women. "Miss Nesbitt, Miss Tomlin, welcome. You honor this humble house with your presence."

Elizabeth Nesbitt curtsied, her eyes on Bones, who had turned nearly as red as Letty's hair. "Mr. Gauthier," she said in a whisper so low Armand had trouble hearing her, "we are honored indeed to have been invited."

"And the man standing beside me is ecstatic that you have been invited, Miss Nesbitt. Bones? Could you possibly escort the ladies into the ballroom? Oh, and lead off the dancing, would you? I think I'm going to be otherwise detained."

"But . . . but you can't do that, Armand," Bones protested. "It's your ball."

"Mr. Gauthier, I do believe," Lettice Tomlin said quietly, "has decided to retire from Society and, to be blunt about the thing, doesn't give a tinker's dam about what's right or proper. Am I right, Mr. Gauthier? Otherwise, I should probably turn around and leave now, before anyone else sees me."

"You're out to shock a few people, Letty?" Armand asked her.

"See and be seen, just for a moment," Lettice said, lifting her chin. "And then just as quickly be on my way. Do you mind?"

Armand shook his head. "I don't mind at all. Have fun, Letty. And now, if you'll excuse us, I've just noticed that Lady Allegra is rather insistently pressing her dancing slipper down on my instep, which I take to mean that she wishes for the two of us to go somewhere and . . . talk."

"Yes," Lettice said with a wink. "Ruthann penned me a note late this afternoon. She told me your *talk* had been quite successful. There will be an announcement, Mr. Gauthier?"

"As soon as the earl shows up, yes."

"Oxie's not coming," Allegra said, then frowned. "You were going to make an announcement? Of what?"

Armand looked down into the face of the woman who would probably drive him crazy on a daily basis, hopefully for the next fifty years, at the least. "Excuse us," he said, still looking at Allegra or, more precisely, at her kissable mouth, as he led her down the hallway, toward the balconies overlooking the gardens.

Once through the French doors, and cloaked in the semidarkness of a moonlit night, Armand pulled Allegra into his arms and kissed her; deep, hard, and long.

"God," he said, crushing her against him, "you're beautiful. How long has it been since I've seen you? A week? A year?"

"Five hours," Allegra said, stepping up on tiptoe, to kiss his cheek. "Five years. Were you really going to make an announcement tonight? You haven't asked Oxie, you know. Or me, for that matter."

"Will your father give us his blessing? When he knows what I suspect?"

"Oxie? He'll fall on your neck in gratitude, if you also give him an allowance. He's gotten rather used to solvency, if not being called your lordship."

"So you keep saying, but I wonder. And I still don't know, *we* still don't know, if I'm really Harry's son."

"We don't know that you're not. Besides, I have something to show you. Later, when everyone's asleep. I'll let you in through the kitchens."

Armand cocked his head to one side. "If you mean to show me your bedchamber, Ally, I have to tell you that . . . oh, hell, I'm tempted. But first—will you marry me? No matter who or what I am?"

"Will you take me to that warm, sandy beach?"

"You'd marry me for a beach?"

"I'd marry you if we had to live here, in the heart of Mayfair. But I'd really love to see that beach. You looked so happy today, thinking about Barataria, about America. Oh, and I've figured out who the Captain is," she ended, dancing away from him, leaning back on the balustrade, grinning at him.

"You did, did you. How?"

"I found the information in a book."

Armand shook his head. "You did not."

"Oh, all right. I had Letty come knock on the back door and ask to see Mr. O'Neill. He told her. Letty says men tell her most anything she asks. Mr. O'Neill did, even with her hair still black as coal. Anyway, it's Lafitte. Jean Lafitte. A French name. He named you, didn't he? That's why you have a French name."

"Lafitte, the Captain, the *bos*. My friend. Yes."

"Will I ever meet him?" Allegra asked, pushing herself away from the balustrade, to stand close in front of Armand, her fingers plucking at the folds of his neckcloth.

"I don't know. Conor says he's not happy where he is, working for the Mexicans. I've always thought that one day he'd just disappear, become in truth the legend men have already made him." Armand lifted Allegra's fingers to his lips. "He would have adored you. Now come with me. I have to at least make an appearance at my own ball."

"Not yet," Allegra said, and her smile had disappeared. "There's a problem."

"A large problem?" Armand asked, suddenly uneasy.

"With a halo of white hair, yes," Allegra said, taking Armand's hand and walking with him toward the far end of the balcony. "Someone threw a knife at him today, in the mews, while he was smoking one of his cigars."

"He's all right?"

"For now, yes. When I questioned him, he told me the knife had stuck in the door behind him, but had missed him by at least three feet. More of a warning, I'd say, than a serious attempt to kill him. Lord knows he's a large enough target. Mama has him locked in their bedroom, fussing over him. I wouldn't let him come here tonight. Gauthier? Are you thinking what I'm thinking?"

"If you're thinking that someone else received the same note I did, that this someone wasn't amused and would like Oxie to either disappear or die? Then, yes, we'd be thinking the same thing."

Allegra blinked back tears. "I've told him and told him. One day he'd prank the wrong person. But he didn't listen. He pranked all three of them, Gauthier—

Sir Guy, Mr. Jagger, and the viscount. Who do you think it is? Which one of them?"

Armand shook his head. "I have no idea." He held out his arm to her. "Come on, let's find your cousin, and you can keep her company while I talk to one man who will know."

"Mr. Boothe?"

"Bones, yes. His mama is London's biggest gossip. Anything she knows, Bones knows, although he's always very closemouthed about such things. Now come on. We need this settled before I have to tell your father what I suspect about my identity. We'll solve our problems one at a time, all right?"

"As long as we solve this one quickly," Allegra said, squeezing his forearm. "If whoever threw that knife hoped to rout Oxie from London, he was successful. Mama wants us to leave for Sunderland tomorrow morning, at daybreak. I can't go, Gauthier. I can't leave you."

"That's not going to happen, Ally, I promise." Armand, feeling a small tic working in his cheek, escorted her into the overheated, overcrowded ballroom, on the lookout for Bones.

Behind them, lost in the darkest corner of the farthest balcony, Conor O'Neill moved back from the woman he'd been hiding against the wall, the woman in the scarlet dress that would have been visible in the moonlight.

"Sounds like the boyo has his problems, Letty. I should go help."

"Later, Conor," Lettice Tomlin said, snaking one hand

behind his neck and drawing him toward her waiting mouth. "Much later. Now take me down into those gardens and make love to me." She sighed as his hand captured her breast. "Oh, Conor, you fine, strapping Irisher, it's amazing what we think we can live without, isn't it?"

Chapter Eighteen

ONE THING ARMAND HAD KNOWN about Bartholomew Boothe within moments of their first meeting was that the man's sentences could all quite easily end with the words "I told you so."

This time, after being almost forcefully removed from Elizabeth Nesbitt's side and nearly dragged into Armand's small private study on the ground floor, after listening to Armand's explanation of Oxie Nesbitt's latest prank and his own subsequent questions, Bones *began* his sentence with those words: "I told you so."

"Feel better now that you've said it, Bones?" Armand asked, handing his friend a wineglass.

"Much, yes. Nesbitt, Armand. It doesn't rhyme with disaster, but it very well could. I told you so."

Armand settled himself in the chair behind his desk, the noise of the musicians sawing away on their fiddles filtering down from the ballroom and through the open window. From the sound of things, he must give one hell of a ball. Pity he'd yet to step inside the ballroom.

"So, these three men have deep dark secrets? The sort that might even lead to murder, in order to keep those secrets safe?"

Bones took up a chair on the other side of the desk, sipped at his wine. "I'd really rather not say. I was told in confidence. And m'mother always told me, never betray a confidence. She doesn't, you understand. She just *shares* with me, because she says she'll burst if she can't tell someone what she hears, and she hears *everything*. Aunt Henrietta did though, m'mother told me—told her sister's biggest secret, to the vicar, no less—and the upheaval in the family was something to—"

"Bones," Armand said, drawing out the man's name.

"Oh, all right, all right. But isn't it enough to know that, yes, all three do have secrets? Do you really have to know what they are?"

"I'm a curious sort, yes. Now, and I can't believe I'd ever say these words to you, old friend—what did your mother tell you?"

Bones shifted uncomfortably in his chair. "She really isn't a bad sort, Armand. Just doesn't have enough to keep her interested. Doesn't embroider, doesn't paint, don't warble or play the harp. She just *knows* things. Keeps her in demand, no doubt about that."

"Bones, you're stalling. Start with Walter Jagger, if you please."

"Jagger? Very well, as I can see you're going to be persistent. Remembering that these are things only a few, select people know, and no one speaks of."

He took a sip of wine. "Let's see, Walter Jagger. 1811. Twenty-fifth of September, to be precise. I know, because I remember dates very well. Ran from the ranks at El Bodon, hid himself in a ditch until the battle was over. Said he misunderstood a command. Wellington stayed, General Craufurd didn't. Pity was, Jagger wasn't with Craufurd, he was with Wellington."

"Jagger was with Wellington?"

"Long in the tooth for it, but yes. M'mother said he liked the uniform. He sold out right after El Bodon, but the day he was there, he ran like a rabbit. Though, as I said, only a few know for sure. My uncle Horatio, for one, because he got drunk with Jagger that same night. See? M'mother doesn't go *hunting* for gossip. It, well, it finds her. Really."

Armand scratched at a spot behind his left ear. "A white feather man. No, I can't see Jagger wanting that bruited about. How about Sir Guy? What's his secret?"

Bones sniffed. "Not much of a secret there, except to his wife, I imagine. Don't need to rely on m'mother for this one. Berkert's put a bun in his wife's maid's oven. Quick married her off to one of the stable lads, but everybody knows. Except, as I said, the wife. She controls Berkert's purse strings. The man's walking a fine edge, Armand. He could be dangerous."

Armand pressed both hands to his temples. "God, I feel like I should be sitting in a circle with a bunch of nattering women, embroidering slippers." He put down his hands, picked up his wineglass. "That's two, Bones. What about the viscount?"

Bones drained his wineglass and went over to the drinks table, to pour another measure. He kept his back to Armand.

"Bones?" Armand prompted.

Slowly, Bones turned around. "I don't like Eaton. Not a bit."

"You're an astute judge of character, Bones, and you haven't even seen the man in the nude."

Bones smiled at that, then returned to his chair. "This has to stay between the two of us, Armand. M'mother would have my head, because she likes the man. Says we're related to him, how I don't know, and don't wish to know for that matter. He's got a title, has invited m'mother to his estate from time to time, lends her cachet. M'mother dotes on cachet."

"I won't repeat anything you're telling me, Bones. I just need to get a better idea as to which of the three may be tossing knives at Oxie's head. So far, it could be either Jagger or Sir Guy. They both have what, to many, would be a compelling reason."

Bones pressed his elbows on the arms of the chair, leaned forward. "Not like Eaton's. He's the viscount, soon to be the earl, if m'mother's right, and the old boy really is close to slipping his moorings. Should be, he's got to be as old as dirt, hanging on to the point where Eaton has probably thought about helping him untie the knot in order to get his paws on the earldom."

"Go on," Armand said, sensing that Eaton's secret might make Jagger's and Sir Guy's seem inconsequential.

"Well, m'mother said she had it from the dead countess herself—before she kicked off, understand, not since. I know some ladies like to join hands and talk to the dearly departed, but m'mother doesn't do that. Probably could, though. Make 'em sit right up and speak. Anyway . . . according to m'mother, the countess told her that Eaton isn't really the earl's son. He's a product of a liaison with one of their footmen, and not even an upper footman at that."

"A bastard from the wrong side of the blanket? Interesting. Does Eaton know?"

Bones shrugged. "His mama was dying, trying to set things right. That's what m'mother said. She might have told him, doing that setting things right thing? Once the earl is dead, it won't matter, Armand, but if he were to find out while he's still able to cut Eaton out? Eaton could be a very, *very,* dangerous man to tweak right now, Armand."

Pushing himself up out of the chair, Bones said, "And now, if that's all you wanted, I'd like to get back to the ballroom. You should, too, Armand. You are the host, remember. Half the people upstairs think it's my ball, and can't understand why m'mother isn't here. I've already had to listen to two sermons on being an unnatural son."

"Yes, yes, you're right," Armand said, slowly getting to his feet. "Oxie had no idea of the mess he'd land himself in sending those notes, you know. Which means I'm going to have to clean it all up for him."

"Because you're in love with Lady Allegra," Bones said, nodding.

"Because he may be my heir," Armand said, then smiled as Bones abruptly sat down again, goggling at him. "Oh, hadn't I told you? Well, never mind. I know you're anxious to get back to Miss Elizabeth."

"Sit . . . down," Bones managed to squeak, pointing toward the chair behind the desk.

"Of course," Armand agreed, knowing he'd have

Bones dragging from his ankles if he tried to leave the room without him.

"I wrote to Simon, Bones, with a particular question, and he answered. Simon provided quite a few answers, actually . . ."

Allegra headed toward the balconies, knowing she shouldn't desert Elizabeth, but also aware that she might have to stuff her cousin rump down in the nearest potted plant if the silly girl didn't stop waxing poetical over the unmitigated glory that was one Bartholomew Boothe.

It wasn't as if Elizabeth was left alone, either, because the ballroom was clogged with people, so that it was easy enough to drag Elizabeth over to a group of turbaned ladies and sit her down in their midst before . . . oh, all right . . . before deserting her.

There were several couples walking the balconies, but Allegra ignored them, strolling along the inside of the ballroom, peeking out at each balcony, looking for an unpopulated one. When Armand found her out here, she'd rather he found her alone, in the dark.

The very last balcony was free of guests, and she walked out to stand at the balustrade, near a set of steps leading down to the gardens. She pressed her gloved hands on the cool stone, and looked out over the dark gardens lit here and there with flambeaux. It was a fairyland by moonlight and torchlight, but Allegra didn't really see it.

She was too full of thoughts of Armand, too full of worries about Oxie.

Too excited about a future that excluded curtsies and rules, and included barefoot walks on sunny, sandy beaches, Armand Gauthier at her side, their children dancing with the waves that kissed the shore.

Maybe Oxie and her mama would come to America with them. Anything was possible, and she would dearly want to have them there. Not too close, of course, unless Oxie kept his promise of this afternoon, and cried off his pranking . . .

"Lady Allegra? Excuse me, please. May I speak with you for a moment . . . on a private matter? A rather delicate matter?"

Startled, Allegra turned around, to see a well-dressed gentleman, a stranger, approaching her. "Yes, I suppose," she said warily, gathering her soft shawl more closely about her. He looked and sounded too young to be any of Oxie's old schoolmates, wanting her to deliver a message to him. So what did he want?

"Thank you, my lady," the man said, coming out of the half shadow and stepping into a small puddle of moonlight that filtered through the branches of trees planted near the balcony. Allegra saw a handsome man, blond, with startling blue eyes. He seemed harmless.

He held out his hand to her, as if expecting her to take it in greeting. How very modern. Allegra complied . . . and the next thing she knew, she had been spun into the man's arms, her back to his belly, and a cloth was being jammed into her mouth.

She used to carry a long hatpin everywhere she went, just because it seemed like a good idea.

But not tonight, not to come here, to be with Armand.

Allegra tried to kick back at the man's shins as he lifted her off the ground, but he was too big, too strong, and her breath had been nearly cut off by the cloth. She knocked her head back against his chest, once, twice, a third time, before his forearm went across her throat, cutting off even more air . . . until she felt dizzy, and her vision clouded.

She was limp in his arms even before he'd made his way down the steps into the garden, and never knew that she had been tossed into a small coach, which quickly drove away.

Conor O'Neill, cursing a blue streak and still trying to button up his breeches, ran along behind.

Bones was still doing what he did best, worrying, as he and Armand mounted the stairs from the study, heading in the direction of the ballroom.

"Frederick Nesbitt will fight you, even if Lady Allegra says Oxie won't. A handkerchief? A story about a well-born infant found adrift at sea beside the bodies of his dead parents? Sounds like something Byron would scribble on one of his less inspired days. No, Armand. I don't think so. I don't want to be the one to cut up your hopes, but I don't think so. Are you sure you have nothing more? Some more proof?"

"Such as?" Armand asked almost absently, standing at the entrance of the crowded ballroom, scanning it for any sign of Allegra or Elizabeth.

"Oh, I don't know. A locket with miniatures inside it? That would be tidy. A ring with a crest? Six toes?"

"No locket, no ring." Armand craned his neck, the

better to look for Allegra. "And as to the toes, I have ten, Bones, sorry."

"Not on one foot, surely? Well, never mind. How about a mole? On your back perhaps, so that you never noticed it? Shaped like a crown, or a cross, or something mystical? Something everyone knows all Nesbitt men have on their bodies? We need proof, Armand."

"Yes, and all I have for that proof is a jacket and a handkerchief. Depressing, isn't it?"

Bones looked at him through narrowed eyelids. "You don't seem very upset. Why is that, Armand? You should be overjoyed, now that you've finally found what you came here to find."

"Yes, I have," Armand said, smiling. "And I didn't even know I was looking for her." Then he turned to Bones. "The rest doesn't matter, not really. Do I believe I'm Harry's son, the real Earl of Sunderland? Yes, I do. Does it matter? Let me answer my own question. No, it doesn't, not really. Not anymore. Have you seen them yet, Bones?"

Bones shook his head, either in disgust at Armand's offhand treatment of the possibility that he could be an earl, or in answer to his last question.

"Let's check the balconies. Allegra wouldn't be comfortable in here for too long. Not if I know her, and I think I do."

"You go, Armand. I'll just walk around a little, hunt for Miss Nesbitt. Good thing Letty left, isn't it? What was she about, anyway?"

"One of the dreams Letty always had was to make a splash in Society, Bones. I think she's managed it tonight, don't you? You go, and I'll see you later. I want to tell Allegra that I've decided to speak to each of the three men, assure them that Oxie was only pulling a prank."

"Will they believe you?"

"When I also tell them that Oxie will be leaving London tomorrow, never to return? When I also let it be known that even though I was also a victim of this particular prank, he is under my protection? Yes, I think they will."

Armand left Bones where he stood, and headed for the balconies. After checking three of them, a small part of him began nursing a low niggling feeling that it should be easier to find Allegra.

He stepped through the French doors to the last balcony, to find it empty. No, that wasn't quite right. He bent down, picked up a dancing slipper.

The little niggle grew.

He walked over to the steps that led down from the balcony, to see the slipper's mate lying on the bottom step, and he gathered that up, too.

"Ally?" he called out, advancing into the gardens. "Ally, please. This is no time for you to remember that you're Oxie's daughter. No pranks, all right? Ally?"

"Mr. Gauthier!"

Armand turned to his left, hearing his name called, closely followed by the crashing sounds someone made as they barreled through the shrubbery, not bothering to keep to the gravel paths.

"Mr. Gauthier! Oh, thank God!" Lettice Tomlin said, all but falling into Armand's arms.

He pushed her slightly away from him, saw that her gown was only partially buttoned, and hung rather precariously low over her full breasts. "Letty? What the—who did this to you?"

Letty shook her head so hard that one strand of faux pearls came loose, to hang on to her bare shoulder. "No, no, not me. Conor and I—I got dressed as fast as I could. Damned buttons! But it doesn't matter. It's Allegra. He's taken her."

"Conor?" Armand shook his head. "No, of course not. Who took her, Letty?"

"Jagger," Letty gasped out, trying to pull up her gown. "I think . . . I think he knocked her over the head, and took her. We saw him stuff her in a hired coach. Conor . . . Conor ran after it, but I had to get dressed before I could come find you, tell you."

"Jesus," Armand swore under his breath. "Walter Jagger?"

"No, no! Not the father, Mr. Gauthier. The son. Rutherford. I know, because he used to be one of my cust—what are we going to do?"

"How long, Letty? How long ago? How long did it take you to get dressed?"

She dropped her chin to her chest. "Starting from scratch? After I found my petticoat? Not more than a few minutes, Mr. Gauthier. And Conor? Did I tell you he's gone running after the coach, Mr. Gauthier? He'll see where it goes, then come back and tell us. That's what he said to tell you, before he ran off. Run up the Jolly Roger, he said, put a knife between your teeth and a belaying pin in your fist, and be ready to follow him."

Letty looked up at Armand, tears standing bright in her eyes. "He doesn't even have his boots, Mr. Gauthier."

Armand wanted to break into a run, follow after the coach. That would be doing something, but it would be fruitless. Too much time had passed. He had no choice, he had to wait for Conor. The man wouldn't let him down. Not Conor O'Neill.

Armand slipped his arms out of his evening coat and draped the thing around Letty's shoulders.

"Come on, Letty, we'll go in through the kitchens, and you can wait in the ground-floor study while I round up Bones, talk to a few people."

"And we'll wait for Conor? It's best, Mr. Gauthier. Otherwise, where would we look?"

Allegra grimaced as something cold and wet hit her face, putting up her hands to protect herself even as she opened her eyes. "You," she said, recognizing the blond hair, the blue eyes. She struggled to sit up more fully on the rather lumpy chair, gave a quick glance around the unfamiliar room. "Who are you? Where am I? Are you *insane?*"

"Not insane. Insolvent, Lady Allegra," the man drawled, bowing to her, just as if he hadn't just kidnapped her. "But you're going to fix that, aren't you?"

"Me? I don't understand." Allegra kept her eyes moving, taking in the contents of the room, which seemed to be a sort of storeroom, clogged with cast-off furniture and other articles. One window, high on the wall, and a dirt floor beneath her feet.

A cellar. She was in a cellar. But why? Was she being held for ransom? Did people really *do* that?

The man leaned closer to her. Allegra, never a shy sort, immediately slapped his face, then tried to get out of the chair, head for the wooden door in the distance.

She landed back in the chair with a small *poof* of breath escaping her as the man pushed her down.

"Don't make me tie you up, please, Lady Allegra. I'm trying to be a gentleman."

"Then I have to tell you," she said, trying to catch her breath, "that you are failing, miserably."

"Now you sound like my father. But never mind. Information, Lady Allegra. I want—need—information. And you're going to give it to me."

Allegra looked at him for a moment, then shrugged. "All right. For your *information,* Armand Gauthier is going to have your guts for garters."

The man threw back his head, laughed. "Well, I'll say this much, my lady, you're not the fainting sort. I appreciate that."

"You're not welcome."

"Yes, yes, enough of this lighthearted banter, if you please. Now, to get serious. Your father sent threatening notes to three men."

Allegra felt her blood run cold. "I should have known. I've told him, and *told* him. I've said, Oxie, one of these days someone isn't going to think you're funny."

The man grabbed her shoulders, gave her a sharp shake. "Funny? What do you mean, funny? He sent notes. *Your secret is safe with me.*"

"Oh, and it is, because Oxie doesn't know anybody's

secrets." Her eyes widened slightly, as an almost murderous look came over the man's face.

Maybe, just maybe, she shouldn't be so candid. The man seemed to think she knew something. If he found out that she didn't, he'd have no further need for her.

That couldn't be good.

"Well . . ." she said slowly, "he does know a few. But I really couldn't talk about that. I've been . . . I've been sworn to secrecy."

"You'll be found lying dead in an alley if you don't tell me," the man threatened, stepping back from her, beginning to pace, rather like a caged beast.

"Yes, I think I've sensed that," Allegra said carefully. This man might be pretty, and desperate, but he wasn't, she thought, overstuffed in his brain box. She was sure she could handle him. Well, slightly confident, maybe, and not completely sure. "You're talking about Walter Jagger, aren't you? And Sir Guy Berkert? Viscount Eaton?"

Suddenly the man was all smiles. "They were right. They said what the father knew the daughter probably knew as well. You're all in on this together, aren't you? Even Gauthier?"

Allegra shifted her eyes to the left. "Gauthier? No, not him. He's just . . . he's just my lover. A convenience, you might say."

The man sniffed. "You Nesbitts. Gutter trash. Your father probably helped turn down the bed. Why do all the wrong people fall into luck?"

Allegra inwardly bristled, but did her best not to react. He was in front of her once more, his hands gripping the arms of the chair as he leaned toward her. "You can't touch me, you know. I'm not doing anything you and that father of yours weren't already doing. Who would you tell? Nobody. Why, I might even cut you in on the money I get from those three buffoons, if you're nice to me."

He lifted one hand to her cheek, ran his finger down the length of it, across her chin, and down onto her chest, stopping just at the center of her bosom, above the neckline of her gown. "What you give to one, little beauty, you can give to another. You think Gauthier's good? I'm *better,*" he said, leaning even closer, whispering the words into her ear as his hand slipped inside her gown, captured her breast. "Want me to prove it?"

Surprising even herself by her reaction, Allegra leaned forward . . . and rather copiously vomited lemonade and sweet cakes onto the man's black patent evening shoes.

"You stupid *bitch!*"

The man jumped back, stamping his feet, looking down at his ruined hose, his ruined shoes.

He pointed a shaking finger at her. "I'll be back," he warned, sort of *squishing* over to the door. "And when I am, you'd better be ready with some answers for me. Ten minutes. I mean it. In ten minutes, bitch, you either live or you die. It's your choice."

Allegra, wiping the back of her hand across her mouth, didn't bother to answer, and only flinched when she heard a bar being slipped into place on the other side of the door.

She took a good thirty seconds to feel sorry for herself, another thirty to compose herself, and then stood up, began walking around the room, looking for weapons, yes, with which to defend herself.

Happily, the first thing she found was a bucket filled with fresh water, so she rinsed her mouth, splashed the cool liquid on her face.

Then she looked at the bucket. She looked at the ledge over the door. She fingered the length of rope that lay on the table beside the bucket.

And she smiled.

She didn't know who this man was, or how he'd found out about Oxie's silly letters.

What she did know was that this man didn't know who *she* was, either. If he did, he would have trussed her up with this same stout rope and still never, never ever, have turned his back on her.

As the study door closed behind the three men, Oxie Nesbitt wiped his sleeve across his damp forehead. He didn't quite look his best, his halo of white hair a mad tangle, some of the hem of his copiously large nightshirt still sticking out of the back of his hastily donned breeches.

And his complexion, normally ruddy, was as pale as parchment.

"Do you think they believed me, Got-yer?" he asked, collapsing onto the couch in the small study.

"I think they'd all like to break you into very small pieces, then sprinkle bits of me on top before setting fire to the whole pile," Armand said, settling behind his desk, his every nerve and muscle wanting to be up, moving, doing.

"But there won't be any more knives?"

"No," Armand said, dropping the copy of *Smith's Amusements: Tricks, Ploys, and Sundries Mischief* into the bottom drawer of his desk. "No more knives. And no more pranks. You've retired your pranking, right, Oxie?"

"Oh, yes, yes. Definitely. I never meant any harm, Got-yer, never a bit of it. Nothing in the book about meaning harm, you all saw that. It was only a joke. And that's what I'll tell Ally, just the moment we get her back. Why didn't you tell Jagger his son's got her?"

"Because it wouldn't help, Oxie. Jagger's son would never have confided in him. The man's a sot. He was swaying on his feet, Oxie, didn't you see that? Drunk half out of his senses. Besides, the man deserves the son he's got. No, I just wanted them gone, one complication gone."

Because there are other complications. Oxie. You have no idea.

Unable to remain seated, Armand walked over to the drinks table, poured himself a glass of wine he didn't want.

He glanced toward the mantel clock for the second time in as many minutes. Five minutes for Letty to climb back into her clothing and find him, another ten to rouse Oxie and get him and his pranking book across the Square, another twenty to corral Oxie's victims from the ballroom, show them the book, then explain that the man, quite succinctly, was a harmless idiot not worth their worry—or their retribution.

They believed him. They must have. Eaton even apologized for the knife.

And their secrets were safe with Armand, who didn't give a damn about any one of them.

So where was Conor?

What if Rutherford Jagger hadn't taken Allegra somewhere close? What if he was driving into the countryside? What then? He'd still be sitting here tomorrow afternoon, twiddling his thumbs?

No. Rutherford wouldn't put down the blunt necessary to take a hired coach into the country. He was close. Allegra was close.

So where was Conor?

"Oxie, there's something I have to tell you," Armand began, trying to fill up the moments, so that the ticking of that damned mantel clock didn't drive him, screaming, into the Square.

"You want to marry my Ally, don't you, Got-yer? Well, if it's my blessing you want, you've got it. Her mama and I already talked about it, and we both agree. Just promise to find her, Got-yer, and then protect me when she goes for my throat."

Armand smiled in spite of himself. "Thank you, Oxie. I'll do that, protect you. But there's something else. Something Ally already knows."

"She knows I shouldn't have sent those notes," Oxie said sadly.

"I might be Harry's son, Oxie," Armand said baldly, then waited for the man's reaction.

"Harry Got-yer? No, can't say as I know the man. Don't have to impress me by trotting out the relatives anyhow, seeing as how I already said you could have her. She wants you, so I have nothing much to say in the thing anyway. It isn't why I brought her here, but her mama's over the moon, so that's all right."

"Thank you again. But not Harry Gauthier, Oxie. Harry Nesbitt."

"Oh, Harry Nesbitt. That sounds more familiar. Harry Nesbitt." Oxie's head shot up, his eyes bulging as he looked at Armand. "Harry Nesbitt?"

"Married to one Sarah Charlene Tate, yes. Sailing home after two years visiting one of the family holdings, never to arrive. Sailing home with their infant son."

"No, no, that can't be right," Oxie said, shaking his head. "Harry had no children. I would have known. Well, not me. But the old earl? He would have known if he'd had a grandson."

"Possibly. Or possibly not. If the letter carrying that information never made it back to England, he might not have known. Or Harry and Sarah may have wanted to surprise everyone, coming home, producing the heir."

"There is that, I suppose," Oxie said, and Armand knew the man was only listening with half an ear, his mind concentrating on his missing daughter. "But what of it?"

Armand sat himself down on the edge of the desk. "It's as I said, Oxie. I may be that infant. There's . . . there's some proof. Not a lot, but some. It's possible. Possible, Oxie, that you aren't the earl at all." He took a deep breath, released it. "That I am."

Oxie crossed one pudgy leg over the other, and looked at Armand. "You? Not me? The devil, you say. And Allegra thinks so, too? Well, if that don't beat the Dutch . . ."

The door to the study banged open, hitting against the wall, and Bones stuck his head in. "He's back, Armand. Conor's back."

Leaving Oxie Nesbitt where he sat, vaguely smiling into the middle distance, Armand stuck a brace of pistols into the waist of his breeches, and bounded from the study, out into the Square, where four freshly saddled horses waited.

"Conor!" he exclaimed, grabbing the man at the shoulders, all but holding him up. "God, man, half of anything I own—it's yours for the asking. Where? Where is she?"

"Not . . . not far, boyo," Conor said, attempting to get enough breath to be able to speak. "Can't . . . can't tell you, but I can show you. Not far. No more than five minutes on one of those things," he ended, pointing to the horses.

"Is she in a house? Could you see her?"

Conor nodded, then broke off as Quincy appeared, carrying a full glass of beer, which the seaman poured down his throat in one long swallow. "And it's a saint you are, Quincy, I swear it on m'mother's head."

"Conor?"

"What? Oh. Yes, Armand, I saw her. I got there too late to try to make a grab for her, but she's in a cellar. I saw her through the window. She's not tied up, nothing like that. They were talking. Man who talks usually doesn't act, right, boyo? I could have played the hero, but what if I failed? So I left, marked the house with one foot, to remember it—all I had with me, boyo, unless I wanted to piss on it—and hied myself back here, lickety split."

"Damn, Armand, look at his feet," Bones said in some shock. "He's bleeding like a stuck pig."

Armand looked down at the Irishman's feet that, indeed, were cut and bloody. "Should I have the carriage brought around? Or can you ride?"

"No time for a carriage, so I'll be riding. To hell and back if I have to, boyo," Conor said, grinning. "And you sure do know how to show a fella a fine time, don't you now. Except I have a little unfinished business waiting on me here, so let's get started."

Bones was already in the saddle, holding on to the reins of the horse with the sidesaddle attached—Quincy, bless him, seemed to think of everything.

Conor mounted, wincing slightly as he slipped his foot into the stirrup, and Armand tried to remember if he'd ever seen the Irishman on horseback. He decided that he hadn't. Bless the man.

Once on his own mount, he motioned for Conor to lead the way out of the Square, then bit back a grin as Conor's rump and the saddle dueled with each other as the horse broke into a canter.

Even having to ride close beside the Irishman, holding him safe in the saddle by the back of his coat, they made it to the dark house in Gurzon Street in less than five minutes.

In the moonlight, Armand could see the Irishman's bloody footprint marking the white marble steps leading up to the house.

"Conor, you've done more than enough," he said, patting his friend on the shoulder. "Stay here with the horses, all right?"

"I help, and now you punish me, boyo, want to leave me with this beast? I've rode out hurricanes with less bite." Conor groused, gingerly holding on to his mount's reins as he rubbed at his backside. "Letty's going to be one disappointed woman tonight, boyo. Isn't that bad enough? Let Bones here stay, I'm going with you."

"And I'm going with all of you, Gauthier, if that's all right with you."

Armand whirled about, to see Allegra, minus her dancing slippers, the flounce at the hem of her gown half ripped off, but with her shawl neatly draped across her shoulders, holding open the door to the small house.

"Ally!" He vaulted the steps in one bound, pulled her into his arms, kissing her face, her hair. "Oh, God, Ally. He let you go? How? Why?"

She pushed at his chest, stepping back slightly as she looked up at him. "Let me go? Of course he didn't let me go, Gauthier. He wanted to know the secrets Oxie was supposed to have known. He—whoever he is— wanted to use those secrets to wring money from those three unfortunate men. He wasn't about to let me go."

Armand couldn't get enough of looking at her, his mind made stupid by his fear that was now sweet, blessed relief. "But, if he didn't let you go—?"

"I decided to leave," she said, lifting her chin. "But perhaps I'm glad that you're all here, because I don't think I know my way back to Grosvenor Square. And my slippers have somehow gone missing. Although I was certain you'd be along, sooner or later."

"Ally," Armand said, his voice pained. "We came to rescue you. Why don't we need to rescue you?"

She went up on tiptoe, kissed his cheek. "Oh, Gauthier, that's so sweet. And if I was ever in any real danger, it would have been wonderful. But, as it happened, I rescued myself."

"Where's Jagger?"

"Jagger? Is that who he is? Isn't he too young?"

"The son, Ally. Rutherford Jagger. He must have overheard his father and the other two, moaning about Oxie knowing their secrets, and decided he should know them, too. Where is he?"

"Is he still breathing? That's the question you might be asking, boyo."

"Shut up, Conor," Armand said as Allegra took his hand, led him into the house, the Irishman and even Bones following behind after the latter had tied the horses to a nearby post.

She picked up the single candle that was burning in a rude pewter candleholder, and lit a nearby brace of candles in a small candelabra. "This way," she said, handing the candelabra to Bones.

They all passed down a narrow hallway, to an open door and a set of creaky steps leading downward, to the cellars.

The area lit in eerily moving shadows by the candles,

Armand could see that there was a door halfway along the cellar, standing open.

"In there?" he asked Allegra, who nodded.

"Who's there? Help me! Damn it, help me!" The voice was hollow, not quite muffled, but definitely strange.

"Oh. He's awake," Allegra said. "I suppose it's nice to know I didn't hurt him too badly."

Armand halted, putting out an arm to gather Allegra close.

"Jagger?" Bones called out, holding the candelabra in front of him as he advanced toward the doorway. He stepped through the narrow entrance, lingered for a moment, then half staggered back to Armand, grabbed on to his shoulder, laughing like a loon. "You've got . . . you've got to see this! We're not here to rescue Lady Allegra. We're here to rescue Jagger."

Armand took the candelabra from Bones and, holding Allegra's hand, entered the smaller room.

There was a puddle of water on the floor just inside the doorway, and a few small candles scattered about, giving a faint light.

The room was crowded with odd bits of furniture, cooking pots, an old spinning wheel, some rusted tools. Armand paid them little attention.

Because it was difficult to think about looking at anything other than the man lying on the floor, his legs tied together at the ankles, a large rope coiled around his sopping wet torso, holding his arms at his side . . . and with a wooden bucket jammed down over his head.

"How . . . ?"

"Oxie taught me," Allegra said, grinning rather wickedly. "A bucket filled with water, carefully placed over a door. A rope attached to the bucket. The door begins to open, the rope is pulled, the bucket falls, bam, right on his head. He fell like a tree, Gauthier. Very satisfying. I learned to tie the knots myself, when I was a child. I think they're tight enough, and then I poured water over them, to be sure."

Conor limped into the room, stared his fill at Rutherford Jagger, then went to sit down on a nearby chair.

"Oh, Mr. O'Neill, you don't want to do that."

"I don't? And why would you be saying that, m'lady?"

Allegra made a face. "Because I couldn't be sure the bucket would knock him senseless, that's why. So I . . . made other provisions. Two of those chair legs are just about sawed through, Mr. O'Neill, and, trust me, you wouldn't want to be falling into what's under that seat. And then there's the mallet I've got tied to the beam over there, by a length of rope. If anyone were to move that candleholder over there, the mallet will come swinging down, to take off the top of your head."

She turned to Armand, who was looking at her with open admiration. "I thought that one up by myself," she said proudly, but then her smile faded and she swayed where she stood. "Could we go back to Grosvenor Square now, Gauthier? Suddenly I'm not feeling quite as brave as I was a moment ago."

Armand bent down, swept her up into his arms, and strode for the stairs, calling over his shoulder, "Untie his legs, Bones, and deliver him to the Watch. But don't take off the rope around his arms—or the bucket!"

Allegra, pluck to the backbone, even as she melted against Armand's strength, giggled.

After assuring her mother and Oxie that she was little the worse for wear, Allegra insisted that Armand take her outside, into the Square, to find a few moments together before anyone could tuck her into bed to "recover from her ordeal."

But first, once her mama and Oxie had kissed her good night and gone back to their beds, Allegra took Armand's hand and led him toward the library at the back of the mansion.

"Do you remember that I said I had something to show you?"

"Vaguely," Armand said, bending to place a kiss against her nape. "I thought it would be your bed-chamber. But then, I'm a wicked, wicked man."

"You're also the earl, Gauthier, whether you like it or not. Look," she said, picking up a brace of candles as she walked over to the fireplace. "Remember that first day we met? The day I said you looked familiar to me?"

Armand nodded, looking up at the portrait that hung over the mantel. "Who is she?"

"There's a small plaque on the frame, bearing her name. Sarah Charlene Tate Nesbitt. Your mother, Gauthier. You can't deny it, nobody can deny it. You don't look like a Nesbitt. You look like your mother. Those eyes, that chin. Do you see it? I did, this afternoon, when I finally looked, really looked. I couldn't wait to tell you tonight."

She watched, tears coming to her eyes, as Armand slowly approached the portrait, reached up a hand to touch the canvas that had captured the smiling face of a young woman happy with her life, looking forward to the future.

Allegra could see his throat working as he swallowed several times, his gaze locked on the portrait. "My mother," he said quietly. "How could I have thought, even for a moment, that I could walk away from the possibility of this moment? Walk away from her?"

With a soft cry of her own, Allegra moved into his arms, held him, waited for him to come to terms with his now certain knowledge, his ancient grief.

"We'll do whatever you want, Gauthier," she said at last. "I'll talk to Oxie, make him understand."

"I've already spoken to him," Armand said, at last turning away from the portrait. "I think you're right. He seemed . . . relieved."

He took her hand, led her back down the hallway, toward the door to the Square. "It's going to take some time for all of this to sink in, Ally. Time for me to decide what I want to do. What *we* want to do."

Allegra squeezed his hand, then pulled him through the doorway as the butler swung back the door, tripping down the steps in her bare feet, onto the cobbles.

"I know what I want to do, Gauthier," she said, taking hold of his other hand as well, pulling him with her as she backed toward the fountain. She wanted to see him smile, needed for him to smile. "I want to go wading. It's not a beach, it's not sand, and it's not particularly warm—but I am barefoot. Say yes, Gauthier. Say yes."

She threw back her head and laughed as he picked her up, still dressed in his evening clothes, whirled her around in a circle, and then stepped into the fountain.

Epilogue

𝒯HREE MONTHS LATER, in the perfectly manicured rose gardens of Sunderland, Allegra Nesbitt and Armand Gauthier, fourteenth Earl of Sunderland, were married.

In attendance were the bride's parents, Letty and Conor O'Neill, Mr. and Mrs. Bartholomew Boothe, and the new Mrs. Boothe's parents, who were soon to move in as the caretakers of Sunderland.

It hadn't been easy. It hadn't been quick. But now it was done.

In two weeks, Armand, Allegra, the bride's parents, and the O'Neills would embark for New Orleans. Once there, Armand and Allegra would hunt for land upriver for the house they would build, the home they would make.

Oxie and Magdalen would have their own house elsewhere on the property, but Letty and Conor had already decided that what New Orleans needed was a fine establishment to serve drinks and supply card tables to the local gentlemen.

Letty had already found the perfect name: *The Sea Horse*.

Frederick Nesbitt, a man with daughters but no sons, had agreed to come live at Sunderland, care for the estate, inhabit the Grosvenor Square mansion whenever he and his wife chose, and collect a most generous allowance.

It seemed only fair.

Fairer still, as Armand was many things, but not a fool, Bartholomew Boothe would be keeping very close tabs on both his new father-in-law and the Sunderland finances, and reporting on both to Armand.

The Nesbitts would go on, for Armand had officially taken the family name, even if Allegra persisted in calling him Gauthier and he never wanted her to stop. Armand and Allegra's children would carry the Nesbitt name, the title, perhaps even come to live at Sunderland one day. It would be, Armand had stated adamantly— and Allegra agreed—their choice.

But the portrait of Sarah Charlene Tate Nesbitt, and the one of a young Harry Nesbitt surrounded by his favorite hunting dogs, were both already crated and ready to go to America.

There was still much to do, including a farewell visit to Simon Roxbury, his wife Callie, and their new son, but for tonight at least, Sunderland belonged to the newlyweds.

Oxie and Magdalen had taken Letty and Conor to the village pub, to celebrate the wedding with a few pints. Oxie had given his daughter a hug before he left, quietly telling her that he "was done now. I promise. But I needed just one more, pet, you understand."

So it was with some trepidation that Allegra took Armand's hand and led him upstairs, to the master bedchamber.

"Oh, Oxie," she said as Armand opened the door and she walked inside to see . . . nothing. The room was empty to the walls.

Armand stepped up behind her, put his hands on her shoulders. "Darling, I do believe our furniture has gone missing," he said, a smile in his voice.

"You noticed?" she countered, leaning her head back against his chest, to look up at him. "Are you angry?"

"No. To tell you the truth, I've been waiting, wondering what he'd do. His last prank was a fiasco. He had to try one more. So? Do we adjourn down the hall, to my former bedchamber? I believe you already know the way, madam," he ended, kissing her nape.

"Shhh, Gauthier," she teased. "Someone might hear you, and know that we've been . . . naughty."

"And tonight, darling, we'll be even naughtier. Unless you think that being an old married couple now, we'll turn stodgy? Shall we find out?"

"No, not yet." Allegra took his hand, led him back into the hallway. "First we'll decide if Oxie's idea is better," she said, pulling him toward the door that led up to the attics.

Once there, she found the door that opened to yet another flight of stairs, this one leading up to Sunderland's flat roof.

There, just as she'd suspected, sitting beneath a starry sky, and arranged very neatly, sat nearly everything that had so lately resided in the master chamber. The carpets. The clothespresses. The vanity table. The desk. The candelabras.

The huge four-poster bed.

"I thought as much," Allegra said. "Do you mind?"

"No, I don't mind. I don't mind at all."

"Thank you. I do love you, Gauthier." Then she added, with only a faint hint of reluctance on her voice, "Well, I guess we can probably go back downstairs now."

"On the contrary, my dearest wife," Armand said, lifting her high in his arms, then depositing her on the turned-down bed, following her down. "After all, it is a lovely evening . . ."

Center Point Publishing
600 Brooks Road ● PO Box 1
Thorndike ME 04986-0001 USA

(207) 568-3717

US & Canada:
1 800 929-9108